OFF THE BEATEN PATH

WOFFORD LEE JONES

I dedicate this collection
to my beautiful and amazing wife,

LAURIE JONES

who dubbed my stories as
Dark, Delicious, and Disturbing.

I hope you find these tales to be some of
the darkest, most delicious,
and disturbing stories you've read
even on this second and third time around
as you are the one who read them first.

Thank you for your love, support, and encouragement,
and for always being my number one fan.

All my love, Always,

WLJ

CONTENTS

Dear Reader,

I wanted to write a short letter to explain a few things before you delve into these little creations I've written primarily for you.

First, I want you to know how important you are to me. I know some of you personally, but there are many of you I have never met. I genuinely hope to meet you one day, whether it be at a book signing, a conversation between us on social media, or a simple chat in person on the street somewhere. It would be my honor to know you in some small but unique way. But even without knowing you, you are no less important to me than my family and the friends I personally know.

If I only sold one book to one person and that individual read and enjoyed the stories within, I would consider myself a successful writer. I do not need the fame of well-known writers, though if that comes to me one day, I will certainly welcome it with open arms. It has always been my hope that everyone who reads my tales will enjoy and love them, but as we all know, a writer can never please everyone. Still, we always try, and I would certainly love to be the first. If, for some reason, there are a couple of stories within this collection you don't like, I hope the remaining ones affect you in some way and that you find them thoroughly thought-provoking, entertaining and unnerving.

Second, there are eight novellas within these pages (seven if you count *Off the Beaten Path – the Ending*, as it goes along with the opening story). If after the opening story, you can't wait to read the last book-ended tale then, by all means, feel free to jump to the end and read *Off the Beaten Path – the Ending*; the rest of the book can be read in any order, but please read those two stories in sequence.

Again, thank you so much for reading this horror collection; you don't know how much I appreciate your investment of time to read my stories. It is one of the best gifts you can give this writer.

Now, sit back and relax with that special blend of coffee and snack or with a chilled glass of wine (if that is your poison), as you settle into your favorite reading chair and wrap up with a warm blanket. Take some deep breaths and brace yourself, because these paths are long, and the woods are dark. Dig in, my friend, and dig deep. Are you ready? I hope so, because I now present to you *Off the Beaten Path*. I indeed hope these tales bring you beautiful nightmares. I will see you in your dreams.

All the best,

Wofford Lee Jones
Upstairs Writing Nook
Saturday, September 5, 2020

OFF THE BEATEN PATH - THE BEGINNING

Rachel Kirkland looked down and saw that her left hiking boot had come untied. She had felt it slowly loosening, becoming more and more annoying, for the last two to three hundred yards. As she finally stooped to retie it, she glanced up and saw that Stuart Monroe had continued to walk on ahead of her.

Her eyebrows creased in confusion as she stared after Stuart. He had been quiet for some time now as they hiked this trail. She knew he wasn't just taking in the scenery. Something was on his mind; his silence was beginning to annoy her as much as the boot.

Rachel stood again and placed her hands on her hips. Without releasing too much malice into her voice, she asked, "Where in the hell are you taking me?"

"Nowhere special." Stuart's short reply came back quickly, as though he'd answered without even hearing what she'd asked.

"You've already said that."

He seemed to rouse from the fog of thought surrounding him. "Did I?"

"Uh, yeah, you did. About twenty minutes ago."

"Then *somewhere* special. We're just hiking. You like to hike, don't you?"

"Sure. That's what I had in my personal ad when you answered it nine months ago."

He turned and gave her an alluring smile. "Then quit worrying about it."

"Can you at least tell me how much further? How much longer will we be hiking?"

"I have no idea. We could be hiking for hours yet. It's all part of the fun. Relax; enjoy the view."

Rachel took a moment to look around. She couldn't help but admit that the view was actually breathtaking. The woods were overlaid with a cornucopia of fall colors. Blood reds, pumpkin oranges and sunflower yellows, with some pine greens as highlights; they all screamed for visual attention. The rays of sunlight filtered through the leaves and branches of the forest like stationary searchlights. The autumn weather was crisp and clean.

Even though it was seasonally cold, Stuart and Rachel were coated with a fine sheen of sweat. The trail itself meandered through lush under-growth. There were easy straightaways and slopes, while other parts of the path seemed downright difficult.

They had just climbed a steep incline and were on a level stretch when Rachel wiped her brow and asked, "Can we at least take a breather? I'm kinda tired here."

"Of course we can."

"We've been hiking, like, forever and to be clear, my profile said 'strolls in the woods'."

They stopped. Stuart found a fallen tree at just the right height to lean on without actually having to sit. He surveyed the surrounding trees and took in their beauty as Rachel had done. "Let me know when you're ready."

Rachel didn't sit but continued to stand with her head up, eyes closed and hands perched on her hips. "What's the rush?"

He didn't answer right away but glanced at his watch, then said, "No rush. No rush at all."

"Shhh. Do you hear that?"

"Did you just *shush* me?" Stuart asked with a chuckle.

"Yeah—you got a problem with that?" she teased.

With a bad southern drawl, he said, "Of course not, darlin', I was just, uh, checkin' to make sure."

"Seriously, shhh. What do you hear?"

"Um—"

"Don't answer right away. Listen first."

"Okay."

A long moment passed between them. Stuart looked around again. Rachel took some shallow breaths. Her ears were pricked to the forest sounds.

Finally, Stuart broke the silence. "I don't hear anything."

"Then you're not listening hard enough. *I* hear the faint sound of a brook off in that direction." She pointed to the left. She listened again, her eyebrows crinkling in concentration. She threw a thumb over her shoulder. "Squirrel. Or maybe a bird. Trying to find something to eat." On the next sound, she didn't motion toward it but simply stated, "Wind. Rustling the trees."

She turned toward Stuart, keeping her eyes closed. She heard another sound but didn't call attention to it; Stuart was patting his thighs. It was barely audible but she could hear it distinctly. When Stuart was nervous, he always patted his legs—or the table or the steering wheel—to a rhythm in his head. It was one of the many cute mannerisms that made Stuart the adorable man with whom she'd fallen in love.

Wonder what he's so anxious about today. Cute mannerism or not, he had been acting strange all day, from when they'd left the house for this hike. It was just small things, but she could tell he was different. She let her mind drift back to her listening game again, motioning again to the right and toward the sky.

"Plane, probably a twin-engine."

"You know planes?"

"I don't know, but it sounds like a small one—not like one of those big commercial airliners, but a plane."

"Uh-huh," Stuart said, then smiled as he watched her intently.

A bead of sweat on Rachel's forehead connected to another and then another, until it traced a line down the side of her face. Stuart watched the rolling sweat drop pick up speed and continue down her neck and into her cleavage. She didn't seem to notice it, but Stuart swallowed hard.

The moment was broken when Rachel came out of her superhero pose. She slipped off the green and blue plaid work shirt she had borrowed from Stuart earlier that morning when the air had been chillier, unrolling the sleeves and tying them around her waist.

Stuart admired her body, as he often did when she wasn't looking. She was always oblivious to his admiration. His eyes trailed lovingly over her figure.

She was wearing hiking boots, and her socks were pushed down to her ankles. Her short-but-not-too-tight shorts revealed beautiful, tanned, muscular legs that stemmed from weekly rituals of jogging and dance instruction at the local ballet school where she taught. The tight green muscle shirt clung to her form from the sweat of the hike. It had a print of a cartoon dragon holding up a singed knight impaled on the end of a jousting spear. In front of the bibbed dragon was a jar of peanut butter and some small chocolate rectangles. The shirt simply stated, 'MAKING S'MORES'.

Shaking his head at her comedic fashion sense, Stuart smiled again. *I have to hand it to her. She always makes me smile.*

Her curly brown hair, which usually framed her face and hung a little past her shoulders, was pulled back with a clasp. A few spiraling curls had escaped and now hung loosely around her ears. Rachel was strong, silly and sexy all at the same time.

She rolled her shoulders, then her neck. There were a few crunches as her neck bones popped on one side.

"Shit. That was a really good one," Rachel said.

"I heard *that*," Stuart said, trying to save face from having failed her listening game. Rachel laughed. "Sounded relaxing."

"It was. I could deal with another one of those." She tilted her head the opposite way, but her neck didn't crack on the opposite side. She tried again. "If I could just get this side to do the same."

"You want me to pop your neck?"

"Hell no—you're not a chiropractor!"

"Suit yourself. You'll be passing up the massage that goes along with it."

"I'll survive without it, thank you very much." She turned and raised an eyebrow. "Maybe later?"

"No," he said firmly. "There won't be a later."

Rachel glanced over at him, looking slightly concerned. He kept his face solemn. She gave him a sarcastic eyebrow lift. He folded his arms, shifted away from her and played like his feelings were hurt.

"You can't turn me down once the offer is made. You have to take me up on the offer when it's given."

She tilted her head up to the sky as she laughed him off. "Yeah, right."

Stuart turned back to her. He noticed her eyes were closed again. He stood and moved toward her. Leaves crunched beneath his hiking boots.

Rachel said, "Now *you're* moving. I can hear you loud and clear."

"Don't move," he said. "Stay right where you are."

"Is that an order?"

"Yes, ma'am, it is."

"Ohh, nice. I like it when you're forceful with me."

"You do?" he asked, wrapping his arms around her waist.

Rachel smiled and turned in to him; he pulled her into a tight embrace. Tilting her head up, her lips found his. His hands dropped low on her hips, and he pulled her even closer so their bodies were pressed together as tightly as possible. Her arms slid under his light jacket and closed around his torso, her hands meeting between his shoulder blades. He responded to her affection, and the passion in their kiss grew into full-blown urgency. Stuart's hands slowly began to roam over her body. Always slow caresses at first, which usually grew into feverish stokes.

Rachel smiled at the thought that she could always entice him with the smallest hint of seduction. She was something he could never turn down.

As their kiss grew, one of Rachel's hands dipped low into the small of his back. Stuart felt her body go rigid in alarm as her hand found the holstered revolver attached to his belt. Before he had a chance to say anything, she pushed him away.

"What the hell are you doing with a gun?"

"Rachel. Calm down. It's nothing to be alarmed about."

"Damn it, Stuart. You know I hate guns!"

"I know. That's why I didn't tell you about it. I knew you wouldn't approve. It's only for our protection."

"Protection?"

"Yes. I don't know what kind of animals are out here in these woods. Or people, for that matter. You don't know what might be lurking around out here. I never go into any situation without protection."

"Is it loaded?" As soon as Rachel asked, she knew it was a stupid question. He looked at her with a smirk that carried the same inward expression she had just given herself.

Rachel spun on her heels and started back down the trail the way they had just come. "I'm going back to the truck. *This*"—she spun her finger in a loop-de-loop as she passed—"all of a sudden, has stopped being fun."

Stuart quickly jogged after her, grabbed her arm, and spun her back to face him. "Rachel, please, don't do this. We're just out taking a *stroll* through the woods. Please don't be mad if I want to protect you from anything out here that could possibly harm you…" He paused for a moment, looked down and placed his hand on her belly button. He smiled, then added, "And eventually our little one."

She looked down at his hand on the flat of her stomach. She saw the silver ring on his index finger and the small cross that had been punched through. The skin of Stuart's finger showed beneath. The small cross threw her mind back to a recent memory. It had only been a few days since she had stared down at the plus sign on the pregnancy test. She had yet to start showing.

Smiling and giving a sigh, she nodded and looked back up at him. "How can I argue with that?"

"You can't," he said, grinning down at her. He gave her a quick wink.

"You're right. I'm sorry."

"Just forget I have it. If we need it, we have it. If we don't, it won't be moved from where it is now."

"Alright." She gave him a playful punch in the chest. "I still don't like it though. Just keep it away from me."

"Fair enough. I will." He moved his hand from her stomach and took her hand in his. "Come on. Let's finish this hike, then go home. Maybe take a nap or watch a movie. Or make love, if you're up for it."

She winked back at him then pushed her hips into his, running a light, loving caress down the side of his neck. "I think maybe you're the one who will have to be *up* for it."

He grinned again. "I will be. You just need to be ready to *hike up it.*"

She burst out laughing. "Oh! I cannot believe you went there."

"Oh, I'll go there. In a heartbeat, I'll go there."

She playfully slapped his chest again. "Good one. C'mon, Casanova. Let's go. Maybe if you're lucky I might be enticed into *doing it* somewhere out here in the open, in front of God and everybody else."

"Ready whenever you are, babe."

They walked for a bit, sometimes talking about nothing in particular, but quiet most of the time, just enjoying each other's company. At certain points along the trail, he would help her across a creek or up a steep slope. Sometimes she would do the same for him.

Eventually, they crested a small rise. It sloped downward for a hundred yards or so before angling off to the left and disappearing around an outcropping of boulders that jutted from the ground. Halfway down the straightaway, Stuart stepped to his right, onto the small sub-trail that branched off into the woods, without thinking twice about it.

Rachel did a double-take at his abrupt decision to change directions. She stopped, gripping his hand tightly, pulling him back to her.

"What are you doing?"

Stuart looked back in Rachel's direction, turned to the side trail and threw his hand out in front of him. "I'm, uh, following the trail."

"Uh, hello," she said, mimicking him and indicating the wider trail they were currently on. "It obviously goes this way. Straight down that way and around to the left."

"Who says we have to stick specifically to that one?"

Rachel laughed aloud. "That? That barely qualifies as a footpath."

"Where's your sense of adventure?"

"Uh, not that way. Stepping off the main trail always gets you in trouble. I don't want to get lost." She motioned to the main trail again. "That's why they call *this* a *trail,* because *it* leads somewhere."

"Oh, c'mon, let's just see where it goes."

She gave him a disgusted look, jerked her hand out of his and shook her head. "No. It's not a trail. It doesn't lead anywhere." Still, she looked down the main path, considered it, then looked back to the rabbit trail where Stuart was standing. He took a step or two further away from her, farther along the path.

"Look, you stay here." He threw a thumb in the direction of the path less traveled. "I have to piss like, you know, right now."

"So piss. You don't have to go through there. It's not like I haven't seen your dick before."

"You know how I am with bathroom stuff."

"Oh yeah. That." She made a little frustrated rumble in her throat. "I'll turn my back," she said, and turned away from him.

"Rachel."

"Okay, okay. Jesus. Just go." She folded her arms. "Have fun with that. I'll see you when you come back. I'll be right *here*. On the *trail*."

"I will. Be back in two shakes."

"If it's more than two shakes, you're playing with it," she called after him as he pushed through the thicket of shrubbery. "And playing with it is my job." Under her breath, she added, "Asshole," then laughed a little at the craziness of the conversation.

She watched him go. When she couldn't see him anymore, she followed him with her ears; his footsteps receded until all was silent around her.

How deep in the woods does he need to go to pee? Is he playing some sort of game with me? Whatever; who cares? I'll wait him out. Jesus, he really is weird about his bathroom stuff.

Rachel was tired. Her legs ached from the hike. She sat down in the middle of the trail, kicked her legs out in front of her and leaned back on her hands. She tilted her head back and stared up at the trees that seemed to stretch toward infinity. There was a space between the leaves and limbs that showed a perfect patch of intense, cobalt sky. She closed her eyes, breathed deeply, and inhaled the clean scent of forest pine and evergreens.

Eventually, she lay back on the bed of leaves that covered the forest path. She folded her hands over her lower belly and smiled. She thought again of the little one growing inside her and how excited she was about having a baby.

"I'm going to be a mother," she said to herself. "A mommy." She giggled, then squealed with excitement. "I can't believe it. I'm going to be a mom!"

With her hands still on her stomach, she fervently hoped she would feel a slight heartbeat or a small kick within her belly. She willed the baby to move. Then she laughed at her silliness. She knew there was no way to feel the baby this early. It was nothing more than a bundle of genes, cells and a twist of DNA. But eventually, it would become—

"A girl," Rachel said aloud. "I want a baby girl."

She let her mind drift. *I don't know what Stuart wants, but I'm so happy he's excited we're pregnant.*

When she had first found out, she had gone three days before telling Stuart. She'd been afraid of his reaction. What would he say? What would he do? Would he be happy? Sad? Disappointed? Would he kick her to the curb?

The pregnancy had been a shock to her system, and she'd known it would be the same for him. She hadn't even known if he liked kids or whether he wanted them. The subject was something they had never really discussed in great detail, but she had had an intuition that he wasn't that into children. Still, it was something she couldn't hide from him forever, and she knew she would eventually begin to show; she had to tell him.

When she had finally got up the nerve, Stuart had beamed with genuine excitement. He'd seemed even happier than she was, and that had made it all the more special; perfect, even.

She remembered her earlier thought. *Oh, wow, nine months!* Had it really been that long? Or short? *That's a pregnancy term.* A full nine months. Yeah, it might be a short length of dating time. Maybe being pregnant now was a bit too soon in a relationship, but Stuart truly seemed excited about the news. *Jesus, we aren't even married yet.*

The word 'married' suddenly bloomed as a huge realization in her mind.

"Married!" she said aloud as she opened her eyes and sat up in surprise. *That's why he's acting so strange.* She laughed aloud as the moment hit her full force. *He's trying to get up the nerve to propose to me. Oh, wow, what a weird way to propose. Up here on a hike. Jesus Christ, I'm making it so much more difficult for him.*

Her laughter faded into a smile as her thoughts circled back. She paused for a moment, listening again, and finally noticed how loud the silence was in these woods. She couldn't hear anything. Well, not *anything*; she could hear the forest sounds, but she was mainly listening for one sound in particular.

Where was he? How deep in the woods had he gone? *And exactly how long does it take this man to piss? Has something happened to him?*

Suddenly motivated, she stood.

"Stuart?"

A pinprick of fear as well as excitement pierced her heart. She was, all of a sudden, desperate to find him.

She looked again at the barely visible trail he'd started out on. Reluctantly, Rachel stepped onto that trail and followed. As she left the main trail, she muttered under her breath, "Oh, I don't have a good feeling about this."

How long had he been? Five minutes? Thirty minutes? She had no clue. She had lost all track of time. She didn't have her cell phone; she'd left it in the truck, thinking it would only be a quick hike. She hadn't wanted to ruin this romp in the woods with social media. She also hadn't wanted to be burdened with carrying anything. She cursed herself for not bringing it along.

"Stuart! Where are you?"

She looked down but didn't see any semblance of a trail at all. She glanced back the way she had come. There were only pine needles, intermingled with a patchwork quilt of fallen leaves. She knelt to study the ground. She saw an area of leaves that appeared to be disturbed, as if someone had taken a step, maybe, but it was very faint. It wasn't much, but it was something. She saw another displacement a few feet ahead of the first, then another.

"Stu? Where are you!?"

Rachel continued, blindly walking and then jogging, hoping and praying inwardly that she was on the right path—if you could even call it that.

In a playful, sing-songy voice, she called, "Stuart, I think I know why we're out here. Are you down on one knee?" Then she shook her head, feeling stupid for saying it.

Stuart didn't answer.

Rachel moved on, simultaneously hating him for doing this to her and loving him all the same. In her mind's eye, she saw him somewhere nearby, laughing at her stumbling about on a blind hunt to find him. She stopped and studied the nearby trees to see if she could see him peering out from behind an elm or snickering at her in the undergrowth.

"This isn't funny at all! I'm going to kick your ass when I find you!"

Eventually, the faint suggestions of footprints led her to a thick wall of pines that seemed to have grown too close together.

That's odd. Didn't know Mother Nature could be so precise.

Rachel peeled the branches back and pushed through them. Slipping on some leaves, she fell through the dense foliage and into a clearing.

"Congratulations. You found me," Stuart said. His voice held no emotion.

Rachel quickly looked up, expecting to see Stuart silently laughing at the joke he'd just played on her. Instead she saw him sitting solemnly on a large rock jutting out of the ground. He was leaning over, his elbows perched on his knees. His chin rested calmly on his knuckles.

"Stuart?" she said, standing as she dusted herself off. "What's going on?"

"What do you mean?"

"What the hell do *you* mean by *what do you mean?* Why did you leave me back there?"

"I had to piss. I told you that."

"Well, it doesn't look like you're pissing now. How long have you been finished? How long have you been sitting—" Rachel looked around, noticing for the first time exactly where she was. "…Here? Where exactly is *here*?"

Even before he answered, Rachel knew it wasn't going to be good. She saw the hole, and a shovel stabbed into the mound of dirt piled high to the right of it. A lantern sat perched at the head of the opening. Her mind was working toward a conclusion, but she didn't quite make it there before Stuart's voice pulled her out of her thoughts.

"It's my—" He paused, and seemed to relish the word: "Haven." He corrected himself quickly by adding, "My *Sanctuary*," as though the word would explain everything.

"Your haven? What the fuck does that mean?"

"This is the place I go when I need to think."

"You come all the way out here… in the middle of nowhere… digging holes… to *think*?"

"On certain subjects, yes. It's where I can focus all my thoughts and attention and consider the best solution to my problem."

"What has you so troubled that you have to come here to think?"

"You," he said, almost before she finished her sentence.

"Me? What the hell is wrong with me?"

"You're pregnant."

"Pregnant? Is that what this is about?"

Standing, he said, "Yeah. I've decided it's not going to work out between us."

She laughed out loud, then became immediately pissed. "So you bring me out here in the middle of nowhere to break up with me? I thought you were going to propose, you asshole! Let me make one thing perfectly clear to *you*, Stuart. I don't need *you* to take care of the baby and me. If you don't want to have anything to do with us, just say so and we'll be out of your life forever. I'll disappear completely."

Calm and cool, Stuart said, "I couldn't have said it any better myself. But I wouldn't call it breaking up—"

"What the fuck would you call it then?"

He gritted his teeth and gave an agitated huff. "If you let me finish, I'll tell you. I'm not breaking up with you. I'm severing the ties completely."

The realization from moments before finally crystallized in her mind.

"You're going to kill me, aren't you?"

"You always were a smart one."

She kept thinking this was some sort of elaborate hoax.

Any moment now, my friends are going to jump through those trees and yell SURPRISE! But my birthday isn't for another four months. This is all way too weird. Shit like this doesn't happen to average, everyday people like me. Things like this only happen in stories and movies and really fucked-up dreams.

She willed herself to wake up. She came back to reality and stared at the solemnity of Stuart's face, now tilted in concern the way a dog tilts its head when it hears a sound it can't quite discern. She caught herself already shaking her head. She wasn't going to put up with this shit anymore.

"Fuck you, Stuart. I'm leaving." She turned on her heels. Over her shoulder, she added, "I don't ever want to see you again."

She was about to push through the wall of pine trees when the shot rang out. She heard the whine of the bullet as it whizzed by her ear and burrowed into a tree ahead of her.

Instinct took over Rachel's body, and she immediately dropped to the ground.

Birds scattered from nearby trees as the gun blast echoed through the forest, then died away. She heard a startled animal dart into the underbrush to her left.

As she turned over and looked back, Stuart said, "Uh-uh-uh. Get back here, bitch, or the next one enters the back of your head... maybe between your shoulder blades. I can put a bullet anywhere I want."

Rachel stared at Stuart from where she lay with an open-mouthed, wide-eyed expression. Stuart stood with the gun in his right hand and shook it slightly, as if to remind her he still had it and there was another bullet in the chamber.

"The gun. It had nothing to do with protection from animals out here, did it? It was for me..."

"Yeah, so let's not start any of that bullshit. Why don't you come over here and have a seat?" Stuart indicated the rock where he'd been perched.

"I'd rather not."

He shook the gun at her, a little more threateningly. "I would prefer that you do. Let's not have an argument about it, because you will lose."

Reluctantly, Rachel obeyed. She stood, brushing herself off as she moved to the requested sitting area. She viewed the 'sanctuary' in more detail.

It was lovely, and Rachel assumed many hours had been spent here doing more than just thinking—grooming this place so as not to let it be overrun by forest growth. An immense oak tree stood beside the long flat rock where Stuart had been sitting. The tree's limbs fanned out above, keeping the whole area shaded and cool. The carefully planted pine trees grew straight up, intersecting the oak's limbs completely, intertwining with them. There was little else; no stray briars or brambles, and it had been raked so no leaves were visible. It was just the plain forest floor.

Rachel noticed something else, and she froze as a breath caught in her lungs. "What are those?"

Stuart followed the direction of her gaze. On the other side of the open hole, two slightly mounded areas were too parallel to be produced by nature itself; each was about six feet in length.

"Oh, you mean Lynette and Evelyn," Stuart said, instantly excited. He quickly and gracefully moved to the space between them, holstering his gun as he stooped, then put his hands over their graves and simultaneously stroked the dirt on each. He seemed to regress into his memory.

Rachel pulled him back. "Who are they? Or should I say, who were they?"

A long moment.

"Girlfriends. From my not-too-distant past."

"You've got to be kidding me."

Anger instantly flashed on his face as he jerked his head in her direction. "I've had other girlfriends beside you. You aren't the only fuckable chick out there."

"What? Why did you—? You brought them up here and you…" She paused, unable to say the words.

He said them for her. "Killed them? Yes. Something like that."

Rachel couldn't believe what she was hearing. Stuart was talking so nonchalantly, as though he were discussing the weather with a stranger in an elevator. It was impossible.

Invasion of the Body Snatchers, she thought. The real Stuart had been stolen or cloned and replaced with this evil Stuart. This Stuart was one-hundred-and-eighty degrees from the Stuart she had dated for the past nine months.

Even through her haze of shock, she couldn't hold back the fear creeping through her veins. That pinprick had turned into an icepick and was sliding deeper into her insides. Rachel felt faint and queasy.

Stuart picked up a few leaves that had landed on their graves and pitched them to the side. He lovingly smoothed the dirt on Evelyn's grave.

"It took me forever to convince Evelyn to come up here with me on a hike." He mimed having a pregnant belly. "She was reeeeally big by the time I did. But it was quick." He adjusted the other grave's headstone. "Lynette, on the other hand, just wouldn't stop talking about kids. It became so tiresome; I had to shut her up before too many other people found out our news. I couldn't have that." He paused, then added, "But I loved them. God, yes, I loved them."

"What the fuck is wrong with you?"

Another, stronger flash of anger flitted across his face as he stood, pointing at her for emphasis. "There is nothing wrong with me."

"Right, because it's normal to bring your pregnant girlfriends up into the woods to show them a grave because you can't man up to your responsibility as a father. You may not want to get married—I understand that. You may not want the responsibility of a child, I get that as well, but you can't just kill us and get away with it!"

Stuart smiled and indicated the other two graves. "Well, you know, I've done it twice before. And I'm about to do it again."

Rachel plunged ahead, ignoring his threat. "Here's a thought for you, asshole. Instead of getting whatever girl you're dating pregnant, why not wrap your dick? You ever thought about safe sex? Better yet, why even date? It's obvious you don't want to get married or have kids. So why don't you save yourself and whoever you're attracted to the trouble?"

"It's complicated."

"No fucking shit, *bitch*. I suspect it is *complicated*. But why don't you let me be the judge of that?"

"I wouldn't expect you to understand."

"Try and explain it to me. I want to know why I'm sitting in front of a fucking hole, Stuart."

"Look, I love being in a relationship. I love being in the company of a beautiful woman. And dating. But I don't want the responsibility of a family."

"A more in-depth answer would be great, but all I'm getting is that you're a fucking pussy."

Stuart rubbed his head in frustration.

"Come on, Stuart. You can do it. I need more than that."

"I have to be with someone. I *need* to be with someone."

"So why not get a dog? They're loyal. You don't have to worry about them getting pregnant—unless I find a few smaller graves out here as well." She began to look around as though there just might be some.

Stuart laughed out loud, then immediately became solemn again. He jerked his gun from the back of his pants and whipped it up, aiming at Rachel. "Now you're just making fun of me. I don't have to explain myself to you." He indicated the grave with his gun. "Just get in the fucking hole."

"If you want me there, you're going have to put me there yourself."

Stuart moved toward her with irritable determination.

Rachel had been toying with an idea during the past conversation, but had no clue if it would work. She had to try. Before Stuart could reach her, she stood quickly and moved toward him in a non-threatening manner with her arms out in front of her.

Stuart wasn't expecting her movement. Startled, he stopped and raised his gun in self-defense.

Just as his demeanor had changed, so did hers. "Put the gun away, Stuart." It wasn't spoken as a command, just a comment, and with all the calmness she could muster. "You don't need it." She was surprised at how calm her voice actually was.

"What are you doing?"

"Nothing that warrants you pointing that gun at me. I'm not a threat to you. I just wanted you to hold me one last time."

"What?"

She ignored his question and stepped closer to him, then slowly and cautiously moved past the gun and into his arms. She wrapped her arms around him and gave him a tight hug, stiffening slightly as his arms slowly wrapped around her. He held her close.

With her head against his chest, Rachel said, "If this is it, then I at least want to feel how much you love me." She braced herself for him to push her away. When he didn't, she pressed on, grasping for anything that might help her sell these lines of bullshit falling from her mouth. "You obviously love Lynette and Evelyn. I can tell by the way you've taken care of this place." She felt Stuart's heart racing beneath his shirt. "I can only assume you'll continue to take care of this place once I'm buried here as well."

A slight pause; he was wary of her. "Of course. I'll probably take even better care of it." Stuart kissed the top of her head.

Rachel wanted to vomit. She couldn't believe she was saying and doing this, but she could think of no other way out. She prepared herself, then looked up into his eyes. Standing on her tiptoes, she quickly forced her mouth over his lips. She kissed him hard and as intensely as she could with her stomach churning and the icy fear in her veins.

Grabbing her shoulders, he pushed her away. "What are you doing?"

She knew this was it. He was on to her. She plunged forward and moved back into him. "I'm doing what you like." Rachel snaked her arms around his neck and pulled him back toward her, kissing him long and deep. He accepted her kiss and returned the passion. His will was weakening. He was succumbing to her. She had to be quick.

With desperation in her voice, she said, "Make love to me."

He pulled away again. "What?"

She spoke urgently. "You heard me. Right here, right now. One last time. Do it now before I change my mind."

He looked around as though people were standing at the edge of the Sanctuary, staring at them. The idea of a public display of affection all of a sudden seemed to make him extremely shy.

"I can't do that. Not here."

"Of course you can. There's no better place to do it than here. Here, in your safe haven."

"Sanctuary," Stuart corrected.

"Yes. Your sanctuary. At least you would have another memory to remember me by when you came up here to think. Wouldn't you like that?"

"Sure. Of course." Stuart paused. He looked down at Lynette and Evelyn's graves.

Rachel wondered briefly if his mind was so far gone that he actually saw the ghosts of Evelyn and Lynette standing somewhere in this clearing, watching him with hateful abandon. He hadn't totally backed down. She grabbed his face gently and pulled his gaze back to hers.

"Don't think about them." Her hands went to the belt of his pants and forcefully pulled him toward her. She dropped her voice slightly to a deeper, more sultry tone. "They can't see or hear you now. You should focus your attention completely on me. You still want me, don't you?"

"Yes, I want you. Bad."

"Then take what is yours. Do with me whatever you like."

A slight pause.

"C'mon, Stuart. Don't ever keep a woman waiting when she's all worked up. There's no one watching. You've done it before; let's do it again," she said, echoing his words.

She moved her hands to his chest and fumbled with his shirt buttons, her insides churning and their contents threatening to spew out.

"Rachel, don't."

"Why not? It's funny that you're all of a sudden shy on me. You enjoy sex with me, don't you?"

"Yes, but not—"

"Don't hesitate. Do me right here and now. I want you inside me." She was running out of things to say, options that would appeal to him. She pulled at his clothes as she dropped to the ground. "Ravage me, Stuart. Come here." She mentally shook her head. *That was dumb,* she thought, but continued as she tapped the slope of her neck. "Start with my neck. Right here. You know how that drives me insane."

Stuart hesitated, then reluctantly obeyed. He knelt and moved in on her neck as she leaned back.

Rachel cooed softly, "Oh yes, Stuart. That's what I like."

She saw Stuart's arm move, the one holding the gun; it quickly snaked around to his back, where she could only assume he was shoving it into the waist holster on his jeans. Stuart leaned back into her again.

As she faked ecstasy, she fumbled around blindly to her right where Evelyn's headstone lay. It was just a simple, rounded rock—about the size of a softball—that had gingerly been placed at the head of the grave. Stuart had probably found it in a creek bed during one of his long hikes up here by himself. It would be an effective weapon, if she could just find the damn thing. She clawed the ground in a desperate search for it. Could she risk a quick glance to her right? But before she needed to look, her hand closed around the rock and relief flooded her body.

She moved the hand that was around Stuart's back up and in between their chests and pushed him away as she struck him across his face with her other hand. The stone hit the side of his head. There was a slight crunch-crack underneath Stuart's yelp of surprised agony, then he fell away from her and landed in the dirt, holding his head.

Rachel scuttled backward to put more distance between them. She glanced at Stuart, thinking she had knocked him out cold or maybe even killed him. To her surprise, he had already moved onto his hands and knees, shaking off the unconsciousness threatening to take him under.

The hit had connected solidly; she was sure of it. Blood was already running down the side of his face. Part of his ear was split where the corner of the rock had lacerated it.

He shook his head again and glanced her way. He actually smiled at her. "Good one." He started to laugh. "That hurt like a son-of-a-bitch." He shook a finger in her direction. "You're very good. Thinking with the wrong head and all that. I actually thought you..." He trailed off as he fought to stay conscious. "I'll never do that again."

As she stood, she noticed the gun in the back of his pants. She wondered, *Is he dazed enough for me to grab it?* Without realizing it, she had already made up her mind and was charging him.

Stuart had expected her full-on body charge and braced himself. She came at him, swinging the small headstone again. He stood and caught her arm in mid-swing with one hand, wrapping her body up in a half-bear-hug with the other. Rachel's natural instinct brought her knee up hard into his crotch as her untrapped hand slithered over and far down his lower back. She blindly searched for, finally found and grabbed the gun, jerking it free.

The force of the crotch blow forced Stuart to let go of Rachel as he covered his groin and doubled over in pain. She took a step back as she brought the gun down level with his head, dropping the headstone and bringing that hand up to steady the shaking pistol.

Stuart was already lunging forward and to the side, out of the way of the pointed gun, as best he could with an aching crotch. Encircling Rachel's hands with his, he pushed the gun up and away from his body.

The gun went off.

Keeping a solid grip with one hand, Stuart pulled the other hand away and punched her in the lower abdomen. Releasing the gun into Stuart's hands, Rachel stumbled backward and landed on the mound of dirt piled near the empty grave. The impact caused the dirt to shift and the shovel to fall over.

Forgetting about Stuart, the gun, and everything else, all Rachel's attention went to her unborn child. Tears instantly burst from her eyes as she wondered if the punch had been a death blow to her little baby. Her stomach burned hot with a throbbing ache.

Hope went out of her; she didn't know if there was still a chance her baby was alive. And if she couldn't have the baby, she didn't care if she lived or died. She looked up at Stuart with murderous eyes.

Before she could say anything, Stuart said, "Hurts like hell, doesn't it?"

"You could've killed our baby."

"Now. Later. It's going to happen eventually."

Her mind reeled; she couldn't wrap her brain around how Stuart could be so two-faced. "Shoot me if that's what you want. God, I wish I had never met you!"

"Come on, baby. Don't be that way." He glanced down at the gun. "I'm not going to shoot you. I'm going to give you what you wanted earlier. You did ask for it. Practically begged for it, remember?" He moved toward her, casting the gun far enough away that Rachel couldn't grab it.

She struggled to her feet, still stooped over from the punch to her stomach. "Get the fuck away from me! Don't you fucking touch me!" Her voice had taken on an edge that scared even herself.

Stuart lunged. Rachel spun away, but Stuart wrapped her knees in a football tackle and she fell backward across the shovel. Their weight was enough to snap it in two.

Spider-quick, Stuart scuttled on top of her, pinning her to the ground. He spread her legs with his and pinned both of her hands over her head with one of his own. With the other hand, he grabbed a fistful of her green muscle shirt and jerked back, ripping the s'mores-making dragon into two halves and exposing her bra. Throwing the material aside, he immediately started to undo her belt.

"You don't mind if we skip the foreplay, do you?" Stuart muttered as if to himself, leaning in close.

"Stuart!" she yelled, distracting him from her mid-section. He glanced up as he continued fumbling with her shorts.

As soon as they made eye contact, Rachel grabbed his shirt and pulled him closer to her, then slammed her forehead into his face. Stuart screamed. He was dazed; his hands released her and went to his face. Rachel wriggled free, flipped over and moved away from him again. Stuart sensed her escape, grabbed her ankle and pulled her into him again, this time on her stomach.

"Not a very wise choice, Rachel. You're just making things worse for yourself. I'll put you in the fucking hole in pieces if I have to."

He reached for the waistband of her shorts and jerked at them again.

Rachel panicked. Earlier she had been more shocked and amazed than scared. Now true horror was intertwining itself between her muscles. That icepick of fear had turned into a butcher knife, and it was stabbing her repeatedly with each beat of her adrenaline-pumping heart.

He is not going to rape me. There is just no fucking way I am going to let that happen.

She floundered around on the ground until she found a smooth wooden stick.

The broken shovel handle, she thought, and hope bloomed inside her.

Once her hands wrapped around the handle, something within her mind snapped. With every ounce of strength she could harvest, she abruptly flipped over and with a banshee cry, blindly shoved the jagged handle forward as hard as she could.

There was a wet puncturing sound as though she'd hit a soaked punching bag.

Stuart let out a surprised yelp as his whole body stiffened. He instantly stood and stumbled back. All at once, everything stopped and became intensely silent except the surprised gasps from both of them.

It finally caught up with Rachel, and she realized what she'd done.

Stuart swayed slightly, as though lightheaded, now breathing in surprised hiccups. He stared down, mesmerized, at the shovel handle protruding from the left side of his abdomen. He lightly grasped the wooden shaft a few times before releasing it, as though touching it had assured him that it was indeed real.

As Stuart moved away from her, Rachel saw she'd hit him with such force that the rod had punched completely through his body. Fear continued to possess her, but she didn't let it cripple her; if anything it empowered her. She stood with newfound courage.

Stuart saw her coming and seemed to think she was going to help him pull the stake out, but she grabbed the handle and pushed it deeper into his abdomen. He tried to protest, but the shock had stunned him into silence.

Rachel added more force to the initial stabbing and starting walking forward, causing Stuart to stumble backward. The shovel handle continued to slide through his body. Rachel's fist was now up to his abdomen, his blood seeping out and covering her hand, but she barely noticed. She marched him to the base of the grave that had been dug for her.

"That'll teach you to fuck with me and my baby."

She placed her left hand on Stuart's chest and pushed him backward as she jerked the wooden handle out of his gut with her right, instinctively hoping it would cause more pain.

Hands grasping for anything but finding nothing, Stuart fell backward and landed with a hollow thud in the bottom of the deep pit.

Rachel stood, heaving with mortified sighs, as his blood dripped from her hand and the jagged end of the shovel handle. Her life, as well as her baby's, had been moments from ending. She unconsciously stroked her lower abdomen with her unbloodied left hand.

"If you are still alive, and I pray to God you are, I will never let anything happen to you. I will never let anything happen to you. I will never let anything happen to you." She stared down at Stuart for a long moment, frozen in shock as she prayed for her baby. "Please be okay. Please be okay. Please be okay."

She half expected Stuart to spring out of the grave and attack her again. She even braced herself for it, but he just lay there, staring up at her with a wide-eyed gaze.

Why, Stuart? Why were you like that? Why didn't I see any of the signs? Even though she asked, she knew why. *It was because you didn't want me to see them.*

A shiver rippled through her, and that brought her out of her thoughts, the involuntary movement motivating her body. She realized she was still holding on to the shovel handle with a death grip. She couldn't get rid of it fast enough, so she pitched it into the grave beside him.

She untied the plaid shirt from her waist and slipped it on to cover her exposed body. With shaky fingers, she struggled with the buttons but finally managed to button it all the way up. She felt vulnerable under Stuart's stare. Even in death, the sleazy look on his face creeped her out.

She knew she still had plenty to do before she could leave this place. She looked around quickly, making mental notes of the things she had to get rid of—the gun, the lantern, her torn T-shirt, Lynette and Evelyn's headstones, and the shovel head. She couldn't leave anything exposed. If she did, it could come back and disrupt whatever new life she would have in the future, and she simply wasn't going to let that happen. She knew there were eventually going to be questions, but she would make sure everything pointed to the fact that Stuart did not want to have kids and had moved away. He had just disappeared out of her life. It was the only way. She retrieved the gun and torn shirt and pitched them into the grave as well, then did the same with the lantern.

Rachel looked over to the two smooth headstones; one was still at the top of its grave. She picked up the one she had used to brain Stuart, then moved to the head of both graves. Replacing the headstone, she tentatively placed her hands on each of them. Grief for these two ladies and their unborn children welled up inside her, bursting forth in a torrent of tears. She sank to her knees and wept for them.

Her apologies came in jerky sobs. "I am so sorry this happened to you. I wish I could do something for you." She thought for a moment. "I suppose… I suppose I did. I killed the one who murdered you and your ba-babies. That should count for s-something, I guess." She continued to rub the smoothness of the stones in slow circles. "I wish I could've known each of you. I think, maybe, we could've been friends. I wish… I wish I knew your l-last names or who your families are. I-I kn-know they are grieving as hard for you as I am now, and I don't even know you." She paused again, unsure of what to say next. She wiped her tears away with a dirty hand. "I will never come back here again. I don't think I could ever bring myself to return." She hesitated, somewhat ashamed of her promise. "I guess this is goodbye."

As she stood, she picked up each headstone and dropped them into Stuart's grave. A huge pang of guilt swept through her body. With that simple movement, she was erasing these women from existence forever. Their bodies would never be found, and their families would always wonder what had happened to them.

Today was nothing but survival; she kept telling herself that. It was simply the continuation of her existence for normal life. It had to be this way, because the smallest piece of evidence could be linked to her.

She immediately picked up the broken shovel. Without looking back at Stuart's body, Rachel started shoveling dirt onto him. Shovelful after shovelful was awkwardly thrown back into the grave as quickly as she could manage. Memories of him flooded back into Rachel's mind, and she realized the past nine months had been nothing but lies. Her pace quickened with each heap of dirt, until she was simultaneously crying and cursing him. She worked in a flurry until the job was completed. She began slapping the dirt with the back of the shovel head to pack it down so there wouldn't be a hump in the earth. Each slap of the ground brought the whole fight back to her system as she relived the memory over and over. The movement turned from a flat slap to a pointed stab as she brought the blade end down repeatedly in the center of the grave. Pent-up frustration poured from her body as she stabbed an imaginary Stuart, killing him again and again. Once her arms were fatigued, she gave one last stab, then stood and screamed at the top of her lungs, venting the last bit of frustration from her body.

When she finally fell silent again, she stood at the foot of the grave, breathing deeply as her tears dropped on the fresh dirt. She felt... purified. Totally exhausted from the burial, she crumpled to her knees and sobbed quietly to herself.

She cried over many things. What she had done, the prospect of still having a child, the nine months of a wasted relationship, her having missed the signs of Stuart's mental condition, the fact that the families of these two women would probably live the rest of their lives not knowing they were here in these cold, wayside graves. But mostly she cried over the simple fact that she had survived a brutal fate and was still among the living.

When she had no more tears inside her to release, she dried her face. She tried to camouflage everything to make it look as though it was just a random clearing. She didn't want anyone to make their way off the beaten path and discover this graveyard. Double-checking that the 'sanctuary' was closed forever, she grabbed the shovel handle and began the long trek back to Stuart's truck.

Rachel had always thought that in any journey, the trip back was usually shorter than the journey to the destination, but not so in this scenario. The hike seemed unbelievably long. On a few occasions she thought she had lost her way, but then something would indicate that she was headed in the right direction.

She had initially enjoyed the hike, even though they had walked for longer than anticipated. Going back down the trail, she barely noticed the scenery; she walked—and sometimes ran—in a daze. Her mind kept replaying the confrontation over and over. She tried to block out the images and sounds by thinking of her unborn child, but the memory battered her relentlessly. She focused her mind on the trail as she rubbed her lower belly. She just wanted to get to the truck and back home to put this whole nightmare behind her. A million thoughts shot through her mind as she blundered forward.

How am I going to explain what happened to Stuart? What did *happen to him exactly? A fake story that I have to make seem real without questions or doubts. How can I explain to everyone without suspicion coming back on me? Who knows I was up here hiking with him? No one. At least, none of my friends. God, no one would've known where I finally ended up. Is it possible to cover this up? And do I really want to? Yes. God, yes, I want to. No doubt about that!*

With these wild thoughts and thousands of others racing through her mind, she finally emerged from the woods at the beginning of the trail. She crested the small rise and saw Stuart's truck on the other side of the small parking area. Nothing had ever looked more beautiful to her—that, and the fact that no one was parked alongside it. She broke into a run to get to the truck. She darted around to the driver's side, dropped the shovel, and jerked up the door handle to jump inside. The door didn't open.

Locked.

What the fuck?

She instinctively reached into her pockets and came up empty. She slid her hands across her ass, checking her back pockets.

Nothing.

Panic immediately set in, followed by a realization. She paused and slowly looked back to where the trail started, mentally tracing the exhaustively long journey, ending up in the sanctuary where she had just buried Stuart.

"FUCK!" she yelled aloud as she tried the door handle over and over again. With each jerk of the handle, a "fuck" or "no" or "God damn it" accompanied the action.

How could I have been so stupid? I didn't even check his pockets to get his wallet and who knows what else. I was in such a hurry for it to be over. If someone stumbles on his body, they'll find his driver's license and that could be traced back to me. Probably. Maybe.

She threw herself against the truck in frustration, then turned and slowly slid down the door panel until her butt hit the pavement; she sat weeping, rivulets of tears washing her face.

Pull it together and think, she told herself between sobs. *What are you going to do? Are you going back up there? And if so, what? Dig Stuart up and get the keys? Or are you going to just walk away and hope for the best? Is his wallet in the truck, or is it buried with him?*

"I have no idea," she answered herself aloud. *But there are too many unknowns to just leave his truck here.* She knew she had to make as much of Stuart disappear as possible; that included his truck.

An image of her own hand placing her cell phone in the glove box before their hike flared in her mind.

Fuck! I can't just walk away with my phone in there! If someone finds my phone, they could easily trace it back to me. I have to go back.

This realization solidified her decision. It would be another long hike back up there. *Will I be able to find the place again?*

Maybe?

Yeah.

She looked toward the mountains in the distance and made a judgment call via the sky. It was edging toward late afternoon, but there was still time. The sun would start setting soon. She might be able to get to the sanctuary, dig Stuart up, get his keys, bury him again and get back here by sundown, but she would definitely be hiking back close to dusk.

Cursing herself for being so careless, she didn't hesitate any longer, knowing the daylight was too precious. She jerked the shovel back up and reluctantly began the long trek back to the sanctuary.

This would be the last time, she told herself.

Rachel ran; she was a runner. It was much more difficult in her hiking boots, but she made the best of it. She had to beat the sun if she was going to find her way back before complete darkness set in. As she ran, she began figuring out what she had to do. She would make sure every loose end was tied up and that Stuart was erased from this world forever. She would burn his wallet and IDs. She would get rid of his truck later on when all this was behind her. Piece by piece, bit by bit, the truck would disappear. Eventually, he would just be a faded memory, and then he would be forgotten forever.

Rachel became lost in her thoughts as they turned angrier. She began making all sorts of promises to herself: promises that men wouldn't play an important role in her life ever again and that her unborn child—if still alive within her—would never be harmed by anyone. She swore she would never go hiking again, as each pounding footstep and heartbeat brought her closer to the grave.

She finally ploughed through the low-hanging boughs of the pine trees of the Sanctuary. One cursory glance of the clearing, and her breath double-clutched inside her throat.

There was a hole in the middle of Stuart's grave.

Had Stuart crawled out? *That's a crazy notion.* Had someone else pulled him out? *No, no one saw us up here.*

A heightened sense of panicked terror spun her in all directions. Her head whipped back and forth, looking everywhere for any sign of Stuart, but she couldn't see anyone, let alone him. Her mind was reeling, and the shock of it all was threatening to make her faint. She could feel her body rebelling against her.

"No. No! NO!" she said as she moved mechanically toward the grave to get a better look and figure out what the fuck had happened.

The wind picked up and mussed her hair. She shivered, but it wasn't from the autumn chill.

When Rachel heard the tinkling of a wind chime to her left, her body went rigid and the shovel slipped from her grip. No, not a wind chime exactly. She knew instantly what it was, and her head jerked in that direction.

A labored voice—now deeper than its usual timbre—called out to her. "Looking... for... these?" A choked laugh accompanied the broken words.

She only saw a dirt-encrusted hand sticking out from behind the oak tree that split the center of the Sanctuary. The hand shook the set of keys it was holding, then moved out a little farther, revealing a dirty arm. Stuart stumbled out from behind the oak and leaned against its trunk. He was covered from head to toe with dirt. He was holding his side tightly with one hand, but blood was still seeping from his wound. He held the keys up at eye-level and shook them again in her direction.

"Can't get. Too far. Without... these keys."

"I buried you."

"And a damn fine... burial it... was. Save for the fact... that your corpse. Me. Wasn't dead. You were just... going to leave me... here... all by myself?"

"You wouldn't be alone," Rachel said, anger bubbling beneath her words. She crossed her arms and hitched her chin toward the graves. "You have Lynette and Evelyn here to keep you company."

A hiss of air blew through his clenched teeth, then he yelled, "Don't you fucking patronize me! You cunt!"

Stuart had reached an all-new level of pissed-off that Rachel had never seen before. He had just reached DEFCON 1, and he was emptying the missile silos. She stared back, mesmerized. She was scared, but now it was more fearful awe.

Stuart began retching, then spat out a huge amount of bloody phlegm. He looked back at Rachel, taking a moment to really focus on her. He pocketed his keys, then took a few wavering steps toward her. He began to stand taller and take deeper breaths as he walked.

"I'm surprised... you came back. When I dug myself out... and realized I still had my... keys. I was about to start back down the trail... to my truck... when I heard someone—*you*—coming. I would've bet money... that you would've just left."

"I wish I had, but it's a good thing I didn't."

"I know. It saves me... the trouble of finding... you... later on."

He took another few staggering steps toward her.

"What? To finish me off?" Rachel asked.

"Yeah... something like that."

"You think you're going to survive that shovel-handle-stab-wound I gave you?"

"What? This?" he said, pointing to his side, shaking his head. "This is... nothing."

"You're delusional."

"I've survived... so far."

"You're coughing up blood, you asshole. You can hardly walk. No doubt you're bleeding internally. You're not going to last much longer."

"You going to stay… here with me… until I – until I—"

"Die? Yes. If that's what it takes. And I'm going to make sure that you do. And then I'm going to bury you again. For the last time."

"That is… soooo… romantic. You staying with me… until I breathe my last… breath."

"Trust me. There's no fucking romance in it whatsoever."

He took another step, stumbled and fell to one knee. He gave a pitiful cry.

Rachel didn't budge from where she stood rooted to the ground.

Stuart took another deep breath and pushed off the ground. He took two steps, lost his balance, and fell on his side; he rolled over in pain as he cried out again. Slowly, he moved into a kneeling position and then stood on shaky legs. As he did so, he put his remaining strength into an 'all or nothing' charge and lunged at Rachel. She only had enough time to take two steps away from him before he snagged her arm and turned her back towards him as he swung a hard punch with his other hand.

Rachel was only focused on getting away from Stuart; she had no time to think about self-defense and left herself wide open. Her world exploded into stars and pain unlike anything her face had ever experienced. She felt blood in her mouth as she dropped like a sack of rocks.

Stuart yelled with excitement. "And she's down for the count, ladies and gentlemen!"

She heard him make a fake cheering sound, as if the crowd in the arena in his mind were indeed going ape-shit over the blow he'd just given her. She looked up to see him give the empty air a few quick boxing jabs, then raise his arms over his head in a champion's pose. He didn't pose for long, though, as the stretch obviously caused more pain to the wound she'd given him. She smirked at that.

Stuart looked down at her with a grin, in spite of the pain, that wiped the smirk from her face. She shook her head as she fought to stay conscious.

Rachel saw him move toward her. She tried to pull away, but he knelt over her middle. Taking a fistful of her hair, he pulled her closer to his dirtied face and said, "Two can play… that game. You tricked me… earlier. Consider us even."

He flung her back to the ground and wrapped his hands around her throat. He pulled her up and slammed her down… one, two, three times. The loose dirt under her head still packed a decent punch.

Stuart's hands were tightening, and she knew that this time he was going to continue until her life was choked into submission.

I'm not down for the count, she thought. *I still have something to live for. I have to live for my baby.*

She was trapped under the weight of his body. Her mind searched frantically for a way out of this trap; her hands flailed about his body, trying to move him off her. Then her hands felt blood and she remembered the wound she'd inflicted earlier. She blindly shot her hand forward in what she hoped was the direction of the stab wound. It wasn't a direct hit, but it was enough for him to wince and loosen his grip. She leaned forward as best she could, saw the open wound, and shoved her hand forward again. Her thumb went deep into the opening, and she forced her hand into him as hard as she could.

Stuart couldn't get off her fast enough. He scrambled away as Rachel sat up, trying to hold on. She wanted to hurt him more, but her hands were slick with his blood, and her grip slipped. She rolled over, stood in a hunch, and tried to move away.

Stuart was already lunging for her. He dropped into a low crouch as he reached out and snagged her ankle. He jerked her back quickly, and Rachel went down hard.

She turned away and feebly tried to escape his grasp, but he had latched on to her like a Rottweiler to a burglar's crotch. She kicked blindly at him and felt her foot connect with something. There was a muffled cry of pain.

She turned to crawl away from him and searched the ground for something, anything, to get him off her. That was when she saw it. Hope had never looked so sweet. In a last-ditch effort, she flung herself away from Stuart one last time and it was just enough. She landed hard on her stomach and chest. Her hands wrapped around the shovel head. She grabbed it as though she was drowning and it was her only lifeline.

Rachel had just enough time to register how uncanny this sense of déjà vu was before Stuart jerked hard, pulling her back toward him.

She turned over and sat up as her arms came over her head in a stabbing motion.

Stuart, seeing the upside-down end of the shovel coming directly at his face, screamed out in terror. Simple, instinctual reflexes made him release Rachel's legs, and he brought his hands up and caught both sides of the shovel just as it entered his mouth, but not before the blade sliced cleanly through both of his cheeks. Stuart's scream was cut short, the rest of it emitted as a gagged and muffled yell. Blood immediately began to run out the sides of his mouth and down the outside of his jaw.

He tried to pull the shovel from his mouth and draw his head back. He was so focused on getting the goddamn shovel away, he didn't realize the peril of their situation.

Rachel, however, felt most of Stuart's weight hovering over her and was held up by only his hands, which were trying to prevent the shovel from going further into his mouth.

For a split second, Stuart and Rachel locked gazes. Rachel saw his eyes shift down to her lips. She saw him notice the slight smirk playing at the corners of her mouth.

Rachel said, "Not today, and never again."

His eyes quickly shifted back to hers as the realization of what she already knew bloomed inside his mind. He started to move to counterbalance himself, but there was no time. She simply let go of the shovel and rolled out of the way as quickly as she could.

As soon as she was clear, she turned and looked back in time to see the broken end of the shovel stab into the ground as he fell forward. The force of it hitting the ground, combined with the off-balanced weight of Stuart's body, forced the shovel blade straight through the back of his neck, severing his head completely. A sickening sound, as though someone was kicking through a thick tree root, accompanied Stuart's body as he fell forward and crumpled to the ground. Arterial blood splattered over the Sanctuary ground.

Rachel turned away from the ghastly sight and immediately lost everything she had eaten earlier that day. Needing to get away from the grisly scene, she crawled away as quickly as she could. Wave after retching wave cascaded from her body until all she could do was dry heave.

Eventually the spasms subsided, but she remained on her hands and knees for a long time, shaking uncontrollably. Once she felt somewhat in control of her body, she stood, fortified herself, turned and walked back to where Stuart lay. The top portion of his head had only rolled a few feet from the rest of his body. Rachel was thankful it hadn't landed bloody side up. Stuart now looked as though he had been buried vertically up to his upper lip. He was staring straight ahead at her feet through droopy eyelids.

She stood near his corpse, staring down at what she had done. She couldn't look away. She thought again about the way he had been killed and couldn't help but think, *Equal and opposite reaction, and all that jazz.*

Finally, making herself end the moment, she grabbed the blood-covered shovel and made her way to his grave to begin the arduous task of burying him again.

This will be the last time, she thought.

"One thing I know is true," she said, directing her comment over her shoulder to Stuart. "You won't be coming back this time."

She was about to begin digging, but another thought entered her mind—the real reason she'd come up here a second time. She dropped the shovel and went back to Stuart.

"Before I forget," she said, digging into his jeans pocket, "I'll take these from you now." She grabbed his keys, then rolled him onto his side and dug into his back pocket. "And I'll take your wallet. You won't need that where you're going." Rachel made sure to check all his remaining pockets. Satisfied there was no other evidence that could link back to her if he was ever found, she stood. She spat on his corpse, then kicked him hard in the ribs as an extra 'fuck you' for what he had done to her and to the other two women.

"I hope there's an extra-special place for you in Hell, and I hope to God it's extra hot. Goodbye and good fucking riddance to you, you piece of shit."

But even as she said those words and turned away to begin digging the final hole that would erase Stuart Monroe from existence, she knew she would never truly be rid of him. He would always be in her memory, lurking on the edge of her consciousness. She knew her mind would play tricks on her and conjure him up. She would glimpse him in a crowd, but then he would be gone. She would see movement from the corner of her eye and think it was him. And it *would* be him for one heart-stopping moment before her mind flipped back to reality.

But most of all, Stuart would frequent her dreams and turn them to nightmares. She might've taken care of him physically, but she would never be completely rid of his haunting presence mentally. Rachel knew this was something she would have to live with for years to come. If that was the cost to continue living, she knew she could and would get through it. She was a strong, capable woman; she had just proven that to herself.

"I'm going to be alright," she whispered to herself as she dug. "I'm going to be alright."

She had to believe that.

STRANDED

THE BAR WAS called The Station. The establishment doubled as a gas station during the day and a local bar at night. Tonight it was packed to the gills, as it was every weekend. This was the place everyone went to unwind with a couple of drinks and conversation with old friends or co-workers. The crowd housed people from all walks of life. The Station catered to no one in particular, and welcomed anyone and everyone who was like-minded.

It was nearly midnight on this Saturday night in late October.

Pete Morin and his old high-school classmate and long-time friend, Thomas Collins, were both leaning against the bar, taking in the view. They were scoping out the hot chicks for a potential late-night conversation over drinks and anything else that might happen.

The band, Itchy and the Chiggars, was in full swing. The drums and guitars—even a harmonica thrown in at times—made the most noise as the band played covers of popular songs. They were currently in the middle of their bluesy rendition of "Sweet Papa John" by Johnny Winter. Some of the crowd bobbed along to the song as they conversed between themselves. Some patrons were even down front dancing in a small area that was kept clear for that. One drunk fan kept yelling out the title of the song at random times; his placement didn't exactly go well with the band's version.

Itchy was singing, "Well, they call me Sweet Papa John. My candy is known for miles around. Lord, baby when you lick it, it makes my love come tumbling down."

Pete and Thomas were each five beers into the night. They were tipsy and teetering on the edge of that downhill slope that rolled into sloppy drunk.

Pete drained the last bit of beer from his mug and turned around to find the bartender. "Britney!" he yelled over the band's music and the elevated conversation, waving her over.

Britney was at the other end of the bar. She nodded to Pete and held up her index finger to indicate that she would be with him in a moment and for him to not get his panties in a bunch. When she'd finished fixing drinks for her current customers, she set them up on the bar and walked Pete's way, wiping her hands on her bar towel.

As she approached, Pete held up two fingers. "Two more. One each for me and my boy here. But this time make it Jägerbombs."

"No way, Pete," Thomas said, pulling his arm down. "You crazy? I'm not doing a Jägerbomb after all we've drunk already."

"Quit your bitchin'," Pete began. "You *are* going to do this with me because I'm buying and you never turn down booze, especially when you don't have to pay for it." To Britney, he said, "Make the drinks. He'll drink it. He's just being way too cautious."

Britney gave them a curious look. "You sure you two can handle these? They're pretty *explosive*." She gave them a 'see what I did there' look, then gave a slightly stilted laugh.

In spite of Britney's odd laugh and slightly lame joke, the guys joined in and acknowledged her little pun.

Britney snagged two pint glasses, popped the top on a Red Bull and poured half the can in each glass. As she grabbed the Jägermeister and two shot glasses, she said, "You two are starting to look a little wasted to me."

"And you, doll-face, are looking sexier by the glassful." Pete held up a finger to make sure she didn't get offended before he could clarify his statement. He flicked his finger forward and pointed at her. "Not that you don't look sexy as hell without my beer goggles on."

Britney laughed and poured two shots of Jäger. She set the pint glasses up on the bar in front of them. "Pete, you always say the sweetest things." Britney added the two Jäger shots beside each glass. "Enjoy, boys, it could be your last." She didn't sound as chipper as usual, but she gave them a wink.

"You okay, Britney?" Pete asked. "You sound a little off tonight."

"I'm just not feeling myself tonight. Other than that, I feel fine."

"You should knock off early and go home with me."

Smiling, she said, "I'll put it on your tab, Pete." She turned away to tend to the other customers.

Pete grabbed her attention by quickly asking, "When are you going to marry me, Britney?"

Britney paused and turned back to him. "You ask me that every weekend you come to The Station." It had become their playful banter, always non-threatening and fun.

"And you always turn me down. What do I have to do to convince you that I want to spend the rest of my life with you?"

"We'll talk seriously about the subject when you get me that diamond ring I always suggest and that you always promise to bring."

"I'll get you the ring, baby. Just go home with me for tonight. We could test out how great married life would be."

Thomas butted in. "You must not want lots of sex, because that is when you get it the least. You know, when you're married."

Britney laughed out loud. Her natural, infectious laugh was back. "That's so true." Then she added, "In some cases." She looked back at Pete. "In your wildest dreams, big guy. In your wildest dreams." She walked away to make some drinks and serve other customers.

"Ahh, she kills me when she does that," Pete said, shaking his head.

Thomas shouted over the music, "You've been asking her that for weeks. Ever thought of surprising her by actually bringing a ring in and giving it to her?"

Pete was still looking at Britney. "Yeah, actually, I have. That would really blow her mind, wouldn't it?"

"Maybe then she'd blow yours."

They both laughed at the perfectly timed innuendo.

They were silent for a few moments, then Thomas dropped his voice into a perfect imitation of Ron Burgundy from *Anchorman* and said, "I don't know if you know this or not but, uh, she winked at me when she served us these drinks. I don't suppose you happened to see that? Did you? Did you see that?"

"Yes, Ron, I saw it. Maybe you should marry her."

Thomas quickly changed back to his regular voice. "Oh no, she's *your* girl. I wouldn't *dare* dream of crossing that line by asking *your* girl out." He paused, then slipped back into his Ron Burgundy impression once again. "But, uh, don't think I haven't thought about it. Because I have. I've thought of it a lot."

"Don't let me hold you back, *Ron*. You want her? Go get her. I'd be happy if someone was getting some action tonight, even if it wasn't me."

Pete grabbed his highball glass and Jäger shot, holding them beside each other as he turned to Thomas. Thomas mirrored his actions, facing Pete.

"So, what should we drink to?" Pete asked.

"What? Why not who?" Thomas answered. "Why not drink to Britney?"

"Hell yeah. I'll drink to her any day of the week. Or drink any drink off her. I like drinking her in. Hell, I just love to drink."

"Cool it, Romeo. It's just a toast."

"I know, I know. I'm just kidding." Pete held his glass up to Thomas and said, "To Britney and the man who finally wins her heart."

They clinked their glasses together, dropped their Jäger shots into them, and immediately chugged away.

When Thomas was halfway through draining the contents of his drink, he glanced from Pete to the inside of his glass and saw what he thought was a hair floating in his Jäger bomb. The hair was black—barely visible in the dark liquid—but the bar lights that shone through the bottom of his glass reflected off the roundness of the follicle. It wasn't a regular-sized strand of hair; this one looked to be a little thicker, almost the thickness of a strand of angel-hair pasta.

Thomas blinked in surprise when he thought he saw a flicker of movement from the strand. It was like the hair follicle had wriggled—or maybe the more correct term was *swum*—toward where the contents of his glass were headed. It could have been the tipping motion that had caused the illusion of movement.

Startled, Thomas quickly tipped his glass back and pulled it away from his lips. He looked into his glass, but didn't see anything stuck on the side or floating in the remaining liquid. The hair was gone.

Then Thomas felt the hair in his mouth; he felt the thing move. It made him think of an earthworm and how it wiggles when you're about to bait a hook. He coughed, spluttered, then reached up into his mouth to grab the strand, but before he could it was gone. Thomas didn't know if it was his imagination, the effect of all the drinks he had consumed, or a combination of both, but he was half-convinced the hair had thrashed around on its own and moved to the back of his throat.

He tried to pin the strand with his tongue against the inside of his cheek, but the hair-thing slipped between the back wall of his mouth and his tongue, then skittered down his throat. It felt like he'd swallowed a length of thick dental floss that was now hanging on to the wall of his esophagus.

Thomas leaned over and purposely coughed as hard as he could to hack the thing up so he could spit it out. That action seemed to make it worse. The hair went rigid and coiled up halfway down his throat. Thomas coughed hard again, as he now felt like something was actually choking him. It was as if the hair was so far down his throat that he couldn't get a cough deep enough to expel the damn thing from his body.

Alarmed, Pete said, "Woah, shit, man. What's the matter? Too much of a drink for ya?"

Thomas held up his finger, indicating that Pete give him a moment.

Ignoring Thomas's silent request, Pete asked, "What, you choke on something?"

Thomas shook his head and swallowed hard in order to get the hair the rest of the way down his throat.

To Pete, it looked like Thomas was just answering no. He offered a suggestion. "Finish the rest of your drink, man."

"Th-that's how it all st-started," Thomas managed to say as he stood again. Despite his reluctance to finish his Jägerbomb, he tilted his glass up and drained the remainder of it. The last mouthfuls of Jäger and

Red Bull flooded his throat and washed the hair and the tickle in his throat away.

When Thomas was finished, he coughed hard again. He felt around in his mouth for any sign or sensation of a hair. Finding none, he turned to Pete and said, "What the fuck was in that drink?"

"Jäger and Red Bull. So damn good. Pretty awesome, wasn't it?"

Thomas gave Pete a look that matched his reply. "Thank you, Captain Obvious."

"What? How do you mean?"

"Nothing. Never mind. It's just… I think I swallowed a hair."

"A hair?"

"Yeah, a hair. But this hair seemed thicker than any normal strand of hair."

"What, like a pube?" Pete asked.

"No, dumbass. Don't be crude. It wasn't curly. It was a long, straight, black hair. I couldn't stop it in time."

"You want another drink to wash it down? I'll buy."

"No. I do not want another drink. It's gone now. It's in my stomach. But I think that was my last drink for tonight."

Thomas shivered in disgust, remembering the frenzied movement of the hair inside his mouth and the creepy feeling as it skittered down his throat. He worked his tongue around in his mouth to erase any trace of the phantom follicle and forced his mind to think of something more pleasant. The hair thing had killed the mood of the evening. All he wanted to do now was just get home.

～∾～

The itching started shortly after two o'clock in the morning. Thomas scratched absently at the tiny pain as he placed a bag of popcorn in the microwave.

As he waited, Thomas sang, "You know they call me sweet papa… cause my candy is the best. You know it melts right in your mouth… yeah, I sure don't leave no mess… I ain't sloppy…."

"Sweet Papa John" was the last song the band had played before

Thomas had left The Station, so it was playing on an endless loop in his head.

After Thomas scratched his belly, the itch went away for a minute or two, but as the last of the kernels popped and the microwave dinged, the smallest hint of the itch returned. After about the seventh time brushing his abdomen with the palm of his hand—sometimes his fingernails—he looked down at his belly button to see if there was anything there. He tilted forward as far as he could, rotating his hips up so he could see his midsection better. The skin was slightly red, but that was from his scratching. There was no puffiness or bump to suggest that any type of rash had begun or that an ingrown hair had become lodged beneath his skin.

Thomas thought back to the last time he'd worked in the yard on the off chance it might be a delayed case of poison oak or ivy. But he seldom worked in the yard. He actually had a landscaping company come around on a regular basis to do maintenance, so he didn't have to waste his valuable weekend hours with those chores.

He double-checked the area around his belly button again, pushing and pulling his skin up, over and in every direction, but found nothing alarming.

Thomas dropped his shirt as he gave the area a vicious scratch with his fingernails. He paused, expecting it to come back, but there was nothing.

Good, he thought. *Got it that time.*

Thomas retrieved his bag of popcorn, dumped the contents into a plastic bowl, and walked to the living room. He sat in his leather recliner and kicked the footrest out in front of him. He grabbed the remote, flipped on the television and began the painful process of going through hundreds of cable channels to find something to pass the time while he waited for his insomnia to fade. Apparently, Pete's bright idea of a Jäger-bomb had zapped the sleep right out of him.

Thomas settled on one of those lame-ass sci-fi movies where the government takes two dangerous animals and crossbreeds them to create a super-hybrid monster-animal they plan to use as a secret weapon against some foreign country. The son-of-a-bitch always, *always,* escapes and wreaks havoc on some small, outlying town. But, of course, you can count on the specialist who knows exactly how to track down and kill the hybrid in a secret or specific way. Thomas thought these movies were hideously made, with really bad acting and even worse computer graphics. But for some reason, he usually stopped his channel surfing on one of these S-rated movies—'S' standing for *shit*—just to watch the ridiculousness play out.

Shortly after Thomas finished his popcorn and drained the last of his Mountain Dew, he drifted off to sleep.

He was startled back awake by the sound of gunfire. He jerked upright in his recliner, right into a close-up view of the hybrid monster the specialist was trying to kill so he could save the big-boobed damsel in distress. The creature's open mouth was wide and coming in for a quick chomp as the music swelled to accentuate the excitement. Even though it was bad graphics, Thomas jerked back in fright. The monster was in the process of taking out the equivalent of a *Star Trek* red-shirt character.

"You got me," he said to the creature. "You got me good that time." Then, as he scratched absently at his bellybutton again, he muttered, "Son of a bitch. Poor guy didn't even have a chance." He pushed back again in his recliner to drift off to sleep again.

Thomas had just gotten settled when he jerked awkwardly in his recliner. There was a small pain in his stomach around his belly button. It felt like something had bitten him. Though he was startled, it wasn't so bad he had to sit up in his chair. His hand immediately went to his belly button, and he scratched his stomach again. The pain went away, but as he scratched the itchy section, he noticed something different. It felt like there was a long hair growing out from the middle of his belly button.

"What the hell?" Thomas muttered as he pulled his shirt up on his chest with one hand and grabbed the hair with the fingers of his other hand. The hair was much thicker than the other follicles on his body. It felt like a limp spaghetti noodle. Thomas tilted his head up so he could look down the length of his body to try and see what the hell this thing was.

In the backlight from the television screen, everything near him showed up as a silhouette—the roundness of his tummy, his hand and the hair strand he was currently holding. As he pulled at the hair, it didn't break off at the root where it was attached. It actually continued to slide out of his belly button.

"What the fuck?" Thomas whispered.

He squinted as a mixture of confusion, fear and uneasiness settled over his body. He was pulling something out of himself. He didn't like the look or the sensation of what he was seeing and doing, but he couldn't stop.

Could be an ingrown hair, Thomas thought, trying to make sense of this matter. *How long has this thing been wound up inside me? God, it's so gross!*

Finally deciding to just get rid of it, Thomas gave it a hard tug, thinking it would just break off or pull free when it got to the end.

When he jerked at it, the hair strand—or whatever the hell it was—jerked back away from him and out of his grasp. It whipped back and forth around outside his stomach. Thomas actually felt and heard it slap against his belly a few times; it also retracted, quickly slithering back into his stomach.

As if stung by an electric cattle prod, Thomas shot to his feet and ran to the bathroom.

"Oh, Jesus Christ. What the hell is that? What the fuck is inside me?"

In his haste to check himself over, he banged his knee on the coffee table and accidentally kicked the doorjamb with his bare foot.

"Damn it," he said between gritted teeth. He grimaced through the searing pain and hobbled the rest of the way to the bathroom.

He flipped on the bathroom light and stripped out of his shirt; in the mirror, he looked at his belly. It was redder than before, but there was still no sign of a rash or bumps to warrant it being poison ivy or an infection of some sort. Nothing was oozing from out of his body either. Everything looked completely normal.

Thomas stood there, staring at himself in the mirror, more at his belly area than anywhere else. He didn't know what to do. He knew something was inside his body, and he wanted it out.

How am I going to do that? he wondered.

The itch started again, but it was barely a tickle. It was like his skin was being brushed by an invisible feather. He felt the sensation on the surface, yes, but as he concentrated on it more, he had the uncanny realization that it was actually on the inside of his torso, rubbing against the lining of his skin. The itch grew little by little, but he forced himself to stay relaxed and keep his hands at his sides. The itch was getting worse. Then, in the mirror, he saw it; a ripple on the surface of his skin as something shifted beneath it.

Thomas's blood ran cold and drained from his face as he felt the sick squirming of whatever was inside him. It took every bit of self-control to calm his body; he had to mentally fight the urge to flip out and just fucking lose it.

What the fuck was that? Do I have worms... like a fucking dog? Tiny miniature snakes. The fear crept in and squeezed; his panicked state heightened.

Then the hair appeared again. One end of it slowly slid out from the space in his belly button. It reminded Thomas of a coarse piece of thread being fed through the eye of a needle. The end of it—what Thomas now thought of as the head, even though the whole strand was the same diameter—looped up into an 'S' shape, like a snake. It appeared to be looking around and checking out its surrounding environment. Thomas thought it extremely odd that he was standing there right in front of a mirror but the hair-creature didn't seem to see or notice him. It was as though it was blind, maybe. Although there was no forked tongue like that of an actual snake, it looked like the creature was testing—or maybe *tasting*—the air. Thomas finally realized it was trying to see if it was safe to venture out of the warmth of its current host.

Apparently sensing this alien environment was safe, the thread-creature slid out a little further and paused again. It seemed extremely wary, like a doe when it tentatively steps from a dense forest into an open field. The slightest little sound puts the deer on edge and on high alert. A deer always makes sure it's safe before she bows her head to graze. That was the way this hair creature was; it would slide out a bit more, pause, and then listen. It flinched away to the right at the almost inaudible sound of the house settling, then moved out a little more. It shied away again, this time to the left, from the sound of the air conditioner automatically cutting on, then it hovered back to the middle, letting its guard down once again.

Thomas was steeling himself the whole time he watched the spa-ghetti-strand creature. Once the hair-thing levitated back to a relaxed state, Thomas struck like a snake himself. He shot his hand in near his bellybutton and clamped down on the extruding hair with three fingers. He was about to pull hard on it, but the hair was quick and jerked back against where Thomas had grabbed it.

"Oh, shit! Motherfucker!" Thomas exclaimed as he snatched his hand away and shook it.

The pain came from the sliced pads of his thumb, index and middle fingers, with which he had pinched the thread-creature. It felt like he had just slid each of his fingers across the length of regular bond paper as hard as he could and received simultaneous paper cuts, deep enough to draw blood. They felt more painful and bled more than simple paper nicks.

"Okay, you little shit," Thomas said, looking down at the hair-thing. He hadn't seen or felt it, but it must have slithered back into his body. "I got you. I so got you. You wanna play nasty, I'll fucking play nasty. You just wait. Sweet Papa John's got something for your ass." The music was still playing in the back of his mind.

Before Thomas could put his spur-of-the-moment thought into action, he knew he had to stop the bleeding of his sliced fingers. He shifted his position over to the medicine cabinet housed in the wall to his left, opened the door, and pulled out a box of Band-Aids. He really didn't have the time to doctor his fingers with Neosporin or Peroxide, even though his mind was screaming at him to wash out all the impuri-ties that could've infected the ends of his fingers. He had bigger problems to attend to, like getting this huge fucking worm-like impurity out of his body. He could worry about the pads of his fingers later.

Maybe if I just drink the whole bottle of Peroxide... How would the worm-thing like that action? *Yeah, Einstein, and kill yourself in the process? Not worth it. Find another way.*

He pulled three Band-Aids from the box and unwrapped each one as best he could with his bleeding digits. He wanted to have them ready to bandage each of his fingers and do it all at once. The cuts weren't bleeding profusely – just enough that the blood pooled on the ends of his fingers.

When he finally had all three Band-Aids unwrapped, he took his time washing each finger and then bandaging it tightly so it would stop the bleeding altogether. As he wrapped each one, he felt his own heartbeat throbbing in the end of each injured finger.

After this arduous task was completed, Thomas put his other thought into motion. He moved quickly to the kitchen and pulled a pair of scissors from a kitchen drawer. He also grabbed a pair of chopsticks he'd gotten with his last carry-out order from Yellow Ginger, his favorite restaurant down the street.

In the bathroom again, he placed the scissors on the counter in front of him where they would be within reach, then tore open the wrapper holding the chopsticks. He crumpled the wrapper, pitched it aside, and broke the chopsticks apart like a wishbone. They didn't break evenly.

"Fuck," he muttered under an agitated breath. He fucking hated it when his chopsticks didn't break apart perfectly.

He put them between his thumb, index and middle finger and readied himself like Mr. Miyagi trying to catch a house fly in the classic '80s movie *The Karate Kid*.

The writhing became worse as it slithered around beneath his skin. The itch came back in an agonizing way. It felt like an itchy butthole when you don't wipe very well. He wanted to claw at it to quell that itch in just the smallest of ways. It was all he could do not to dive in, scratch around his navel like crazy with sandpaper and go to town, but he remained focused. He knew it wouldn't be long before the hair-strand would slither out again.

And when you do, I'll grab you, you little spaghetti wannabe. I'll get you this time, you fucker.

Eventually he felt it worming its way out. The feeling was barely noticeable; the surface of the hair-strand was perfectly smooth. He wouldn't even have noticed had he not been watching it in the mirror.

When he'd grabbed it with his fingers earlier, it must have gone rigid with some sort of defense mechanism. Maybe little miniature spikes could flare out from the hair's sleek surface, Thomas thought. His belly button showed no signs of being cut up.

The hair now looked to be at least nine inches out of his body. It hovered out of Thomas's belly button but was angled up, much like a cobra—minus the hood—when it was coiled and ready to strike. The front part of the strand wove back and forth as it tested the air. It was insane how long it was.

It was no more than three or four inches when I swallowed it. Jesus Christ, how fucking long is it now? Is it growing? And if so, how fast? Doesn't matter now. It's coming out of me right fucking now.

Thomas struck at it like Daniel-san and snagged it on the first try. He immediately grabbed the other side of the chopsticks and clamped both ends down hard, trapping the hair between the two sticks. He began rotating the chopsticks in a clockwise direction, like a little kid bringing his kite back in on a windy day. He wound it as tight and fast as he could.

The hair-creature didn't like what was happening to it. It writhed like a worm on hot concrete. The head part of it lashed back and forth as more of it was pulled from Thomas's abdomen. It seemed to be working. A spark of hope flared within his mind, but was gradually extinguished when no end pulled free from his body. Mother of God, how long was this damn thing now?

Then the chopsticks were jerked violently from Thomas's hands as the hair-strand pulled itself back toward and inside Thomas's body. The thing got caught up on re-entry when the chopsticks were pulled flush against Thomas's belly. It pushed itself back out and tried harder to wiggle itself free from the wooden sticks that had it knotted up. It was like one of those dogs who try to bring a stick into the house that's too long for the doorway.

Thomas watched in horror as the pain around his bellybutton increased. The opening the hair was coming out of was very small; far too small to get that balled-up big knot back inside. For a few pregnant seconds he thought his belly button was going to rupture, allowing the whole thing back into his stomach.

In a flurry of agitated movement, the hair-strand tightened around the chopsticks like a mini boa constrictor. They snapped easily, like pieces of kindling, and fell away. The hair-strand unraveled and shook itself free from the wooden splinters, unknotted itself, then retracted back inside Thomas's body. It reminded him of the electrical cords to one of those old Electrolux vacuum cleaners, the ones that suck back up inside themselves.

Thomas barely heard the sound of the destroyed chopsticks rattling as they settled on the tile floor. He looked down in amazement as the last of the hair-thing zipped back inside his body and out of sight. He stood there, stunned.

The scissors were his last resort.

Should've cut it off when it was coiled up in a knot with the chopsticks, Thomas thought. *By God, I will next time.*

He was going to have to cut the thing out of him piece by piece. That was it. Eventually the strand would venture out of his body again and when it did, that was when he would get it, or at least a part of it.

Why does it keep coming out of me? Why the sudden need to be out of my body? Is it producing other hair-strands inside me? Jesus Christ, my body must be infested with those things.

He didn't like the questions cropping up inside his mind or the answers that went along with them. He shivered uncontrollably at the thought of his body being an incubator for those little fuckers. Thomas grabbed the scissors and readied them in the open position, right near his belly button.

I don't give a fuck about this thing or what it's trying to do to me or inside me. The next time it sticks its head out of my body, it gets cut off. I don't care if it's an inch or a foot, it's getting cut. I'll take it out little by little if I have to.

It took a long time. Thomas stood there for what seemed like thirty or forty minutes; he had never been so focused.

His hands were sweaty. He wanted to wipe them on his sweatpants, but he refused to move. He knew the moment he moved his hands away from their ready position, that was when the hair-creature would slither out from its hiding place again. Feeling his movement, it would just retreat back inside his body and it would be another eternity he would have to wait out.

Perspiration dotted his forehead. Some of the beads of sweat connected to others and ran down the side of his face and into his beard.

Others dripped directly from his forehead to the floor as he looked down to view his bellybutton.

Then, ever so gently, the hair-thing slowly squirmed out again. It was quite slow and deliberate this time, even more cautious than before.

Thomas was so excited and keyed-up about the possibility of getting rid of the strand, he jumped the gun and snipped before hardly any of the hair was out of his body. He was successful, though; he'd cut off a piece, he was sure. The scissors had had difficulty actually cutting through the thread-thing. Even though it moved like a flexible piece of cooked spaghetti, it was as hard to cut through as a toughened piece of wire.

The end he'd snipped off dropped to the floor and bounced somewhere Thomas couldn't track. The hair-strand whipped and slithered back and forth beneath his skin.

In agony? Or was that frustration? Thomas thought. *Maybe both.*

Then, out of nowhere, two things happened simultaneously. A cold, numbing liquid seemed to be released into his nervous system. The chill started at the very base of his spine, or maybe it was the middle of his core. In either case, the iciness spiraled up his spinal column, wrapped around the sides of his head and permeated into his brain. The liquid chill seemed to flow through his veins, shooting out the length of his arms into his fingers and down his legs into his toes.

Then the hair on his head, face, chest, arms and legs rose in gooseflesh as the chill moved up from his core to the outer surface of his skin.

A paralyzing feeling came over his body as the coldness slipped through his veins and into his outer extremities. Instead of the intense terror dissipating, it seemed to freeze along with his body and intensify.

He swayed on his feet and felt himself start to fall. He stepped back to regain the balance he thought he still had, and realized he had overcompensated for that step. He tried to take a bigger step to adjust to the imbalance, but was unable to keep his footing, his body still paralyzed. Thomas fell forward, banging his head and left shoulder on the countertop. He bounced off the counter and slid backward, landing on his butt, then rolling to his side and finally lying half curled up.

A veil of unconsciousness overlaid his eyes then lifted briefly. Before he surrendered to the darkness, he saw one thing that chilled his blood, making it colder than the iciness that had started his paralysis.

Immediately after his head smacked off the bathroom tiles and dizzying spirals exploded in his vision, the hair-strand-creature slithered out of his body. It seemed to explode from him, as if shot out of a mini-cannon. It arced over the tiled floor, dropped, and lay still on the opposite side of the bathroom.

The last thing Thomas realized was that he no longer had an itch that needed to be scratched.

⌇

When Thomas woke from his unconsciousness, he was looking across the tiled floor. The squares nearest him were gigantic diamond shapes, being so close to his eyes. They gradually became smaller the further away they went across the floor, until they disappeared altogether on the horizon line near the bathtub.

Thomas realized he was in a somewhat half-assed fetal position. He was bent slightly at the waist, and his shoulders were rounded. He was lying on his right side, and had landed with his right arm pinned behind him. His head was flush with the floor. From his vantage point, he could see from the tops of his thighs all the way down to his feet.

He could see the hair-strand. He didn't know if it was still attached to him, as he couldn't see his belly button. It seemed like it was still hooked to him or in him, but he wasn't exactly sure; he simply had a strange, uncanny feeling that it was. The hair-strand was exorbitantly long, zig-zagging back and forth across the floor. The frightening thing now was that it was pulsating slightly in different places.

He tried to get up, but his legs and arms wouldn't move. He only had minimal movement of his extremities. He *could* blink.

Oh, Jesus. Thank you, God, for small favors, Thomas thought. *The thought of not being able to blink my eyes and them just going dry in my sockets! That would be the worst hell. Not that this isn't crazy as fucking hell in and of itself, but that would just be the icing on the damn cake.*

He could move his ears, his nostrils and the tips of his fingers. He could just make out movement on his left hand, but he had to concentrate on the fingers to do so. He tried to lick his lips because they were dry, but he couldn't move his tongue out of his mouth.

Next he tried to close his mouth, but his jaw wouldn't work. The saliva he wanted to lick across his lips and tongue was slowly running out the side of his mouth and pooling around his right cheek. It was a feeling that made him want to fold in on himself. He always hated the sensation of waking up in the middle of the night because he had drooled on his pillow. That same gross feeling gripped him now, but he couldn't do anything about it. He just had to lie in the growing wet spot.

Thomas also saw a tinge of red on the floor tiles. He'd noticed it as he'd strained his eyes to look around the bathroom. The red was growing ever so slowly. It finally dawned on Thomas that he must've broken the skin around his eyebrow, and blood was oozing out of the wound, pooling around his head.

He continued to try to move any and all parts of his body, but there was no major movement of anything else. All he could do was lie there and stare at the pulsing hair-strand not five feet from him.

Thomas watched it carefully for a long time; it could've been an hour, for all he knew. Time was passing by at a snail's pace. Then he saw a thin line slowly slice down the middle of the hair. It started in a number of different areas, and as the split grew, it joined other parts that had already divided. The split sections unfolded from within themselves and pulsed more strongly.

Thomas was mesmerized, albeit with horror, at what was happening; it was agonizingly slow. He had no idea what was going on. He was mostly just relieved that so much of the hair-creature now lying on the floor was no longer in his body. He marveled at the amount that had been inside him at one point.

The hair-strand wiggled, thrashed around on the floor for a few moments, then lay still again.

Thomas's heart seemed to jump inside his chest. Trepidation caused something to flood his body. It mixed with the heightened fear that had never subsided. Maybe some chemical release in his brain, he didn't know. But the movement had definitely spooked him.

He watched the strand carefully. Nothing happened.

Another minute went by. Two minutes.

Just as he relaxed—as much as his body could relax—the strand jumped and writhed again.

Some grayish substance punched out from the split and become visible on the hair-strand. About a foot or two away from it, another gray section bloomed out and slowly started growing. Two more feet away, another section of gray budded. Then another section opened, close to the first two buds. All along the six-foot hair-strand, more sections of what looked like gray popcorn opened and started growing. They grew until all the sections were finally connected.

Thomas was puzzled; he closed his eyes to concentrate better and to reason out this situation. He'd strained them looking all around the room. What the hell was this thing growing into?

When he opened his eyes again, he saw the grayish section was even larger. It continued to expand, like one of those long, slender balloons a clown blows up and transforms into an animal for a child.

Thomas could barely see through the parchment-thin membrane, but what he could make out was a liquid filling it up as it grew. The liquid didn't seem to be any particular color—perhaps a light gray, or maybe that was just the stretching membrane. He lay there in his paralytic and horrified state as the rounded tube grew. More liquid was produced from somewhere and continued to trickle in.

Eventually, the tube stretched as big as Thomas thought it was going to get. And then it just sat there, half-filled with its gray liquid. For an unbelievably long time, nothing happened. It seemed like hours had passed, but it could have only been minutes. Thomas shut his eyes briefly and exhaled as best he could. He was trying to rid himself of the terror gripping his body. If he could have just one wish, besides not being paralyzed, it would be for this feeling to release him.

When Thomas finally opened his eyes again, he studied the cylindrical tube more closely. It wasn't exactly smooth. There were seams, and a patchwork of ridges that arced down in different directions.

Then he saw an object floating in the liquid: something that was just a little bit darker than the water. It was small, but seemed to be growing very rapidly.

His mouth was already half-open, drooling saliva, but shock had temporarily overtaken the horror. He tried to say, 'No.' It came out as a one-syllable, mournful dirge. His mind was reeling, and his body was itching to run as far and as fast as he could from this thing.

Is that some sort of… cocoon? How the fuck is any of this possible? What's growing inside that gray liquid? How long is it going to take to be fully grown? Is that… is that… amniotic fluid? For the love of God, don't tell me that's the equivalent of a fetus! Jesus, God, no!

But even as he saw the growing shape taking form, he knew it was true. The state of his paralyzed fear seemed to grow—if that was at all possible—though it had never subsided. His heartbeat was thundering inside his chest so hard he could feel it echoing in his ears. It felt like he'd had one too many cups of coffee and his body was vibrating from the caffeine.

The thing in the cocoon elongated as millions of cells on a microscopic level multiplied and those new cells in turn multiplied again, then bound together on top of themselves.

As he looked on, Thomas's mind drifted back to his seventh-grade biology class. His teacher, Miss Hayes, had assigned them insect collection as homework. During his exhaustive search for bugs, Thomas and his dad had found a cicada larva clinging to a pine tree outside their front door. At first they thought it was just the husk the larva always leaves behind once it has hatched, but as they looked closer, they saw it was one actually getting ready to molt. He and his dad stood there as twilight fell around them, and by the light of the front porch, they watched the back of the cicada larva split down the middle. It took the cicada a while, but it eventually emerged out of that slit and stood on top of the shell. They had watched in fascination and wonder as the shriveled wings filled with fluid and expanded to the luminous wings for which the cicadas are known. Once they had formed and grown to the correct size, the cicada had fanned its wings to test them. Then, finally, when it trusted itself enough to do so, the cicada took to the air and disappeared into the darkness. The whole process had taken a few hours, but it had probably been one of the best learning experiences and most amazing moments of his seventh-grade year.

Thomas's mind spiraled back to the present and he realized this was somewhat the same thing, although he didn't know what the hell was going on inside the murky tube on the other side of the bathroom. All he could do was look on in wonder and amazement.

◈

The figure—now seemingly fully developed, about the size of a man—lay motionless in the dirty liquid, enclosed in its covering. Thomas never took his eyes off the thing. He couldn't.

Maybe it's stopped growing, he thought. *I swear to God, if that thing moves—*

There was a ripple on the water inside the murky cocoon. Thomas focused his attention on the surface of the dim water again to make sure he'd actually seen it. The ripples leveled out, then they were there again. The water shook once more.

Thomas shifted his line of sight down the torso of whatever was in the cocoon and toward the bottom half of the figure. And there it was: a slight movement from the appendage at the far left side of the enclosure. The thing jerked again, a little harder this time. He could see the water shifting.

An appendage from the creature shot up into the middle of the cocoon. Five individual points stroked the inside of the membranous covering. The rounded points pressed up against it and continued to feel around the inside of the sack. Then another appendage shot up and joined the other one.

The ten rounded points scratched along the inside of the hull in a frenzied movement. Then, abruptly, the scratching stopped, and the points came together and pushed up hard against the roof of the cocoon, concentrating the pressure in one spot. The cocoon held tight for a moment but then stretched away from itself. Thomas thought the thing inside was about to relax, but the focused pressure pushed through and broke apart. The web-like enclosure popped as the appendages—which

Thomas now realized were the arms of a humanoid figure—pulled the opening wider.

The cocoon split straight down the middle. As the figure rolled over and spilled out of the pod, the brackish liquid poured out over the bathroom floor. The gray water rushed toward Thomas. He had just enough time to close his eyes before the small incoming wave hit him dead in the face and body. It actually moved him back along the bathroom floor a little from where he'd lain throughout the night.

As the water washed over him, Thomas heard a sound like a loud exhalation of air. The thing—the person—sounded like it needed CPR.

After the shallow water receded and evened out across the floor, Thomas opened his eyes again. His gaze landed on the thing that had rolled out of the cocoon. The creature's eyes were open and staring directly at him. Thomas now saw that he was looking at an exact replica of himself.

Realizing he had been holding his breath since the hand had exploded from the tube, he released a lungful of air.

The mirror image of himself continued to stare back at Thomas as it rolled out of its cocoon. Its feet got tangled up in something Thomas couldn't see. The doppelgänger kicked its feet free from its bindings and rolled over onto its chest.

The eyes of the new Thomas-thing never wavered from Thomas's. There was no expression on the duplicate's face—just unnervingly blank, placid features.

The other disconcerting thing about this new creature was that he looked as though he didn't have an ounce of fat on him. His legs, torso, arms, chest, calves and abdominals were perfect. The kind of perfect you'd get if your nine-to-five job was to be in the gym eight hours a day. Tack on the no-nonsense, restrictive diet of the exact calorie intake you would need for that specific regimented workout with no cheating whatsoever.

Thomas was almost enamored with his new self—except that thing wasn't him. He was still the paralyzed Thomas; the one who was slightly overweight, maybe with high cholesterol and high blood pressure. Not the worst physique, but certainly not like the perfection beginning to stand before him.

Thomas didn't think his elevated state of uneasiness could possibly worsen, but it did. The trepidation that had already spiked within him ramped up to an even higher state of fear. His heartbeat was thundering within his chest. He could actually hear and feel the pounding within his ears. He felt as though his heart was going to simply explode.

Standing to its full six-foot-one-inch height, the thing swayed slightly as it tested out its new, muscular legs. It stumbled awkwardly for a few steps, then finally found its balance.

The creature glistened from head to toe with the gray, gooey substance in which it had been immersed. Pieces of the goo dropped from the alien being and splattered on the floor around it as it ambled a few steps toward Thomas. It was a weird, zombie-like shuffle. The thing stopped in front of him. Thomas noticed that its feet seemed huge so near to his face.

The new Thomas continued to stare down at him with an unemotional detachment. It angled its head, as if trying to understand what it was looking at.

Then the doppelgänger stooped quickly. The sudden movement made Thomas close his eyes as tightly as he could. His natural instinct was to shield himself from the onslaught of a possible attack, but his hands and arms still wouldn't move. He could only close his eyes. Oh, God, how he wanted and wished he could move, to fight back or lash out in some way.

Surprisingly, no pressure or hits came to Thomas's body. He tentatively looked up at the creature out of the corner of his eyes.

The thing was just staring down at him with a cold, empty gaze.

Thomas tried to say something, but his vocal cords wouldn't work. His mouth, lips and tongue wouldn't cooperate. A long, unintelligible stream of sounds came out.

The Thomas-twin abruptly stood, turned from him and stepped toward the shower. As it did, more gray globs of goo dropped from its body and peppered the area around Thomas. Some bits even dropped onto Thomas's face. Thomas had the urge to reach up and wipe them from his cheek, but his arms still wouldn't budge. The new Thomas stepped into the shower and turned on the water. It didn't even have the know-how or courtesy to slide the shower curtain closed.

Thomas had no idea what setting the shower was turned to, but he could never just step in and turn the water on full force; it always came out ice cold. He always had to let it warm up first. This being, however, didn't even flinch. For all Thomas knew, it had kept the temperature on the cold setting. That thought quickly faded when Thomas saw steam start to rise from the water and off his doppelgänger's body.

But how can he just stand there in it? Thomas thought. If he had turned the handle all the way over to the hot setting, it would be scorching his body. *Those dials are so damn finicky. I always have the hardest time getting the right temperature set. One of my biggest pet peeves with this place.* Its skin should be scalded and maybe even bubbling up, or at the very least turning bright red. But there wasn't even a tinge of color change to its skin.

The thing grabbed the shampoo bottle and squeezed a more-than-enough helping onto the palm of its hand. It put the bottle back in the shower rack, then lifted the handful of shampoo up to its nose and sniffed long and hard. A hint of a smile creased its lips.

Thomas thought his twin was about to open its mouth and start eating the stuff, but it finally lifted its hand and dumped the shampoo onto its hair. The thing worked up a lather on its head and beard then ducked its head under the shower's spray, just as any other human would do.

How did it know to do that? Thomas wondered. *Is it going off past memories of things I've done all my life? Do all my memories exist within that thing now?*

After the lather was washed away, the Thomas-twin duplicated the process. Got more shampoo, sniffed it, then worked it into a lather and rinsed its hair and beard clean. Once the hair was completed, the thing grabbed the bar of soap and went to work on its body. It was very methodical about cleansing itself. It worked from its face down its torso, past its waist, and finally finished with its legs and feet. All of the gray goo was gone by now. After it had rinsed, it began and completed the process again.

The Thomas-twin finally finished cleaning and rinsing its body, and Thomas thought it was about to turn the water off and step out, but the creature kept standing there, letting the unbelievably hot water sluice over its body.

Thomas had a brief thought of how big his water bill was going to be if his new self stayed where he was for much longer. It was ridiculous how much water it was wasting. Thomas noted how much was ricocheting off its body and splattering all over the bathroom floor. If he could have voiced his opinion, he definitely would have said something about it.

Finally, the thing seemed to come out of its trance. It turned the water off and stepped out of the shower, taking a moment to look down at its mirrored self.

Thomas thought, *Did he actually forget I was lying here? He? Listen to me. Personifying him. Fuck! Him? I mean it, damn it. It's an* it. *A fucking* it!

After taking Thomas in, the thing simply turned—almost in military fashion—and walked out of the bathroom into Thomas's bedroom. Thomas closed his eyes in relief. He kept them closed for a few moments but was too wired to fall asleep.

After about thirty minutes, Thomas heard movement coming from his bedroom. He opened his eyes a couple of seconds before the thing entered the bathroom again. When the Thomas-twin did enter, it paused once more to take in the scene before it.

Thomas's twin now wore a pair of his casual shoes, his nicer jeans, a T-shirt, and a matching sweater with the sleeves pulled up on its forearms. Thomas barely had enough time to take in his new self before his twin stepped toward him again.

It stooped and grabbed Thomas's left wrist, which had lain unmoving in his eyesight for so long. Thomas's arm moved up as the thing stood again. The Thomas-twin stepped toward the open enclosure of the cocoon from which it had recently escaped. As it moved, it dragged Thomas behind itself over the cold-tiled floor. Thomas didn't like this movement, and had a deep-seated feeling of dread for what was coming next. The thing pulled Thomas until he was lying perpendicular to the slime-dripping, ragged opening of the deflated sac. Thomas fought to move his body, but he was still paralyzed and couldn't budge, no matter how hard he tried. He couldn't even scream out in protest; he tried but, again, it only came out as an inarticulate, guttural grunt.

The thing moved around to Thomas's feet, grabbed his ankles and calves, and rotated them up and over, inserting them into the opening. The alien sac and the remaining dirty water and goo felt cold and slimy on Thomas's skin. His body shivered involuntarily in disgust.

No wonder it wanted to take a shower so bad. That shit is only on my feet and legs and I want to take a long, hot shower as well.

Then the creature moved to Thomas's head and grabbed his arms by the wrist, lifted his body up and over, and lowered him into the opening. It grabbed Thomas's hands and folded them over onto his chest.

The thing grabbed hold of the hair-strand that was indeed still hooked to Thomas's belly button and gently pulled it free. Unlike when Thomas had tried, the strand now slid from him with ease. The disconnection was accompanied by a pop-wheeze burst of air, along with some droplets of odd, whitish-gray fluid that spewed from the end of the strand as it exited his body.

Finally, the doppelgänger grabbed both parts of the split cocoon at the very far end of the tear and began to fold it back together. Thomas could see the membranous covering reattaching itself as it was pressed back together, the cells re-binding themselves to the ones they touched.

Absolutely out of his mind with terror, Thomas panicked as a claustrophobic feeling enveloped his body completely. As his twin continued to close him in, he reached up without thinking, and was amazed to find that his hand actually moved away from his body. It wasn't much, but he was able to move his arm now.

What the fuck? Thomas thought. Then the reason hit him pretty hard. The hair-strand had something to do with it. He remembered the liquid chill that seemed to have been released inside his body when he had been fighting with it. *It was during that fight that I couldn't move. That was only when the strand was attached to me. This thing just pulled the end free from my body. Maybe the paralyzing agent is dissipating from me just as quickly as it locked me down.*

Thomas quickly moved his other arm, flinging it outside the opening, and tried to sit up. It was a meager attempt, but he managed it. His twin grabbed his arm and stuffed it back down inside the enclosure, grabbing great big handfuls of the cocoon lining and pinching it shut. The flaps bonded together again quickly, making the hole even smaller.

Thomas knew that if he didn't get out of this cocoon-thing, he would be trapped forever. *I'll suffocate and then, days or weeks later, someone will find my rotting corpse inside this bathroom. What an awful way to go. Definitely not how I planned on leaving this world.* He was getting more movement back and started moving different parts of his body. He kicked as hard as he could against the sides of his container. The cold water—which now seemed a little bit deeper—sloshed around inside the cocoon. Thomas fought back and pushed another arm free of the enclosure.

The creature grabbed his arm in a vice-like grip with one hand near his wrist and the other halfway up on his forearm. It gave its own fists a quick torque in opposite directions, and Thomas's ulna and radius bones splintered in half as they twisted away from each other. It was an Indian burn from fucking hell. The pain was so overwhelming that Thomas let out a howl louder than he had ever screamed. The yell even startled him, as his voice box was now working. The instantaneous pain also caused Thomas to involuntarily sit up in the cocoon's opening.

The Thomas-creature followed the arm break with a quick backhand punch to the center of Thomas's face. Thomas's nose exploded in agony and Thomas—dazed and head spinning from the doubled pain—fell back into the cocoon's breached opening.

The doppelgänger, still unfazed, continued to close the opening as though nothing had happened.

The white fire in Thomas's arm and blunt force trauma to his face kept him from passing out. The cold water sloshed over his face and revived him even more. When he opened his eyes again, he saw his twin—blank-faced and unemotional—peering down at him as its hands worked feverishly to close the gap. Thomas had just enough time to lock eyes with his evil twin before it pinched the last of the opening completely shut. A split second before it closed, Thomas screamed as loud as he could and shot his hand forward again. A portion of his scream escaped, but as the last of the opening closed tight in the creature's hands, the scream was also pinched off and couldn't be heard past the lining of the enclosure. His hand crumpled against the underside of the container in which he was now trapped.

Double-checking the membrane to make sure it had sealed together completely, the new Thomas finally stood and stepped back from the duplicating chamber.

As it looked on, the figure inside—his carbon copy, his other self—continued to kick, writhe, punch and scream in an effort to escape. Although Thomas was screaming within his confines of his prison, no sound escaped the cocoon. There was utter silence in the bathroom.

The creature looking on knew the membrane was too strong for humans to escape. It had been tested time and time again. His species had collected plenty of specimens.

Inside his small prison, the claustrophobia that had threatened earlier had now completely settled deep within Thomas's bones. He searched feverishly for a way out. Slapping uselessly at the sides of the cocoon, his hands splashed down into liquid. That was when Thomas noticed that the water level was higher than when he had first been trapped. The three to four inches of liquid had now crept up to his belly button. This sent him into an even more desperate search for a weak point in the lining as he fought to keep as much of his body as he could above the ever-climbing water line. The lining had grooves in it that looked and felt like a web of old, healed scars, but he couldn't dig his fingernails in deep enough to tear a hole.

What the fuck is going to happen to me now? Thomas thought. *How much air do I have inside this damn thing before I deplete it with all this hyperventilating? Now that I'm in here… where is it going to take me? What is it going to do to me? Is it going to bury me in a small grave in the backyard? Or stuff me in a closet or the attic and wait for me to—* Thomas forced the panicked stream of questions from his mind before he thought the word 'die', but they came flooding back instantly. *Will I suffocate in here before he lets me out? Is he ever going to let me out?*

The questions zinged around inside his mind as quickly as his hands darted around the cocoon's inner surface, looking for a weak spot. His mind was searching for a reason, a solution, but no answer came to his frantic mind. The membranous covering was translucent enough that the light from the bathroom shone through, but it was just thick enough that he couldn't see out of it clearly.

Please, God, Thomas prayed. *Don't let that thing turn off the bathroom light. I think I would go insane if there was no light coming through into this... this... what the fuck is this thing?*

Everything on the other side of the sac appeared as blurry shapes and unrecognizable objects. It was kind of the way it felt when Thomas was at the lake in the summer and went underwater, but very close to the surface, looking out. It struck him that only hours ago he had been the one on the outside, watching the blurry silhouette of the man-form growing within the cocoon, and now their positions were reversed.

When the answer to 'what's going to happen to me now?' finally came to him, it was in physical form. A stinging sensation started at the base of his left foot.

"What the—" Thomas said aloud as he jerked his leg back toward his chest. He quickly looked down the length of his body toward his feet. There it was again. A pain in his right foot and ankle, this time, like someone had grabbed his lower leg and twisted the skin hard to give him another Indian burn, though not enough to break bones. He jerked his right leg away, as he'd done with his left. Then the pain attacked his inner thighs and butt, because that was where the water level had moved to. Thomas squirmed his body away from the pain to the end of the container he was in, which wasn't very far at all. The enclosure now seemed... smaller... and the gooey liquid level now seemed even higher.

No—no—no. Please, God, no, Thomas begged, as he began frantically pounding on the lining. *Is this thing shrinking?* A ball of dread formed in the center of his chest.

With his body now packed on one side of the enclosure, his feet were completely submerged in the gray liquid. It was up to his knees at this point. Thomas saw what seemed to be mist coming off the top of the liquid. Along with the misty vapor trail, he saw specks of something pale floating on the surface. It took him a moment to realize they were bits of his own flesh. Thomas's feet weren't just stinging; they were burning. It was as though an army of fire ants was teeming all over his body and biting him at once.

He tried to lift his legs out of the liquid. The movement caused him to rock back on his side. His feet came out of the liquid, but the gray water rolled back into the area where his body fell. As he became prostrate on the bathroom floor again, the water ran underneath his back and sloshed up and over his chest, coating most of his torso. Thomas looked down as more mist rose from his body.

His eyes widened and his breath became ragged as pure terror washed through him. In the dim light shining through his enclosure, he saw tiny holes opening up on the skin of his chest as whatever was in the liquid began to eat away at his flesh.

Thomas's mind screamed, *It's fucking acid! It's eating me alive!* He bit down hard on nothing. His teeth snapped together and he gritted them against the pain that was burning throughout his body, building in intensity.

Blood oozed out of those tiny holes, and the openings continued to enlarge. Some of the wounds joined others to create small craters all over Thomas's chest. He glanced down at other areas of his body. His legs and arms had the same horrific thing happening to them, ever-widening, hideous wounds opening up and leaking blood.

His body jerked uncontrollably, reacting to the pain as he tried to get away from it, but there was nowhere to go in his shrinking coffin. Sections of his flesh melted through as some of the gray liquid washed over him and poured down into his body. He had no doubt that he was being eaten away on the inside as well. The torment in his core was evident of that. He felt as though his blood had been exchanged with gasoline and someone had lit a match to it. The liquid fire was burning through him and hollowing him out.

Layers of skin slid from his body. He made a meager attempt to grab hold of one piece and pull it back into place, but his body spasmed again and he couldn't snag it in time. His fingers—now without skin and barely any muscle—missed anyway. All he could do was watch it slide away, like a layer of snow and ice sliding off a windshield.

He looked to the side and saw more bits and pieces of himself floating in the now bright-red-tinted fluid. The pieces shrank quickly, eaten away into nothing by the chemical within this liquid. His flesh was evaporating before his very eyes into a light fog that drifted up, then disappeared completely.

The container *was* quickly closing in around him. He had nowhere to go. The shrinking cocoon caused the liquid level to rise, allowing it to cover more and more of Thomas's body and breaking it down even more quickly.

Then, all at once, the pain became too much. His mind steeped in agony from the ordeal, Thomas surrendered to his fate, unable to sit up anymore. He dropped back, level with the bathroom floor. The acid washed in around him and surrounded his head. It poured into his ears, nose, mouth and eyes and ate away everything at once. In one moment, his face—his very identity—was dissolved, leaving nothing but the muscle, cartilage fibers and nerves that made up his features. In the next instant, they were wiped away too, leaving nothing but his skull pulled tight against the lining of the shrinking cocoon. The thrashing abruptly stopped as the enclosure constricted quickly, like a snake around his body.

An impression of Thomas's skull had been frozen in an open-mouthed scream against the side of the cocoon. Thomas's lower jaw snapped off under the weight of the shrinking enclosure, and with a final pop and shifting of bone, the rest of his skull shattered. Those final pieces disintegrated in the liquid acid, burning the last of Thomas into nothingness.

The creature was almost back to its long form. The cocoon shrank away very quickly; it stretched, twisted and elongated as it moved the last of Thomas's nutrients along and throughout the alien hair strand.

For a long time, the hair-strand just lay on the bathroom floor, writhing around as it squeezed bits of itself together and elongated to its final, inordinately long extent. When it finished dissolving what it had been fed and had broken its subject down to the smallest nutrients, fully satisfied and content, the hair-strand started to divide itself into short sections.

When the new Thomas stepped back into the bathroom, it knew what it would find. The bathroom floor was now littered with hundreds of tiny hair-strands writhing all over the floor, identical to the one Thomas had swallowed at The Station the night before.

The new Thomas stooped near the closest wriggling strand and gently picked it up. It examined it for a moment, then placed it in the container it had found in Thomas's kitchen. It proceeded to pick each of the others up with a gentle hand and place them in the container with the others.

When the new Thomas picked up the last hair, he heard the sound of the doorbell. He turned and paused for a moment. Taking a second look at the wriggling follicle, a hint of a smile curled the corners of the Thomas-twin's mouth—much like it had when smelling the shampoo in its cupped hand.

Instead of placing the hair in the container with the others, the Thomas-twin enclosed his fingers around it in a gentle fist. Then it placed the lid over the container and snapped it closed ever so carefully.

As the new Thomas moved from the bathroom into the kitchen, it placed the container on the kitchen counter and moved to answer the door.

"Hey, Thomas," Pete Morin said when the doppelgänger opened the door. "What's up? How you doing?"

"Hello, Pete," the new Thomas-twin said. It came out in a monotone, devoid of emotion or inflection.

Pete just stared at Thomas. "You okay, man?"

"Yes. I am fine. Why do you ask?"

"Well, for one, you sound weird today. Why you talking in a monotone voice?"

"I wasn't aware I was talking in a monotone voice, but if it bothers you, I can stop."

"You sound like a damn robot."

"I can assure you I am not a damn robot." The corners of the creature's mouth turned up with a hint of a grin.

"I see what you're doing. You're doing that shit Britney was pulling on me at The Station last night. One of your damn jokes again."

"Yes. One of my damn jokes. Why are you here?"

Pete looked at him weird again.

"I was in the neighborhood and thought I would drop by to see how you were doing. Don't you ever answer your damn phone? I've called you like ten or eleven times today already. You seemed a little pissed after last night's round of drinks when you choked on that Jägerbomb. That was some crazy shit, right?"

The doppelgänger was taking in how Pete used tones and inflections to color his voice. The more Pete spoke, and the more the Thomas-creature listened and replied, the more natural its voice became.

"Yes, crazy shit, but no, I am fine. Nothing to worry about here," it said. "You want a beer or something to drink? I have a cold one in here just for you."

"After last night, probably not a beer, but if you have a Coke or Dr. Pepper that would be perfect."

The Thomas-twin smiled and said, "Okay. C'mon in."

As it turned and moved toward the kitchen, it moved its hand close to its chest and opened its fist. It smiled down at the wriggling follicle, the one so eager to get to work.

"One Coke coming right up."

⌘

Later that night, Pete Morin's belly button, as well as those of numerous other citizens in the lazy town of Bournemouth, Louisiana, began itching as well.

FROSTBITE

FANTASY'S STOMACH WAS mad; it was growling at her again. The hunger pains were protesting the recent 'real food' strike. To satisfy their cravings, if only for a little while, Fantasy took another huge bite of her juicy cheeseburger.

Jade, a stripper sitting two dressing areas away from Fantasy, paused as she put the final touches to her makeup, looked over and asked, "Was that your stomach again?"

Fantasy nodded, but held up a finger. The bite she had taken was extremely large and she couldn't talk around the food. When she finally swallowed, she said, "Guilty. I'm just starving so bad. I had to get a quick bite in me before I go on."

"Girl, I do not see how you eat the kind of food you eat and stay as fucking sexy as you are. What the hell is your secret?"

"Oh, I could tell you, but if I did…" Fantasy said, but paused for emphasis.

They both finished the well-known phrase in unison. "Then I'd have to kill you." They shared a laugh.

Fantasy continued, "I guess I've just been blessed with a crazy high metabolism."

That wasn't really the case, but she couldn't tell Jade her secret. She didn't know how Jade, let alone anyone else, would react to the information; she was still trying to figure it out herself.

"Oh, I would give anything to have that," Jade said. "I have to watch every little thing I eat, count every fucking calorie that goes in. I'm in the gym all the time. Jesus, staying in shape really sucks."

"You look fan-fucking-tastic to me."

Jade was obviously taken aback. "Wow. Hey, thanks. You have to do what you have to do to keep that money flowing, right?"

"That you do," Fantasy agreed.

As she took another bite of her burger, her stomach protested again. This time it wasn't as loud, but Fantasy glanced in Jade's direction to make sure she hadn't heard. Jade was now looking in her dressing-station mirror, continuing to apply her makeup.

Good, she thought. *It's subsiding. Thank God.*

Fantasy began to eat again.

The dressing room was a cluttered mess of various skimpy stripper outfits on hangers, hung on nails that were hammered willy-nilly into the walls. There were two hanging racks that held other outfits, colorful feather boas and other accoutrements of the trade. The room was bright from the overhead florescent fixture and the makeup lights that accompanied most of the dressing stations. All of the dressing stations had an assortment of lipsticks and eyeshadow cases that were shared by all the performers.

Jade asked, "You're due up in a few minutes, aren't you?"

"Yeah, right after Marshmallow. Just going to down the rest of this," Fantasy said, pointing at her burger, "touch up my makeup and head to the stage."

"Well, I'm sure you're going to kill it out there again tonight. You always do."

"That really means a lot. Thanks, Jade."

"Never seen moves like the ones you do. You are so goddamn limber. I bet all the guys want to fuck you."

"Yeah, and some of the girls. I have to break so many hearts, or I'd be really busy and my pussy would be insanely sore."

"Wouldn't be too much of a bad thing, I guess."

"Just tiring. There are a number of guys out there that really want to hit this." Fantasy playfully smacked her own ass.

They shared another laugh. Jade went back to putting on her makeup but kept talking. "Jeez, watching you devour that damn cheeseburger is making me want to eat something naughty. I'm so hungry, I could probably eat *you*. I may just have one of those myself, then jump back on my diet tomorrow. I've been craving meat so much lately, and not of the dick variety either."

Fantasy laughed. *Me too,* she thought.

Jade looked over at her and saw Fantasy staring wide-eyed at her. "What?" she asked. As soon as she had asked, she realized what she had said. "Oh, shit, that came out wrong."

"Not really," Fantasy said. "Depends on how you really meant it. Was it a Freudian slip from what you're really thinking? Or wanting? Or was it just a way to describe how hungry you are with no double meaning?"

Jade gave her a quick smile, pausing and thinking before answering with a blush. "Both, I guess. Sorry about that."

Fantasy put down her burger. She stepped over to Jade and whispered in her ear. "Don't be. Just go with it."

Fantasy kissed Jade full on the lips as she wrapped her in a lover's embrace. She was careful not to get any grease or ketchup on Jade's skin or outfit, but pulled her closer with the heels of her hands as she kissed her deeply.

When Fantasy ended the kiss and embrace, sucking Jade's lower lip hard, she stepped back and looked deep into Jade's eyes, which were now wide in surprise.

Before Jade could say anything, Fantasy said, "That can happen if you really want it to. I'm game. I didn't French you just now because I've been eating that." She threw a hand back in the direction of her plate of fast food. "But what I really wanted to do was tongue-fuck your sexy mouth."

Jade barely found her voice. Her sentence came out in a breathy whisper that ramped up to her regular voice as she said, "I've never really heard it put like that, but I wish you had. I, um, just, you know, didn't think you were into girls."

Fantasy gave her a look that said otherwise. "Oh, more than you know."

"You're new to this strip club. We just haven't figured you out yet. You're kind of a loner—you sort of keep to yourself. It's like you're hiding something from us girls." She gave a laugh. "Guess I figured out what your deep, dark secret really is."

"That's one of them," Fantasy said. *But not the main one.* She took an extra-long look at Jade then turned, moved to her chair, and began to eat again. An awkward but not entirely uncomfortable silence settled around them.

The dressing room door flew open and banged against the wall.

"Motherfuckers!" Baby Cakes said as she entered the room. "Goddamn it! Who the fuck do those animals out there think they are?" She turned back and yelled out the door, directing her comment to someone out in the main room, but her yell was swallowed up by the music. "Fucking rednecks!" She slammed the door behind her and put her hands on her hips.

"What happened?" Jade asked.

Baby Cakes turned toward Jade, took a moment to compose herself, then moved to the chair that separated Jade and Fantasy and sat, facing Jade.

"Fucking lap dance got out of hand is what happened. Or should I say, *too handsy.* Jesus, I don't make enough money to grind all up and down on a pair of grease-monkeys. They smell like oil. The least those assholes could do is take a fucking bath and look presentable before they come in here to get their cocks off on us. It would help me get a little more in the mood, that's for damn sure. Just look at my new outfit; it's ruined. They kept pawing at me, even though I told them there was a 'no touch' policy in this nice Christian establishment. They nearly finger-banged me before the song was finished, so I just left them high and dry. They took their money back, or at least the thin guy did. Can you believe that shit? I should fucking get half that money! I gave them half a fucking lap dance, right?"

Before Jade could comment, Fantasy asked, "Who were these guys again?"

Baby Cakes glanced up at Jade, then turned slightly and peered over her shoulder. "Um, hey there, Fantasy. Ah, it was two guys sitting over near the fish tank. You know, near the main dance platform."

"Why didn't you get Buddha involved in the situation? Maybe get those guys kicked out."

"Buddha was across the room, dissolving a different situation that was getting a little carried away. I didn't feel like bothering him."

"What did these guys look like?"

"Assholes."

Fantasy laughed aloud. "There are a lot of assholes out there tonight, I'm sure. I need to know specifically which two assholes it was so I can get your money back from them."

"Look, Fantasy, no offense, but I don't need anyone to fight my battles for me. I'm a strong enough woman to do it myself. I'll make the money up by doing a few more lap dances for some other guys or gals. It's okay. I just felt it wasn't that important to pursue this time around. You know, take the high road and all that."

"I know you're a strong woman and you don't need anyone to fight your battles. But you were wronged, and if you don't stand up for yourself when you feel you've been wronged for whatever reason, then you won't stand up the next time something happens and you'll just cease to be a fighter. I have a bit of fight in me tonight, and I'd love to take care of this matter for you. That is, if you'll let me. Maybe it'll give you the strength to stand up for yourself next time. We gals have to stick together, don't we?"

"Um, yeah. Sure. Okay. If you want to, be my guest. Ah, just two dirty guys wearing car mechanic uniforms. You know, the usual dark blue kind. They probably came here right after work. One is decently thin, athletic, rugged good looks—if you like that type, which I do—which is why I started bumpin' and grindin' on him first. The other guy is a bit chubbier. Fat, actually. Very non-sexy, if you get my meaning. I was hoping I could get some money and hit up another table, but they both wanted lap dances from me. You know, the type who like to partake and then watch as they mentally whack off on what they want to do to me—us. I was just trying to drum up enough courage and the stomach to grind on Tubby McTubberson."

"I don't blame them for wanting a dance from you," Fantasy said. "You are stunning." She winked at Jade and smiled.

Baby Cakes looked at her more directly for a moment, then glanced at Jade, wondering suspiciously if something had gone on behind closed doors. She turned back to Fantasy. "Where did you come from? And why haven't you been dancing here longer?"

Jade piped up, "She could tell you, but if she did she would have to kill you." She thought for a moment, then added, "And me too." She and Fantasy shared another smile.

Baby Cakes said, "Well, I needed to hear that. I'm going to put you in my pocket, and when I don't feel so hot about my body, I'll take you out so you can give me all sorts of compliments to boost my self-esteem."

They all laughed.

"Okay, so we have a thin guy," Fantasy said, getting the conversation back on track. "A fat, tubby guy. Both in dirty, greasy car mechanic uniforms. Got it. I'll get you your money back for you; maybe a little more if possible."

"What? Really?! You are? What are you going to do to them?"

"I'm just going to go sex them up."

Fantasy pushed the last bit of cheeseburger into her mouth along with the last two fries, then moved toward the bathroom, saying no more.

After she had thoroughly washed up, she moved back to her dressing area to add the final touches to her face. She took a long look at herself in the mirror. She adjusted her breasts in her outfit, her nipples hardening in arousal.

God, I'm sexy. I love my body, Fantasy thought. *I can't keep my hands off myself.*

She left the dressing room area and stepped into the short hallway that led to—as she liked to refer to it—'The PDA Section', or 'Sextion'. As she entered it, the lighting dimmed drastically, but the music ramped up in volume. The sound was a deafening assault to her ears, but she knew it was just the Changing coming upon her again. Her hearing became more acute when it was about to happen.

When she reached the end of the hallway, she paused at the cloth drape that was the only barrier between her and the audience members.

She pulled back the fabric and walked through, then paused again to survey the grand room of this establishment.

"Hey, Fantasy," a man said, leaning a little sideways to direct his greeting down to her. "You're looking beautiful and sexy as ever."

Fantasy looked up to see a beefcake standing sentry to the left of the entryway. "Hey, Buddha. Thanks."

It was the compliment he'd given her every night she had performed, and Fantasy thought it was probably the same one he gave every stripper that came out to dance. Buddha was the bouncer, always on watch to stop anyone who got out of control or too handsy with the ladies. He always took up this position to protect the strippers from any assholes that tried to go down the hall and enter the dressing areas to get an autograph, phone number or something else.

"No problem. You up next?"

"Yeah, in just a few. Right after she finishes mesmerizing those dolts."

Buddha chuckled at the comment. "She's been at it a while. That's a long song she chose. I'm sure your dance is going to be amazing."

"We'll see."

"It will be. It always is," he assured her.

Buddha was always professional with every woman who entered and exited. Most of the time he kept to himself. He only made polite conversation but was always business-like, a perfect gentleman, and never gave the women any reason to feel creeped out. They always felt safe with him on guard.

The lights jittered, flashed and strobed to the beat of the music. The lighting for the most part was subdued, so patrons had some sense of privacy as their lap dance happened, but there was enough to illuminate the strippers and the action going on inside Lust tonight.

Right now, Marshmallow was center stage and in the spotlight. She was very good at keeping the men's attention. She had perfected the skill of giving the men glimpses of her body and then covering herself up again. Sometimes it was a longer, calculated glimpse of her perfect curves—then she moved away, leaving the guys to groan and complain that she wasn't giving them more.

Guys are so easy to entertain, Fantasy thought. They would live like a king for one night and throw away a week's wages for a few beautiful sights of mental ecstasy. They were ridiculous. *But if they're going to pay for it, we're certainly going to give it to them.*

Fantasy looked away from Marshmallow; her moves were starting to make her horny. With the promise of snowfall in the air, there were fewer men here tonight than usual. Definitely a slow night. Still, there was work to be done and money to be gained. By her count, there were twenty to twenty-five men spaced throughout the club; maybe some more were having some fun in the VIP rooms. Most of the men had a stripper before them in various stages of undress, moving sensually to the beat of the music. A couple of men were here with their wives or girlfriends—those women who liked to watch their men as they got lap dances and ogled the sexy girls. A few of the women were even getting a dance of their own. The women were able to get away with touching the strippers a little more than the men, because the dancers knew they weren't a threat. Waitresses in skimpy outfits were busy servicing everyone with their drink and food orders.

Fantasy said, "Wish me luck."

Buddha replied, "Gorgeous, you don't need luck. Knock 'em dead."

She moved away from Buddha with stealthy purpose. The music was banging and so was her body. In the two days Fantasy had been performing here, she had already gained fans who were back and ready for more. They left their seats and came to try and entice her to come sit with them or give them a lap dance. She promised she would as soon as she performed, and invited them to come down to the edge of the stage to get an eyeful.

She was dressed in a pink-and-blue plaid school-girl outfit, complete with white garters, white fishnet stockings and matching light-blue fuck-me pumps. Her tight white top was tied into a knot under her breasts, which strained against the thin fabric. The bra underneath matched her skirt, which barely covered her ass. There was a little sway to the skirt that matched her sashay as she moved toward the main stage. Her olive skin glistened with a hint of glitter. Her long, black hair was pulled into two ponytails that bobbed on either side of her head. She wore black-rimmed glasses to give that hint of the 'sexy secretary' look.

All eyes were on her; they followed her every move. She smirked, winked and blew kisses to her new adoring fans. She felt eyes undressing her and ripping off what little clothing she was wearing. Fantasy felt the thoughts of all the men and women in this place mentally pawing at her body, saw them bending her into every imaginable angle so they could greedily insert a part of themselves into her. She knew every explicit action and animalistic urge they wanted to do to her. It was a huge turn-on, and she started to get wet. She smiled.

She could smell the musk that hovered in the air. She was aroused and wanted to fuck something, anything. She felt the Changing quivering and shimmering just beneath her skin. It was so hard not to just let it happen, but she knew if she did, it would be bad for everybody in this place. She couldn't let that happen. Not here, not yet. But soon.

Above the sexual urges pulsating through her, she was still hungry—practically starving. Apparently the burger and fries hadn't been enough, only a temporary deterrent until she could get a real meal. Her stomach growled at her again, but the music Marshmallow was stripping to was more than loud enough to cover it. She needed something else to eat; something of substance. She knew there was only one thing that would satisfy her insatiable hunger.

Jesus, how long has it been since I've eaten? she asked herself. *I mean, really eaten? Seven, eight days now?* She couldn't really recall. *I can't dwell on that right now. I'm up. Time to perform. Time to put my game face on.*

As the last notes of New Order's "Shellshock" ended, the DJ's voice came over the sound system. "Ladies and gentlemen, give it up for Marshmallow! That's right. You know Marshmallow well, because she's white and she's sticky. You just saw her dance, and I *know* you all want to take her with you on your next camping trip. But why wait that long? Let her take you to the closest VIP room. You never know how sticky you'll get."

A wave of laughter rippled through the dive.

The DJ's voice dropped to a deeper register. "And now, new to Lust, and coming to the stage right now..."

Fantasy was already walking up the steps. She wiped down the stripper pole with a towel.

The DJ continued. "You've been waiting for her your whole life. You've seen her in your wet dreams. Let's give it the fuck up for FAAAAANTASYYYYYY!"

Fantasy pitched the towel down the runway and struck a pose against the stripper pole—legs spread wide, hips cocked to one side and her hands above her head—as the last syllables of her name faded away.

The DJ's voice was replaced with the infamous panther cry that began Janet Jackson's "Black Cat". As soon as the beat of the song boomed through the speakers, Fantasy turned and jumped onto the stripper pole, spinning into an inverted split. She wrapped her feet around the pole and held herself upside down, ripped off the knotted shirt, and tossed it into the face of a guy who had just come down to the edge of the stage with a few dollar bills in his hand.

She winked and blew him a kiss, then continued with her dance without missing a beat.

As the song played, one by one, pieces of clothing were peeled sensuously from her body with alluring seduction. Every ass-shake, sexy pose, boob-grab and stroke to her body was choreographed to perfection. The dance was a tease, and more and more men moved down to check out this new dancer. As they worshipped her, they all were adding another fantasy to the mental spank-banks.

Stripping always turned Fantasy on. There was something about giving all of herself, baring it all in front of a group of admiring and lustful men and women, that made her feel euphoric. She wasn't stupid; she knew what they all wanted to do to her, and in the most hardcore of ways. She knew they wouldn't mind passing her down and around as they took turns making their sexual fantasies come true, whether it took a few strokes or many.

Hell, that might even be an interesting night, Fantasy thought as she cat-crawled around on the stage floor. In the back of her mind she knew that would be a bad idea for everyone involved.

Better keep that little fantasy in my head. The Changing is upon me, and very close; so close I can hardly contain myself. As she danced, she let her mind drift into various other thoughts—anything to keep the Changing at bay.

Janet Jackson was singing: *"Better watch your step or you're gonna die."* *Great,* Fantasy thought. *It's near the end.*

All of a sudden, the film over her left eye broke free and gave way to a whole new visual clarity. One side of her vision instantly became colorful and much more vibrant.

She quickly shut her eyes, thinking frantically, *NO! NO! NO! Not now! Not here!*

Finally, the last beats of "Black Cat" died away, and she struck her final sexy pose. She held it a moment longer, so the ending of her dance wouldn't look rushed. She had an image to uphold. The DJ's voice came back on, but she heard nothing of what he was saying. She quickly grabbed her few skimpy items of clothing and the money discarded on the stage floor, then moved down the small runway and behind the curtain that was rarely used.

There, amid numerous crates of beer, discarded stage lighting and other miscellaneous boxes of bric-a-brac, Fantasy leaned back against the wall and willed the Changing into submission as best she could. She took deep, calming breaths, and after a few minutes, she felt the split in her eye merge back together. Only then did she open her eyes.

"Oh, thank God. Thank God," she repeated. *That was close. Way too close. It wouldn't have been good if I had allowed it to go any further. I'm going to have to work hard on controlling that.*

She slowly got dressed in the abandoned backstage area as she continued to calm herself, then finally worked her way back through the storage area to a door that led to the main dressing room. Jade and Baby Cakes and the other strippers weren't there at the moment. They had probably stepped out to see her dance. She was sure Baby Cakes was in the main area, watching to see what Fantasy was going to do to the two dicks that had cheated her out of her money.

Let's just see what I'm going to do, Fantasy thought. With one final look to make sure her makeup wasn't messed up on the eye that had changed, she ventured back out to the PDA Section.

The huge hunger cravings were getting worse. She had to satisfy them now, or something insane was going to happen inside this strip joint. Knowing this, Fantasy was immediately on the prowl again. She moved directly to where she had spotted the two guys that had felt up Baby Cakes as though she was a magnet pulled in their direction, destined to make a connection.

She came up on them from behind. They were busy talking dirty about Busty Tina, whose head was currently thrown back in peals of laughter as she let some frat boy motorboat her tits three tables away.

Fantasy walked around and stood in front of them, blocking their view of Tina so they would have to look up at her. She struck the sexy pose from the beginning of her dance.

Before she could say anything, one of the guys, the fat one, said, "Oh, shit. It's Fantasy."

"That's right, boys, the one and only. But tell me this—why do you want to do that with her," she said, tilting her head in Busty Tina's direction, "when you can do the same with me?" She pointed at herself. "I mean, my tits may not be as big as hers, but I do have a beautiful set that needs some lips on them."

The two men looked at each other in confusion. The thin guy said, "How did you know we were wanting to do anything with her?"

"I've worked in places like this long enough to know that you boys don't want to start a book club with her."

They only smiled slyly.

"You boys want or need a dance from me?"

They didn't answer.

"Let me rephrase: you *want* a dance from me." It came off as a command.

That familiar sensation was running the length of her body. It was just beneath the skin. She mentally fought against it. It was almost too much for her, like an orgasm on the verge of release. She had to get out of here.

She continued to stare deep into their eyes, mesmerizing them as she swayed slightly to the music thumping in the background. She was like a cobra charming its prey.

She continued before they could answer, "I could rub you both the right way." She ran her hands over her body. It was mainly to quell the sensation running along her skin, but it was helping with her sales pitch as well. Her voice was husky now; deeper. "And maybe if you're lucky and treat me right, I might just rub one out for the both of you. How does that sound?"

"Fuck yeah. I'm game. Bring it on, gorgeous," the thin one said, and slapped his thigh. "Sit down on my lap, and we'll talk about the first thing that pops up."

Jesus Christ, you're not Santa Claus, Fantasy thought. How many times had she heard that lame-ass line? *They all think they're so cute and clever.*

She leaned over and wrapped her arms around his neck, pushing her breasts up into his face close enough for him to smell her essence. "I need to see the money first. Money always talks me into doing things—dirty things—that I don't normally do."

The thin man looked over at his fat friend. They smiled at each other, then the thin man leaned up enough to pull his wallet from his back pocket. He looked through the bills and then back to Fantasy.

"How much will a hundred dollars get me?"

"Not as much as two hundred, but it will get the party started. Definitely my dirty side."

The thin man laughed. "You drive a hard bargain, lady. Okay, so—"

The fat man had already pulled his wallet out and was holding up a handful of bills. "How much will two hundred get *me*?"

Fantasy looked back at the thin man and smirked, then moved over to the fat man's lap. "I can guarantee it will get you off," she said, sliding a finger down his nose. "But we can't do it here. We would have to go someplace special. Someplace more private."

"TJ, you son-of-a-bitch. Quit cock-blocking me."

"Calm down, Slade. Man, you have to talk serious with sexy ladies like Fantasy here. You have to go with the big bucks if you want them to open up their legs to you."

"That's right, Slade," Fantasy said. "Money is the sweetest but dirtiest talker."

"I've only got two hundred and fifty on me."

Fantasy kissed TJ on the check, stood and moved back toward Slade. Before she could sit down on his lap, TJ blurted in a last-ditch effort, "I have two-fifty as well. Plus, an extra twenty in my emergency stash."

Slade placed his beer glass back on the table a little harder than necessary. "Motherfucker," he said, glaring at TJ.

"What, dude? Don't get pissed at me. I want to make it with her as much as you. If the money talks, then I'm going to talk my way into her panties as best I can. Look at me. Money is the only thing I have going for me at this point. If paying her two hundred and seventy dollars will give me a little joy tonight, help me sleep like a baby and give me an amazing memory that I can jerk off to for years to come, I'm going to take it. So fuck you."

"Boys, boys," Fantasy said, grabbing their attention. She was now standing between them. They looked up at her. "There's enough of me to go around. I'm not opposed to doing you both at the same time."

TJ and Slade exchanged slack-jawed glances.

"Get you both off at the same time." She gave them each a seductive smile. "How's that for a *fantasy*? Yeah, you like that, don't you? Here's the deal—for five hundred dollars, you two can have me any way you want me, but after you've had your fun, I get to have mine. I get to have you two any way I want *you*. Does that sound fair?"

TJ and Slade looked at each other again and grinned. They were obviously both thinking they were going to get off twice. Their heads bobbed up and down on their necks, as though they were infants trying to concentrate on something of interest for the first time.

Fantasy continued, "Two hundred fifty each. Do you know how much of a fun time that will get you with me?"

Slade said, "No, but I'm willing to find out." He pulled the bills from his wallet and handed them up to her.

"Put your money away for now, boys. As you can see, I really don't have a place to hold it with this outfit. You can pay me later. I want to make sure you're satisfied with my service."

Slade looked over at TJ as he replaced the bills in his wallet. "Okay. Sure. Play now, pay later. I like your policy, babe. I can deal with that."

Fantasy didn't like the look shared between the two men. She knew Slade didn't have any intention of paying her if he could get out of it. He was the one who had taken his money back from Baby Cakes. TJ was a different cookie altogether, though. She sort of felt sorry for the schlubby guy. She felt he would gladly pay the money for the sex and the memory that came along with it. It was going to be one of the most cherished moments of his sad and lonely life.

"So, where are we going?" she asked. "We can't do it here or in one of the VIP rooms. It's against company policy to have full-on sex in the rooms. They want you to have fun, but not that much fun."

TJ said, "How 'bout your van, Slade?"

"Sure. Let's go have a party in my van."

Fantasy took two steps away, then glanced back at them. Both men were staring at her with dumbfounded looks on their faces.

"Are you *coming* or not? Pun intended—or should I find someone else in this rat-hole that's going to fuck me tonight?"

They looked at each other. Fantasy was now standing with her hands on her hips. The tip of one of her fuck-me pumps was impatiently tapping the sticky floor, waiting for them to make up their minds.

They will, she thought. *They always go for the pussy. They just can't help themselves. And I don't blame them. I am so goddamn sexy that everyone wants a piece of my ass.*

"You boys have to ask each other's permission? Or are you going to be men about this, step up to the pussy plate and make it a night we'll all three never forget? It's a deal of a lifetime, and one I offer only once. Take it or leave it. Make your choice, but remember the deal. You can have me any way you want, but I also get to have my fun and have you two any way I want. So, what's it going to be, gentlemen?"

"No, we're going to take you up on your offer," Slade said. "We're just being careful. We're just making sure this isn't a trap."

Fantasy burst out laughing. "You two are so cute. I assure you, it's not a trap. I'm no cop, if that's what you're worried about. I just want to get out of here for a while. Have some fun. Cool off. It's a little warm in here."

"That's probably your fault, because you certainly are hot," TJ said.

Mentally, Fantasy rolled her eyes at the comment but thought, *I'll give him points for trying.* She stepped toward them, grabbed their hands and jerked them up out of their chairs.

TJ was immediately on guard. He'd felt Fantasy's unnatural strength as she'd pulled them into a standing position. He glanced over to see if Slade had noticed.

But no, Slade wasn't that observant. Maybe it was because he was staring down into Fantasy's deep cleavage. He took an extra-long look at her tits, then turned back to the table to grab one last sip of beer before they left. Maybe Slade was a little more drunk than TJ was.

TJ, still wary, thought, *How did she pull my fat ass out the chair so easily? With her small frame and in those FMPs? Something's odd about her. That wasn't normal.* He quickly adjusted his hard-on and stood the rest of the way up.

Fantasy said, "C'mon. Let's do this if we're gonna do this. I'm sure there are other men in here that would gladly take your place."

They turned and grabbed their jackets, following Fantasy as she led them to the side door and pushed it open.

As they exited, the arctic chill hit them like a punch to the gut. Snow had already started to fall in the late evening. The flakes backdrafted underneath the awning and spun around them.

"Jesus Christ on a crutch, what the fuck?" TJ gasped. "Why does it have to be so goddamn cold out here?"

"What are you talking about? This feels amazing," Fantasy said, leaning forward on the banister right outside the door. She breathed deeply.

"What am *I* talking about?" TJ shot back. "What are *you* talking about? This is bullshit weather. It's fucking freezing out here."

"You barely have anything on," Slade said, and smacked her hard on the ass. He slid his finger between her ass cheeks then up between her legs.

Fantasy spun and played like she didn't appreciate his forwardness, but TJ could tell it was an extreme turn-on.

Slade continued, "And I will hasten to say, I am very appreciative of that fact—but how the fuck are you not cold, sweetheart?"

They descended the three steps from the side entrance landing to the parking lot asphalt. Fantasy began spinning in slow circles with her arms outstretched, staring up at the stars.

"I grew up in weather like this. This is nothing. I'm used to it. It feels so good." She looked like a little child who was seeing snow for the first time in her life. TJ was still weirded out by her and the sheer strength she had displayed.

The three of them moved across the parking lot toward Slade's van, Fantasy still slowly spinning as she moved. As they neared it, she noticed it was shit-brown in color and had a good number of dents in the lower panels. It was also rusted through in places around the wheel wells. There were bubbled-out teardrop-style windows in the upper back corners of the van's sides. She couldn't help but think, *Drive this around too many neighborhoods, and kids are going to start disappearing. Where's their candy stash for luring kids into this piece of shit?*

Looking TJ and Slade over inside the strip club, she hadn't exactly got a child molester vibe from them; they were more the type of shit-heads to kidnap young women and take them to a hideout cabin deep in the woods to make snuff films before making them disappear for good. What she *did* know was that they were a couple of complete assholes that needed to be taught a lesson because of what they had done to Baby Cakes. They probably had committed their fair share of petty crime at some time in their lives. Still, this van sure gave off a really bad feeling at first glance.

Watching Fantasy spin in the falling snow and without thinking of his choice of words but not meaning to be offensive, TJ said, "You're weird. Beautiful. Amazing. Alluring. Sexy. But really fucking weird."

Pulled from her thoughts about the van, the guys and what crimes they might have committed, Fantasy turned cat-quick toward TJ and was immediately in his face, glaring at him. Her eyes were full of fire. "Be nice, TJ, or I won't let you play with my tits."

Thrown by her quick movement, TJ took a quick shuffle-step back. "Okay, forget the weird comment, but the rest is definitely true."

As quick as the flash of anger had lit her face, it was gone. She smiled and looked up to the sky, starting to spin again. "Thank you, TJ. You will now be allowed to play with my tits."

TJ looked at Slade to get a read on what he was thinking. Slade shrugged his shoulders as if to say, *I have no fucking clue what the hell just happened.*

They arrived at Slade's van and he opened one of the fold-out side-panel doors. The interior dome light came on and dimly illuminated the back area of the van. Fantasy glanced in. Other than the front windshield and the driver's and passenger side windows, there were only two small square windows in the top of each of the back doors and the small teardrop windows in the back corner. All were tinted. Once the doors closed, the dome light would go off; there would only be the pale evening light to illuminate the action.

Slade noticed Fantasy's hesitation. He stepped back and held his hand out in mock chivalry as he helped her into the van. "Don't be afraid. We're going to take real good care of you."

I'll just bet you are, Fantasy thought. She wasn't the least bit scared. She was going to be able to see perfectly in the dim interior of his fuckmobile.

"Why thank you, kind sir," she said playfully. "My knight in shining armor."

"Not that shiny," TJ said, butting in. "More like a greasy mechanic's outfit. It's cloth. No armor."

"Shut up, dickhead. Who asked you? Did you happen to look at the way you're dressed? Exactly the same as me. You're no better than me."

TJ's laughter trailed off. He shot a glance toward Fantasy, but she looked as though she hadn't heard Slade's comments.

She crawled right in and looked around the van compartment, nodding her approval. There were no chairs in the back. It was completely empty and decently clean compared to the outside. The floor was covered with a soft, dark blue shag carpet. The metal hardness of the floor underneath was there, but at least there was a little bit of cushioning for however rough it might get, if she ended up on her knees or back—or both. She moved from her knees and leaned back against the driver's seat, waiting for them to make their move.

This won't take long, Fantasy thought. *These guys will probably blow their load after only a few strokes, then I'll be able to have my fun.*

TJ crawled in, sat on his butt and leaned against the van doors in the back. Once he was settled, he watched Fantasy and her reaction to what was about to go down.

This is almost too good to be true, he thought. If he hadn't been as beer-buzzed and thinking so much with the wrong head, that statement just might have been enough for him to nix this little rendezvous.

Slade stepped in and moved to his knees as he jerked the side door closed. It banged shut with a loud metal-on-metal sound which caused Fantasy to cringe and jerk her head in that direction. When Slade turned toward her, he saw her startled face.

"What's the matter?"

"Oh, nothing. The slamming door just scared me, that's all," she lied. It hadn't; the loud sound had been jarring to her in these close quarters. With the Changing so close on her, her ears were ultra-sensitive.

"Sorry about that. It has a catch and it's hard to close. I have to slam it hard all the time. Sorry. I should've given everybody a heads-up."

"Yeah, a warning would've been nice."

Fantasy shifted her gaze to TJ, and Slade followed suit. TJ glanced back and forth between the two of them. Nobody said anything.

Fantasy finally broke the silence as she took off her fuck-me pumps. "Gentlemen, don't everyone jump on me at once. How do you want to get this party started?" She put her shoes in the driver's seat and then began to remove her stockings and garter. She placed them in the front seat as well to protect them from any stains. She didn't want to return to the strip club with anything questionable on them.

"You said we could have you any way we wanted," Slade reminded her, glancing to TJ, then back to Fantasy to get her approval. "Right?"

"That I did." She held her finger up and added, "Only if *I* can have the both of *you* any way *I* want."

"Well, I don't know how you can have *us* any different than we'll already be having *you*, but I can't wait to find out," Slade said.

"Neither can I," Fantasy said with a sly smile.

Slade and TJ looked at her, unsure of her meaning. She winked.

"How would you like us?" TJ asked.

She smiled broadly and said, "Oh no. I won't come out and tell you. I'll go with my animal instincts and just do you. So, what great fantasies are you guys going to play out on me?"

"I don't know about you, but I would really love a blowjo—"

"Don't say it out loud," Fantasy said, interrupting Slade. "Just do it.

Put a little romance into the evening." She started moving toward him on her knees. "Move me into the position you want. Let me be your real live blow-up doll."

Slade said, "Blow-up dolls are pretty bendable, and you are amazingly flexible. The way you worked the stage tonight during 'Black Cat', I about had a heart attack."

"I am pretty flexible, aren't I?" She started playfully kissing him, darting her tongue in and out and over his lips. "Do me any way your heart desires. Just go with it."

Slade buried his tongue within her mouth and kissed her deeply.

Fantasy's hands dropped from his hair, down his chest and to the buckle of his blue work pants. She grabbed the end of the belt, flipped it open, unhitched the buckle, then unbuttoned and unzipped his pants. Working her hand inside his underwear, she pulled back the elastic band and released his cock.

"There it is," Fantasy cooed. "There's the big boy I've been looking for."

She immediately lowered herself and stuffed him deep into her mouth, then ran her tongue and lips along his thick shaft.

Slade groaned with pleasure as he threw his head back and looked at the ceiling. His hands went to the ceiling to steady himself. "Yes, yes, yes!" His fist pounded on the van's roof with each word.

When Fantasy came up for air, she turned to look at TJ, who was still sitting there, leaning back against the van doors with a surprised look on his face.

"Are you a watcher, TJ? Or a doer?"

"Huh?" he said, tearing his gaze from her ass to her face.

"Do you just like to watch?"

"No."

"Then do me," she commanded. "You can join in on the fun too, you know. I'm kind of busy with Slade's big guy here, but there's more of me to go around."

"I know," he said. He pointed at Fantasy's ass. "I'm worshipping it right now as we speak."

Fantasy glanced around even further. She gave him a slight smile, then shook her ass at him.

"Well, worship it closer. My pussy and ass aren't gonna take care of themselves, if you know what I mean. Do you think you could help me with that? The choice is yours, but don't just sit there."

Slade's hand grabbed one side of her face and pulled her back toward him. "Come on, TJ. If you're going to be in on this then do it, but don't be talking and ruining my fantasy. Don't make me show you how it's done."

He shoved his dick back into Fantasy's mouth and started gyrating back and forth. He leaned over and ran his hands down the length of her back, massaging as much of her as he could. He grabbed her tiny skirt and gave it a quick jerk. The velcro attachments released easily.

"Hey," Fantasy said quickly, taking his cock from her mouth again. "Be careful with that. I only have two outfits."

"I'll buy you a new one with the two-hundred-plus dollars I'm giving you. Don't worry about it."

"Well, put it in the front seat. I don't want to get anything on it."

"And what do you think is going to get on it?" TJ asked, knowing good and well what she meant.

"Yeah," Slade said. "What's going to get on it?"

"I certainly don't want to take it to the cleaners and have to explain any crusty white stains that need to be removed."

"Just so you know, if my spunk goes anywhere, it's going to go directly on your face. I'm a really great shot. That's my *fantasy*, Fantasy."

"Oh shit, now we're getting creative," Fantasy said.

Not breaking eye contact, Slade pitched her skirt over his shoulder into the front seat.

"Now my glasses." Fantasy pulled them from her face and handed them to Slade. "And don't throw them into the front seat," she added quickly. "Be careful with them. Those were expensive."

"Yes, ma'am," Slade said with a small salute. "Whatever you say."

"Thank you," Fantasy said.

"No, no. Thank *you*." Slade kissed her deeply again as he quickly unfastened her bra. She pulled back, opening her mouth to say something. "I know, I know. The front seat." Without looking, Slade pitched it over his shoulder again, then grabbed her head and lowered her onto his cock again. He slid his hands down the length of her body until he could grab two solid fistfuls of her ass. He reached as far around her as possible and fingered whatever hole he could find.

"TJ. C'mon, boy. This bitch is so wet. Just look at that. Better get in on all this, or I'm going to have her all to myself."

He smacked her ass a few times, then ran his hands back up the length of her body. He slid his hands underneath her arms and grabbed her breasts, kneading them fiercely.

TJ rocked himself to his knees and moved in behind her. He pushed her feet to either side of his knees and grabbed the small waistband of her G-string, helping her get it off without stopping Slade's ongoing blowjob. Knowing the protocol by now, TJ threw it onto the front passenger seat.

He knee-shuffled up closer to Fantasy's backside, then unbuckled, unbuttoned and unzipped his pants. He was already hard from watching Fantasy deep-throat Slade, and he slid inside her with ease.

Fantasy's stomach growls were back, but they weren't audible to the men yet. The Changing was upon her. Nothing like a little hardcore sex to spur it along and to help her fully blossom.

This is just what I needed, she thought as she relaxed her body and welcomed whatever was going to happen next. It was an amazing feeling, more exhilarating than sex—if that was possible—and she loved it. The Changing was very new to her. She never knew when it was going to happen; she hadn't transformed enough times to know how to control it well or change at will. She just knew the feeling that accompanied it, and right now it was very close.

She knew men's groans of ecstasy, and Slade was ramping up to climax. He was pounding deep within her mouth. TJ wasn't far behind him.

Her body was simultaneously hot and cold at the same time. She was so wet from arousal, she was actually dripping. Her body had broken out into a small sheen of sweat.

And there it is, Fantasy thought. *My eye. It always starts with my eye.* The Changing happened in a split second; in an instant, whatever she was looking at was infinitely sharper and more defined in brilliant colors. Everything was so much more vibrant. It was as though a film over her eyes was peeled back to reveal the yellow eyes of the creature she always became.

She remembered how it looked to see herself change. Her body erupted into millions of minuscule pinpricks as individual strands of hair simultaneously shot through her pores and grew. One second she was looking at her beautiful, tanned skin, and the next she was covered in a glossy coat of dark, short-haired fur. It always amazed her, and it all happened in the blink of an eye. If you weren't watching closely, you would miss the abrupt growth. It was just all of a sudden there.

Her ears always felt like they were being pierced, the tops pulled upward and back as the ends grew pointy and elf-like. Her hearing suddenly became much keener, as though someone had thrown a switch inside her head. She could even hear her own heartbeat and the blood pumping within her veins. She was so alive.

TJ was looking up at the van ceiling as he pumped in and out of Fantasy's body at an awkward, unsteady pace. His hands were gripping Fantasy's hips tightly as he did so. At first he didn't notice anything, but then he moved his hands to gain a better grip on her hips and realized he wasn't exactly touching skin anymore. He looked down, but couldn't process what he saw. He was almost mesmerized, like a kid seeing something for the first time, and had to touch it. He moved his hand to another area of Fantasy's back and felt her fur. He involuntarily stroked her back, and realized he was actually petting her. Her whole back was a sleek coat of black fur.

Slade's voice brought TJ out of his mental questioning. "What the hell are you doing to my cock? Are you purring? I've heard of a hummer and I've had them a time or two, but you have to be the best fucking hummer of my entire life. Oh shit! Don't stop."

"Purring?" TJ asked.

"Yeah, she's fucking purring, dude. It's the best. You have to get her to do you next."

"Fantasy?" TJ asked. He expected her to turn around and smile at him with her beautiful, sexy smile, but that illusion was shattered when two yellow, sulfurous, cat-like eyes whipped around and locked on to his. They stayed frozen on him, unblinking, studying him.

Horror unlike anything he had ever encountered in his shitty little life coated his body. He actually thought he might be changing into something himself as his whole body broke out in gooseflesh. His hair stood on end, and a wave of fear washed over him, rippling from the top of his head through the length of his body and out his toes.

"What the fu—?" he started, but couldn't finish the sentence. He tried to move away from Fantasy, but he was frozen where he knelt.

"What's the matter, TJ?" Fantasy purred in a low, guttural tone.

"Yeah, TJ, what's the matter?" Slade chimed in. "C'mon, man. You're messing up the rhythm we had going. I was almost ready to come. Why'd you stop?"

TJ hadn't realized he had stopped, but knew he wasn't going to start again, no matter how amazing it felt being inside her.

This isn't normal, he thought. *This is so fuckin' crazy.*

He pulled himself the rest of the way out and was pulling up his underwear and pants when Fantasy's voice stopped him.

"Don't you fucking dare think about leaving," she growled. "You wanted me this way, you're going to finish me this way. Now drop your fucking pants and put your dick back in me." He realized her voice was different now. It was still beautiful and sexy, but it had taken on a deeper tone with a silky quality to it.

"Goddamn, your voice is so sexy," Slade said. "C'mon, TJ, she's giving up that ass. What's your problem?"

"We gotta go," TJ blurted.

"Go?" he barked. "What the fuck you talkin' 'bout? I'm not leaving till I fuck this bitch seven ways from Sunday. If you don't want to join in on the fun that's fine, but don't fuck up everyone else's vibe."

"Slade. Really. We gotta go."

"Go then!" Slade yelled, and threw his arm up, pointing in the direction of the strip club. "Get the fuck out of my van so Fantasy and I can have some privacy. I'm tired of your goddamn bullshit."

He grabbed Fantasy's head roughly and pulled it back in line with his crotch so he could finish where they had left off. He inserted himself back into her mouth and thrust deep. He just needed a few more strokes, and he could ejaculate down her throat or on her face with pleasure.

As he did so, he noticed something different about the part of her face he now held. There was something wrong with it—a new texture. It was no longer smooth skin, but something soft and velvety to the touch. He noticed this at the same time he saw her arched back, now a sleek, dark pelt. Her skin—pelt—seemed pulled even tighter over her athletic body, the muscles even more defined in the dim light.

Slade's statement of horror started much the same way as TJ's did— "What the FUCK?"—but the last word of the sentence was screamed as Fantasy bit down with her new, razor-sharp teeth. Slade's cock was all the way in the back of her throat, so as he pulled back, a spray of blood ejaculated onto her face.

Slade's screams of agony filled the van. He tried to grab his crotch, but Fantasy batted his hands away. She shoved a clawed hand up to the center of his chest and forced him roughly against the van's wall, holding him firmly so he couldn't move. To get her point across even further, she dug her claws in as she palmed his chest. The five claw-marks started oozing blood.

She stayed down near his spurting crotch for a few moments, letting the warm blood wash over her newly formed snout. She breathed the scent of his blood in and opened her mouth to let his severed penis drop to the floor, then she drank deeply as the blood sprayed down her throat.

AB negative, she thought. *Ahh, so delicious.*

Slade's castration was more than TJ could handle. Bile erupted from inside him and bubbled up in the back of his throat. He choked it down as best he could, but some leaked out his lips, dribbling down the front of his greasy mechanic's shirt. Desperately, he pulled up his pants and buckled them. He couldn't do it fast enough; his overweight frame complicated the matter.

Fantasy rose slowly from Slade's crotch and looked Slade dead in the face. She smiled, but to him her blood-coated, cat-like features looked more like a snarl.

"Oh God, oh God, oh God," was all he could say in a panicked whisper-chant.

She licked around her snout and said, "Now *that's* what I call a facial."

Her fur rippled in anticipation of the upcoming kill. Slade had lost too much blood. His eyes rolled back into the top of his head as he fainted, and Fantasy shifted to the side to allow him room to fall face-first onto the carpeted floor of the van.

"Pity," Fantasy whispered in a guttural tone. "I was expecting so much more of a fight out of you. So disappointing."

TJ couldn't take any more. He had to get out of here quick. He didn't try to be stealthy, but bounded to the back door. He jerked the handle up and swung it open, then crouched to jump when he heard the inhuman cry of frustration behind him. He jumped from the back of the van, but clawed fingers scraped the back of his neck and wrapped around his coat collar. The grip jerked him up in midair, much in the same way a dog is snatched up when he reaches the end of his chain. TJ expected to land on the gravel driveway, looking up at the stars and the falling snow. Instead, he was immediately jerked back into the van. The force of the pull was enough to roll him all the way to the driver's seat.

When TJ looked up, he saw the silhouette of Fantasy hanging sideways in the van door opening. Snow spun in around her. She stepped into the van again, grabbed both doors, slammed them shut, spun on the pads of her newly pawed feet, and crouched at the back of the van.

"Tsk, tsk, tsk," she purred as her new, yellow eyes glimmered in the shadows. "TJ, TJ, TJ. What did I tell you before we came out here?"

TJ was blubbering, and his nose was running. "That—that if—that if we had *our* way with—with *you*, then you could have *us* any way you wanted."

"That's right. Looks like you were trying to get out of our deal by running away."

"I just—I just had to get some air. It was getting hot in here."

She began to crawl slowly toward him on all fours. When she got to him, she said, "I'll agree with you on that. It is a little warm." She leaned in close and purred in his ear. It sounded a little like honeybees swarming around deep in her throat. "But I can't just leave the back of the van open to let some air in, can I?"

TJ sobbed, but shook his head. "No," he croaked. "I guess not."

"Other people might see the party we're having and might want to break up all the fun." Fantasy ran a clawed finger down the side of his face. She was careful to do it gently, but there were a few places where her sharp claw sliced the skin and made TJ wince. Droplets of blood oozed out and slid down his face. "Oops, I'm sorry. Allow me to get that." She moved in close and licked the length of his cheek with her warm tongue.

TJ winced at the rough, sandpaper sensation. Fantasy made sure she didn't miss a drop.

She slid her clawed finger into where the buttons fastened TJ's shirt and sliced them away. The girth of his stomach forced the shirt open and popped the buttons off in the process. She continued all the way down his chubby chest and stomach until the shirt disappeared into his pants. "And right now," she paused and dropped her voice to a whisper, "I want you all to myself."

She slid her claw underneath his belt and jerked up on it. It sliced through it cleanly. She began cutting away more of his garments.

"You don't mind me being a little selfish, do you?"

"I guess not," he said reluctantly. "What—what are you going to do?"

"You didn't finish what you started. I was going to continue what we had going on in here earlier. You know why?"

"No. Why?"

"Because I'm so fucking horny I can't stand it."

"Are you—are you going to castrate me too?"

"No. Not unless you want me to."

"No, for the love of God, no. Please don't castrate me. I'll do anything."

"Okay, I won't. Besides, it would be a little hard for you to get me off if you had nothing to stick inside me, right?"

"Yeah. Yeah, I guess so."

"Okay. So you're going to make love to me?"

"I—I don't want to."

"Why not?" Fantasy played up her disappointment. "That's not how you and Slade were feeling thirty minutes ago inside the club. It was like you boys couldn't wait to slide your boners into something warm. Don't you like the way I look?"

"Yeah."

"And feel?"

"Yeah."

"I could be your very own sex pet. Wouldn't you like that?"

"I guess so."

"I bet you've never fucked anything like me before in your life, have you?"

"No. No, I haven't. I mean, I've never *seen* anything like you, let alone—" He let the rest of the sentence fall away into nothingness.

"Well, just let me help you out of these clothes." She began to cut away at the cloth of his pants until he could feel cool air on his penis again. She lowered her crotch to his and began sliding her sex over his. Despite his fear, he instantly became aroused.

Fantasy said, "Oh, yeah. There we go. There's your man. We're going to give him the workout of his lifetime."

Fantasy seized his hands and made him grab her breasts. She kept her hands over his and made him squeeze them hard.

He still stared in awe at the fur that covered her body. He didn't know what it was about her, but somehow the fur added to her allure. He didn't know if it was how dangerous she was, how strong she was, or how sexy she still was as a—what was she? *A cat creature? A mix of some feline and human DNA?* He didn't know, and he sort of didn't care.

"Am I beautiful?" she asked.

TJ nodded.

"Tell me you love my body."

He looked her over again. "I—I love your body."

"Tell me you love me."

He looked deep into her glowing eyes. "I... I love... I—I love you."

"Tell me when you're going to come."

"What? When I'm going to—Why?"

"Because I asked you to, and it will be an ending you'll just die for."

"Okay. I will. I'm almost there as it is," TJ said.

"You are?"

"Yeah. You're so very sexy. It doesn't take much to get me off."

"Ohh, so quick."

She moved her right hand behind his head and readied her clawed left index finger for the exact moment.

"Okay, I'm almost there," TJ warned her.

"Yeah? You almost there, big guy? You going to erupt into me?"

"Oh yeah. Yeah. Yeah. Okay, oh God, I'm coming. *I'm coming.*" He let out a groan as he ejaculated into her.

At the same time, Fantasy jabbed her clawed finger deep in the side of his neck and cut across and down toward his Adam's apple. The claw severed his carotid artery. She was already leaning in to accept his ejaculation of blood. She caught the geyser as it erupted from TJ's throat and drank greedily from the newly opened tap. Her mouth covered the gaping wound, and as she closed her lips around it, Fantasy sank her teeth deep within his neck.

TJ let out a scream of abject misery and tried to push Fantasy off him, but she had already wrapped her arms around him in a death grip. There was no escape now, and he knew this was the end of his miserable, shitty life. But leaving this world in the throes of sex was one of the best things that had ever happened to him. A slight smile played at the corners of his mouth.

Fantasy drank deeply and swallowed greedily. She sucked hard and fast again and again, as though desperate to quench an undying thirst. TJ actually felt his life's blood being pulled from his body. With each sucking motion, he felt the blood being drawn in the direction of his neck. When Fantasy paused to take a deep breath, he felt some flood back into his body. That feeling was short-lived, as Fantasy latched on and sucked deep again. He was feeling lightheaded and faint from the severe loss of blood.

In one last desperate attempt to be rid of this leech-cat, he leaned forward and pushed against her breasts with all his might. This only caused her to lean back, which made them top-heavy, and his weight came crashing down upon her.

Fantasy released her mouth's grip on him, but she dug her claws into his back and wrapped her legs around him tightly. She lapped at the hideous open wound that was still gushing blood. It covered her face and splashed onto the van wall.

She was about to bite down again when a knife-blade stabbed down into her right shoulder. Fantasy let out an anguished, cat-like cry, unlike anything TJ had ever heard.

Fantasy thought, *Slade. Obviously fainted, but certainly not dead; must have woken up again. He'll pay for that little move.*

Slade was yelling in her ear. "Take that, bitch! Yeah! Take that! You fucking took my cock! I'm gonna take off your goddamn head!" Slade jerked the blade from her shoulder in a high arc and plunged it down again with all of his might as he aimed for her neck. He thought he was about to drive it home too, but at the last second, Fantasy shifted TJ's body up right in line with the knife. The knife disappeared up to its hilt in the center of TJ's upper back.

TJ seemed to come alive, screaming, and shot to his knees. He leaned back, flailing his arms behind him to try and grab the knife, but there was no way he could reach it.

Slade said, "What the fuck? Oh, Jesus. I'm sorry, TJ. I'm sorry."

TJ fell forward again on his face, still trying to reach the knife sticking out near his neck.

Fantasy had scooted out from under his weight and come up on the other side of him. She planted her paws on the floor and wall of the van and vaulted over his body, turning in midair and driving her feet into Slade's body before jumping to the back of the van. Slade hit the van wall hard, and his head glanced off something metal.

Fantasy clutched at her wounded shoulder. The blade had gone in solid and deep. The son-of-a-bitch hurt too.

"Yeah, that's right, bitch. That's what you get. I drove it in deep, didn't I? Same way I did with my cock."

Fantasy countered, "Yeah, you went real deep, but I took care of that problem, didn't I? You won't be doing that to me again, or anyone else. Since you no longer have a dick."

"Fuck you. Just fuck you." Slade grabbed the knife-handle TJ was still feebly trying to grasp and ripped it out of his back. "Come at me again and see what the fuck happens. I'll cut the shit out of you, whore."

Fantasy pushed hard on the knife wound in her shoulder as she paced back and forth, beginning to shiver. The shaking was uncontrollable and had nothing to do with the cold. As she shook, she stared at Slade, then down at her wound. Almost as soon as Fantasy had started shaking, she stopped. She removed her hand and dropped it to her side.

Slade stared in awe as the already-healing wound miraculously repaired itself completely right in front of his eyes.

Fantasy looked up from the wound, fixed her eyes on Slade again and smirked. "You were saying?"

Not giving Slade any warning, she charged him.

Slade was anticipating an attack. He had just enough time to grab her wrists as she jumped toward him. There was a lot of strength behind Fantasy's advance, and it slammed him back against the passenger's seat. The force was just enough that Slade had to release her wrists. He was still on his knees, but prepared himself to stand his ground against the feral-cunt-she-bitch.

Fantasy came at him again, hissing and flailing her arms. There was a quick flurry of motion. Slade threw his hands up and blocked what he thought were most of her movements. Fantasy let out a banshee cry of victory and retreated to the back of the van.

Thinking he had connected with her in some way, Slade said, "What's the matter? Too much for you this time?"

She paced back and forth, glaring at him in the darkened interior of the van.

Slade held the knife out in front of him and said, "Fuck you, bitch."

In a low, guttural tone, Fantasy replied, "No. Actually, it's fuck *you*."

Slade finally noticed the deep grooves in his arms. When he had blocked the quick swipes of her paws, he hadn't realized she had sliced his arms up pretty bad. Blood was dripping from some of the wounds, but pouring in steady streams from others. That was when the pain finally set in. His arms and abdomen felt like they were on fire.

"You fucking bitch, I'm gonna gut you like a goddamn fish."

She only smiled in amusement. "I highly doubt that. I was just a little bit quicker than you."

"What the fuck are you talking about?"

She waved her bloodied claws in the direction of his lower extremities.

By the pale evening light coming through the tinted windows, Slade noticed the blood as he moved into a kneeling stance. Something felt wrong about his body. Intense pain radiated from the center of it, then engulfed him. He looked down in time to see most of his guts roll out of his shredded abdomen and smack the van's carpet with a sickening splat.

The sound was nauseating, and the sensation of his stomach rolling entered his mind, but it was only from memory. He had just enough mental capacity left to realize his stomach was already sitting on the floor of the van. His body erupted into new and instantaneous agony as he saw his open, eviscerated cavity.

He immediately started whimpering, "Oh Jesus, oh Jesus, oh Jesus," as he grabbed feebly at the steaming pile and tried to scoop his intestines back up into himself.

There was a mountain-lion cry of fury as Fantasy lunged for Slade from across the van. She hit him with the full force of her body, causing his head to snap back against the van wall.

The last thing Slade saw was that cat-like visage, ultra-close and staring at him with feline curiosity. Slade barely registered her voice as the dizziness of death started to engulf him.

She was saying, "No need to do that, sweetie. I'll just have to scoop them back out of you again once you're dead."

As Slade fell over on his side, he felt one last excruciating ripple of pain as Fantasy reached up inside his body cavity, grasped his heart, and tore it from his mangled body.

Fantasy feasted until she had her fill. The sport of this hunt was now over, and she was the winner again.

She tore the last strand of muscle from one of TJ's ribs and pitched the bone over her shoulder, licking the last bit of blood from her clawed fingers.

She took a deep breath, inhaling the mixture of musk, blood and death into her nostrils.

Such a delicious scent, she thought. Fantasy felt full and satisfied, her hunger sated—for now. She crawled over the bodies and up onto the passenger's seat, and began the process of cleaning herself.

She was glad the fallen snow had blanketed the windshield and most of the windows. The heat from their bodies and panting breaths had fogged up the glass. Combining that with the tinted windows, Fantasy knew no one had seen what had gone on inside the vehicle.

She took her time as she cleaned herself, relishing the last flavors of her kills. She wasn't in any hurry. She had to remove all the evidence from her body. As she licked her fur, her body began its slow change back to her old self. The short hairs that made up her sleek fur retracted until she was licking her normal skin. As the fur disappeared, it absorbed the remaining bits of blood, leaving her skin clean and refreshed with a renewed glow.

Her facial bones crunched, then shifted behind her skin as the Changing left her. Her elongated snout retracted into her face and her sharp teeth became flat. As her jaw realigned, she worked her lower jaw back into its natural setting. Her ears lost their keen sense of hearing as they reshaped to her regular human form.

She pulled on her thigh-high stockings and slipped on her high heels. She always felt sexy, but slipping into lingerie made her feel sexier. She was glad she'd moved her clothes out of the way of the spray of blood. Lesson learned from seven or eight days ago.

She was starting to get horny again. She slid her G-string up and pulled it tight and high on her waist, then fastened her plaid skirt around her. Her bra went on, then her shirt, tied in place with a knot under her breasts. Her pony-tail hair ties had been lost in the transition and were somewhere in the back of the van. She wasn't going to worry about those. She could find more. She found her glasses and was about to put them on when she noticed a few smears of blood on the left lens. She ran her tongue over the glass surface and wiped them clean.

Carefully, she grabbed both of the men's wallets, which she had pitched up into the driver's side floorboard while she had been feasting, and relieved them of their earnings.

Here's the amount they owed Baby Cakes, with a little extra for her trouble, she thought as she stuffed bills inside her left bra cup. *And I'll take the rest.* She tucked the remaining bills in the right side of her bra.

Before Fantasy left, she glanced one last time into the back of the van.

Slade and TJ were now nothing more than discarded scraps of human remains. Their bodies had been split, pulled apart and divided to the point where no one would be able to tell where TJ started and Slade ended. Their skin had been sliced cleanly through and peeled from their muscles. Their bones had been broken open, the marrow sucked clean, ravaged until there was very little meat attached. There were blood splatters on the walls and windows from when she had flung parts of their bodies aside that contained no nourishment for her. Anyone viewing this carnage would have a hard time looking at it for long, but Fantasy simply smiled as she remembered her fun.

Not wanting to get blood on her baby-blue pumps, she exited by way of the passenger door.

She shivered when she slammed the door, but it wasn't from the intense cold. The cold—to her—was exhilarating. It was just the after-effects of the Changing—the final shaking off of the animal that had emerged.

She had feasted and groomed herself for quite a while now. She looked all around to make sure nobody had witnessed her exiting this van. The parking lot was desolate; a few cars remained, but nobody was milling about. No one knew what had just gone down inside the small realm of this beat-up brown van.

At least I have wheels to go to my next destination, she thought.

Fantasy said to herself, "I doubt anyone else will be coming out in this snow, no matter how sweet the tits and ass are here at Lust."

As she walked back to the side entrance, she realized her whole body was calm. Settled. Satisfied. Her stomach was no longer mad at her. The growling had stopped—for now.

She thought again of Jade and how aroused she had become when Fantasy let her know she was into women as much as, if not more than, men.

Maybe I could change her into what I am, Fantasy mused. *It might be nice to travel with someone else of my kind. Whatever my kind is. Maybe I'll see if she wants to get together tonight. We'll see how she feels about the idea. I could try to make the Changing happen and reveal myself to her.*

If she's not into the true me… well, at least she'll be a nice dessert.

TEN-PENNY NAILED

BILLY BARBARY. WHAT an asshole, Jacob thought as he made his way across town to his neighborhood. *He's the biggest shithead in the sophomore class.* Voicing his thoughts aloud, he said to no one, "So, why did he choose me? Can you tell me that? Anyone?"

Nobody answered him. Jacob was alone, as usual.

Jacob Cantrell wasn't the biggest loser of his tenth-grade class, but he was certainly down there on the totem pole. It wasn't because he was unattractive; he was from a lower-income background than some of the wealthier kids in his school. Jacob had friends, of course—they just weren't here hanging out with him at this particular moment. They all had some sort of family member—a mom, dad or older sibling—to pick them up after school.

Jacob kicked a half-crushed Sprite can that he pretended was Billy's face. The can skittered ahead of him, then jumped the curb and spun off into the woods near the road he was walking.

A smile broke out on his face; he liked the feeling of denting Billy's face.

Jacob was wearing a pair of ratty white Nikes with a black swoosh symbol. The baggy pair of light denim jeans he wore was threadbare around the knees. He also wore an oversized black Halestorm hoodie with the band's graphic across the back.

The afternoon sun was hot during this late summer day. There weren't many trees on this stretch of street, so there was no shade. Jacob was sweating underneath his sweatshirt, staining the armpits. Little rivulets ran out of his armpits and down the length of his arms. A few more trickled down the center of his back.

Yeah, that's not pleasant at all, he thought. *Too hot to be wearing this damn hoodie. I'll be glad when I can start wearing lighter clothes, but I gotta keep up this charade I've been playing. Hopefully I won't have to do it for too much longer.*

He stepped over the curb and walked to the edge of the woods, then paused and looked behind him to make sure no one was watching or following him. Seeing no one, he quickly turned and ducked into the space between two pine trees. He made his way through the woods until he stepped onto a thin rabbit trail. He walked this trail on the days he took the long way home from school, as he was doing today. He looked right, then left, turned left, and moved further down the trail.

The temperature in the woods had dropped as soon as he'd stepped off the main road. It was so much cooler down here. Every so often, the late afternoon sun punched through the green canopy above him in a few places where the tree limbs didn't completely connect, creating a filigree design on the path. Though the leaves now protected Jacob from the sun, they also kept away the breeze. There wasn't much wind blowing through here to stir the stagnant air that seemed to hover throughout like a clear fog. But it was cooler, and Jacob was thankful for that small blessing.

He grabbed the left strap of his backpack and hoisted it further up on his shoulder. The backpack was heavier than usual today; he was carrying other things in it along with his school books.

He kept his right hand in his sweatshirt pocket. There was only one reason he would take it out, and that was if Billy had been stupid enough to track him down and give him a reason. Jacob was really hoping Billy *would* start something with him today, because this time he was prepared for him. He had actually been planning a meeting with Billy for a couple of weeks now.

One thing about it, Jacob thought. *This is gonna be the last day Billy ever fucks with me again. I can guaran-damn-tee it.*

He made a tight fist inside the pocket of his hoodie. The fist felt good. Strong. It felt even better as it tightened around the metal he was holding. His palms and fingers were sweaty, but that didn't worry Jacob at all.

He smiled and said to himself, "Yes, sir. Billy's neva-eva gonna-eva fuck-with-me-again."

He liked the way that sounded, and chanted it again. "Billy-Barbary's neva-eva gonna-eva fuck-with-me-again." The singsong sentence morphed into a half-sung, half-rapped mantra. "Billy-Barbary's neva-eva gonna-eva fuck-with-me-again."

He laughed at his little saying. He stopped singing and rapping the statement out loud, but it echoed in the back of his mind. His head bobbed to the beat of his mental phrase as he walked, looking around constantly to see if anyone was following him. He scrutinized every possible hiding place in the surrounding area.

Billy's a sly motherfucker. He could be hiding anywhere.

Seeing no one in the vicinity, he relaxed a little but picked up his pace. He didn't feel safe out here alone. He wouldn't feel safe until he was behind the locked doors of his house.

"Hey, asshole!"

Billy Barbary's voice came out of nowhere and sent a chill through Jacob. Startled, Jacob spun around and looked behind him again, but no one was there.

"Up here, numb-nuts!" Billy shouted down to him.

Jacob looked up and saw Billy crouching on the lowest limb of the tree he'd just walked under. He was dressed in tennis shoes, brand new jeans and a blue polo shirt.

Jacob hadn't expected Billy to come from a high elevation. Usually, Billy would just lunge out of his chosen hiding place and tackle his intended target. Jacob didn't stop to reply; he just ran.

Billy jumped from his roost in the tree, landed softly on the path and ran after Jacob. He caught up pretty quickly. Billy was the main wide receiver on their high school's football team—the Sidewinders—so he could move pretty quickly when he needed to. Billy nabbed Jacob by the hood of his sweatshirt and jerked him back hard.

"Oh no ya don't."

Jacob's feet flew out from under him. He landed on his back, staring up at the interconnecting limbs of the trees above him.

"Get the fuck back here. Where the hell do you think you're going?" Billy asked.

"Away from you," Jacob said. He rolled over and tried to stand. It was hard with his right hand still in his sweatshirt pocket.

"I don't like the tone of your voice," Billy said.

"Tough shit. I can't do anything about the way I sound."

"Yeah, I know *that*. But the tone you're using isn't very respectful."

"I'm not going to give *you* any respect, *Billy*. You don't deserve it."

It was a simple verbal lash-out, but for once in Billy's life, he didn't have a comeback. He stood there above Jacob, seething. He was bewildered as to why Jacob was all of a sudden mouthing off to him; he'd never done that before. Usually Jacob was quiet during his beatdown sessions and just took what Billy dished out.

Jacob asked, "Where are your goons today?"

Billy was thrown by the question. He was the one who usually did all the talking. Making up something on the fly so he wouldn't look like he was losing this conversation, Billy replied, "I gave them the day off, asshole. What's it to you?"

"That was nice of you," Jacob said.

Billy continued, "I wanted to have some quality time with you today, Cantrell. Just you and me. Nobody else."

"You know what, Billy? Me too. I was thinking the exact same thing." Billy didn't understand what Jacob was talking about, but Jacob didn't give him the time to throw a comeback line. "But you know what? This is the worst day you could've picked on me without the backup of your Goon Squad."

"What do you mean?"

Ignoring Billy's question, Jacob said, more or less to himself, "Better for me, I guess."

"What's that s'posed to mean, Cantrell?" Billy asked again.

"That I'll just get a beatdown from one of you instead of four. Or maybe, it'll be a little more of an even fight this time."

"You trying to stand up to me, bitch?" Billy said, a snide laugh engulfing his statement.

"Yeah, today I am. Today, I take back *my* life, Billy."

Jacob's comment really pissed Billy off. He stooped, grabbed two fistfuls of Jacob's hoodie, and jerked him to his feet.

"What are you going to do?" Billy asked. "Huh?"

Jacob said nothing, but stared hard at Billy, as if trying to figure out the best place to hit him if he ever got the chance. Billy was still clutching two fistfuls of Jacob's shirt. He started walking backwards toward the tree he'd jumped from. He walked quickly, and Jacob's feet could barely keep up with Billy's pace.

Billy continued, not giving Jacob time to answer, "That's right—you're not going to do shit." He scoffed and repeated Jacob's last line. "Take back my life. How the fuck d'you think you're going to do that? Huh?" Billy finally reached the tree he'd jumped out of and slammed Jacob hard up against its trunk. "I own you, Cantrell. I own your ass."

"Let go of me," Jacob said evenly, then in a barely audible whisper added, "Or you'll wish you had."

"What was that?"

Jacob looked up into Billy's face again and really studied it. He repeated his sentence, enunciating every word clearly so Billy wouldn't misunderstand him. "I said, let go of me or you'll wish you had."

"What are you going to do to me if I don't?"

"You'll see."

The punch to Jacob's abdomen came out of nowhere. It was hard and swift. The air immediately left Jacob's lungs. He doubled over and dropped to his knees, gasping, and heard Billy's voice above him.

"You're not going to do a goddamn thing to me. You know why, Cantrell?"

Through heaves of stale forest air, barely getting the word out, Jacob asked, "Why?"

"Because you haven't done shit about me in the past. You haven't even tried. You're such an easy, pansy-ass target."

Jacob was still on his knees, hunched over, looking at the leaves. He smiled through the pain.

He felt Billy's hands on his shoulders, grabbing two fistfuls of Jacob's hoodie again. Jacob lost the grin pasted on his face and replaced it with a grimace of pain.

Billy pulled him up and pushed him back against the tree. He cocked his arm back to deliver a simple, hard and effective punch to Jacob's face.

"Hey, Billy, wait. Just—just wait a minute," Jacob said, bringing some panic into his voice. "Can we make a deal?"

"A deal? What the fuck are you talking about, Cantrell?"

Jacob added a little nervousness to the panic and said, "Ju-just hear me out. And if you don't like it then you can do whatever else you were going to do to me, and I'll do whatever the fuck I was going to *try* to do to you."

Billy gave a frustrated breath, but slowly lowered his fist to his side. "Okay. Sure. I guess I can do that. But make it quick; I have shit to do. Believe it or not, kicking your ass is not the only thing on my agenda today."

Jacob wasted no time in getting right to the heart of the matter. He dropped the fake panic and the nervousness. "I want to give you the opportunity to just walk away. Walk away and never pick on me again."

Billy gave him a half-scoff, half-laugh. "What? You kidding me?"

"No. Not at all. I'm giving you the chance to do the right thing. Right here, right now, just leave me the fuck alone. I won't hold a grudge about all the other shit you and the Goon Squad have done to me in the past. You and all your buddies get a free pass. If you let me walk away right now and never come after me again, talk to me again, or even look in my direction again, then I'll pretend like nothing has ever happened between us."

Billy laughed out loud at Jacob's proposal. "God, you're such an asshole. You're an even bigger dickhead than I thought."

"So... I take that as a no," Jacob said.

"Yeah, Cantrell, it's a big fucking no."

"I thought you would've been a bigger man about this. I should've just gone through with what I was going to do to you. But I promised myself I would at least give you the opportunity to choose."

A measure of curiosity and panic seemed to penetrate Billy's tough facade. "Gone through with what? What the hell are you talking about?"

"Oh, don't worry. You'll find out eventually, because you didn't take me up on my offer. Now I'm obligated to show you and follow through with my plan." Jacob smirked.

Jacob saw the look on Billy's face and knew he didn't like the smirk. It was most likely the equivalent to a real slap to Billy's face. Billy was obviously itching to lash out at him, but then his eyes shifted down to Jacob's pocketed hand. His right hand was in the right pocket of his hoodie and had been there the whole time of this confrontation. Suspicion crossed Billy's face.

"What's in your pocket, Cantrell?" he asked.

"Why do you need to know, *Barbary*?" Jacob asked, dishing out an even bigger helping of sarcasm.

"Lose the attitude and quit asking dumb fucking questions! Just take your hand out of your pocket and show me."

"I can assure you, you don't want me to do that." Jacob continued to stare into Billy's eyes; then he studied the rest of his face.

"Well, you're gonna show me. You're gonna give me whatever's in your pocket."

"You're not going to like it."

"I'll be the judge of that, fuck-face," Billy said, and relaxed his left hand. He released Jacob's sweatshirt, turned it over and opened his hand palm up. "Give it to me."

Jacob smiled within himself at the words Billy had chosen and repeated them in his mind. *Give it to me. Yeah, I'll give it to you alright.* Then he shrugged, as if the request were no big deal. "Okay, but remember, you asked for this."

In one quick, smooth, perfectly-timed movement, Jacob jerked his hand out of his pocket and cocked his arm back as far as it would go.

Billy had just enough time to register a hint of metal at the top of Jacob's knuckles. *Gun,* Billy thought. *He's going to shoot me with a gu—*

Then Billy saw Jacob's fist and the piece of metal flash forward, and it made contact with Billy's jaw.

He felt like he'd been struck with a metal baseball bat. Dizziness overwhelmed him. A blackness covered his eyes, then dissipated gradually. Billy released Jacob's shirt, stepped back and wobbled on unsteady feet as he fought to stay standing. He looked back at Jacob, who now had a look of shock on his face. Jacob split into two images, then slowly slid back together again. Billy tried to say something, but his mouth wasn't working properly.

The only thing Jacob could make out was a very slurred, "Mo… ther… fuck… er," then Billy crumpled to his knees and fell forward in the leaves.

Jacob blinked the shock out of his eyes and closed his gaping mouth. He said in a whisper to himself, "It worked. It actually fucking worked. I punched the shit out of Billy Barbary." Then, in a bittersweet afterthought, he added, "And no one was around to see me do it."

He brought the fist that held the brass knuckles up near his face and kissed the metal his index finger was looped through. He smiled, looking back down at Billy, and said, "Lights out, asshole. Should've taken my offer. Now it's my turn to play bully."

When Billy blinked his eyes open again, he found he was looking straight down the length of his body to his feet. He slowly lifted his head and saw a figure sitting on a fallen tree in front of him. He finally realized the figure was Jacob Cantrell.

Jacob was looking down at something in his hands; it was a piece of metal. Billy focused and strained to make out the metal object. He recognized it as a pair of brass knuckles, but something was different about this pair. It seemed thicker than the ones he'd seen before in magazines, online and in the movies.

Must've been what he hit me with, Billy thought. *Wasn't a gun after all. Oh, fuck; he nailed me good with that thing.*

He shook his head to make the fuzziness go away, but this did nothing except agitate the growing ache throbbing on the side of his face where Jacob had hit him. Billy groaned at the renewed pain.

Jacob glanced up and saw Billy staring at him.

"Good morning, sunshine," he said, standing and slowly walking over to Billy. "I was beginning to think you weren't going to come around. You've been out for quite a while."

Billy groaned again and said, "What the fuck happened?"

Smiling, Jacob said, "Some people call it a knuckle sandwich. Some call it a sucker punch. I call it an attitude-adjustment of Biblical proportions. Looks like it worked, too. You're definitely more docile than before I punched you."

"Why did you do that?"

"You serious, Billy? You seriously asking me that question? After all the weekly shit you and your friends do to me at school and after school? Are you really going to pull that card with me?"

Billy didn't reply, still woozy from the punch. He tried to take a step, and noticed something odd about his feet. Loops of rope were tied around his ankles and then wrapped around the tree. His feet were tied about shoulder-width apart.

"Wha' the fuck?" Billy slurred. He tried to lean over to see his feet better, but couldn't move in that direction either. He realized his arms and wrists were pulled back and tied around the tree as well. "What's going on?" he demanded, alarm creeping into his voice.

"Oh, right," Jacob said, snapping his finger. "You're not understanding what's happening to you. Well, let me remind you. Before your blackout..." Jacob gave a little laugh, remembering how everything had gone down. "I mean, before I *blacked you out,* I offered you a simple deal. You remember that? You know, for you and your boys to just quit picking on me. And I, in turn, would forget you guys ever messed with me in the first place. Well, you didn't take too kindly to that deal, so now you have to suffer the consequences."

"You can't be serious."

Jacob gave another half laugh. "Oh, I'm afraid I'm as serious as that punch to the face I gave you earlier. There's no more playing around, Billy. I have asked you time and time again to just leave me alone, but you refused. So you've left me with no other choice. The gloves are off now. Literally."

Billy shook his arms as best he could to get free, then said, "C'mon,

Cantrell, this is silly." He tried to kick the ropes loose from his legs, but they held fast. "Dude, I didn't know you were really serious."

"Didn't think I was serious? You think I actually enjoy getting pummeled week after week? That I enjoy all the gags you and your shithead friends play on me?"

"Well, no, I don—"

"You're damn right I don't. You should think about your actions before you go through with them. Because those actions may turn around and bite you in the ass, like what's happening to you right now."

Billy didn't yell out for anyone in particular to help him, but he did scream in frustration as he jerked hard and kicked against the ropes that bound his wrists and ankles. Jacob silenced him with a hard, swift blow to the abdomen. The air was driven out of him, and he coughed hard and wheezed as he tried to regain his breath.

Jacob said, "You might as well stop struggling with those ropes. I tied those knots pretty damn tight, so they aren't going to come loose."

Catching his breath, Billy leaned his head back again the tree. "Why did you use your brass knuckles on me?"

"Oh, well, funny you should ask. See, you and your goonies have been punching me off and on for most of this school year. I've actually lost count, and just figured I would pack all my return punches into one session and get them over with all at once. I'm not one to drag shit out, you understand. I'm currently on a deadline." Jacob laughed. "I figure one hard, focused punch with my brass knuckles is equal to about five to seven of the ones you and your friends dished out on me. Does that sound fair to you?"

Billy groaned, looking down at the ground again.

Jacob continued, "Doesn't matter if it's fair or not; it's what I've decided to do."

When Billy looked up again, he noticed that Jacob had removed his hoodie while he'd been unconscious. Jacob's muscular form—underneath the Wolverine T-shirt he was wearing—was different from the Jacob Billy remembered from six months ago. This Jacob wasn't a weak, puny kid. This Jacob actually looked athletic, or like he'd been in the weight room for quite some time. He looked like he'd put on at least twenty pounds of muscle. Billy hadn't noticed his physique at all, since Jacob usually wore oversized sweatshirts and baggy jeans to school every day.

Billy demanded, "What happened to *you*?"

"What do you mean?" Jacob asked.

"Have you been working out?"

A broad smile broke out on Jacob's face. "A little." He chuckled. "Just kidding; a lot, actually. Thank you for noticing. I've been putting forth an effort." He pushed out his lips as he gave the regular muscle-man pose. He turned his head to the side as he flashed his guns briefly to Billy, then slapped at his bicep. He puffed out a breath of air as he admired his biceps. "Sometimes, I just don't know what to do with these things."

Billy didn't understand his comment, but he continued watching as Jacob admired himself. Jacob lifted his shirt briefly and flexed his abs. Billy was surprised to see the very good beginnings of a six-pack peeking out from Jacob's slim but muscular waist. Jacob dropped his shirt again and slapped his abs a few times. He was happy that his news was out and he wouldn't have to cover up this secret anymore. No more sweatshirts, hoodies or baggy clothes after today.

A cool gust of late afternoon air blew through the woods and chilled the beads of sweat that lingered on Jacob's body. It stirred the muggy air that had settled in this section of the woods, bringing with it a hint of grass and pine. A simple thought came to Jacob's mind as he stood there enjoying the moment. *Out with the old and in with the new.*

"If you look like that, why didn't you ever fight back? Why didn't you ever challenge me and the other guys?"

Jacob turned his attention back to Billy as the breeze came to a standstill. "There's this thing called conditioning. If a person gets beat up enough times, like I was by you and your boys, it takes that person a long time to come to terms with it and actually believe in himself enough to fight back. I never felt I was ready." Jacob let the sentence hang in the air, then added, "Until today."

Billy looked confused but said, "I see." He looked down at Jacob's hands again. "Where did you get a pair of brass knuckles like that?"

"Made it myself. You like? I bought a few pairs of the same kind off this guy at the flea market. I welded about four of them together to make one really wide set. It's like I'm wearing a fucking metal glove."

"Feels like it too," Billy said as he worked his jaw on the side of his face where he'd been hit. It was a half-hearted compliment.

Jacob beamed on the inside with pride. *Finally a little respect. That's probably the nicest thing Billy has ever said to me.*

"Yeah, this one's alright," he said aloud, admiring his own handiwork. "It did the job I needed it to do. But this isn't my masterpiece. *That's* over there in my book bag. I call it my problem solver."

Billy's forehead became lined with concern. He looked over at Jacob's book bag, but didn't comment.

Jacob added, "Don't worry about that right now. I'll show it to you a little later."

"What are you going to do to me?" It was evident Billy was scared. His voice had taken on a real edge of the panic that Jacob had faked earlier.

Jacob wasted no time in answering him. "I'm going to take your life."

Billy couldn't believe what he'd just heard. "You're *what?*"

Jacob held up a finger to let Billy know he was going to explain further. "What I meant to say is…I'm going to take *your place* in life."

"What the hell's that supposed to mean?"

"I'll tell you; just be patient and listen. Oh, hey—are you thirsty?" Jacob asked, as if it had been rude of him not to ask earlier.

Billy didn't answer. He was unsure about the events playing out.

Jacob turned from him, stooped to his backpack, unzipped it, and grabbed a water bottle from within. He quickly re-zipped the backpack again and stood, unscrewing the lid as he approached Billy.

Billy pulled away from Jacob as he held the bottle up to his lips, unsure of the motive behind the gesture as well as what might be in the bottle.

"It's just water, Billy. It's not poisoned, if that's what you're worried about."

Billy finally nodded, and Jacob tilted the bottle up for him to drink. "There you go."

When Billy had had enough, Jacob replaced the lid and pitched the bottle behind him near the fallen tree where he had been sitting. He took a few moments to figure out where he wanted to start. Finally, he looked up at Billy again and said, "Have you ever looked at your life in long terms?"

"What do you mean?"

"Like where you're going to be in five years. Or ten years. Twenty years. Hell, even fifty or seventy-five years from now, if you get to live that long."

Billy didn't know where Jacob was going with this. "Sort of. Maybe. I don't know."

"Well, let me help you out with that. See, for a long time, I've been a little envious of you. Hell, why be modest? Okay, I envy you a lot. God, you are so talented, Billy, you really are. You're actually pretty amazing to watch. You may not know this, because I don't tell a lot of people, but I love football. Probably more than the average person. See, I go to most, if not all, of our high school games. At least the ones around here. I see you out there. You're living the dream, man. You're awesome. You've got it all: the looks, the talent, the physique. And no, I'm not gay by noticing your physique. I'm respectfully complimenting you on it. You always get the most beautiful girls. I guess you could say… I'm your biggest fan. There's nothing you couldn't do if you put your mind to it."

"Thanks, Cantrell, but you're not making a whole lot of sense."

"Oh, I will. It'll all be clear eventually." Jacob paused for a moment to collect his thoughts again. He paced back and forth in front of Billy, then turned to him and continued. "Take *your* life, for instance; look at it in the long term. If you stay on your current course, I can easily see you playing football for the remainder of this school year and the next two consecutive years. You'll graduate, then go to college—any college you want, if your grades are there. Then you'll play ball for four years of college, then you could easily go pro after that. Endorsements from commercials and athletic companies. After you retire from your pro career, you could be a coach for one of the top NFL teams, or a TV analyst, if you're interested. Fuck, can you imagine the possibilities? Damn! Invest that money wisely and you're set for life. You'll be swimming in the money. You'll probably get the model wife any guy would kill for."

"What's your point, Cantrell? What are you trying to tell me?"

"I just told you, *Barbary*. It's all right there in front of you. But maybe you haven't looked that far ahead into your life. I don't know why you haven't or why you can't see it. Take a moment and just listen to me, and you'll understand what I'm trying to tell you."

"I'm listening."

"Good. Now. Look at *my* life. If I stay on my current course and just let life itself sort of pick what I'm gonna do, most likely I'll end up following in my dad's footsteps. He's a welder at Blackstone Metal and Steel Corporation. He makes decent money. But every day he goes to work and comes home, I know he's not happy." Jacob's emotions broke through, and tears welled in his eyes. He paused for a moment, then took a deep breath, wiped his tears away and continued as if nothing had happened. "I know... I know he's not happy. I see it in his eyes all the time. I don't necessarily know what he would really want to do with his life if he wasn't welding. He's sort of, you know, just going through the damn motions, hoping something else will come along, or that something good will happen for him. He's never taken the time to plan a future that would make him happy. Sad, I know."

"I still don't understand what you're getting at."

"That's probably 'cause I haven't finished explaining it to you."

Billy didn't like the dig, and gave Jacob a 'go to hell' look. Jacob stared right back with one of his own, as if saying, *you first*.

Breaking their staring contest, Jacob continued, "I'm talking about our futures, shit-ass. Yours is going to be great, but you don't even realize it. You're just sort of going through the motions like my dad. But that's okay for you, because of how good you are at everything already. Even if you don't plan well, you'll be swimming in everything good because it comes so naturally for you. It makes me sick sometimes, how good you'll have it. My future is going to be shit, but I'm wise enough to see that now, and I'm working hard to turn it around. I started first and foremost with my body. And it's looking damn good. I love it."

"God, you're so obscure, Cantrell. Quit speaking in riddles and just come out with it."

The frustrated punch to Billy's abdomen came out of nowhere, much like the punch he had given Jacob earlier. The brass knuckles were around

Jacob's fist, and the force of the metal blow was enough to drive most—if not all—of the air from his lungs.

Billy doubled over as far as he could—which wasn't far, since his hands were tied—and gasped for air. When he was finally able to raise his head, he leaned it against the tree and stared back into Jacob's face.

Jacob looked pissed, and his face was red. He didn't say anything to Billy for a long while, seeming to go into a daze. His only movement was the wind blowing his hair as another breeze swept through the forest, and his right hand, spinning the brass knuckles around his index finger. Eventually the flush faded from his face.

Billy was about to speak, but Jacob beat him to the punch. "I've always wondered why you picked me."

Billy was quiet for a few moments, thinking of the best answer—an answer that wouldn't piss Jacob off.

Jacob repeated the sentence, a little more emphatically. "I've always wondered why *you* picked *me*."

"I don't know. You're just *you*, Cantrell. You're such an easy target to mess with, I guess."

Jacob blew out an agitated breath. "That's the only reason you can come up with, Billy? I'm an easy target?"

"Yeah."

"That's stupid."

"Yeah, maybe. Who cares?"

"See, I always thought maybe I was a little outlet for you. With all the pressure of winning the games for the high school and keeping your grades up, I thought I was just a way for you to let off some steam. Like, maybe the coach was too much of an asshole to you every now and then during practice. A couple of punches to the *personification of your coach*." Jacob air-quoted. "You know, *me*." He indicated himself. "You take out on *me* what you want to do to *him*. Or maybe your parents put too much pressure on you to be the all-American football star *they* want you to be. Same scenario—I'm the equivalent of your parents and you can work the anger and aggression they build up in *you* out on *me*. I'm your emotional punching bag, so to speak."

"Huh. Never thought of it that way."

"It makes sense, though, doesn't it? It's the way I always looked at it. But now I'm tired of it, Billy. They always say when you get mad enough about certain things in your life, that's when change happens, and it did for me. I started re-evaluating everything in my life and what I wanted. And I figured it out. It's all clear as a crystal ball in my mind right now."

"What *do* you want?"

Jacob scoffed. "I certainly don't want the life I have coming to me. Oh, Jesus. God, no. To be a welder for the rest of my life for very little money—fuck that noise. No, thank you; I can't do that." He thought for a moment. "You know, I even made a promise to my dad that if I couldn't make this football thing work for us, I would gladly give it up to go to school to be a welder and follow in his footsteps. There's nothing like a little motivation to drive you to do the things you *want* so you can get out of doing the things you *don't* want." Jacob crinkled his forehead, wondering if he had explained that clearly enough to his captive. "Did that make sense?"

Billy ignored his question. "What do you mean, 'make this football thing work'?"

Jacob turned and looked hard at Billy. "You know what I really want?" He didn't give Billy time to reply. "I want *your life*. I want the life that *you're* destined for."

Billy gave a short burst of laughter. "You can't have my life."

"Oh, but I can. It's already in motion. That happened the day you started picking on me. It just took me making up my mind to change that. I can have whatever I want, and I intend to get it. Everything from playing football the remainder of this school year and the next two years. It won't be easy, but I know I can do it. My grades are high enough; I'm an A and B student already. I can get into any college I choose, and I'm already looking ahead to that. Right now, I'm thinking either Alabama or Notre Dame. I just have to figure out which school I want to be part of my legacy. Play ball there for a couple, maybe three or four years. Then go pro, and the rest is history. Provided I don't get injured along the way."

"But there's a big problem with your plan."

"What's that?"

Billy laughed again. "*You* don't play football."

Jacob gave Billy a broad smile. "Doesn't mean I haven't been secretly practicing with my dad for the past six months. He used to play ball in high school, and a little in college before someone blew out one of his knees in a bad tackle. He's teaching me everything he knows. It also doesn't mean I haven't been studying plays during your practices after school and during the games. You guys never noticed me up in the bleachers, but I'm always there, watching."

Billy's mind drifted back to some of the days during football practice. He remembered seeing a figure sitting in random areas on the bleachers. The figure was usually higher up on the seats and always in some sort of hoodie or jacket with the hood flipped high up on his head so his face was mostly covered. The figure had never really drawn attention to himself. Billy had only noticed him a few times, but he'd never felt threatened by him. After practice was over, on occasion, he'd glance up into the stands and the person watching would always be gone. Billy had always thought whoever was up in the bleachers had come there to get away from everybody to study; it now hit him that Jacob had come there *to* study. Study *him*. A deep dread formed within him.

"That was you?"

"Always me. Looking down from above. They say when someone wants something bad enough, they'll do crazy things to get it."

"And you are crazy, Cantrell. I'll give you that."

"Wonder who made me that way?" Jacob asked, and gave a long stare into Billy's eyes.

Billy didn't say anything. He was all of a sudden even more uneasy about everything than he had been earlier. He pulled hard against the ropes that kept him rooted to the tree.

Jacob continued, "I'm going to talk to the coach and get him to put me on as wide receiver for the Sidewinders in your absence."

"You can't just walk on and expect to get my position. You haven't worked with Anthony Miller, or Paul Bryant, or Scott. Any of those guys. Besides, I'm going to be there."

Jacob cast a doubtful look Billy's way and said, "You sure about that, Barbary?" There was a long pause that hung between them, Jacob giving Billy enough time to internalize the question. "You've been holding me back, Billy, so I thought I would get rid of you. If you're not at practice, someone's gonna to have to take your place. Might as well be me. All Anthony has to do is get it in my vicinity, and I'll catch it. My life depends on it. I'll do just fine come Monday. I know there'll be a little homework to get used to the rest of the team. I'll need to work with them a little before the big game on Friday, but I already know the plays. And I'm damn good. I'm pretty fast. I've been running sprints in my backyard at night. You should see me. I think you would be a little jealous."

"Untie me. I'm tired of your bullshit."

"Sorry, Billy. My *bullshit* has just begun."

There was another silence as Billy thought about what Jacob had said. Jacob broke it by changing the subject entirely.

"How's Amber doing?"

"Amber? What about her?"

"Oh, I don't know. Been thinking about her a lot lately. God, she's really gorgeous. You're a lucky guy."

"I don't like what you're saying about her."

"I'm not saying anything negative. It's only compliments, Billy."

"Doesn't sound like it. Sounds like you're implying something different. Like you have a secret agenda for her."

Jacob just stared at Billy and smiled. "Maybe I do, Barbary. Maybe I do." He paused, then added, "Seriously, though, how's she doing?"

Billy didn't answer. He was getting angry. Jacob could see the buildup beginning.

Jacob continued, "What's she up to these days?"

Billy just stared at him, shaking his head, and waited for him to change the subject again.

Jacob said, "Did I strike a nerve with you?" He laughed, then winked. "I struck something earlier when I knocked you the fuck out, that's for damn sure." He came back to the subject at hand. "Is Amber happy?"

"Yes, she's happy," Billy said reluctantly. "She's really happy. Now drop it."

"How do you know?"

"Look, I'm not going to talk about Amber with you."

"Huh. Then I guess I'll have to ask her myself in a few days."

"What do you mean by that?"

"I just think she's going to be really sad when you don't call her." Jacob paused, letting the sentence hang in the air, then added, "Ever again."

In a slow, deep whisper that was edgy with vehemence, Billy said, "I swear to God, if you do anything to her…"

"Whoa, Billy; just whoa! What the hell are you talking about? *Do* anything to her? I'm not going to do anything to *her*. I just think she's going to need some major consoling, because *you're* about to have an accident. *You're* about to disappear off the face of the earth forever."

"What do you mean?" Billy suddenly sounded like a little kid.

"I'm not going to do anything to *her*. I'm going to do something to *you*. No one will know where you end up, except for me."

"You're goddamn crazy, Cantrell. So help me God, if I ever get out of this, I'm going to fucking kill you."

"No, you're not. You're not going to do shit to me. And rest assured, you won't ever get out of those ropes. I've studied the art of tying knots ever since I began planning this meeting with you. The ones that have you tied up are pretty secure, so I have no worries that you're going to get free."

"So why all this talk about killing me? If you're going to do it, just do it."

"This is a big step in my life, Billy. I'm relishing this moment. Remember all those times you made me squirm like an ant under a magnifying glass on a hot summer day? I'm just enjoying this in the same fashion. This moment will be the turning point when everything *turns* around—ha, pun intended—for the better in my life. Also, this is the longest conversation you and I have ever had and, believe it or not, I'm kind of enjoying it. You know, we could've turned out to be pretty good friends."

Billy said nothing in regard to the last couple of sentences. Instead he asked, "What are you going to do if someone comes down the trail?"

"Dude, we've been down here for a few hours now. Nobody's going to come down here. I've walked this trail plenty of times, and I've never seen anyone but you on it at the same time as me. You're only down here because you wanted to beat the shit out of me. But if someone *does* come down here while we're having our discussion…" Jacob paused, brought the brass knuckles up to his face, kissed the index finger loop again, and said, "I'll improvise."

Billy fell silent. He didn't have a decent comeback. He didn't know what he was going to do. Jacob was certainly way off his rocker. There was only one thing he could do.

The longer I can keep him talking, the longer I'll stay alive. Maybe that's my way out. Eventually Jacob's going to screw up and give me some time to get loose. Someone will come along. Something is going to give for me; I have to believe that.

Jacob noticed his silence. "What's the matter, Billy? Why so silent all of a sudden?"

Billy ignored his comments. "Since you've been talking, I've been putting two and two together, so let me ask you this."

"Shoot."

"Did you let me catch you earlier today?"

"What do you mean?"

Billy felt like Jacob knew exactly what he meant. "Did *you* let *me* catch you?"

"Well, you did jerk me up by my hoodie and slam me to the ground. I wouldn't exactly call it *letting* you catch me, but you did."

"That's not what I'm talking about. You've been working out, but you're not bulky like a lot of the power lifters in the gym. You're athletic. If you've been working out your legs as much as your upper body, then you should've been able to move fast."

Jacob stood there with his eyebrows raised. There was a hint of a smile playing around his lips.

Billy continued, "You should've been able to give me a longer chase than you did. What the hell are you smiling about?"

"You got me," Jacob said. "I'm guilty. I did let you catch me. I mean, you always do. Why should today be any different?" He added, more to himself but loudly enough for Billy to hear, "Maybe I should've played it up a little more."

"Why?" Billy asked. "Why would you do that?"

"Why not?"

"Quit being so damn obscure!" Billy shouted. "It's so goddamn frustrating. Just stop it."

"I had to get you into a position where I could give you the ultimatum."

"You mean this whole thing was a trap?"

"Sort of."

"That's not fair."

Billy's comment instantly pissed Jacob off. Seething, he locked eyes with Billy as he took his brass knuckles off and shoved them into his pocket. Then he lunged forward and sucker-punched Billy in the face again. He didn't stop there, but released a fury of body blows into Billy's abdomen as well.

Billy was shocked at how fast Jacob had actually moved. "Wait, wait, wait!" he cried through gasps of air. "Stop, Jacob! Just fucking STOP!"

Jacob rose again to Billy's level, grabbed his lower jaw, and stared deep into his eyes. "Don't fucking talk to me about what is and isn't fair. You know all about playing unfair. I'm just giving you a shot of your own medicine. But there's going to be one fatal dose."

Billy's voice took on a weak, breathless tone. "C'mon, Cantrell, this isn't funny. Quit threatening me like that."

"I'm not threatening you. I'm promising you. It's going to be very fatal for you when this conversation's over."

Billy didn't know what to say. He was speechless. He bowed his head; he was still gasping for air. He didn't see Jacob pull the brass knuckles from his pocket again and slip them over his fingers. Jacob moved further around to Billy's side and punched him high on his exposed side.

Something cracked and shifted slightly underneath the force of the blow. Billy jumped like he'd been shot, then screamed out in pain.

"Oh shit," Jacob said. "Was that your rib? Did I just break one of your ribs? That's gotta really hurt. How are you going to play football now with a broken rib? Guess I'll really have to fill in for you now."

Jacob took a moment to let Billy take some ragged breaths. It took a lot longer to get his breathing under control this time.

Billy asked through his wheezes, "When you hit me... why didn't you... punch me in the face... with your brass knuckles?"

"Would you prefer that I did?"

"Hell, no! I was just curious… as to why you chose… not to."

"Jesus, Billy, I didn't want to knock you out again. I don't want to have to wait close to another hour for you to wake up again. It would be just like that first time I hit you with them. I don't have that kinda time. Gotta get this show on the road. Move it along."

Billy looked at him, stone-faced, trying not to let his emotions show. He still half believed that all this was a crazy joke, and that Jacob had taken it way too far but wasn't going to actually kill him. With the punch to his ribs, though, that hope was slowly draining from his mind, replaced with the thought that he was never going to leave these woods alive.

"You and your boys have been gunning for me for about two to three weeks now," Jacob commented.

"I know. You've been ducking us pretty well lately. We did get you good last Wednesday though."

"Yeah, I know. I'll give you guys that one. That's why I had to do this. And it's working out pretty well for me so far. I'm really glad your goon dogs aren't here today. I don't know how I would've pulled this off with them around. I might've had to postpone my plans for you if they were."

"What do you mean?"

"The whole ducking thing was just a maneuver to suck you into this plan. I know you've been following me. I strategically went home different ways for the past two to three weeks just to throw you and your boys off my trail. That's why you got me last Wednesday. I should've gone home by a different route a day earlier than by the back side to the old factory on that third day. That was bad on my part. So high-five to you and your bitches for getting me then."

"You serious? This whole sissy game of cat and mouse was just a ploy to get me down here?"

"Here, or down by the old factory, or wherever was secluded enough to do what I need to do."

"That's really not fair."

"If I were you, I wouldn't use the word *fair* ever again. I gave you a perfect opportunity for this whole scenario between us to end when I asked the main question at the beginning of this meeting. But you made your choice."

Billy butted in. "So what would you've done earlier? You asked me to leave you alone. What if I said yes, or okay, and just turned and walked away?"

"To be honest, I would've been shocked that you actually agreed to the suggestion, but I would've let you go"—Jacob snapped his finger—"in a heartbeat. I would've looked at figuring out some other path for my life. That was the deal I made with myself. I might've just tried to get on the football team myself, instead of taking your place. I know it doesn't seem like I would've let you go, since you're all tied up the way you are. I mean, I really didn't think of anything I wanted to do in life other than football, because that's the destiny I really want. But all that doesn't matter now. My plan has been set in motion, and I can't stop it, no matter how hard it is for me to go through with it."

"So what happens after   ah, jeez, I can't believe I'm even asking you this… What happens after you kill me and do whatever it is to me that you're planning on doing? What about the guys?"

"Oh, well, with the ringleader—*you*—out of the picture, your boys probably won't mess with me. After all, you're the one who instigated most of the fights. If they're unwise—as you've been—then I'll offer them the same deal I gave you. If they take it, that'll be the end of it and they'll have a bright future. If they don't, then that'll be the end of them as well. I'll have to devise a plan for each of them, according to their decision. But those are plans for a different day. Right now, I have you to contend with, and sadly, I believe our time has come to its conclusion."

"What are you going to do with me?" Billy asked.

"Oh, don't worry about that. I already have a deep hole dug further down the trail, off the beaten path, to drop you." Jacob threw his hand out to his left and indicated the direction Billy's final resting place would be. "You can't see it from here, so don't try. It's way out of the way. But don't worry; I dug the hole deep enough that no one will find you, and no animal will be able to dig you up. I'll make it cozy for you."

"God damn you. You're a sick son of bitch, Cantrell."

"Just doing what needed to be done a long time ago. I'm *carpe diem-*

ing the shit out of this day and your life." Jacob laughed. "I just made that up. I'm seizing my day by taking yours." He turned his back on Billy and stooped to grab his book bag. "My destiny. My legacy. It starts right here. Right now. In this moment. By removing you from the picture." Jacob stood with his book bag in his left hand. He unzipped it with his right, then reached inside. When Jacob grasped what was inside, he let the bag drop, revealing his masterpiece all at once.

A breath caught in Billy's throat. This was the moment he knew his life was fucked. He started shaking his head back and forth as he mumbled a pitiful, "No-no-no-no-no-no-no-no-no-no."

It was another pair of brass knuckles. This pair was bigger and badder than the one Jacob had been fiddling with throughout their conversation. The only similarity between them was that they both had the same base—three to four brass knuckles—welded together as one unit. Mounted across the top of these knuckles was some sort of flat plate that was slightly bigger than the flat part of Jacob's fist. The worst things about these new brass knuckles were the five ten-penny nails welded to the front of the flat plate. Each looked to be at least three inches in length. Two of the nails were welded near the index finger side, two on the pinky side, and one directly in the middle.

When Jacob slipped his problem solver on, it fit his fist perfectly. It was obvious Jacob had worked on this piece for a while. Billy had to hand it to him—it was perfect, a work of art.

Jacob started walking toward Billy. "Pretty sweet, huh?"

Tears had already started brimming in Billy's eyes. As Jacob approached, he tried to pull away. He couldn't go very far; his head was pressed back hard against the bark.

"Oh, c'mon, Billy. Don't start crying. You'll make me feel bad, and I don't want to feel like that."

They stood there, staring each other down; Jacob, solemn in his decision of what he needed and wanted to do, and Billy, who stared back at Jacob with dread in his face and leaking eyes.

Billy's face all of sudden took on a look of embarrassment. Jacob didn't know why until Billy looked down. Jacob's eyes traveled down his torso and stopped on Billy's crotch.

"Ah, c'mon, Billy. Really? Why the fuck you gotta go and piss your-self? You know, you should be embarrassed doing that in front of me. You know why? Because all the times you and your bitches came after me and beat the shit out of me, I never once soiled myself. I took it like a man. You should do the same. Take what's been coming to you like a man. Don't cry. Don't piss yourself. And for the love of God, you better not shit yourself either."

Billy shook his head quickly, then bowed his head in shame.

"Alright, I'll do you a solid here. You can tell me where you want me to hit you first."

"Just do it. Just get it over with," Billy said in a broken voice.

"What, you want me to decide?"

Billy gave him a pitiful shrug. "Doesn't matter."

"Ah, jeez. Okay, here goes." Jacob drew back. Billy shut his leaking eyes tightly and tensed, waiting for the death blow to come, but Jacob continued speaking.

"You know, I could drag the shit out of this moment and start punching away at your legs or your arms just to make it crazy painful for you for what you did to me. You think I should do that?"

Billy said nothing.

"No, probably not. I've had enough fun for today. Better get on with this so I can get on with my new life. I have some training to do. You know, some more plays to learn. I have to go shopping and get some new clothes so I can look my best when I meet up with Amber a little later this week. Ah, I'm going to have such a good life. And I have you to thank for it. If it hadn't been for you beating the shit out of me from week to week, I might never have come up with the idea to take your life. And take *your life*. If you know what I mean. So, that said, I want to thank you for everything I will have in my not-too-distant future."

Jacob drew back his arm and thrust it forward, much in the same way he had when he'd punched Billy at the beginning of their scuffle. The punch was hard, and Jacob's fist connected perfectly.

The knuckle sandwich sucker punch came swiftly, and didn't give Billy time to close his eyes. The ten-penny nails were huge as they entered his field of vision and punched into him, high on his face. Billy's whole head lit up in a sudden, intense ball of agony, and then the pain was no more.

Jacob expected some sort of recoil, but there was none. This one drilled deep into Billy's head and stuck true. He didn't even need to deliver any consecutive hits. The one punch was all it took, and Billy was gone.

Jacob stood, staring in wide-eyed shock at Billy's face. A few streams of blood trickled out from beneath the flat plate of the brass masterpiece, ran down Billy's cheek and dripped onto his blue shirt.

Jacob's fist was still holding the knuckles that were stuck firmly into the upper left side of Billy's face. He released his grip on them and wiggled his hand free, then dropped his arms and let them rest at his side.

He stood there, staring at Billy, for a long time. He was coming to terms with what he'd done. He wasn't sad, and there was no remorse; just an incredible sense of awe.

When he had finally accepted the moment, he cut Billy's limp body from the tree and set to work, making Billy disappear forever.

∽

Later that day—almost at dusk—Jacob emerged from the edge of the woods. He now wore a pair of grey Reebok tennis shoes and a pair of dark jeans. These jeans didn't have any holes in the knees; they were much nicer than the ones he'd worn before. He also wore a green and orange T-shirt that stated: FOOTBALL IS LIFE. THE REST IS JUST DETAILS.

Jacob wasn't carrying anything in his hands. He still had his backpack, with his books and today's assigned homework yet to be done. Everything he'd taken into the woods was down there still, buried along with the body of Billy Barbary.

If someone were watching and could compare Jacob's walk before he'd entered the woods to this moment when he stepped out again, that someone would've said he had more of an energetic walk. There was more of a bounce in his step. They would've noticed his footsteps were lighter. They might even observe a skip every now and then.

Jacob reached into his jeans pocket and pulled out the only thing he'd kept—his original pair of brass knuckles—and slipped them on. He gave a few small punches into the open palm of his left hand.

He smiled and said to himself again, "Yes, sir, Billy-Barbary's neva-eva gonna-eva fuck-with-me-again. Billy-Barbary's neva-eva gonna-eva fuck-with-me-again."

Jacon began to make his way home, shadow-boxing to the tune of his sing-song rap as it played over and over in his mind.

He glanced back toward the two pine trees where he'd entered and emerged from the woods. He gave them a final look and a slight smirk, then turned and walked away into Billy Barbary's life.

THE SCUTTLING

THERE WERE CRABS on the beach. Most of them were small or medi-um-sized, but every now and then, Andy Whitmore and Marcus MacAlister would see 'a big motherfucker', as Marcus liked to call them.

The midnight walk was perfect. There was only a half-moon, which didn't give much light to see, but the sky was clear of stars and clouds. It didn't matter that it was so dark at this late hour, because Marcus and Andy had their flashlights.

"This beach reminds me of being with your mom last night," Marcus said, then gave a suppressed chuckle.

"Shut up talking about my mom like that."

"Why? She's got a bangin' bod, man. I'd *sooo* do your mom."

"Jeeesus," Andy said, dragging the word out in frustration. "You're disgusting." He thought for a moment, then said, "Hey, if you were with my mom last night, then you wouldn't even be here, since she didn't even come on this beach trip."

In a slightly deeper register, Marcus said, "Oh, she *came* alright."

Andy blew an annoyed breath of air his way. "And furthermore, if you were with her, you'd have crabs too, dumbass."

"Awww, jeez, you're right. Yeah, that is disgusting." Marcus walked in silence, then said, "Crabs or no crabs, I'd still do her."

"C'mon, man," Andy said. "Get off my mom. Literally and figura-tively." He laughed at his own quip.

A breeze blew off the ocean and buffeted their hair; Marcus's, black and naturally curly, Andy's, chestnut-brown, straight and a little longer. They were barefooted, shirtless and wearing swim trunks. Marcus's were aqua-colored and adorned with pink flamingos, and Andy's dark blue with yellow sea turtles and white starfish. Both boys were sixteen, and ready to have sex with any female who showed them the least bit of interest.

"How's that flashlight working out for you?" Marcus asked.

"It's fine," Andy replied. "I can see perfectly."

"Only because I'm lighting up half the beach with the one I brought."

"Shut up. What, you compensating for something?"

"At least I can see where the hell I'm going. You look like you're about to go to a crime scene with your little purple beam of a flashlight. Where'd you get it anyway, from my sister?"

"No," Andy retorted, then as an afterthought said, "It is a pretty shitty flashlight, isn't it?"

"Uh, yeah."

Marcus shone his light on the waves coming in on their left and moved it in a clockwise direction. All the boys saw in the halogen beam was the surf coming in on a constant roll, then the beach seemed to stretch ahead as far as the light could illuminate. The beach was smooth except for a few scattered shells, random pieces of driftwood, small, tangled masses of seaweed, and the washed-up remains of a horseshoe crab or two. The weirdest thing they saw were sections of trees that seemed to have been planted in random areas of the beach. They realized the tide had rolled in earlier, delivering and half-burying these trees before rolling out again.

Marcus rotated the beam and his body as he turned to his right and then around behind them. There were only the white dunes, the bungalows and villas, and the wooden deck entranceways that led to and from the beach. He completed the circle around to his nine o'clock again.

"There's nobody out here except us," he said. "How cool is that?"

"The best," Andy replied. "Hey, you know what would be even better?"

"What's that?"

"To be out here alone with that waitress from the restaurant tonight. You remember that hot little brunette in the baby-blue shorts?"

"Oh, she was hot as hell. I loved her."

"You love anything with tanned legs and shorty-shorts," Andy said, punching him playfully in the bicep. "Even my mom."

"Hell, yeah. But she was extra special. She was an eleven."

"You sure she was an eleven?" Andy asked. "You know the scale to rate women only goes up to ten, right? Dumbass."

"You know what I mean."

Andy laughed. "Oh, I know." In a pretty good British accent, he said the famous line from the cult movie *This is Spinal Tap* that his dad always quoted: "'These go to eleven.'"

"What?" Marcus asked, having no idea what Andy was talking about.

"Nothing. But yeah, she was awesome."

"I couldn't get enough of her. Hard trying to check her out with my parents and sister sitting at the table with us."

"I know. Me too," Andy said. "Too bad your parents were there. Maybe you could've asked her out. That is, if you could've gotten up enough nerve before I did."

"Yeah, we both had a thing for her," Marcus said. He was quiet for a moment or two thinking. "Damn, to be out here on this desolate beach. Just her and me."

"And the damn crabs," Andy added.

Marcus looked over at him with an appalled look on his face. "Jeez, you really know how to kill a guy's fantasy."

"No, if I really wanted to kill your fantasy, I would've said something like, 'And me—where do you want me?' You know, like a threesome."

"Aww, damn it, man. Really? That's even worse." They both laughed.

The crabs were the only constant thing on the beach. Every fifteen to twenty paces, Marcus's flashlight would reflect off them or they would see small mounds that would eventually scuttle up toward the dunes or down to the surf.

Still thinking of his ruined fantasy, Marcus said, "Those damn crabs are literally everywhere."

"Ah, they're not hurting anyone," Andy replied. "They're more afraid of us than we are of them."

"They're just creepy, is all, you know?"

"Yeah."

"I feel like they're going to run straight toward me when they start scurrying like that."

"Me too."

"Where the hell is everyone?"

"Who cares. We have the beach all to ourselves. When has that ever happened?"

"Hey, look! There goes another one. That motherfucker is booking it."

He was too. The crab scuttled sideways away from them and down to the beach, its legs all a blur in the flashlight beam.

"I can barely keep track of him," Andy said.

The crab disappeared in the surf that had just washed up on the shore.

"That's because you have that shitty flashlight," Marcus teased again.

"I know, I know. I didn't think of everything before this trip. I just had enough time to grab a few clothes before you guys left. You could've given me more of a heads up about it."

"Hey, talk to my parents about that shit. They suggested it at the last minute. I thought they wanted to do a 'family vacation'"—he made air quotes—"this year. You know, just Mom, Dad, my dumbass sister, and me. God, am I glad you got to come along. The beach is awesome, but so much better with my best friend."

"I'm really psyched I got to come." They bumped knuckles. "It couldn't have been a better weekend. I'm glad your sister didn't pitch a bitch to come on this walk. Jesus, she whines. *A lot*."

"Tell me about it. She gets on my damn nerves all the time."

Marcus's flashlight beam caught two more crabs. They skittered in opposite directions for a few fast paces, then hunkered down in the sand as though they were escapees caught in the glare of a prison searchlight. Eventually, realizing that the flashlight beam was still on them, they shot away from each other—one into the surf, the other up into the dunes.

"Look at them. They're fuckin' moving," Marcus said.

"How do they not fall down, running so fast and sideways like that?"

"Beats the hell out of me."

Andy asked, "Remember that old fisherman at the restaurant this morning?"

"Yeah. Creepy old fucker. What about him?"

"You think what he was saying was true?"

"About what?"

"All that shit about us not going on this beach after midnight."

Marcus gave Andy a single bark of laughter. "What do you think?"

"I'm guessing no, or that you just don't give a shit."

"No, I don't believe him," Marcus said, casting a disapproving look Andy's way. "He's just an old pedophile who wanted to either get close to one of us, or to my sister."

With disgust in his voice, Andy said, "Uhh, you think he would even want your sister?"

"Hey, man, that's my sister you're talking about."

Andy laughed, then continued in a more serious tone. "Yeah, you're right. He probably wanted to stroke one of us over your sister."

"Aww, jeez, you're *sick*, man," Marcus said. Andy was well and truly crossing the line, the way he always did. "That's just plain *nasty*."

Andy laughed again. He rarely ever pulled one over on Marcus, so he felt damn proud when he did.

"That's a good one though," Marcus acknowledged, and they bumped knuckles again.

When their laughter died away, they walked in silence for a while. Each of them took in the scenery of their midnight walk in their own way. The sea breeze buffeted their hair again; they turned their faces toward it and reveled in the ocean smell. The sand where they walked was compact and wet, not the dry, fluffy kind a little further up on the shore. Every now and then the surf would roll in, nip at their ankles and retreat again.

Andy broke the silence. "So, what, you think that old man was just trying to scare us?"

"No doubt in my mind."

"Kinda odd that no one is out here except us, huh?"

"You *scared*, Andy?" Marcus jeered.

"Nah. Just a little weirded out, is all."

"Yeah, it is weird, but it's cool. Tonight we own this bitch," Marcus said, pointing down at the sand. "Nobody else's but ours."

"So why aren't there more people out here taking a late-night walk?"

"I don't know. Maybe because we're smart, and they're stupid."

Trying to spook Marcus a bit, Andy dropped his voice and spoke in a low whisper. "Or maybe the legend is true, like the old fisherman said."

"Legend my ass. That old codger didn't know what the fuck he was talking about. He was half drunk. You could smell it on his breath. Or at least I could."

Andy laughed. "Maybe that's why your sister didn't make a fuss about coming with us tonight. You know, maybe she's just a scared little bitch."

Marcus chuckled and nodded. Deep down, he truly loved his sister, but he also enjoyed talking shit about her with his friends when she wasn't around. Andy knew this and was always happy to play along.

"Could be," Marcus said. "Hard to tell with her, though. She's so damn finicky. But you're probably right. She doesn't like the scary stuff."

"You let me know when you want to turn around. You know the further we go, we'll just have to walk that same distance back."

"I'm in no hurry. It's nice out here."

"The soles of my feet are starting to hurt some," Andy said. "My feet aren't used to this hard sand. We've been walking for a while."

"We can go higher on the beach where the sand is softer if you want."

"Maybe on the way back. I'm good for now."

Four more crabs zigzagged ahead of them. They were trapped in the bright beam of Marcus's flashlight. For a few seconds, all the crabs stopped and hunkered down in the sand, then three of them shot off in different directions across the beach.

Marcus continued to pin the remaining creature with the flashlight beam until they neared him. They stepped to either side of the small crab and stopped to observe him.

"He's a brave little sucker, isn't he?" Marcus asked.

In a dopey, cartoony voice, Andy directed his next comment down at the little crab. "Hey, you little shithead. What the hell you doin' out so late?"

The little crab turned back and forth between the two giants on either side of him, apparently trying to decide what to do. Then, without warning, he made a run for it, shooting off sideways toward Andy and skittering over his bare feet.

Startled at the sudden movement and feeling all the tiny legs scrabbling over the tops of his feet, Andy jumped up out of the way of the hyperactive crab.

"Oh shit. He's got me!" he yelled.

Unable to contain himself at how ridiculous Andy looked and sounded, Marcus dissolved into peals of laughter and stepped backward.

Andy landed in the same spot from where he'd jumped. There was an audible crunch as all his body weight came down on the crab that had startled him. The crab itself, frightened by Andy's sudden movement, had frozen in place beneath him.

Realizing what had happened and feeling the ooze of the crab's insides on the sole of his foot, Andy jumped again, this time moving backward.

"Oh, you little shit," he said to the crab. "Why did you do that? Ughhh, that felt nasty." Andy's body involuntarily shuddered as he relived the sensation of the crab crunching under his foot. He wiped his foot on the damp sand, trying to remove the slime of the crushed crab as best he could.

Marcus was still laughing. Andy was still caught in being scared and disgusted, but an added layer of anger overcame him. He was pissed that such a little creature could strike such terror within him. He turned away and snatched up a piece of driftwood lying in the vicinity of the flashlight beam. He turned back and beat the already crushed crab further into submission.

"Fuck you, crab! You dumb little piece of shit. I hate you!"

"Andy. Whoa, whoa, whoa, Andy!" Marcus said, grabbing his arm after the second hit. "Calm down. It's just a crab. He's dead now. You got him."

Still angry at himself for being so frightened, Andy jerked his arm away, turned from Marcus, and threw the piece of driftwood into the ocean.

Marcus gave Andy time to calm down, then lowered his voice again. "Oh, you've done it now, Andy."

Andy turned to Marcus in a huff. "What do you mean?"

Marcus had already transformed his stance and posture to that of the old fisherman from the diner that morning. He stuck his pelvis out to one side, bent over, and hunched his shoulders. He held the flashlight up under his face and transformed his facial features into an evil grimace. He slowly shuffled toward Andy with his arm outstretched, his fingers quickly opening and closing with crab-like pincers. Marcus dropped his voice even lower to attain that deep, gruff, sea-worn growl. "Dey gwonna come fo' you now, boy. Hee-hee-hee. Dey gwonna come fo' you. Dey gonna getcha. An' dey gonna eatcha."

On the word 'eatcha,' Marcus lurched toward Andy and tried to grab him around the throat with his pincer fingers.

Andy was right there on the cusp of the grab and slapped Marcus's hand away. "That's not funny."

Marcus had started laughing, but immediately dropped the act. "You're right. It's not funny because…" He paused for comedic flare. "It's *hilarious*."

Marcus then lost it again, jumping around on the beach. He relived the hilarity of how Andy had looked, his legs kicking out in all directions as he jumped off the crushed crab. When Marcus finally had his laughter under control, they looked down again at the broken crab.

"What do you think we should do?" Andy asked.

"What do you mean?"

"I don't know. Shouldn't we bury him or something?"

Marcus gave him a look of contempt. "He's not your damn pet. Just leave him. He'll be a good early morning breakfast for the first seagull that flies by. Come on, this is as good a place as any to turn around. Let's head back."

They began to walk back the way they had come.

Seagull, Andy thought. That single word bounced around in his head for a while, then it hit him like a frozen water balloon to the face. He realized what had been nagging him during this whole walk. *Where are the birds?* he wondered. *No seagulls are flying around out here. Well, it's dark; we wouldn't be able to see them even if they were flying. But wouldn't we be able to hear them crying out? Wouldn't some still be on the beach?*

Andy wheeled around in all directions. No sandpipers were skittering along the water's edge, scavenging for food; no gulls were hopping along the shore, trying to find morsels of food left behind by evening beachgoers. There were no signs of any birds at all.

Andy had an unnerving thought: *Just crabs.*

He shone his puny purple flashlight beam all around.

"What's up?" Marcus asked.

"I don't know."

"You seemed spooked."

"Maybe."

"Why?" Marcus asked, then changed to a high-pitched voice. "You still scared about that crab and what that old man told us about the legend?"

"A little."

"Dude, it's an urban legend. He was just trying to scare us. And apparently it worked. On you."

"All urban legends have some sort of truth attached to them at first, don't they? Then the truth gets twisted over time. That's what turns them into legends, right?"

"What?" Marcus said, then gave a half-laugh. "You're not making any sense."

"Never mind. I don't know how to explain it." Then, in a frustrated huff, Andy added, "I was just wondering why no birds are flying around."

Marcus went silent. His flashlight slashed about in different directions in front of him. "Huh. You do have a point about that."

"Right? See. Told you it was weird. No people. No birds. Nothing. Just fucking crabs everywhere."

"Maybe there're no birds because it's night and they're all asleep somewhere."

"Don't give me that bullshit. You have to admit it's pretty odd that there isn't one single fucking bird out tonight."

"Sure. Okay, I admit that it's weir—"

A new sound came to their attention, drifting in behind them. At first they thought it was the wind kicking up, but no breeze was blowing. The sound was soft at first, barely audible, but the faint clicking slowly became louder.

"You hear that?" Andy asked.

"Yeah, what is that?"

The sound grew with each step they took.

"I couldn't tell you. Some sort of clicking."

"Where's it coming from?" Marcus asked, but even as he posed the question, he and Andy knew.

The boys stopped and slowly turned to look behind them. As the glare of the flashlight beam rotated around, they saw a whole section of the beach move as one unit, then stop as the light cascaded over its surface. At first they thought it was their imaginations and blinked a few times in confusion, but then the horror of the moment registered in their mind.

Marcus said, "What the—"

"Crabs," Andy whispered.

"No fucking way."

The whole surface of the beach moved again, wiping away any further doubt. The noise they had heard started up once more. It was the clicking of the crab's claws and the sound of their shells clacking into each other as they slowly advanced on the two teens.

Andy and Marcus were suddenly on edge; they began to back away from the horde of crabs in front of them.

"Where did they come from?" Andy whispered.

"Beats the hell out of me, but I'm not gonna stand around to find out."

"It… it's the Scuttling. Like the old fisherman said. Has to be. Remember what he told us this morning? He said if we ever heard the Scuttling, we should never, ever, under any circumstances, turn and face it."

"Well, I've never heard what the Scuttling sounds like," Marcus exclaimed. "So how the *hell* could I know not to turn to that sound?" He threw his hand out, indicating the sea of crabs.

"I know. Doesn't matter. It's too late to figure it out. Let's just run. That's what the old man told us to do."

Marcus and Andy simultaneously turned and ran for all they were worth. The sound of the Scuttling grew louder and faster as more crabs joined the moving surface of the beach.

Marcus arced his flashlight up into the dunes as they ran. He saw more crabs cresting the knolls and scuttling down to meet the army that seemed to be gaining on them. He refused to look back, thinking it would be the last thing he ever did. He turned his beam toward the ocean.

Bursting forth from the incoming water, droves of crabs left the surf as though the sea were deliberately washing them up on the beach. Each of them joined the horde, but not all the crabs fell in behind. Some of them were scuttling out ahead of them, and neither boy liked the look of that.

Seeing a hint of movement ahead of them in the jittering glare of Marcus's flashlight, Andy yelled, "Marcus! Look! Stop!"

Marcus was already looking, and saw the same unbelievable sight.

The open beach ahead of them as far as his flashlight beam illuminated was full of crabs as well. A myriad of sizes and colors. There were even some bigger than the ones Marcus had called 'big motherfuckers'; those lumbered along slightly slower than the others. But all of them were heading straight for them.

The boys stopped abruptly and turned in all directions, shining the flashlight in a frantic circle. Both sides of the oncoming crabs stopped about six feet away from the boys. The space to their right and left quickly filled with crabs.

The boys stood with their backs against each other, slowly turning in a circle. They moved their flashlights as they did, Andy wishing his beam was brighter.

"What do they want?" he hissed.

"Pretty safe to say they want us. I guess. I don't know. I mean, we're out here after midnight. We killed one of their own."

"You serious? That was an accident."

"But you beat the ever-loving shit out of it after that. I don't think they took too kindly to your shit-stomp."

"I couldn't help it. That crab just spooked me."

"Like we haven't been spooking them tonight during our walk."

"What do we do now?"

"Fuck if I know."

One section of the crab circle surged forward from the group and advanced on Marcus, then quickly backtracked. Marcus gave a startled yelp and jumped back, almost causing them both to topple over into the layer of crabs. Andy caught him, held their balance and pushed Marcus back.

Marcus yelled again, directing his anger at the crabs that had just shot toward him. The crabs moved away in an undulation, but were replaced by others. Frustrated, Marcus kicked some sand onto the new ones. The sea of crustaceans parted, making an opening for the sand to settle, then moved back over the spot where the sand had just landed.

"Oh, Jesus, we are so fucked," Andy said. "We are so far from our room. How the hell are we going get back?"

"We have to make a run for it," Marcus suggested.

"You think we can make it?"

"You have any other suggestions?"

"No."

"Then we have no other options."

"What if we try to make it to that entranceway over there?" Andy asked. "If we can get off the beach, maybe we can take the main road back to our hotel."

"Right. Good thinking. That could work."

"It better."

"Why?" Marcus asked.

"Because this fucking circle is getting smaller."

Marcus shone his flashlight around at the circle of crabs. Andy was right; the twelve-foot diameter had shrunk to about nine or ten feet, maybe even eight, and it was getting smaller by the second.

"If we're gonna do this, we gotta do it now," Marcus said.

"On three?" Andy asked.

"Fuck three—let's do this shit on one."

"Okay. But once we start running, we don't fucking stop," Andy decided. "Not for anything or anyone. Not even me."

"Gotcha. You do the same."

"Ten-four. Meet you back at the room, buddy," Andy replied.

"See you there."

"Ready?"

"I swear if I ever get out of this, I'm never going to the beach ever again," Marcus promised.

"Me either. Let's do this shit."

"One—"

Marcus barely got the word out of his mouth before the beach of crabs surged forward as one unit and attacked.

Startled, Marcus and Andy screamed in sheer fright when the circle around them disappeared and the horde covered their feet. Their screams of terror swelled as the first crabs latched on to their ankles. More crabs clamored over the first wave and climbed higher up their legs.

The boys were caught completely off guard. They both tried to slap the crabs from their buried feet, but while one leg was lifted, the other one disappeared as numerous crabs climbed higher and locked on tight with their claws.

At first Marcus and Andy thrashed about, swiping at themselves and kicking their legs back and forth, trying to rid themselves of the growing weight of crabs, but Marcus quit trying to swat the crabs off and started running toward the entranceway. He only took a couple of steps before he realized he was crushing numerous crabs beneath his feet. He winced as the sharp edges of crab shells lacerated his feet. He felt as though he was running across broken glass. Some of the brittle shells broke off inside each foot, which made running all the more difficult. The feeling of the oozing liquid from the crushed shells disgusted him, and that, combined with the swarm overtaking him, was enough to make him throw up. By now, the crabs had climbed to his knees and were starting to latch above his knee-caps. Their weight was more substantial than he had expected.

Andy was pinwheeling in circles, trying his best to kick all the crabs off himself. He became disoriented and just began running. His heart leapt in his chest when he too felt the crunch of numerous crab shells under the soles of his feet after his first few steps. Extreme panic engulfed his body when he felt the surf wash over his feet.

That's not good, he thought. *This was the worst decision I could have ever made.*

Andy stopped and turned around to head back to the beach, but the crabs were everywhere. The water around him churned in agitation. The sound of the Scuttling surrounded him, a mixture of hundreds of crab claws clicking together and their shells scraping and clacking against each other. It made every hair on his body stand on end.

Andy tried to run again, but this time he slipped on the slick insides of the crushed crabs. He fell face-first into the surf. He quickly raised his head above the water, gasping for air, thankful that no crabs had had a chance to latch on to his face and head. That was when he felt the stinging sensation in both of his arms. He stood quickly, and by the pale light of the half-moon, he saw his arms were covered in crab sleeves. He screamed out in sheer horror at the sight. He shook his limbs furiously and three or four crabs tumbled free; most of them had dug in, relentless.

Andy tried to run, but he slipped again in the surf. He stumbled to regain his balance, but that only brought him further out into the water. He couldn't regain his balance, and fell face-first in the ocean again. He felt the swarm of crabs skittering over his body. They traveled up the backs of his legs and underneath his swimsuit. Others scuttled over his backside, onto his back and up to his head. He struggled to lift his head out of the roiling water as still more crabs cascaded over him. The weight of so many crustaceans on his body, neck, and head caused his head to droop. Little by little, it lowered back down into the salty foam. As his face was pulled toward the water, he saw a buildup of crabs growing up out of the churning surface. The sound of clicking, anxious claws reached up to welcome him.

The pain receptors all over Andy's body lit up; it was an instant bonfire that sent his body into an epileptic-like shudder, and with that agony came screams. Instead of the fresh beach air he needed, Andy took in deep, choking mouthfuls of salty ocean water, his own blood, and the sand kicked up by the thousands of crustaceans trying to get to him. Andy hit the peak of his panic and dread; he knew he was going to drown.

All over his body, hundreds of tiny claws dug into his flesh. They worked as a team, snipping, cutting, tearing, and ripping small chunks of his body away and taking it with them, as other crabs moved in to do the same.

His last thought before he gasped his final sea-water breath was: *They're literally ripping us to shreds!*

As Andy was being dissected, Marcus was fighting with every bit of life he had left within him. His only thought was *I am not going to go out like this! I am not going to be taken out like this!*

He grabbed one of his thighs with both hands and pushed down the length of his leg as hard and as fast as he could. The pain was horrendous as the crab's pinchers were ripped away. It felt as though he had pulled the skin of his leg off as if it were only a stocking. In some places, the skin was torn deep enough to draw blood. Those wounds started to ooze blood and run down his leg. He knew the crab's appendages were being ripped away from the crabs themselves too, but he didn't give a shit. He just wanted to be rid of them. He longed to be back in the comfort of his hotel room. He wished for the warmth of the hotel bed and the loving arms of his mom and dad tight around him. Hell, he'd even go for some tight hugs from his stupid sister.

Seeing that his idea had worked on one leg, he quickly swiped the other in the same manner. Marcus could feel more blood running down himself, but it didn't matter; he was free of the crabs.

The crabs were persistent—they had already started to latch back onto the first leg—but his legs weren't heavy enough that he couldn't make a run for it, so he bolted.

As he ran, Marcus heard three distinct sounds. First, the Scuttling starting again as the crabs pursued him. Second, the crunching of more crab shells under his bare feet. He ignored the brittle shards opening up new wounds on the soles of his feet. And third—the sound that unnerved him the most—the dwindling screams of Andy, emanating from somewhere behind him. He was unable to do anything for his best friend, but even if he could, he remembered their promise to each other.

Marcus was nearing the entranceway and smiled at how close he was; almost home free. He didn't know how he was going to explain this hell to his parents, much less to Andy's mom and dad when they arrived back home and Andy wasn't with them. But at least he would be alive, and that was something to hope for. Hope swelled within him at the thought of surviving.

His foot struck something hard on the beach; his toes crumpled against the object he'd accidentally kicked. The pain was insane, like that of really nailing the corner of a coffee table or the leg of a couch while moving barefoot about the house. Marcus fell face first and tumbled over in the soft sand. He rolled over and glanced over his shoulder to see what had tripped him. A half-buried piece of driftwood he hadn't noticed while running blind was now uncovered, lying on top of the sand.

Marcus never had a chance to get up. A blanket of crabs surged forward and crested over him like a small wave onto the beach—only this wave never washed back away from him. Marcus's screams swelled for a moment, then became muffled as the crabs scuttled over his face, burying him in a constantly moving and agitated surface.

They mimicked the same actions they had performed on Andy, who was now face down, unmoving and silent at the water's edge. Each crab ripped a little piece of flesh from Marcus then departed, only to be replaced by another. Some of the bigger crabs tore bigger chunks of the skin and flesh from the boys' bodies. It was a feeding frenzy, plain and simple.

Finally, when most of the muscle had been ripped away from Marcus, the crabs worked together as a team and moved the last portions of his body down to where Andy's ravaged bones lay in the surf, gleaming in the moonlight.

A blood trail led from where Marcus had fallen in the dunes all the way back down to the water, and the sand where Andy had been dissected was covered with it too. The surf lapped hungrily at the blood-soaked beach. When the crabs had taken the boys completely apart—except for their bones and any other pieces of their body they couldn't do anything with—they left both carcasses for the tide to erase. Each time the surf rolled in, it would wash a little more of the blood and remains away.

Eventually, all the crabs dissipated and scurried away. Some left by way of the ocean; others crawled into the dunes and burrowed into the cool sand. Still others moved on to their own small, remote areas of the beach. *Their* beach. Their beautiful, desolate beach.

Just the way they liked it.

RAGE

IT ISN'T ENOUGH—NOT after what he did. It just isn't fucking enough.

These two sentences were what went through Scott Markley's mind when he compared what he was about to do with the incident that had played out between him and Connor McPherson a little over two weeks ago.

Right now, it was some time after midnight and extremely dark, with only the light from the fingernail-clipping crescent of a moon that hung in the warm night sky. If there was any noise to alert Scott that someone was moving about in the darkness, it was covered by the incessant, loud droning of the insect orchestra that was playing their symphony tonight.

Scott was standing with his back against the flourishing oak tree that stood at the edge of Connor's property. He was looking down at the two items he held, psyching himself up. This was something he definitely wanted to do. Make that *needed* to do.

Scott took in a deep breath, and found that the dry night air was redolent of freshly mowed grass. There was a scent of late-night grilling mixed with the twinge of burning leaves coming from someone's backyard.

Jesus, that smells so good, Scott thought as the scent of the nearby cookout filled his nostrils. *I'm going to have to cook me something good after this. Celebrate me getting up the balls to go through with this. Pork chops would be good right about now. Yeah, with rice and green beans and a beer or two. Yeah, I'm gonna do that when I get home, just as soon as I take care of Connor.*

"Connor," Scott muttered to himself in disgust. "Such a damn yuppie name. Perfect name for the complete and utter asshole that he is. An *inconsiderate* asshole, to be precise."

Scott shook his head as he thought again about the little fuck-you salute Connor had given him as he'd gunned the engine of his silver-grey convertible BMW and weaved around the slower-moving traffic a lot faster than Scott could was able to.

There was no way to catch that fucker that day, Scott thought. *But I got you now, bitch, or at least I will when I give you this. You can't be a douche and get away with it.*

Scott looked down again at the items he carried, one in each leather-gloved hand.

"Yeah, this is gonna get you good," Scott said to himself, and smiled.

Just the equivalent of a kid prank in this adult game we're playing. Just a little push-back for what you did to me, asshole.

Scott turned and peered out from around the oak tree to see if the coast was clear.

He was dressed in all black, garments bought with cash from a Kohl's department store for tonight's little prank. The only thing showing out behind the tree was his head. He'd thought about trying to find a ski-mask with eye, nose, and mouth-holes to cover up his face, but then decided against it. He just couldn't bring himself to buy and wear a ski-mask. To Scott, it seemed too much like actually committing criminal activity.

He wore black cargo pants that had a zippered pocket on each side of the outer thigh. The black, lace-up Skechers and the long-sleeved black T-shirt he wore didn't have any distinguishing marks on them. He had also picked up a thin, dark pair of leather Isotoner gloves that he'd found on a crowded discount table. It wasn't the season for gloves, it being the middle of summer, but there they'd been, on a long table with all the other items marked with a 70% off tag. So he'd got these kickass gloves for around $3.00.

Oh yeah, Scott thought. *Tonight's escapade is going to be awesome. This isn't going to be nearly enough to prove my point, but it will help me feel a hell of a lot better about what happened than just sitting around and doing nothing about it. It'll ease my mind until I can think of something better to do to him... or should I say* worse?

He knew he was taking this—whatever *this* was—way too far, but he hadn't been able to just let the incident go. He'd asked himself numerous times: *Why are you doing this? Out of revenge? To teach Connor a lesson? Exactly what is this going to prove once you go through with it?*

He replied now in a whisper to himself, "It's going to teach *Connor*"—the word was spoken with a hatred that was a little unsettling to Scott himself—"that he can't fuck anyone over and get away with it. That *anyone* being me."

Seeing no one out and about, Scott dashed from the side of the tree to the side of Connor's BMW, where he crouched and waited.

He half expected a bright searchlight to flip on and pin him where he crouched. In his imaginative mind, he saw a swarm of SWAT and police, completed with tactical gear, run in and aim their machine guns and pistols down at him. They would've caught him red-handed with the evidence in his hands before the crime was even committed.

Scott felt as if his heart was pummeling the inside of his chest. The dash from the tree to the car hadn't been particularly long and he was in decent shape and health; he was just scared out of his mind by what he was about to do. But he couldn't stop himself. He had a point to prove and a lesson that needed to be taught to this *fucking Connor guy.*

By the BMW, he looked around quickly to check his surroundings but saw nothing. He heard nothing as well—except the unbelievably loud insects. He turned quickly and glanced down at the gas cap. There was no indention for a finger to slip beneath the covering and pull it open.

"Damn it," Scott muttered between clenched teeth. "I was afraid of that. No worries, though," he added as he set the two items he carried down on the paved driveway. "I have this." He pulled a small crowbar from his back pocket and carefully slid the flat end into the space between the car panel and the gas cap lid. He did this as gently as he could, not wanting to set off the beamer's car alarm and wake Connor or the surrounding neighbors. Once he had his crowbar in position, he slowly pushed back on the bar and added pressure until the gas cap popped open. Scott froze for a moment, thinking the alarm might sound; when it didn't, he breathed a sigh of relief and stuffed the crowbar back into his back pocket.

Must be an older model, and the alarm must not be as advanced. Lucky me.

He carefully flipped open the gas tank lid, unscrewed the gas cap, slid the end of the funnel into the gasoline slot, and poured an already open bag of sugar into the fat end of the funnel. He poured as fast as he could, but was careful not to overflow the funnel. He didn't want any sugar to be wasted.

As he patiently waited for all the crystals to sift down into Connor McPherson's gas tank, he said, "Oh yeah. Let's see how far you get in traffic when your engine sucks this sugar into its system. Good luck getting anywhere now, bitch."

When the contents of the bag were in the gas tank, Scott jiggled the end of the funnel in the opening to make sure there was no evidence of dropped sugar crystals for Connor or anyone else to see.

It would really suck if anyone discovered the evidence of what I did here tonight before it really affected Connor.

Making sure the funnel was free of any sugar, he pulled it from the gas tank hole, recapped it, and closed the lid.

"I just gave your car diabetes," he gloated as he double-checked his surroundings one last time.

Seeing no one, Scott retreated from Connor's BMW in a hunched run and made his way back to his hideaway oak tree, then eventually to his Kia Sorento, which was parked in a secluded area about four neighborhoods away.

The next morning, Scott was already sitting underneath the low-hanging branches of an elm tree that grew near the street. The tree belonged to one of Connor's neighbors, who lived three houses down and almost around the bend from him.

Scott had set his alarm to get up extra early this morning. He had showered and gotten dressed and ready for work in time to get out here—to *fucking Connor's* house—to see how this morning's events played out.

He had a feeling Connor's car would start. He didn't think that just by putting a bag of sugar in his gas tank, it wouldn't turn over when cranked. But then again, he'd never done this before and didn't exactly know how all this worked. It would take a little while for the sugar sludge to work its way around the chambers of the engine before it clogged up on him—at least, that was what the internet said, and everything on the internet is true. It would be a couple of miles down the road when it would crap out on him, and Scott wanted to have a front-row seat when that happened.

Scott had been sitting here in his SUV for about ten minutes. Even though he had cooked the pork chops, rice, green beans, and biscuits after he'd arrived home last night, he was now eating a Hardee's ham, egg, and cheese biscuit with hash browns and a Diet Coke. He'd just taken the last bite of his biscuit and crumpled the wrapping paper when he saw Connor step out of his house, then turn and lock his front door.

"Let the games begin," Scott said to himself as he watched Connor jog down the four steps of his house and around to the driver's side of his BMW. Connor bleeped the alarm, opened the car door, and slid inside.

What? No girlfriend this morning? Where's your girlfriend, Connor? *Still sleeping, or did she not even come over last night? The bitch.*

Scott really didn't have a problem with *her*—whatever her name was—other than the fact that she hadn't done what he'd asked her to do during the whole fiasco; at least, he didn't think she had. She *had* leaned over and said something to Connor—he didn't know what—then cut her eyes back to Scott, but how could he have known what she was saying with all the yelling he was doing after the incident?

"And there goes the convertible top. You always gotta drive with that fucking top down, don't'cha, *Connor?* You think you're hot shit with the top down. Well, you are. You're the biggest piece of shit to ever drive a convertible."

The engine cranked as expected, and the car immediately backed out of the driveway.

From his hiding place, Scott saw Connor back into the road, his tail lights away from him. The car's headlights came into view and pointed in his direction.

Oh shit, he's coming my way, Scott thought as he folded himself over onto the console. He held the position until Connor's car roared by.

"Don't gun it, bitch," Scott said to the passing BMW. "You're not going to get very far revving it like that."

When the BMW's engine faded, Scott sat up in his seat and looked into his rear and sideview mirrors. He was just in time to see Connor's car round the corner at the far end of the street.

Once Connor had disappeared, Scott cranked his Sorento and made a quick U-turn, flooring it to catch up. He just needed to see enough of Connor's BMW to find out which way he was going so he could follow him. He definitely didn't want to get close enough for Connor to get suspicious of a tailing vehicle. Scott caught up enough to see him at the far end of the road, braking at a stop sign.

Connor turned right and headed toward the highway that led downtown. As soon as he had disappeared, Scott gunned his Sorento again so he could reach the stop sign quicker. He wanted, *needed,* to see the BMW break down. At the stop sign, he braked for a few seconds, then turned right as well.

They continued this game of cat and mouse throughout the neighborhood until they finally came out to a larger road with heavier traffic. Scott felt great about keeping his Sorento a safe distance from the BMW. He was having fun. It hadn't really registered with him that he was committing a felony or two.

Connor doesn't have a clue about me or what is about to happen to him. Speaking of which—shouldn't something have happened by now? How long does this shit take to work? They do make cars better these days, I guess, so who knows…?

Connor switched lanes up ahead, and Scott knew he was about to get onto the main highway into downtown.

"Fuck. I gotta get over into that lane too," Scott said aloud to the empty SUV. "He's gonna be gone, and I'll never get to see my brilliant and amazing handiwork."

Scott flipped his blinker on and maneuvered into the next lane. The cars had already started turning to get onto the highway. He moved forward, but saw that Connor had already gunned it and was heading down the entrance ramp toward the highway.

Scott was simultaneously watching the car in front of him and the traffic light as he glanced to his left to see Connor getting closer to the merging traffic.

The light in front of Scott turned yellow.

"No-no-no-no. Fucking no," he chanted, but the car in front of him had already braked hard and the light had changed to red. "Fuck!" Scott shouted as he slapped his steering wheel, then he turned to watch Connor disappear for a second time.

But Connor's brake lights came on, and Scott noticed that his car had instantly slowed.

Scott's frustration at having to stop at the yellow light—a light that they both could've easily gone through had the car in front of him just hit his gas—turned into a smile as he realized that his sugar prank had finally set in.

"Holy shit," he whispered aloud. "I just don't believe it. It worked after all. Take that, you asshole."

Connor hit his brakes again. They flared on and off as his BMW slowed in a jerky fashion, then he pulled off to the right into the side at the bottom of the entrance ramp as he was about to merge with traffic.

A car horn sounded behind Scott. He snapped his head back to his rearview mirror to see what idiot was honking their horn and why they were honking it, and saw the driver behind him throw their hands up in frustration, then gesture angrily at him. He saw the pissed-off driver yelling, "GO!"

Scott looked forward and realized that the light had already turned green and traffic in both lanes had already started. The cars were way ahead of him. No wonder the driver behind him had lost it; Scott's Sorento was just sitting there, unmoving. He always hated it when a driver got distracted by something in his car, and he hated that he'd done the same to the guy behind him.

Scott threw up his hand in an apologetic wave and gunned his engine to put some distance between him and the very animated driver. He realized he was going to have to pass Connor, who was now sitting at the bottom of the ramp.

His heart started shadow-boxing inside his chest as it had the previous night. He hadn't wanted to get this close to Connor; he'd just wanted to see the inconvenience happen, take it in, and be gone. Just a quick, satisfied observation of the incident, and then disappear.

The two lanes merged into one right before the bottom of the ramp, so Scott was courteous enough to allow a beat-up, dirty grey truck get in front of him. He was hoping to make his green Sorento less conspicuous.

As he neared Connor's car, Scott pushed the button for the window on the passenger's side to roll down. He didn't know why he did this, other than thinking that he wanted to hear something from Connor and this small episode if possible. It would just help settle his mind about what he had done to Connor that much quicker.

He saw the BMW's driver-side door open and Connor quickly stepped out. As Scott slowly rolled by, he heard Connor shout 'Fuck!' as he slammed his door shut. Scott couldn't help but smile at Connor's frustration.

What Scott didn't expect was the frustrated look from Connor as he moved to the front of his car. It was just the timing of the situation. The quick glance from Connor turned into a double-take. Their eyes locked on each other for a moment, and Scott thought he was going to pass out.

Without fully believing he was doing it, Scott gave Connor a little 'fuck-you' salute as he passed, and then Connor was gone. It wasn't as pronounced as Connor's had been to him two weeks ago, but it just was enough for Scott.

That was when Scott realized he was smiling and how that must've looked to Connor. He immediately jerked his head to the passenger-side rearview mirror to see Connor's reaction to his idiotic hand movement and leer.

Oh, fuck, I just gave myself away. Oh, shit, I just gave myself away.

Connor—apparently thinking nothing of Scott's passive-aggressive hand gesture—was reaching down to pop the hood of his car. Scott saw him pull it up before he turned away.

It was only when Scott had safely merged with the other traffic that he released the breath he'd been holding since he'd turned onto the entrance ramp.

"Holy fuck, I can't believe I just did that and got away with it. Oh yeah, I got you back so good. Fuck you, Connor McPherson," he bragged, and gave another sarcastic salute as though looking at Connor again. "You piece of shit. Oh, I hope your car never gets fixed."

Scott hit the button to turn on the stereo. He found a station with a great song, then sang vigorously off-key as he drove the rest of the way to his work.

✺

Scott remembered that it had been bright the day of the incident. He'd just slid on a cheap pair of sunglasses he'd pulled from a four-sided kiosk inside one of those Spinx or Quick Trip stores a few weeks ago. They weren't the best pair of shades in the world, and he made a mental note that he was going to have to invest in a better pair now that summer was upon them.

Scott was traveling from the Cherrydale area on Pleasantburg Drive—a road that had three lanes of traffic, a median strip, and then three more lanes of traffic traveling in the opposite direction. Scott was in the far right lane—what people sometime call the slow lane, or at least where all the slower cars should always drive. There were many that didn't abide by that highway rule, and it always pissed him off.

On this particular day, traffic was traveling at a pretty decent speed. Scott remembered seeing another car in the lane to his left and maybe one car-length ahead of him—if even that. The car was one of those big land-tanks—one of those old cars from the 70s—and it looked like it had a good many miles on it.

A tub of crap, Scott thought, thinking back to what his friend, Stephen Dunbar, used to always called the piece of shit he'd had to drive back during their high-school days. Scott smiled widely at that phrase and the memory. Yeah, it was a big tub of crap. *Wonder if that's Stephen driving it?*

From out of nowhere, a BMW blasted through the small space

between him and the land-tank. There was barely any room for another car to squeeze through, but there it was, cutting a plane on an advancing diagonal.

Startled, Scott was pulled from his reverie and jerked the wheel to the right as he hit his brakes; there was no time to react properly to the movement of what looked like a car materializing out of nowhere and so close to him. He realized his mistake as soon as the Sorento cut to the right. He immediately jerked the wheel back to the left to overcorrect the severe movement. The Sorento bobbed up slightly on the right two tires for a second, then wobbled back down to the left and leveled out again.

"What the fuck!" Scott exclaimed, his body suddenly cold with fear. "What the hell was that all about?"

Scott saw the asshole in the car and the woman he was with for a few seconds before they moved away from him. The guy, whom Scott immediately pegged as a rich yuppie, was wearing a fucking golf visor. It was the only thing he could register as he fought to correct the almost-out-of-control SUV.

"Oh my God, who the fuck wears those things anymore? Call the goddang fashion police. Take him away."

Scott immediately blasted the asshole with a long, loud burst from his horn. The shithead didn't even look into his rearview mirror, which pissed Scott off that much more. Instead, the guy added even more gas and began to speed away—but not before Scott pressed down on the gas as well.

"Oh no you don't, asshole. You don't get to get away from this unscathed."

Scott didn't know if the asshole knew he'd cut it so close and almost caused him to flip his SUV, but it didn't matter. To not even acknowledge him—even after he'd used his horn—and to not even throw a hand up to give an apologetic gesture: that didn't cut it with Scott. They were going to have it out in some way right here and now.

Up ahead of him, the beamer veered out of Scott's lane into another, then moved ahead again and over to the lane closest to the median.

Scott mimicked his movements and kept up pretty decently with him. There were times when the asshole got away from him for a few moments, but slower traffic and red lights allowed Scott enough time to catch up.

There was a fated moment when the traffic halted just enough to where the asshole had to stop at a red light, rather than running it like the car next to him. Scott didn't hesitate, but gunned it into the other lane and pulled up beside him.

Scott's window was already down, and he yelled out, "Hey, asshole!"

The yuppie and his bitch either didn't hear him, or they were just ignoring him altogether. Probably the latter, but he was going to make himself known. Scott tried again, even louder.

"Hey! *Asshole!*"

He got the same response.

"Yeah, you know exactly what you did, you fucking bitch! You're not going to look at me, you fuck, are you?"

Scott was now sure they were ignoring him. They were obviously just hoping he would go away. This pissed him off, and he yelled again, "I don't know if you know this or not, but you almost clipped me back there! You almost caused me to flip my car, you piece-of-shit asshole!"

The guy's female sidekick couldn't help herself, and glanced over her left shoulder to look back out of the open convertible.

Lot's wife, Scott thought.

"Yeah, I'm talking to you, you she-bitch!" Scott yelled. He pointed emphatically at the stubborn asshole behind the wheel. "Get! That! Asshole! Right there! I want to talk to that whore! Not you!"

The queen bitch hesitated, but finally leaned over. The guy leaned over to hear what she had to say. She whispered something in his ear.

The guy leaned back up and squared himself in his seat. He turned and said something to her, then looked forward out of his windshield again. A smile crept over his face, but he never looked Scott's way, although deep down Scott felt—or knew deep inside—that the guy wanted to.

"You fucking bitch! You get his goddamn attention right fucking now! Have the decency to look at me, you cunt bitch!"

The man remained implacable, staring straight ahead, flexing his jaw muscles and nervously gripping and regripping his steering wheel. His smile became that much broader. The girl gambled another look—she apparently couldn't help herself—and received the biggest, harshest, and most meaningful of all fuck-you birds that Scott had ever flipped to a person.

"Bitch! Get his attention!" Scott yelled. He was seething. "Don't just sit there like a cunt on a log! Make him look at me!"

The light changed. Clearly wanting to get away, the asshole punched his gas pedal. The beamer's wheels spun and kicked up a little smoke before the tires caught, then he was gone.

Scott was right behind him, punching his gas as well, and he stayed on his tail as best he could. Scott was going to get the respect he deserved. He pushed his Sorento harder than it should've been pushed just to keep up with the BMW. He was pretty damn proud of himself for it, though he was mentally cringing the whole way. He was yelling at the top of his lungs, pointing his fingers, shooting more birds, and promising that he was going to 'get him' in some way.

Inwardly, he hated himself for losing control. The ass-clown had been so calm, cool, collected, and laid-back about the whole incident. Scott wished he could've just let it go, but a burning hatred had scorched the nice guy out of him. Nothing but unbridled road rage remained.

At the top of Pleasantburg Drive, they came upon a traffic light pretty quickly. The two lanes turning left to get on Highway 85 were green, but Scott knew it was probably going to change at any second.

"I'm gonna get you if it's the last thing I do," Scott promised. "One way or other, I'll fucking get you." He looked down at the guy's license tag, and read it aloud. "JWB721. JWB721. JWB271. I got you now, you fucking asshole. I sooooo got you. You gonna wish you had never passed me up like that in traffic and ignored me like you did. JWB721."

They were both nearing the traffic light when it indeed turned to yellow.

Scott was so busy staring holes into the asshole's rearview mirror that he didn't notice the light change. He was hoping and wishing—actually willing—the guy to look up into his mirror. Scott's breath caught in his throat when the asshole did in fact look up and caught Scott's gaze. He flipped Scott a sarcastic little salute, downshifted into fourth, then punched the gas, veered into the other lane, and floored it. His wheels gave a slight squeal as he took the turn a little too fast.

Scott's body burned even hotter, rage boiling over when he saw that the light was changing from yellow to red. The asshole had played him again, and the anger poured out of Scott in a torrential wave.

"FUCK YOU!" he screamed. He couldn't do anything about the asshole's actions but sit there and fume at the red light. And fume he did. "JWB721. JWB71."

Scott snagged a pen from his console. He shuffled things around in his front seat, trying to find a piece of scrap paper. He moved his traffic ticket device and placed it on the passenger seat floorboard. He set his book bag in the floorboard as well. He shuffled some papers and fast-food bags around until he found a voided parking ticket. He snatched it up, remembering the poor sap who had begged him to void the parking ticket for him. The guy had actually had a pretty good story, so Scott had had a little compassion on the guy and done it. He flipped the voided ticket over to the blank side and scratched the asshole's license tag down, then stuffed it into the empty cigarette holder for safe-keeping.

He looked back up again and said to the asshole who had already disappeared, "I'll look you up a little later, dick. I'll get your name and address, and then we'll see how cool you think you are when I pay you a little visit. You won this battle today, but the war between us has just begun. It's not over by a long shot. We will meet again, I can fucking promise you that."

There were numerous roads and avenues that branched off from that highway, and the asshole could be going anywhere right now. There was no way to know. Scott had to let it go.

He tried to force himself to calm down, but he was livid, jacked up on an all-consuming hatred that he couldn't put out of his mind.

⌘

Scott was driving in an angry daze, his mind rehashing what had happened two weeks and two days ago. The reason for his current amped-up behavior was that Connor McPherson was in his BMW; he had just blown by Scott less than three minutes ago. His convertible top was down—*as it always is when he's tooling around town*—but this time his music was blaring from his speakers. It looked as though his car was running perfectly now.

"Son-of-a-bitch," Scott said aloud when he saw the BMW. "What does a guy have to do to get back at this fucking guy?"

Scott had been at the drive-thru exit of the Wendy's on Pleasantburg Drive, waiting to turn onto the three-lane highway itself. He had been craving a chocolate Frosty for a few days now and had stopped by the drive-thru to pick up a large one. Seeing Connor moving along as though nothing had happened pissed Scott off again, and he was right back where he'd been the day of the actual incident, reliving that memory burning in his mind. The Frosty sat in the cup holder, untouched and melting; his appetite had been taken from him.

Scott turned onto the Pleasantburg Drive and followed Connor again at a modest distance. Connor didn't seem like he was in a speeding mood today, since no one was chasing him.

Two days, Scott thought. *Less than two fucking days, and he's out free-wheeling around town again as though nothing happened to his car. His car is running just fine now. Well, fuck that. I'm going to have to think of something to give you; something that's going to really inconvenience you, my friend.*

At first he didn't know what he was going to *inconvenience* Connor with, but one idea began to form in his head. It was a little too dark and demented for him. Just the fact that he was slightly entertaining the idea sort of scared Scott. No, not just sort of—it actually scared him a whole hell of a lot. It wasn't the first time the idea had flitted across his mind. He quickly brushed it aside, but not as quickly as the last time it had cropped up.

Scott followed Connor a short way until he turned off the highway onto Villa Road. The road looped around and up the hill, past the entrance to an apartment housing complex, a small Italian restaurant, and a few business buildings before the road turned into a long straightaway. There were a few more apartment complexes and a small par-three golf course off to the left. At the end of the straightaway, the road wound around a sharp curve and up past Bimini's oyster bar and seafood restaurant, then spat you out on Pelham Road.

Connor turned left onto Pelham Road and headed down the hill. Scott did likewise. He had no idea where the fuck Connor was going, but he was game to find out.

Midway down the hill, Connor turned into the parking lot that led to a Publix Supermarket. Scott followed, but he went considerably slower to put a little more distance between him and Connor. He pulled into the first parking space he could find at the far end of the parking lot and coasted to a stop under the shade of small tree planted in the small curbed area to his left. He watched Connor turn into the fourth aisle and park diagonally over two spaces.

All those fucking open spots and you do that shit. God, what an asshole. I hate it when people do that. Not cool, man. Not fucking cool at all.

Connor stepped out of his car and walked toward the entrance of Publix. Scott saw him raise his arm and aim his keys back toward his car for a moment, but without looking in that direction. There was a short bleep as the car alarm was engaged.

"What a fucking dumbass," Scott said, seeing that Connor's BMW top was still down and his car was fully exposed. "You gonna lock your car and alarm it with it completely open? What a *douche*. Don't you know someone can just reach in and grab anything they want—that is, if you have anything exposed for them to grab?"

Scott was frustrated with how careless Connor was with everything he had. Careless when he drove. Careless about leaving his car totally open for anyone to steal anything out of it. Scott didn't want to steal anything from the car. He couldn't care less about anything Connor McPherson had, much less try to steal from him. What he wanted was to do something that would hurt him. He wanted to do something to hurt his pride and joy.

What can I do to him? Scott wondered. *What the fuck could I do to his car?*

Scott's hand dropped from his steering wheel to his lap and brushed against the Wendy's Frosty that he hadn't even touched since he'd pulled out of the drive-thru.

He looked down at the Frosty. Then he looked up at Connor's car, then back down to the Frosty. A huge smile crept across his face, then Scott started laughing.

"Oh, I knew there was a reason I wanted a Frosty today," he said.

He glanced toward the store again and saw that Connor had already gone inside. He didn't have a clue as to what Connor was going to buy; he could've gone in there for a huge list of things, or just for a simple item such as batteries or beer and would be out in a few minutes.

There was only a miniature window of time before Connor or anyone else would exit the store, and that time was growing exponentially smaller with each hesitation, so Scott took it. He drove his SUV over to Connor's BMW, pulling up to the driver's side, which was nearest the Publix front doors. He wanted to block the view of anyone who might be looking out the store windows or exiting the doors—not that they would know anything was going on. It was just a precaution.

Scott double-checked his surrounding and saw that the coast was as clear as it was ever going to be. He hurriedly picked up his large Wendy's Frosty and flipped off the lid. He held his arm out the window of the Sorento, took a measured judgment of the distance, then chucked the Frosty toward the open BMW.

The cup hit the driver's side headrest and bounced into a somersault which caused part of the contents to pour out and splatter over the main console area. It covered the radio and thermostat knobs in a sticky mess. It ping-ponged around in the driver's side area before coming to rest upside-down on a sloped part of the driver's seat. As it rested, the chocolate contents continued to melt. They slowly oozed out of the cup and puddled in the base of the driver's seat.

"Bull's-eye, bitch!" Scott shouted in excitement. "Deal with that shit." His heart swelled with amazement and pride. He couldn't have asked or prayed for a better landing.

That's going to take a while to clean up, that's for sure, Scott thought. *That will teach you to take up two parking spots.*

He pressed the gas to get the hell out of Dodge as fast as he could without drawing attention to himself.

"How's that for inconvenience?" he muttered, hoping this would take Connor off the highway for a little while longer. Another thought flittered across his mind, and he breathed a quick sigh of relief. *Lot of good that fucking alarm did you, Connor. It didn't even go off. I'd forgotten about it. I definitely lucked out. Twice actually.*

But even as he left the scene of the crime, Scott couldn't help but think, *It isn't enough. It just isn't fucking enough. There has to be something worse.* Then that little disturbing thought that had entered his mind twice before drifted to the forefront of his thoughts again.

That son-of-a-bitch needs to die.

Scott didn't immediately push the thought out of his mind. It lingered there, and he dwelt on it a lot longer than he had the last two times. It was a long time before other thoughts took precedence over it.

≼

Scott was driving in circles, going nowhere in particular.

It wasn't enough, he thought again. *It just wasn't fucking enough.* The thought kept running through Scott's mind, even after he left the Publix parking lot.

It isn't enough. Not after what he did. There has to be something bigger. I have to do something worse to him. He thought for a moment longer, then said to himself, "I think it's time to pay Mr. McPherson a home invasion visit."

He couldn't believe he'd just thought it, but he was compelled to follow through with his idea. Scott knew Connor wouldn't be in Publix for very long. He also knew that when Connor came out of the store, he was going to be livid at what he found in his car, and that would tie him up a good deal longer.

I would love to see Connor's face when he looks inside his car, but it's way too dangerous for me to stick around. I'm sure he's going to look around this parking lot for the culprit, and when he does, I don't want me or my car to be anywhere around to jog his memory of me driving past him on the highway two days ago. Connor is going to be out for blood. Come to think of it, that's really all I want as well.

Scott knew exactly where Connor lived. After the initial incident, he hadn't been able to take not knowing what asshole he was dealing with. So, once he had arrived at City Hall where he worked, he took his automobile ticketing device and the voided ticket with the written license-tag number, and punched the letters and numbers into the device.

In just a few seconds, the screen popped up a name and address: *Connor McPherson, 328 Trailways Street.* It gave the city and state, the make and model of Connor's car—sure enough, a silver-gray BMW—and a few other bits of information. This was how he'd known where to go to sugar-daddy Connor's car on that first occasion. Being a glorified meter-maid—meter-*butler,* as he liked to call himself—or a parking enforcement officer definitely had its advantages. This shitty meter enforcement job was just a stepping-stone until he could finish some law enforcement classes in school, go through the training, and take the final test to become a real police officer.

Arriving in Connor's neighborhood, Scott parked two streets over from Connor's house and six houses down into that street. He didn't want Connor to even remotely see that a random beat-up, forest-green SUV was anywhere near his house.

Sitting there in the car, he looked down at his clothes. Regular jeans that were on the lighter side. A light red polo shirt, some tennis shoes, and regular ankle socks. Not exactly the best duds for breaking and entering. He felt ridiculous.

Call the fashion police on me. *I seriously have to get my act together.*

He glanced into the back seat and saw the plastic grocery bag with the clothes he had worn on his excursion to put the bag of sugar in Connor's gas tank. He had placed them in the car to throw away, thinking they were evidence in a crime he had committed. He'd planned on chucking them in the nearest dumpster, but had actually forgotten about them. There they sat, in the back seat of his car, beckoning to him again.

Scott snatched the bag from the back seat and ripped it open. He quickly tore off his clothes and threw them behind the passenger's seat floorboard. He pulled on the dark clothes and felt it was the right decision. He felt more comfortable now, even though there were plenty more hours of daylight to go before dark.

Stepping out of his Sorento, Scott pocketed the gloves—one in each of the back pockets—locked his car, pocketed his keys, then turned to walk the two streets back to see if there was any way he could get into Connor's house. He whistled a little tune as he went, the bridge of the last song he'd heard on the radio.

As he neared Connor's house, Scott heard the sound of a lawnmower. An old man was pushing his back and forth over a pristine, manicured lawn that looked as if it didn't need any yard work done to it. Scott was going to have to walk around the block and come in through Connor's backyard so he wouldn't be noticed.

Must be the one responsible for the scent of the fresh-cut grass from a few nights ago.

Scott continued walking, acting as though he had a purpose being here. He didn't think the old man had even noticed him. At least, he hoped he hadn't—a guy in dark clothes traipsing around this neighborhood looking strangely out of place. The old man looked to be too focused on his yard work. Scott eventually made his way through a small wooded area until he was standing in Connor's backyard.

He checked the back door and all the back windows, but he couldn't find a place of entry. Everything was locked down tight. The only thing he saw that could be a possible entry point was where one of the windows had an air-conditioning unit mounted in it.

Guess that's where I'm going to B&E.

Scott went to the back door and knocked. He wanted to make sure no one was in the house before he did what he was planning on doing.

I have no idea what I'm going to say if someone actually comes to the door. What if his girlfriend is here?!

No one answered the door, which was a relief, but he knocked a second time, a little louder, just to make sure. Sure that no one was home, he went immediately to the window that had the AC unit attached. Pulling the black gloves on, he reached up and grabbed hold, jumped as high as he could, folded his arms over on top of the unit, and bent his body over on top of his arms. His added weight made the block unit shift downward slightly.

What am I doing? he thought. *Am I really going to break into this asshole's house?*

He jumped again and mimicked his earlier movement. It budged a little more each time he tried. Finally, on the fourth try, the unit gave way and rolled out of the window. As it dropped, he spread his legs wide so his feet wouldn't be crushed under the weight of the unit. He was almost too slow, but slid his feet free at the last second as the unit crashed down into the space where they had been. Scott gave a little sigh of relief as he quickly crouched beside it and looked in every direction to make sure no one was coming to investigate the loud noise.

"I guess that answers my previous question," he said to himself as he stood, stepped upon the unit, and peered inside the bedroom. "I'm going to go right in through here."

He scrambled up into the window and crawled inside. The house was unnaturally quiet, and he waited again just inside the room to be sure he was alone.

Yes—alone. At least for now.

As he waited and listened, he looked around the room and found himself in what looked to be the master bedroom. The bed was at least king-sized. The comforter and sheets were in a tangled mess.

You and your girl having fun last night, huh, Connor?

There were matching nightstands, one on either side of the bed. A tall chest of drawers was to his left and another smaller bureau stood to his right. All the pieces matched. The closet was across the room, near the nightstand on the left side of the bed.

Scott walked around the bed and looked out, down the hallway.

Nothing was there; no animals or people were in his line of sight. He stepped through the bedroom door and walked down the short hallway into the foyer. Standing against the foyer wall right inside the front door there was a small table. A minimalistic coat rack sat to the table's right. He stepped past the furniture pieces and to the foot of the stairs that went straight up into the second floor of the house. The dining room was to his left and the living room was straight ahead. He walked forward and took one step down into the living room, then slowly turned a full circle, taking in the lay of this new land. Off the living room, there was a kitchen that connected with the dining room he had just passed.

Scott loved the layout of this house; it was definitely a guy's place, the famous bachelor pad. There were very few feminine touches.

That's going to change soon enough, Connor.

He guessed Connor and his girlfriend had just recently started dating.

Maybe they're at the point in their relationship where she's started having sex with him but not to the point of staying all night with him. Testing the waters, maybe. I hope she eventually dumps him.

He made his way through the house in a very methodical manner. He was sure he had a little time before Connor came home, so he took his time investigating every room and its contents to find out what made Connor tick. He was careful to put back whatever he picked up in its original spot; with the gloves, he didn't have to worry about fingerprints. He didn't want Connor noticing something misplaced.

So what are you going to do about the AC unit? You literally pulled it out of the window. You think he's not going to notice that when he gets home?

I know, but I'll be gone by then.

What are you doing here really, Scott? How long are you going to stay here? What are you going to do if Connor comes back before you leave?

Questions and thoughts like that were popping up inside his mind like popcorn—questions he had no answer to. He didn't know what he really wanted to do; he just kept investigating.

On one of the end tables in the living room, a six-inch folding knife caught his eye, the kind of knife that has a small nodule to assist you in opening the blade very quickly.

"Mine," he said, aloud and abruptly; it just burst out of his mouth. The sound of his own voice startled him. *Yeah, definitely mine,* he thought. *I'm taking this thing. Just a little memento to remind myself of today's excursion.*

He found the knife already in his hand and that he'd already flipped the blade open. The craftsmanship on this knife was good—damn good.

Probably brought it straight from a specialty craftsman online somewhere.

He squeezed the handle tightly; it felt so good. It was comfortable in his grasp, just like the gloves that hugged his hands. He made a few swipes in the empty air, along with a few stabbing motions into an invisible person in front of him. He flipped the locking mechanism and closed the blade, slipping it down into his front right pocket.

After pilfering the living room, he moved on to the kitchen. He opened the refrigerator and saw he had a number of different beverages to choose from. There was some bottled water, a variety of beer—some Stella Artois and Shock Top—some Vernors ginger ale, and a couple of cans of Diet Coke and Mountain Dew.

Scott opted for a Stella and twisted the top off. He was about to move to the pantry to find the trash, but then turned and surveyed the kitchen, thinking. On a whim—and he really didn't know why he was doing it—he stepped to the bar and placed the cap in the center of the counter.

Just a little test, he thought.

He didn't want to give himself away, but he was hoping to maybe unnerve Connor in some way. Would Connor wonder about the bottle cap and why it was sitting there out in the open, plain as day?

It's just a little thing to point out to Connor that he is not the one in control of this situation. Things in his life are just a little bit wonky.

He continued into the dining room off the kitchen, but there wasn't really anything to investigate. Just a nice table with a bench and four chairs. No china cabinet with fine china and nice glassware. Very simplistic, as a guy's dining room would be.

Scott moved back through the kitchen and living room and into another room that he thought would be considered a den. It had two leather chairs and a leather loveseat with cushions, bookended by two little tables. There was also a four-tiered bookshelf with numerous hardback and paperback novels on it. No more than three novels per author, Scott saw, but mostly mystery and suspense novels, such as Silva, Reichs, Crichton, Flynn, Connelly, and Sandford.

What the fuck am I doing here? Scott asked himself again. *This is not going to end well for myself or for Connor if I'm here when he returns.* He didn't have a reply for himself. *This is stupid. Get the fuck out of here before Connor comes home, finds you here and kills you.*

He moved back into the kitchen, draining the last of his Stella as he went. He found the trash can in the pantry and tossed his empty beer bottle. He had just taken two steps in the direction of the open bedroom window when he heard a small squeal of tires on pavement as a car took a turn into the driveway outside too quickly.

"No, no, no, no, no. Please don't let it be him!" Scott begged aloud as he went to the window and peeked out as discreetly as he could.

There he was: Connor McPherson, in the flesh. And he didn't look particularly happy either. A smile crept across Scott's face. He knew it was because Connor had a lot of unwanted chocolate ice cream in his life, especially his car.

"And his girlfriend, too. Are you kidding me? I don't want to deal with her as well."

Connor had already parked, and they were stepping out of his BMW.

Jesus, I can't believe he's already back. God, I thought it was going to be hours before he returned.

Scott glanced down at this watch and gasped at the time. Close to four hours had already passed since he'd left Publix.

What the fuck? Where did all my time go?

They were already out of the car and heading for the front door; Connor was leading the way, and with purpose.

Scott saw he had no time to examine the situation further. He bolted to his left, straight down the hallway and into the master bedroom. He headed for the open window and got as far as putting his hands on either side, but a loud banging sound startled him enough to stop him in his tracks. He turned away from the window to listen.

Connor McPherson entered his house with a little more aggression than he had intended. The front door swung open and banged hard against the wall, and the doorknob punched through the drywall, where previous enraged incidents had already weakened that area.

Winter Mills, Connor's girlfriend, followed him into his house with a small bag of groceries and stepped to the side, not wanting to be in the way of his anger. Connor had never actually struck her, but she gave him a wide berth.

"Calm down, Connor," she said soothingly. "It's over now, and your car looks amazing."

He threw his jacket against the hat rack next to the foyer table. The rack wobbled slightly, but didn't fall over. The jacket itself failed to cling on to any of the hooks and dropped to the floor.

Winter tried again as she adjusted the laptop bag strap on her shoulder. "They did a really great job cleaning it."

"Yeah, they did a beautiful job, Winter," Connor said as he dropped his keys and wallet onto the small table. "But it's a job they shouldn't have had to do in the first place. I just can't fucking believe that someone would throw a fucking chocolate shake into my goddamn car. Who the fuck does that?"

Winter turned away from him to give him a little more room to vent his aggression. She knew his attitude wasn't directed at her in any way. She headed through the living room, dropping her laptop bag on the end of the couch as she went. Connor followed her to the kitchen but at a much slower pace. He had turned inward, probably sulking about the money he'd just forked over for the cleaning job.

"It could have been anybody, hon," Winter said over her shoulder. She shifted the groceries to her other arm as she moved to the kitchen. "It could've been some punk-ass kid who just didn't want to carry his drink anymore. It could've been somebody arbitrarily pitching it out their window as they cut across the parking lot."

"Oh, come off it, Winter," Connor scoffed. "That goddamn cup was filled to the brim with chocolate ice cream. It went fucking everywhere. It wasn't an empty cup that someone was just finished with. They hadn't even started drinking it, for Christ's sake. I have a two-hundred-fif-ty-seven-dollar bill for the fucking clean-up job to prove it. This was no accident. Especially after they sugar-daddied my car on top of that. I was a target. It was a perfectly planned hit."

"I know," Winter said. "I'm just trying to help you talk this out. Don't take what someone else did out on me. *I* didn't fucking do it."

This seemed to take some of the wind out of his angry sails. He blew a frustrated breath. "Fuck. I know. I'm sorry. Didn't mean to yell at you."

From just inside the bedroom door, Scott heard most of the conversation. He was hoping and praying they wouldn't come down the hallway and into the bedroom; he wouldn't know what the fuck to do if they did. There would be no time to run and jump out the window or try to hide.

He snuck a careful peek around the doorframe and down the hall. No one was there. They had definitely moved further into the house. He slowly and tentatively took some huge, cartoonish footsteps down the hall until he was standing next to the coat rack. He glanced down and saw Connor's jacket lying on the floor, so he picked it up and hung it on the hook nearest him. He needed just a little extra cover as he stood next to the hat rack and looked between it and the stairs that continued past his head and up to the second floor. His eyeline was just slightly higher than the eighth step. He stood, looking through the spindles of the banister and over the top of the eighth step, through the living room, and into the wide opening of the kitchen. He could see Connor with his back to him, standing at the bar, but he couldn't see Connor's girlfriend—Winter. Still, he could hear them better from his new position.

In the kitchen, Winter said, "I know. I'm just reminding you it was someone else and not me." She pulled the refrigerator door open and looked inside to see if there was something that interested her enough to eat. Without really thinking, she said, "Could've been that asshole who had a pissy attitude with us in traffic two or three weeks ago. Remember him? You know, that crazy guy who chased us in his car until we lost him getting on the 85. God, that guy was off his rocker. Now, *he* was fucking angry."

Connor was standing with his hands on the back of the bar stools, but froze at her suggestion. He stared at the formica, studying the design in the countertop as his mind drifted back to that day.

Yeah, that guy was fucking crazy.

His eyes shifted from the countertop design to the single Stella Artois bottle cap sitting right in the middle of the counter. Still lost in the memory, his brow crinkled in confusion. He picked it up and flipped it around in his hands as he thought, *Could someone really get that pissed and hold a grudge like that, and for that long, over something so trivial?*

"You think someone would do that?" he asked half-heartedly. He turned and looked around behind him, unsure of his surroundings. Something seemed off, and he wondered to himself, *Why did I do that?*

Winter turned from the open kitchen door and shrugged. "Oh, I don't know. I was actually just thinking out loud, but—" She turned back and looked over the drink selection.

"But?" he asked, coaxing her back to the conversation.

"But now that I'm really dwelling on the idea, it wouldn't be totally out of the realm of possibility. I guess."

"Yeah. Maybe."

Winter continued, "I mean, how many times has someone done some assholey-type maneuver in traffic and you just want to brain that idiot? There's a lot of dumbass drivers out there. I mean, a fucking shit-ton of them. It's on a daily basis I want to fucking kill so many people on the highway. Some days I almost wish there was a law that you could carry a gun while you drive, and if someone did fuck you over in traffic, you would be in the clear just to take them out right then and there. Blam! Blam! A couple of bullets through either of their side windows and then leave them there in traffic to bleed out. It's that bad out there some days." Winter paused. "Oh, wow, if that was the case, that guy would've already wasted you that day when it happened." She gave a half-hearted little laugh.

"That's not the least bit funny, Winter. It's actually a fucked-up thought, to tell you the truth."

Winter didn't really realize how dark her thoughts had sounded. "Sorry, babe, but you did something that day to set that guy off, and if it is him, he's just trying to get back at you for it."

"Well, he's doing a damn good job, isn't he?" Connor said, then thought more about Winter's suggestion. "It has to be that asshole. He was really cussing up a storm at us."

"Us? It wasn't *me* that pissed him off in traffic."

Connor threw his hands up. "Oh, okay, Winter. You're *so* totally innocent in this scenario." His tone became more serious. "You think he's going to just let you off the hook after he gets to me? If he comes after me and you're anywhere around, he's going to take you out too. Believe me."

"Oh my God, Connor," Winter said, suddenly miffed. "What a shitty thing to say to me."

"Oh, you can dish it out but you can't take it yourself? I'm just stating the truth, just like you are with me. He wouldn't let you off scot-free if he did something to me. You would be able to identify him, and he's not going to let that happen."

Winter said, "You make him sound like he's a serial killer or something like that."

"Oh, he very well could be. But I don't really think so." Connor reconsidered. "Oh shit. Wouldn't that be fucked up? Cutting a serial killer off in traffic. I think if he was, he wouldn't have dropped a milkshake in my car and poured fucking sugar into my gas tank. He would've just broken into my house, taken me out and then come gunning for you."

"Oh fuck. That's creepy as hell." Winter's whole body went into an exaggerated shudder. "Oh my God, would you listen to us? I can't believe we're talking like this about him."

Connor took a deep breath, then relaxed slightly. It was silly to think someone was after him, or them, for the almost-accident that had happened the other day. But the fact that he had receipts for flushing the engine and cleaning the inside of his car wouldn't allow him let go of the thought. Something was definitely up.

His mind came back to the item he was arbitrarily spinning in his hand. He looked down again. *The Stella Artois top. Why was there a Stella top sitting on my counter? I can't remember drinking one, and if I did, I would've shit-canned the top itself.*

"Hey, babe, did you drink any of the Stellas that are in the fridge?"

Winter thought for moment. "Uh, no. No Stella for me. Not my drink of choice, remember?"

"Oh, right, sure. I keep forgetting."

"Why do you ask?"

"It's just that there's a bottle cap here, and I'm not the one who drank it. So if I didn't drink it and you didn't drink it, who did?"

"Yeah, that is weird. I don't know what to tell you, babe. Maybe you drank one and forgot you'd downed it."

"Yeah. Maybe."

But Connor wasn't convinced. *I've never left bottle caps just sitting around. I always throw them away. First thing after popping a top.*

Winter asked, "So you think this guy is the same one who put sugar in your car?"

"Yeah—about two to three pounds' worth," Connor said, dropping the top on the counter and forgetting about it. He leaned forward and put his elbows on the bar.

"How weird would it be if that creep was sneaking around our property late at night just to prove a point? Oh my God, that's so fucking scary. Who knows what he would do next?"

"Yeah, who knows?" Connor leaned back, pulled his phone from his pocket, and opened it to dial 911. "I'm gonna call the cops about this."

He had already punched the '9' and the '1' when Winter said, "And tell them what? You have nothing to fucking go on."

Connor dropped his phone onto the countertop next to the bottle cap. With frustration in his voice, he said, "I have a receipt from Cobb Tire telling me that they had to clean everything in my engine to get rid of all the sugar sludge put there by this fuckhead. Rich Cobb would talk to the cops about what he had to do. That's got to count for something." Connor shoved his hands in his pants pockets again. He felt a piece of folded paper there, jerked it out, and held it up for Winter. "Oh, and now I have an upholstery and console-cleaning bill for the inside of my car. This guy is out to get me, and I'm not gonna wait around for him to kill me in some sick way before I tell the authorities."

"You really think this guy is out to kill you? Even if it is that guy from traffic, I'll admit it's creepy, but he's not looking to harm us. Is he?"

"I'm not gonna wait around to find out. I've got to do something now, before this gets any worse. And I'm tired of dealing with things happening to my car."

"It is a slight headache, isn't it?"

"*Slight headache?* God damn it, Winter, comparing it to a *slight headache* is retarded. There are no words to describe what a fucking inconvenience this guy has dealt me."

"Well, excuse the fuck out of me for just trying to talk this thing out with you."

He ignored her comment. "I'll go to the police first thing tomorrow morning. Now, wherever you drive tomorrow, I want you to constantly look around for anyone who might be tailing you. Use your rearview mirrors and your side mirrors, but use them discreetly. This guy has had two weeks and a couple of days to figure out our lifestyle and schedules—that is, if it is him doing this. Who knows what he's planning to do next. I have to figure out a way to find him, track him, and get back at him."

"Oh God, Connor, don't tell me you're going to start a pissing contest with this shithead. That's not smart."

"Well, what the fuck would you suggest I do?"

"You said you were going to call the cops. Well, call them, for God's sake, or go by and talk to them. Let them advise you on how to handle this situation. Please, baby. I don't want you to do anything that is going to get you hurt."

"It's not me that's going to get hurt. It's going to be *me* putting a hurting on *him*."

Winter laughed. "That's some big words coming from you."

Connor looked pained. "You don't think I can handle this piece-of-shit guy?"

"I'm not saying that at all. It's just that you're already talking shit about what you're going to do to him, and that scares me. You don't know who this guy is or how far off his rocker he may be. It makes me think that *you're* not in control. Just think all this through before you do anything crazy."

"Oh, I'm very much in control. I've been thinking about who might have done this to me ever since my car broke down getting on 85 that morning."

Just then, a fleeting thought, a barely remembered memory, fluttered across his mind. It was the image of a man passing him by, waving to him as Connor got out of his car to pop the hood of the BMW.

No, it wasn't actually a wave, he thought, replaying the memory. *He saluted me.*

He thought harder, and the image replayed again. A faceless figure slowly passed him by with a little salute of his hand. But now, looking closer, Connor saw there was a little more behind it. A little more attitude. A little "fuck you," if you will. The memory replayed again, and he saw the man's face appear on the screen in his mind as he flipped the little salute again.

Then he remembered himself a few weeks before, looking up into the rearview mirror and seeing the man in the hunter-green SUV whose face was engulfed in rage, cussing up a storm. Connor remembered the little 'fuck you' salute *he* had given *him.*

"Son-of-a-bitch," Connor whispered to himself.

Winter stepped closer to him. "What is it? What did you think of?"

Still talking to himself, Connor said, "He was doing the same thing to me that I did to him."

"Who? What did you remember?"

"It *was* him."

"Who?"

"That fucking guy in the green piece-of-shit SUV."

"The mad guy in the Yukon?"

"Was it a Yukon?"

"Yeah. I'm pretty sure. Wait! On second thought it might have been a Sorento. Maybe." Winter paused. "Not exactly positive. But I think so."

"Yukon. Sorento. It doesn't matter right now. I never told you, but the day my car broke down, that guy in his *fucking car* passed me by at the bottom of the entrance ramp. I swear to God it was him. And I'm not making this shit up. He was in a dusty, green SUV. I didn't recognize him before, but thinking about all this as a whole, it's all come to me at once. It's like these memories were just sitting on the sidelines, waiting for me to remember them."

As if on cue, an even more distant memory appeared.

The day Connor's car had broken down with sugar sludge, he remembered backing out of the driveway and leaving his house. And about four or five houses down from his, he remembered a dark green

SUV sitting all alone on his street. He remembered thinking, *That car looks strangely out of place. What kind of an asshole leaves their car curbed in this neighborhood? Shithead. He must've got drunk at someone's house and decided to stay the night.*

Could that asshole have been in the car watching my house? Watching to see when my car was going to go belly-up? Maybe he slid down in his seat when I passed by. Connor didn't know for sure, but his gut told him that he was on the right track. Although he hadn't dwelled on seeing the car, it had bugged him at the time.

Not wanting to alarm Winter, Connor whispered to himself, "That son-of-a-bitch has been following me all this time. He's been watching me. He's been stalking us."

All of a sudden, he was deathly afraid. He looked around the room to see if anything else was out of place. He felt as though the top of his head had been opened and impending doom, along with a sense of hopelessness, had been poured into him, weighing him down with dread.

Connor looked over again at the Stella Artois bottle cap and moved to pick it up. Alarm bells were going off in his mind.

He's here. He's here right now.

Oh, don't be stupid. There is no way that some random stranger figured out where you live, broke in and is standing in another room, just waiting for you to come into that room.

He's the one who drank the beer.

While Connor stood there in silence, Winter moved past him and headed back into the living room. She said as she passed, "Well, it's a good thing you know it's him."

From his standing position in the foyer near the coat rack, Scott was still listening to their conversation, shocked into immobility, when Winter came into the living room. Fear sprang up within him, and he bolted back down the hallway with gigantic, flurried steps and into the master bedroom as quickly and quietly as he could.

Scott had three choices. He could jump out the open window, sprint through the neighborhood, get into his car, and forget this whole business of exacting revenge on Connor McPherson. But he knew now that Connor and Winter were onto him. Maybe Connor would find him, report him. Could he prove it? *Fifty-fifty chance of anything.* The odds against Scott were too great.

His second choice was to hide under the bed, but if Connor started searching the house, he would be trapped there. Scott didn't give that too much more thought.

His third option was to hide in the closet. At least if they found him in there he had a fighting chance. He could come out swinging. It was definitely better than hiding like a coward under the bed. He thought of Connor's physique and wondered if he would be able to take him if it came down to it. There was no time to decide anything else. The closet was his only option.

He got to the door, twisted the handle, swung it open and ducked inside, pulling the door to within an inch of being shut. He twisted the handle and softly pulled the door home as quietly as possible. Once it was shut, he rotated the handle back to make sure it was latched.

Connor was still looking intently at the bottle cap and running over scenarios in his mind. It took him a moment to realize what Winter had said as she passed him by.

"What do you mean?" Connor asked as he turned and followed her out of the kitchen. She was heading for the master bedroom. She began taking off her sweater, glancing over her shoulder.

"Well, now that you know who it is, you can do something about him. It will be easier now that we have a face to go with what he's been doing to you. Well, to us, actually."

As Connor watched her approach the bedroom, a strange feeling hit him.

Something's not right.

He glanced at the hat rack and saw his jacket, hanging there on one of the hat hooks. He immediately knew. A thicker feeling of dread filled him.

My coat. It's not on the floor. Didn't it fall to the floor when I threw it at the hat rack?

Connor side-stepped to the coat rack and unhooked it. He glanced back and forth between the bottle cap and his jacket as he followed Winter down the hallway. He arrived at the bedroom door in a mental daze just in time to see her turn from the bed to the closet. She reached out and grabbed the closet door handle.

"Wait! Stop! What are you doing?" Connor asked.

Winter stopped with her hand on the doorknob and turned to him. "I'm just getting my workout clothes. I thought I might take a long run. It's a nice day out and I'm feeling sluggish. Why? What's the matter?"

"I don't know. Just—wait a second. Let me think about this for a minute."

"What's there to think about? I'm just going for a run. You want to go with me?"

Just get the fuck out of here, Connor's instincts were telling him. "Just—hold on. Let me think."

Inside the closet, Scott was sweating; his palms were wet. He wiped them off on the thighs of his jeans. His palm rubbed against something hard. He felt the hardness with his fingers and realized what it was.

The knife. Oh, Jesus, thank God I have his knife. He reached deep into his pocket, retrieved it, and immediately thumbed the nodule. It flipped open so easily. Scott was thinking, *This is the moment. This is what I should've done in the first place. This is what I have to do if I'm going to get away with this and be in the clear. Jesus Christ, am I really going to do this? He knows it's me, but even though he may be suspicious, I still have the element of surprise.*

Scott gripped the knife just a little bit tighter. He slowly moved his hand up, crossed it over his body, and rested it on his left shoulder.

He shook his head. *All this time wasted putting sugar in his gas tank and dousing his car with a Wendy's Frosty. I should've done this in the first place. Gonna make this so quick for him. He's not even going to know what hit him.*

Outside the closet, still standing right outside the bedroom doorway, Connor's mind was racing with a thousand urgent thoughts.

That guy has had so much of a head start on me. Where would he be? What would he do? What would I do, if I was him? That son-of-a-bitch could be anywhere. He could already be here, in the house.

Connor glanced to the far side of the bedroom at the open window. He saw the curtains softly billowing from the outside breeze.

That's odd. The window shouldn't be up. Wait! Where the fuck is my AC unit?

Winter's voice severed his thought process. "Connor, I don't have all damn day. I'm going to get dressed and go for this run, okay? We can talk about this later when I get home."

Connor looked back to Winter, who was still standing at the closet door. She was turning the doorknob.

One final thought screamed out at him from within his mind. *He's in the closet!*

He heard himself say, "Don't open the clo—"

Inside the closet, Scott heard the slight squeak of the doorknob, even over Connor's warning, as it turned and opened outward.

In a smooth, backhanded motion, Scott swiped across the figure's throat as quickly and as hard as he could. The knife blade hit Winter perfectly in the middle of her neck and slid through, then across, with ease. He even felt the knife blade scrape across one of the vertebrae in the middle of her neck. It was a sensation that made him inwardly cringe.

For Scott and Winter, even Connor, who stood slack-jawed in the bedroom doorway, everything happened so fast.

Winter blinked in surprise and horror as everything registered with her all at once.

Who the fuck are you? she thought. *Boy, what bad aim. He didn't even make contact with me.*

Then the figure was leaning close to her, saying, "That'll teach you to cut me off in traffic, asshole."

Winter felt a slight itch in her neck. She moved one of her hands up to scratch the itch away, but became distracted when she felt a strange warm liquid trickle into her cleavage. Her hands reached up and rubbed the sensation away from her chest. As she pulled her wet fingers away, she saw to her confusion that they were coated in blood.

"What the—" Winter began, but was suddenly unable to form any other words.

What the fuck is wrong with my throat?

She got a better look at the figure who had emerged from the shadows of the closet, and recognition hit her hard. *It's him,* she thought as a shiver of dread pierced her chest. *The man from traffic. It's the highway man, and he's here for—*

That was the last thought she ever had, because just then a fan of blood jettisoned from her neck like a kid holding his thumb over the end of a garden hose. The flat fan of blood coated her hands, still held up in horrified wonder, and peppered the black shirt and pants of the man in front of her.

"Oh shit!" Scott said in alarm, taking a quick step back into the closet to dodge the blood geyser. "God damn it!"

Oh, fucking shit. Oh, fucking shit. Oh fucking shit, he chanted in his mind. *What the fuck have I done?*

For a split second, he'd thought he'd dealt a death blow to Connor, but during the stunned silence he realized it was Connor's bitch sidekick, Winter, that was on the receiving end. The woman tried to look to her right, her brows knotted in confusion. She finally gave up trying and rotated at the waist. Her blood-covered hand came up, as if pointing or reaching, then she fell into a crumpled heap at Scott's feet.

Scott slowly stepped out of the closet and stood over her for a moment to take it all in. Then he slowly turned in the direction Winter had been reaching.

Standing right outside the bedroom doorway, Connor McPherson was frozen in shocked silence, with his jacket in one hand and a bottle cap in the other.

"Hey!" Scott shouted.

The shout shook Connor out of his trance, because he didn't remember moving; he was already running. And then he realized the figure that

183

had just sliced and diced his girlfriend was also running after him. He could hear his footsteps behind him, barreling out of the master bedroom and down the hallway. Connor remembered the blade of the knife in the figure's right hand—the one closest to him. The one that had just a touch of blood on it. The blade that had gone through Winter's neck so fast it was as if it didn't have time for any of her blood to adhere to it. Some had probably flung off and dotted the wall considering the force with which the man had swiped.

The hit that was—no doubt—intended for me, Connor thought. He kept expecting to feel the blade stab down between his shoulder blades. His mind was already forming twinges of imaginary pain.

"Fuck!" Scott hissed to himself as he plunged after Connor. *This isn't going as planned. Why did I ever come in here? Was I secretly planning on dealing with him? I could've gotten back at him in so many other ways. Why didn't I just let this shit go?* His mind was wild with thoughts. Then the little gremlin inside his mind who was pitching out these crazy ideas lobbed another one. *But it's not over yet. It's so far from over.*

Scott's heart threatened to punch out the center of his chest. He was more scared than he had ever been in his life. The actual thought of this shithead getting away was more than he could stand.

I can't have that. I won't have that, Scott thought. *I'm closing that window of possibility right fucking now.*

Connor arrived at the front door, grabbed the doorknob, twisted it, and flung it open. The doorknob that had punched through the wall earlier punched through again, got hooked inside the wall, and stuck fast.

The hum of the leaf blower coming from the neighbor's yard assaulted his ears.

Yes! Old Man Dodson is blowing his leaves again, Connor thought. *He'll help me.* Connor plunged out the door.

"Hey!" he shouted. "Mr. Dodson! Help!" He bounded down the steps. He had almost reached the third before he felt Scott grab at the back of his shirt.

"Gotcha, you bastard!"

Scott pulled back hard and relief flooded his body. He was leaning awkwardly out the door, and his right arm was twisted and wrenched a bit too far. A stab of pain shot up his arm. Connor wasn't his prisoner yet. He could feel the grasped shirt slipping through his fingers.

"Mr. Dodson!" Connor screamed as he continued to pull against the fabric that was keeping him from escape. "Help!"

Connor's shirt tore, and the fear of Connor ripping away into freedom made Scott's asshole tighten and his heart plummet into his stomach. He quickly rotated himself back into the doorway. He braced his left hand—the one that was now holding the knife—on the doorframe. He had renewed leverage, and he pulled back again with all his might.

Connor lost his footing as he slipped on the dry leaves scattered on the front steps. He was pulled back even harder. "Mr. Dodson! *HELP!*"

Hearing an off-kilter noise a decibel or two higher than his power tool, Maxwell Dodson cut the power to the leaf blower and slowly turned to that sound.

As Connor was yanked back through the doorway, Scott let go of the doorframe and flung the knife behind him, somewhere into the living room. He grasped another handful of Connor's shirt with his right hand. Connor's body was yanked back inside, and he fell headlong into the table that sat just inside the front door, smashing it into pieces. His head bounced off the wall near the floor.

Scott spun, grasped the doorknob, and slammed the door shut.

Glancing over to see how dazed Connor was, Scott turned his back on him long enough to peek through the slats of the Venetian blinds that were hanging in the window to the right of the doorway. He had to make sure he wasn't going to have another problem on his hands if that old guy came to investigate.

Maxwell pulled his earplugs from his ears as he completed his turn to look toward Connor McPherson's house. He surveyed the yard and surrounding neighborhood. He was still bewildered at the weird sound he'd heard—or thought he'd heard. He saw nothing out of the ordinary, *heard* nothing strange, as he had before. The neighborhood was quiet now.

Maxwell shrugged and stuffed his earplugs back into his ears once again, then flipped the power switch of his leaf blower and began blowing the walkway of any remaining grass strands and leaves.

"That's right, old man," Scott said, staring from the window. "Go back and finish your yard work." He turned right into a swing from a leg from the destroyed foyer table.

The blow caught Scott on his side, high in the ribs. He doubled over, gasping for quick breaths as he stumbled away. He turned and immediately ducked as the table leg came at him again. It cut the air over his head with a loud whoosh.

Fuck, that was a hard swing, he thought. *That would've really scrambled my brains. Didn't even hear him coming at me with that.*

"You think you can come into my house—" Connor hissed as he swung blindly back and forth. "Fucking kill my girlfriend—you piece-of-shit asshole. And you messing with me—"

Though they were extremely hard swings, they were sloppy, and Scott could easily duck them.

He thought, *I gotta get that bat he's using outta his hands.* He thought even quicker and came up with an idea. *Anything to unbalance him.*

He grabbed where he'd been hit, high on his side. He cried out in pain as he faked a hard stumble. Connor paused mid-swing, not understanding what was going on. Anticipating Connor's bewilderment, Scott had already stepped forward. His hands shot out and struck Connor's forearms. The table leg dropped to the floor.

Scott kicked it further away and charged Connor again. He caught him around the middle, forced him back, and slammed him up into the wall.

Connor shoved off the wall, forcing Scott back.

Scott planted his feet and clenched Connor's clothes. He turned his body, trying to throw Connor away again as he had earlier when he'd pulled him back and held fast. They were lost in an 'I push you, you pull me' school-yard shuffle for a moment; then out of nowhere Connor drove a knee up into Scott's solar plexus.

If Scott hadn't had trouble breathing before, he was now. All he could do was fall away, duck and weave until he gained his breath back. He was more terrified than he had ever been in his life—even more so than the night he'd dropped the bag of sugar into Connor's gas tank.

This is what it's come to. This guy is going to kill me, and it was all because of a little highway tiff. Something I tried to let go of but couldn't.

He saw one of Connor's fists coming directly at his face, but he couldn't get out of the way in time. His cheek bloomed in a hard, dull pain as the fist connected solidly. Scott's head whipped to the side and he spun away. He spun back to where he thought Connor would be and swung out, hoping to land a hard punch.

"Not even close, shitbag," Connor said.

Connor had side-stepped and gotten in close again. He came at Scott with a left swing. Scott saw it right before it connected, and he turned his face away as quickly as he could. The punch hit him in the temple and stunned him, but it wasn't a direct hit; it glanced off. He was relieved; it would've dropped him to the ground. Then, when he woke up, he would've been in police custody.

I can't let that happen to me.

Scott ducked away and grabbed anything that could put any distance between him and this fucker.

Oh, if I get out of this one alive, I'm going to—

He had already scooped up a hardback book, spun around, and hurled it in Connor's direction. The book fluttered at Connor like a startled bird, the pages riffling, and hit him in the chest.

"Is that the best you've got, asshole?" Connor said. There was a laugh, then, "A fucking book. I'm going to fucking beat your ass silly and call it a day. Right before I call the cops to come snag your ass away to your new concrete home. I'm tired of your bullshit. Fuck my car up twice gets you fucked up once. Permanently. You're dead, asshole."

The two men charged each other simultaneously. This time it was Scott who lost his footing, and he backpedaled. An extra-hard shove from Connor pushed him back into the entertainment center. It didn't collapse—it was a pretty solid piece of furniture—but the huge television screen spiderwebbed as it was sandwiched between Scott's lower body and the wall.

Connor grabbed two fistfuls of Scott's shirt and jerked him back out of the entertainment center. Ducking low, he caught Scott in the stomach and hefted him up on his shoulder, then spun around and flipped Scott over, slamming him down onto the wooden coffee table.

Scott expected the table to shatter, but his body erupted in pain when the thick wood held fast; his head was flung backwards, whip-lashing against the side of the coffee table. Scott coughed hard and tried to suck air back into his battered lungs. He rolled away to sit up and breathe, but a hand grabbed his shoulder and pulled him back.

"Where the fuck d'you think you're going, asshole?" Connor asked.

All Scott could do was gasp.

"I'll tell you where. *No-fucking-where.* You keep your ass right here."

Scott cradled his head and neck as he leaned up. The table wasn't comfortable, and he tried to roll away again. A hand pulled him back yet again. Connor was still taunting him, but he wasn't listening. He had bigger problems on his mind. His neck was killing him. He was amazed that he could even use any of his neck muscles.

"I said, don't move," Connor growled. "Oh, you fucked up. You fucked up big time coming into my house to play."

Connor was looking around the room for anything he could use as a weapon. His eyes fell on the knife Scott had been carrying. He snatched it up, looked briefly at the blade, which had a few small smears of blood on it, and them back to Scott.

"This is my knife, asshole. You think you can come into my house, slash *my* girlfriend with *my* knife, and get away with it? I'm going to take your head off with this thing, man."

Connor came down on him hard. Scott didn't have a lot of strength left, and there was something definitely wrong with his neck, but he managed to throw his hands up in time to intercept the knife aimed at his chest.

I have to get away from him. I have to get free. I have to do some-thing drastic and very quickly, or he's going to kill me. This is never what I intended. I am not going down like this. No fucking way.

Scott turned his head painfully and saw a black bag—his possible salvation. His last resort, anyway. He didn't know if there was anything in it, but it was the only thing within reach.

The knife that was bearing down on him with Connor's full body weight stabbed a little way into his chest. That pinprick of pain brought him out of his thoughts and back to reality. The knife slid in a little more. Scott looked up into Connor's face and saw the blazing hatred on his face. Connor's teeth were bared, and his eyes were ablaze with murderous contempt.

Scott was tiring fast. Connor was much stronger than him. He made a quick mental note to purchase a gym membership and actually use the thing if he was going to continue doing stuff like this. But he had an idea to escape. That little gremlin who was sitting on the sideline of his mind lobbing ideas his way was working overtime.

Scott released Connor's wrist with his right hand and shoved his index finger up into Connor's mouth. It hit Connor's clenched teeth hard then skittered off down the side of his molars and deeper into his mouth. Scott immediately rotated his wrist, hooked his finger, and jerked hard to the side. Like a large-mouthed bass, Connor's head followed his hooked cheek. At the same time, Scott pushed up as hard as he could and shoved Connor onto the floor beside the table.

As soon as Connor's weight was off him, Scott quickly rolled back the opposite way and grabbed both handles of the bag, which turned out to be a computer case. Knowing that Connor wouldn't stay down long, Scott immediately turned and slung the computer case around with all his might. It connected with the side of Connor's head with a harsh, metallic, shattering crack. Connor's limp body dropped on the far side of the coffee table, hit the edge of the sofa, and landed on the floor.

Scott stood, horrified, as the realization that he'd almost lost his life passed through his mind. He swung the computer bag back over his shoulder, ready to deliver another blow if the asshole tried to get up. He stood there for a long time in frozen readiness, slowly working his head back and forth on the strained muscles of his neck.

I wasn't very smart this time around, Scott thought. *That was pretty dumb on my part. I didn't assess the situation properly. But I'm alive, and being alive is all that matters now. Time to turn this guy's lights out for good, and then it will be time to get the fuck out of here.*

Seeing that Connor was definitely down for the count, maybe even dead, Scott finally dropped the broken computer to the floor. Then he went to assess the damage he'd done to Connor McPherson.

⁘

Connor was startled awake by a harsh burning in his nose. He sat bolt upright in his seat, which he found to be the driver seat of his BMW. His mind was tangled with dizziness and his ears were ringing. His head was pounding with the most god-awful headache of his life.

The slight vibration of his seat seemed to have softly shaken his body out of unconsciousness. He realized his car was turned on and currently idling.

His eyes widened in horror as he remembered everything that had happened earlier. His gaze fell directly on his hands, which were on the steering wheel—not so much on it as fastened to it with electrical cords. His hands were locked tight in the ten-two position.

Confusion set in, but he didn't have any time to process this scene because he heard a voice coming from his left.

"Hey, shit-steak," the voice said in a snide, passive-aggressive tone.

Connor jerked his head to the left and saw that his window was rolled halfway down. Beyond the window was the smiling face of the crazy guy who had lost his temper in traffic a few weeks ago. He was sitting in a lawn chair beside the car. Knots of fear tightened all over Connor's body. He remembered his and Winter's conversation before the figure had stepped out of the closet and sliced open her throat.

"You," Connor said. "I knew it was you."

"You didn't know shit," Scott said. "I covered my tracks the whole time. You had no idea it was me. You don't even know who I am."

Scott was happy to finally be getting a dig in at Connor. He hadn't looked, listened, or paid attention to him that day in traffic, but by God, he was going to listen to what Scott had to say now.

"But yeah, I'm that guy on the highway. The Highway Man." He chuckled. "I like that title. It fits me so well." Scott became serious again. "I'm the guy you almost sent to the hospital. The guy you almost killed."

"But I didn't put you in the hospital. I didn't kill you."

"*Almost,* asshole. That's the key word. You didn't even have the decency to give me an apologetic wave. You didn't even acknowledge me. I didn't like that."

"Dude. Nothing happened. I don't even know what I did."

"Don't fucking lie to me. You know exactly what you did. You cut it way too fucking close and you almost made me flip my goddamn SUV." Scott changed the subject, tiring of trying to reason with this asshole. "Are we comfy cozy?"

Connor glanced down his bound hands. They were wrapped tightly, but there was some sort of padding underneath the electrical cords.

"Washcloths?" Connor asked.

"Well, not to let the cat out of the bag, but I'm trying to cover up my fucking tracks here. I know for a fact you're not going sit still in this car unless you're restrained in some way. After they find your body, they're going to examine it. If they find out that you were manacled to your piece-of-shit car in any way, they'll know you didn't commit suicide. I can't have that. I *won't* have that."

Everything spiraled down and hit Connor all at once: his cushioned but manacled hands, the windows that were rolled halfway down, the slight vibration of his idling car, the strong smell of exhaust in his nose, the realization of where they were—his enclosed garage.

This guy is staging my death.

"Or I guess I should say, *murder*-suicide."

Connor slowly directed his attention back to the crazy guy, who looked past him into the passenger's seat. Connor almost gave himself whiplash turning. A startled squeal of horror escaped his lips as he found Winter's corpse propped up in the seat next to him.

"And the murder I'm talking about," Scott continued, "is your whore of a girlfriend, whose throat *you* slit before *you* placed her in the car next to you and started the engine. Like I said—murder-suicide."

Connor softly and reverently whispered, "Winter. No, no, no."

Winter's head lolled to the side, facing Connor. The huge bloody bib she wore started from the vicious opening in her neck and extended most of the way down her torso, ending near her crotch. There were some streaks of blood down her legs and red splotches on her shoes, but most of the blood had cascaded down the front of her body and soaked her shirt.

Her head didn't sit exactly square on her torso, its weight causing it to shift a little too far to the left. The cut on her neck yawned sickeningly wide like a mouth releasing a silent scream.

Connor turned away from the horrific sight. He worked his mouth and swallowed hard against the bile that was threatening to come up and out.

"Okay, Connor. Hold it together," Scott coaxed. "Don't lose your lunch over this. She went pretty quick. Well, hell, you know that. You saw the whole fucking thing from the hallway, didn't you? Awesome, wasn't it?"

"You motherfucker," Connor said in a harsh whisper.

"Nope. You are incorrect on that accusation. I have never fucked my mom. That would be considered incest. You are a very bad judge of character."

Connor closed his eyes, trying to block out the image of Winter and her drooping head.

"Ah, there's nothing like young love, is there?" Scott mused. "Seeing as how you two always travel together, I felt it only fair that you should die in the same manner."

"What the fuck, man?"

"Hey, that's exactly what I asked the universe when you nearly clipped me and almost made me flip my car in traffic, two weeks and two days ago."

"You killed Winter all because of something I did in traffic? Are you fucking kidding me right now?"

"Nope. Not kidding you at all, and I think you have it all wrong. I didn't kill Winter because of you doing a shit move in traffic. I'm killing you for what *you* did to me. Your girlfriend was an innocent bystander. Wrong damn place at the wrong damn time. Well, now that I think about it, not totally innocent. She was a cunt-whore-bitch-slut that day, and she just got in the way of my knife. See, for a second there, I thought that was *you* opening the closet door. I was determined to fuck your world up and over and inside out, but Winter took that hit for you. And it's probably better for me that she did." He paused for a moment, reliving the swipe of the blade across her throat. "Oh, God damn, you should've seen her face and the mental processing she was doing before she hit the floor. Don't really know if she figured everything out or not, but it was fucking crazy to witness."

"You're not going to get away with this," Connor promised him.

"Oh, I think I'm going to get as far away from this shit as I want. I've been very careful with everything I've done to you. You're the one they're going to think killed Winter before sucking down some exhaust fumes from your BMW. It's only fitting that you assholes go out in the thing that brought us together." Scott abruptly waved a hand in front of his nose a couple of times to fan the growing fumes away, then said, "I'll tell you what I'm going to do." He leaned closer, peering over the rim of the window. "Since this carbon monoxide is starting to kick in, I'm going to give you a little time to think about what you did to me. You can have a last little goodbye moment here with Winter. While you do that, I'm going to make myself a sandwich, have another beer, and probably flip on the TV and watch something good on Netflix to pass the time. Give this exhaust a little time to work its way through your system. Then I'm gonna come back, untie you, and place you in a natural position that'll look like you killed your girlfriend and just did away with yourself."

"You're nuts," Connor said. "You're absolutely fucking nuts."

"No. You're fucking nuts. You killed your girlfriend and decided to kill yourself. What's wrong with you?" Scott grinned, then stood from his lawn chair. "Enjoy your last few minutes on earth, shithead. I'll be back to check on you in a little while."

He drummed a few beats on the roof of the car, then stepped away. He paused in the doorway that led to the laundry room and looked back at Connor one last time. The man had an undeniable look of shock and horror on his face.

Scott moved his hand up to the side of his forehead and gave a little flick of his wrist. The salute came off with a lot of attitude; it ended with his middle finger extended and pointed at Connor. It was exactly the same one Connor had given him in traffic.

"Remember that?" Scott asked, his whole body swelling with satisfaction. "I certainly do."

Connor sat there just, his disbelief palpable.

"Happy trails, hotshot," Scott said, smiling, then stepped through the doorway and closed the door behind him.

Connor sat, gagging in disbelief and wondering how he had got to this shitty moment in his life.

It was that little salute I gave him in the rearview mirror, he thought finally. *I should've taken the higher road and just let it go. I should've looked over at him and acknowledged that I did something wrong. I should've apologized in some way. But would* he *have let it go, or would I still be in the position I am now?* His mind couldn't wrap around the craziness of this guy, or the lengths he'd gone to to get back at him.

Connor swallowed hard, getting up enough courage, then glanced over at Winter.

Her head and body had lolled even closer to him. Her seatbelt was latched, which was keeping her mostly restrained. Connor was thankful for small favors. He felt he would lose his lunch if Winter slumped over in her seat and landed on him. He didn't understand why that maniac—*Who's probably watching God knows what on Netflix now*—would buckle her in.

It makes no sense at all, Connor thought. *But then again, we're talking about the guy who just stepped into my house to eat a sandwich and watch some TV while I suck down exhaust fumes.*

"Well, that's not going to happen," Connor said aloud. "Anybody knows that if you're going to kill someone, you shouldn't leave them alone to escape."

He wriggled his fingers and wrists in a number of different ways to try and loosen the cords that bound them to the steering wheel. He couldn't get to the knots, because they were tied on the back side of the steering wheel and further back on either side of his wrists. There was no way his mouth, teeth, or any of his fingers could reach any of them.

"Smart move, asshole," Connor said reluctantly. "But you didn't think of everything. I'll get out of this, even if I have to drive through my garage door to do it."

Connor worked his knotted left hand over the steering wheel so both were as far to the right as possible. He used his elbow to try to push the gear shift over into reverse, but the wheel just wouldn't let him move far enough.

"Fuck," Connor muttered to himself. "Okay, okay. No problem," he said, and coughed hard as another harsh whiff of exhaust fumes curled up into his nose. "Oh, man, I gotta hurry."

He sat up in the driver's seat as high as he could, needing to give as much room to his legs and feet as possible. He hooked the heel of his right foot onto the toe of his left shoe and pulled hard. His shoe came off fairly easily.

A little squeal of excitement escaped Connor's mouth. "Ha! Yes!" It was a small victory.

His left foot took three tries, but the shoe finally slid off. He shifted his weight as far as he could to his left into the door, then he pulled his right leg up. He used it to maneuver the gear shift into reverse while his left foot pushed in the clutch.

He cheered aloud as he moved his right foot back down to the floor. He took a deep breath—which was a mistake—to psych himself up for flooring the gas pedal. His head spun with the huge influx of fumes, and he went into a spasm of coughs and wheezes.

He hoped he would hit a tree or something that would stop him quickly. He didn't want to get injured; unlike Winter, he wasn't wearing his seatbelt. But truth be told, he could live with an injury. He was so close to dying right now, he just had to escape and get some fresh air into his lungs. He didn't want to hit or hurt anybody, but he was all out of options. He had to do this.

He glanced in his rearview mirror and jammed his right foot down onto the gas pedal.

He expected the car's wheels to spin, grab concrete, burst through the closed garage and hurtle down his short driveway, but the car just revved hard. It went nowhere at all.

"What the hell?" Connor said as he took his foot off the gas again. He looked to his side mirror and then back to his rearview mirror. Nothing was hindering the car from going anywhere that he could see.

He jammed his foot on the gas pedal three times in frustrated succession. Another three loud revs came from the car.

"God damn it! What the fuck is going on?"

There was no use in trying to maneuver the car into drive with his feet. There was a large worktable in front of him, with a number of other discarded woodworking tools sitting around. Even if he was able to drive forward, he doubted that his BMW would have room to gain enough speed to burst through the table and wall. He had to try something else, because time was running out.

He quickly shifted his body weight to the right, which brought him closer to Winter. As he brought his socked foot up to the door handle, his right arm and shoulder brushed her arm and sagging head.

"Ughhhh, Jesus Christ," he said, his stomach rolling over and threatening again to throw up the remains of his last meal. He swallowed the little bit that came up high in his throat and shied away from his dead girlfriend again. Careful not to touch her, Connor crossed his right foot over his left knee. He hooked his big toe into the door handle and pulled back enough to unlatch the door. Holding the handle with his foot, he slammed his weight against the center of the door with as much force as he could in this awkward position.

The door swung out to about a forty-five-degree angle.

"Hell fucking yes. Whatcha think about that, fuck-nugget?" Connor said as he lowered his foot again. "I'm gonna get out of here yet. And when I do—"

An influx of stifling exhaust fumes drifted into the car, ending his spoken thoughts in a coughing fit. Connor sputtered, cleared his throat, and spat on the garage floor.

He wriggled his right hand over to the other side of the steering wheel so he could lean out the door. He was facing the ground, but turned his head to the left and looked toward the back of the car. With his bound hands he couldn't maneuver very far. He caught a glimpse of a rounded bit of yellow that curved out from the side panel of the car.

What the hell is that?

He strained even farther, but his hands and wrists were already bent so much that it was starting to cut the circulation off in his fingers. Confused, Connor pulled himself back up into his seat. He shifted his weight and leaned backwards out of the car. He was able to fold out a little farther and see a little more now.

He froze in stunned horror at the yellow metal attached to the back wheel.

"A boot?" he screamed. "A goddamn fucking tire boot? You asshole! What the fuck are you doing with a fucking tire boot?"

Another thick plume of exhaust wafted over his face, and along with it came the hopeless dread that he was never going to get out of this situation alive. The acrid smell tickled his nose as he breathed in again. It made him even more lightheaded, and his eyelids fluttered.

Oh, Jesus, maybe I've been here longer than I realized.

He felt tired, and shook his head violently to alert himself even more. The dull headache, which he'd mostly forgotten about, awakened and began to throb with the beating of his racing heart. His vision blurred, then came back into focus.

That was a mistake, he mused. *There's no way that son-of-a-bitch got the best of me. I've got to get free.*

He leaned back into the car seat, but it was too uncomfortable with his hands tied like they were. Instead, he leaned forward, placing his forehead against the steering wheel and searching his mind for the next bright idea.

I'm tired, he thought. *I just want to sleep. I need to close my eyes for a few minutes, then I'll figure out my next move. The one that's going to get me out of here. There has to be a way out. I'm not dead yet.*

The toxic fumes continued to billow into the open car door, slowly possessing the interior and Connor's exhausted body. On the brink of unconsciousness, a simple thought popped into his head.

The horn. I should blow the horn. That would get somebod—

The thought disappeared into incoherency as he surrendered to a never-ending sleep.

⌇

Two days, five hours, and thirty-six minutes after he had fixed the McPherson-Mills couple in their murder-suicide poses, Scott was back on the road again. He tried to find something good on the radio, but no great songs were playing and there were too many commercials. He reluctantly gave up and just left it on a station playing the news.

He was now sporting a neck brace, courtesy of his family doctor. During the confrontation, he'd been so scared and on such an adrenaline high that he'd shaken off the whiplash fairly easily. But after he'd got home, once the adrenaline had stopped flowing and he'd fallen into an exhausted deep sleep, his muscles had tightened up on him so much that when he woke the next morning he could barely move his head. The injury had been severe enough that he'd had to call in sick to work and make an appointment with his doctor.

Now his body was on muscle relaxers and his neck was cushioned with a monster brace. It was a reminder that he was going to have to be much more careful from now on.

His mind was pulled back to the news when he heard the news reporter say, "Connor McPherson and his girlfriend, Winter Mills, were found in his car inside their closed garage. An investigation is currently under way, but authorities have concluded that this is a possible murder-suicide after evidence of a fight throughout McPherson's residence was found. The couple were found inside Connor McPherson's enclosed garage with the windows down and the car idling. Winter Mills had been nearly beheaded. Authorities believe she was placed in the car before Connor joined her in this grim death…"

As the reporter blathered on about the police findings, Scott began to relive the events that had played out at Connor McPherson's house. He had to admit, he felt extremely lucky. If he'd been knocked out as a result of that body-slam and fight, it would've been all over for him. He also felt that he was extremely clever to have staged Connor and Winter in a murder-suicide, and the authorities had actually believed it.

Scott's mind was ripped from his thoughts when a complete and utter asshole pulled out in front of him, causing him to slam on his brakes. He had to nearly stand on his brake pedal to stop. His wheels locked up, and his SUV fishtailed back and forth two or three times before he gained control of his car again. Scott immediately jammed his palm against his horn, blaring it long and loudly.

"Oh, you fucking asshole!" Scott yelled. He immediately winced and grabbed the back of his neck.

The asshole jerked his head up and looked in his rearview mirror. Scott saw the figure's arm move out the window, and was slightly relieved that he was about to get an apology wave from this little punk-ass bitch.

That relief was washed away in a river of anger when the hand's middle finger extended in a fuck-you bird back at Scott.

"Oh, hell fucking no. No, sir, you're not going to do that shit to me. I kill people for less than that." He punched the horn again.

The asshole looked back up into his rearview mirror and saw two middle fingers pointed back directly at him. He also saw Scott's face contorted in a mask of rage as he released a stream of vehement curses that would've made any navy captain envious.

"Fuck you, you piece of shit!" Scott yelled at the top of his lungs after his creative tirade. "I just finished killing two assholes for doing shit like that, you fucker. Now I'm going to have to go through it all over again."

Scott checked himself at how naturally that thought had come to him. *It's as if I've been doing this for years,* he thought.

His voice dropped to a low, hateful, calculated tone. "Shitty antics like that will get you killed. Now I'm obligated to fuck your world over like I did Connor and his bitch girlfriend. The question is, what am I going to do to you?"

The little hobgoblin in Scott's mind popped up, and thought after creative thought of what he was going to do to this shithead started playing out in his mind.

Maybe I'll start by cutting your middle finger off with some garden shears and shoving it down your throat. Make you gag on it. That'll teach you to flip me off in traffic.

He looked down into the console of his Sorento, and saw the black-and-red-handled folding knife he'd pocketed from Connor McPherson's house. It was now clean of any of Winter's blood; he'd scrubbed it with different cleaning solutions to make sure there was no trace evidence on the handle and blade. He flipped it open as he looked back at the arrogant little shitbag in the piece-of-shit car in front of him.

"LAS-276. Gotcha, you asshole. LAS-276. LAS-276."

He didn't need to chase this guy as he had Connor the day of the first incident. He eased off the gas pedal, mentally calmed himself, and let the guy go free—for now.

"I have your license plate number, asshole," Scott said. "I'll be seeing you very soon."

DEAD BAIT

JAMES LORY STOOD on the deck of his ship—*The Big One*—and fished his iPhone 10 from out of his front right pocket. It was the only piece of expensive technology he owned, and it wasn't by his own doing. The phone had been a very recent present from his wife, Virginia, who had bought and given it to him as a 'just because I love you' gift.

James examined his new phone's sleek frame. *It's a nice one, that's for sure,* he thought. *I wouldn't have paid for something this expensive. That flip phone I had worked just fine. Virginia's always doing stuff like this for me. Damn, I really need to get her a beautiful gift in return—not that she expects it, but it might be a nice gesture on my part. I definitely don't do as much for her as she does for me.*

Not having set up a fingerprint, pattern, face recognition, or security code to get into his phone, he simply swiped up, and the main menu appeared. This gadget was still new and almost too high-tech for him. He had to think again on what button to tap to get to his address book.

"Let's see here. Oh yeah," he said, remembering and pressing the address book near the bottom of the phone. When his contacts came up, he pressed 'S'. There was only one entry in surnames beginning with 'S' because his other phone was so old all his contacts—there weren't that many—couldn't be transferred over to this one. James figured he would just input the other numbers as he needed them. He clicked to connect to his best friend, Murray Stockton.

As the phone rang, James looked out into the bay that stretched off into the far distance. The mountains beyond were a stark silhouette against this early morning sky. The blended array of tequila sunrise colors—red, orange, yellow, and an added tinge of purple—bled into the sky as the sun slowly edged away from the distant mountains. James drank it in as he waited.

If he knew Murray, he was going to show up half-drunk and headachy from the booze he'd taken in last night down at Bowing's Landing, or at home, or wherever Murray had decided to throw back his drinks. If Murray did make it out today, he would be bobbing and weaving as he made his way down the pier. It was almost a waste of James's time to even bring Murray along if he was going to be inebriated throughout the trip, but Murray was his best friend and had been since they were in elementary school. Lately, Murray had been drinking a lot more than in previous months. Alice—his wife—had voiced her concerns about his *drinking problem* to James a couple of times, when she had called to ask if he had seen Murray because he hadn't yet come home.

The phone continued to ring. *Murray's going to be a no-show again*, James thought. *I just know it.*

The bay was calm this early in the morning. The breeze that gusted over the bow of his ship chilled his exposed face, arms, and legs. He was dressed in Pelagic grey-and-black boat shorts and a worn grey T-shirt of the same brand that stated he had taken part in the 2019 Rock Star Tuna Tournament in Carbo San Luca, Mexico. Even his ball cap, boat shoes, sunglasses, and watch matched his shorts in color and brand. He always tried to match his attire, even if it was well worn; he hated to be a walking billboard of different brands. It would have grated on his nerves to be wearing something like a Billabong T-shirt, Costa Del Mar shorts, Cabella boat shoes, Ray-Ban sunglasses, and a Patagonia fishing cap. His only thought this morning when he'd gotten up was how hot it was going to get during the day; he hadn't realized just how cold it was now until he'd arrived here at the lake marina and stepped aboard his boat.

Should've dressed warmer and brought another pair of clothes to change into later when it does get hot, James thought. "Where the hell is he?" he asked aloud as a trio of birds passed by overhead.

There weren't too many people around at this time of the morning. Some early-rising fishermen had already taken their boats to their favorite fishing spots around the lake to wait for that 'big one.' James wished he was one of them, but he'd graciously waited to hear if Murray was coming or not.

"This is Murray…" a voice said on the phone, then there was a pause.

"Murray! Where the hell are you? We were suppos—"

Then Murray's voice continued, "…And this is my answerin' machine 'cause I ain't here." There was a short burst of laughter, then, "Fooled ya. You thought it was me, didn't ya?" There was another snide laugh, then Murray got serious. "Leave your name, number, and message at that tone, and I'll get back to ya. Bye now." There was a short beep.

James gave a frustrated breath at Murray's message. "Clever," he grumbled. He was about to leave a verbal thrashing on Murray's voicemail for him to enjoy listening to later, but then he heard Murray's real voice coming from behind.

"I'm here, I'm here."

James pulled the phone away from his ear as he turned. Murray Stockton was shuffling toward *The Big One* awkwardly, but this time he wasn't drunk, as far as James could tell. He was just having a hard time walking because of the load of equipment he was carrying. He toted two long fishing poles, his larger-than-life tackle box, an 'almost too big to carry' cooler—it had wheels, but Murray had decided to carry it rather than roll it behind himself—a Chick-fil-A breakfast bag, and a large drink.

Frustrated, James tapped his screen to end the call, shoved the phone into his back pocket and said, "Where the hell have you been? We were supposed to have already cast off an hour and a half ago."

"I know, I know. Sorry, James. Alice and I had a big argument. I had ta sort all that shit out before I could get away."

"Well, you could've at least called me and told me so I would've known you were going to be late. I wouldn't have got so keyed up in thinking you were just going to bail on me as you've done in the past. If you hadn't shown up just now or hadn't picked up the phone, I was going to leave your sorry ass."

"I know. I know. I'm really sorry, man."

"Well, don't just stand there staring at me like *I'm* the dumbass. Hop aboard."

"Here, take this," Murray said, passing James his Chick-fil-A breakfast bag and drink.

James accepted them and stepped to the console, placing the drink in the cup holder near the controls. He placed the breakfast bag on top of the galley roof, where it wouldn't fall over. This flat area was also the enclosure top that opened up to allow access to the bowels of the ship. Below the deck was a small kitchen, bed, and toilet section.

Murray said of the breakfast container, "Alice and I got you a biscuit and hash browns too."

"Murray, y'all didn't have to do that. I already ate breakfast at Russell's Diner earlier this morning before the sun was even up. I've been ready to go."

"Alice insisted. Said it was only right since I was so late gettin' here this mornin'." Murray set his cooler and tackle box on the dock and laid his fishing poles beside them.

"That was really nice of her. Well, in that case, I'll see if I can't eat some of it on our trip out."

Murray turned back to the marina parking area and waved to Alice, who was standing in the crook of the driver's side door. He gave her a big thumbs-up, telling her everything was okay and that he was going with James. Alice waved back and gave him a big thumbs-up in return. Message received.

James saw Alice waving and waved to her as well. Alice went from giving a thumbs-up to Murray to waving again to James. Murray saw the gesture and wondered why the hell she was waving at him again. As he turned back to the boat, he saw James waving and his question was answered. He saw the smile on James's face. He nonchalantly glanced around again at Alice, and although she was far off, he could see the smile she was wearing as well. It was just a little happier than when she'd waved to him. A small flare of anger and pent-up jealousy ignited within him. He shook his head against his emotions and forced himself not to think about that situation right now.

Murray step-jumped aboard *The Big One*, making it a little more dramatic than it had to be, like a little kid afraid to jump into the deep end of the pool for the first time. Speaking again of his gift of breakfast food, he said, "Well, it's the thought that counts, isn't it? Peace offerin', you know?" He retrieved his cooler, poles, and tackle box and set them down near the back of the boat.

James turned away from Alice and the marina parking lot and moved to the controls of the boat. "Sure. Don't get me wrong, I appreciate it."

He gave Murray a sideways glance. He was dressed in a way that unnerved James. Murray was wearing a ripped and very worn aqua-colored Panama Jack shirt from years ago—*Where the hell did he find one of those?*—a maroon-and-white Texas A&M hat that was grime-coated from the machine shop where he worked, and a pair of shorts that had been made from a worn pair of jeans. Murray had just cut the legs off at mid-thigh. The shorts were frayed, with little white strings hanging off all around the bottom of the legs. His outfit was completed with a pair of ankle-high Caterpillar work boots with untied laces.

Not the best color combo in the world, James thought.

"If you're not gwonna eat it," Murray said, bringing James out of his sizing-up of Murray's outfit and back to the subject of the breakfast, "that'll jus' mean, thay'll be more for me."

"You got everything?"

Murray looked around quickly and double-checked his belongings, looking from his breakfast to his equipment. "Yup, I b'lieve so. I'm good to go. Hell, I'm a poet. If I've forgotten anythin', I'll jus' have to do without it this trip, you know?"

Murray turned away from James, pulled his cell phone from his front pocket, and began to text someone.

"Then we're off," James said, and cranked the twin engines of Grady White Freedom 330 Express Cabin. He had almost pulled the throttle into a slow reverse when he looked up and noticed Murray was still focused on typing out a damn text. By this time, Murray usually had the ropes that moored the boat to the dock already untied. James cleared his throat to get Murray's attention. It didn't work. He finally said, "Hey, um, Murray?"

"Yeah," he said out the side of his mouth, still looking down at his phone.

"Uh, you think you could tear yourself away from your social media long enough to untie us?"

"Aw, fuck. Sure, of course," Murray said as he finished typing the last of the message. He hit send, then immediately hit the main center console button on his phone as he looked up. The texting app went away and back to the main screen. He smiled at James, then pocketed his phone. "Sorry 'bout that," he said as he stepped to the mooring line near the stern and untied the rope from the cleat. He quickly wrapped it up and tied it out of the way so it wouldn't be a tripping hazard to either of them during their excursion. Then Murray rushed to the ship's bow and untied the rope that moored it parallel to the dock. He wound the rope up and tied it off, out of the way of anyone's footpath.

With a huff, James gently eased the lever back, and the boat's engines slowly moved them in reverse and away from the dock. Once it was clear of the pier, he swung the wheel more, and the boat took a more severe arc. When the ship was almost pointed in the direction of the open lake, James eased the throttle forward. The Yamaha 300 twin engines reversed course and ramped up—lifting the bow high—and soon *The Big One* was screaming away from the marina and out into deeper waters.

Murray joined James, who was seated at the center controls. He stood beside him and began to unwrap his breakfast biscuit, which was still sitting on the galley roof. He took a big bite of his chicken, egg, and cheese bagel and laid it back on the flat surface again, then reached for his box of hash browns.

As James guided the boat, he eyed Murray carefully, allowing him to get a few bites into his bagel before he began any significant conversation. Wanting to double-check him on his dumbass excuse for being late, he finally asked, "So, what was the argument about? You know, this morning with Alice?"

He wanted to see if Murray was going to pause. Murray had a habit of taking a long pause, or sometimes giving a fake cough, to give himself time to make up a lie—or as Murray called it, an excuse—about whatever they were talking about.

Murray didn't pause this time, though. He began to talk around the mouthful of bagel. "She accused me of fuckin' around on her again."

Well, at least he's not lying, James thought. *I guess*. He asked, "Are you? Fucking around on Alice?"

Murray paused to chew his food a little more, then swallowed a little too quickly—more like gulped—like the mouthful hadn't been chewed well enough. Then he coughed. "No. 'Course not. I'd never do that to her."

James noticed the pause and the hard swallow. Hard to tell on that one. He could be lying, or it could have just been a bite that was too big for him to swallow. *Murray doesn't have the best etiquette when eating...* James shook his head.

"Good. Because you've got a good woman there. Alice is quite the catch. You know, she's beautiful, and... and she's fun. And amazing. She's awesome. What's not to love about her?"

Murray was chewing another big bite of his breakfast bagel, and his chewing slowed. He looked over at James with slightly confused eyes. He pushed the mouthful of food into his left cheek and asked, "Are *you*, James?"

James looked over at Murray and saw him staring directly back with a suspicious look on his face. "Am I what?"

"Uh, duh. Fuckin' Alice."

"What?" James asked in an appalled voice. A little incredulous laugh escaped his mouth.

Murray chewed his food, swallowed, then asked again, "Are you fuckin' Alice? Because it sounds like you're in love with her by the way you're talkin' about her."

James realized Murray's first accusation had been sort of off the cuff and really didn't know if it was a legit allegation. He decided he would play around with Murray for asking such a stupid question. He gave him a slack-jawed, disparaging look.

"Uh, yeah, Murray. I'm fucking your wife. Fucking her in every Kama Sutra position. We're doing it every chance we get. I've even taken her out on this boat a time or two, and I fucked her right back there"— he threw a thumb to the back of the boat—"on the transom of *The Big*

One." He paused for a moment, then added, "With my *big one*, if you get my drift." He grinned. "No, of course not," he said more seriously. "Don't be ridiculous."

"Good," Murray said in a very focused manner. "That's real good. 'Cause if you was, I'd have to make a move on Virginia, right? Turnip about is fair play, you know?" He smiled.

There was a little more going on in Murray's grin, but James couldn't accurately read his obscurity. "Sure, Murray," he said, a slight smile of his own playing at the edges of his lips.

He realized Murray had quoted the saying wrong, but the meaning was there. He tried to imagine Murray and Virginia together in any way and just couldn't wrap his head around it. They were from two totally different classes. Murray had a lot of Southern redneck in him, and Virginia was from a Southern family that had a good bit of money. She was upper-crust, a couple of classes above Murray—hell, she was even a few classes above James himself. Virginia and Murray couldn't possibly happen; there was just no way that combo would match up. James put them out of his head and changed the subject. "There is another thing I'm curious about, though."

"What's that?"

"Why're you not drunk today? Most every time we've gone fishing, you've either shown up half-drunk and sobered up during the trip, or you don't even show up at all. I thought you were going to be a no-show again today."

"Awww, that's Alice's doin's. She gave me an ultimatum. Said if I didn't stop drinkin' so much and makin' a fool outta myself and her, then I would be doin' without her. So I've dialed it back jus' a li'l bit." He paused for a moment to let the statement hit, then he reiterated, "Notice I said, 'jus' a 'li'l bit.'" He held his right hand up, his thumb and index finger held about an inch apart.

"Well, that's good. We're definitely going to have a better time fishing today than the last time, that's for sure."

"Don't remind me 'bout that. I'm eatin' right now."

"Well, *you* weren't the one who had to clean up your lunch from off the deck of my ship."

"Right, I 'member. That was real nasty. Tasted even worse."

James pushed the throttle forward another notch and swung the steering wheel to the left, guiding the boat toward Foster's Cove. He wanted to investigate that area and find out if the rumors about big fish biting over there were actually true.

When they arrived at their destination, James slowly pulled back on the throttle and finally docked it into neutral. He rarely just slammed it from 'full-tilt-boogie' mode down to an abrupt-stop. James had always hated a sudden stop when riding in a boat. The propellers slowed, and *The Big One* rode out the mini swell of the wake that came up behind them, lifted the boat up, and finally settled it back on calm, level waters. He finally killed the engines, and silence fell over the lake.

A loon on the distant shore cried out. It was an ominous sound this early in the morning.

Murray was already kneeling on the deck, working on his line to get it ready to cast. He had spent some of last night carefully tying his newest and biggest hook onto the new 120 monofilament line of his latest reel. He opened the cooler that James always had filled with the headless and tailless fish they used for bait. Hooking one of the decapitated fish onto his hook, Murray carefully rotated it and his pole behind him and gave it a gentle toss. He didn't want to abruptly fling it hard and risk the hooks ripping through his bait and falling off. They were out in open water, so there was no need to throw it far from the boat. The bait dropped about twenty yards out.

James grabbed his fishing pole from its usual location on the boat. As Murray had done a few days before this trip, James had also checked his weights and lures, having it all ready to go. Baiting a hook of his own, James mimicked Murray's action and cast into the lake.

As Murray toyed with his line, his attention was drawn to something else James had added to his boat. He'd been eyeing it ever since he'd climbed aboard, but hadn't gotten around to asking about it yet.

"What the hell is this?" The metal contraption was bolted down in the very center of the deck.

"I've been waiting for you to ask me about that. *That*... is my new downrigger unit, which I designed and installed myself."

Murray rapped his knuckles on the steel pole that shot up from the deck. It was sturdy, as it was welded to some other metal pieces attached to the roof of the boat. Jutting off from the central pole was another arcing piece of metal. It looked to have been made from three separate metal parts that had been welded together to form one central piece in an arc that pointed away toward the back of the ship. It made the curved 'J' shape that a regular fishing pole takes when someone is reeling in a big one.

Murray saw a large metal reel mounted on the vertical pole at waist height. To him, it looked like one of those circular contraptions a garden hose would be wound up in if it was near an outside faucet. The metal reel had been beefed up with other metal pieces, so Murray knew it wasn't going anywhere. He moved his hand to the black line and examined it. It looked and felt to be a high-test weight of some sort of thin but durable mountain climbing rope. The rope had been reeled very meticulously on the spool, and from the looks of it, there was an ass-load of it. It had been threaded up through into the roller ball-bearing loops that were attached by welds along the underside of the metal arc. The end of the rope was tied around the handle of a large hay-baling hook with a simple but effective slipknot. The hook itself looked as though it had been sharpened explicitly for this contraption. It was slipped into the largest of the bottom loops to hold it in place until James was ready to use it.

"Uh-huh. Yeah. Okay, James, don't'cha think this is a bit overkill? We're not tryin' to catch a big-ass shark, are we? I mean, sharks are saltwater fish, anyway. We're in freshwater, brother. I don't really think you have a need for somethin' like this, do ya?"

"We do if we're going to catch Methuselah today."

Murray busted out laughing. "No one's ever gwonna catch Methuseler. That fish is just a *legend* anyway. The stories of that big fucker have been around ever since we was kids."

"So? Some say the lifespan of a catfish, or whatever-the-fuck-type fish he is, is sixty years or more. I'm thirty-five. So if you do the math, it seems to me there are a couple more years before Methuselah kicks the bucket."

"Yeah. Maybe."

"Okay, Mr. 'I'm the Best Fisherman in the Whole Goddamn World,' if you don't believe in Methuselah, then why the hell did you go and buy that new Fin-Nor rod with that Santiago reel, huh? Don't give me that look; you know what I'm talking about. I saw it when you loaded your equipment aboard back at the marina. A rod and reel like that would be more suited for saltwater fishing rather than here on Silver Ridge Lake. Talk about your overkill. You already had a nice Shimano rod with a Tiagra reel that would last you a long time. Why did you think you needed to upgrade?"

"I just wan'ed a new rod and reel, and I got a good bargain for it too from my boy Ryan Taylor, down at Outdoor Sportin' Goods."

James gave him a look as though he were shoveling bullshit out of the boat and into the bay.

"Okay, okay, you got me," Murray admitted. "I'm always hoping to catch Methuseler. And I'm gwonna get him today. Or one of us is."

"We'll see. I have an excellent feeling today is going to be a perfect fishing day."

"Hope so. Been hearin' a lot more stories about Methuseler lately. You know, more sightin's an' shit."

"Uh-huh."

"Tom Watersbee said it came right up to his skiff and ate his whole goddamn sandwich."

"I heard that too."

"He jus' opened his mouth, and Tom dropped that peanut butter and jelly sandwich right inside. Then he jus' closed his mouth an' disappeared back under the water and swam away, just a' pretty as you please."

"Yeah, well, Tom has been known to stretch the truth at times. He cheated in the last tournament we were in, remember that? He said he wrote his poundage down wrong by accident, but I think he added a four in with the numbers when he calculated, just to get that trophy. Tom's a sly son-of-a-bitch."

"Aww, he's alright. Hey, Maynard Tillotson told me down at the Feed 'n' Seed that that big fucker just stuck his head out of the water and fuckin' winked at him."

"If anything," James said. "Maynard probably meant 'blinked.' I'm sure that fish wasn't telling him a joke and winked at him when he told him the punchline. Methuselah's so damn big Maynard probably couldn't see the eye on the other side of its head."

"Yeah, I know. Maynard's a dumbass, but he did say that Methuseler had a buncha lures and hooks stuck in his lips, you know, that different fishermen had hooked when he'd taken their bait. Methuseler's such a big som'bitch that all the lines broke. Maynard said that his mouth was lined with an ass-load of 'em."

"Yeah, well, fish are stupid," James agreed. "Methuselah may be the dumbest fish of them all if he never learns his lesson with all the hooks he's eaten over the years. Fucker's going around eating any type of bait he sees." James went into charades mode, acting out the rest of his story. "Fisherman jerks the line." He changed his voice to a deeper, dumb, backwoods, redneck voice, giving a voice to Methuselah. "'Oh shit! That hurt.'" James quickly switched back to his normal voice and continued, "Then he goes about looking for more food. Eats another fisherman's bait. Fisherman jerks the line." He dropped back into the deep redneck voice. "'Oh shit! That fucking hurts. Why is all this food in this lake loaded with barbs? This is bullshit.'" Normal voice again. "And on he goes, just forgetting that certain bait hurts him and eating it up whenever he sees it. Just a big dumb fucking fish."

Murray sniggered. He continued, "Maynard also said his lips looked all infected from the lures that had bin hooked in there for so long, you know, all rusted up an' shit. I don't know. His lips probably growed over the rusted hook part, and it's just in there all festerin' up and shit, with pus leakin' out all over its lips and all."

"Oh, God; I get it, Murray. I see it clear as day in my mind. You don't have to draw me a fucking mental picture."

"I'm jus' sayin'. Hey, you know, Methuseler might not be fit to eat if his lips is all infected like that. It coulda spread to other partsa his body, ya think?"

"I don't care to eat him. I just want to catch the son-of-a-bitch and take some pictures with him so we can put this legend shit to rest once and for all as truth, you know?"

"Yeah, I know." Murray paused for a moment, then switched gears. "Still weird what happened to Old Bags, you know?"

"Old Bags?"

"Yeah, you know, Harry Bagwell; that old coot that loved goin' out night fishin' by hisself?"

"Oh yeah, I remember him. Nice old man. I always loved talking to him. He could tell a joke."

"Yeah, he was funny. Weird he jus' up and disappeared, you know? Jus' left all his belongings on his li'l johnboat, then poof, just vanished. Some say he was jus' done with life and committed suicide late at night and drownded hisself."

"But there would've been a body, right? His body would've resurfaced."

"I guess so. But that's creepy, though, isn't it?"

"Hell yeah, it's fucking spooky as shit."

"Only thing that was missing from his boat was his fishing pole. The fishermen that found his boat found his bucket fishin' hat jus' floatin' on top the damn water."

"I can tell you have a different theory about what happened to him."

"Oh, hell yeah. I know what happened to him, but nobody'll b'lieve me."

"What's that?"

"Methuseler got him. Ate his ass."

James laughed out loud. "That's bullshit, Murray, and you know it."

"Well then, if you're so goddang smart, what happened to Old Bags?"

James had no idea, but to be eaten by Methuselah, an overgrown fish—he couldn't even fathom the thought. Methuselah wasn't *that* damn big. There might be some crazy stories of his size, but he was simply wasn't big enough to eat a man. "Fuck, I don't know what happened to Bags, man. I'm not a detective."

"Old Bags hooked Methuseler. He couldn't handle the fight with him, an' he was pulled overboard. Then Methuseler snatched his ass up, an' that is all she wrote. That's why his reel was missing, an' his hat was jus' floatin' there on top the damn water."

"That does conveniently button everything up, doesn't it? Makes it perfect material for an urban legend."

"Tellin' ya, no urban legend 'bout it. It's the truth. Methuseler got him. End of the story."

"Okay, Murray, okay," James said. "Don't get so worked up. Methuselah got him. We only have the eye-witness accounts that people have seen this big guy, but no one has ever thought to take any pictures of him. So, that's what we're going to do."

"Sounds good to me. We'll be famous."

"Oh, I don't know about famous," James said. "But it will be a fun catch, no matter how big Methuselah really is. It's only a matter of time now before we get a nibble."

"Yeah, but even if we don' get a bite, it beats workin' a reguler job today, right?"

"Oh yeah, any day of the week I can be out here on the water in the sun just enjoying this view and the possibility of hooking something. It's definitely the high life."

"Preach on, brotha."

Knowing Murray was just agreeing with his statement, James fell silent and focused on the action at hand. Murray fell silent as well, and both men toyed with their lines just a little to create some sort of interest for the fish below.

After a long moment, Murray looked over at James, who was intently watching his line for any sign that some fish down there was fucking around with his bait.

"Hey, James?"

"Yeah?"

"You still mad at me?"

James gave him a quick glance. "No. I'm not mad at you. Never was. Why you ask?"

"I don't know. Jus' wan'ed to make sure."

"I'm just focused on catching these fish, since we got a late start."

"Sorry for bein' late and all… and not callin' ya to let ya know what was goin' on."

"It was just frustrating, since we'd talked about leaving at an earlier time. But I'm over that now. We're good. Don't worry about it."

"Okay. Thanks, man."

"Don't mention it."

They fell into another silence, and both men watched and played with their lines again.

"Hey, James?"

"Yeah, Murray."

"How you think Methuseler got so damn big?"

"I don't rightly know. Never really thought of any reasoning behind it. We really don't have any proof that Methuselah's a giant. But if he is, I just think he's probably a fluke of nature."

Murray thought about James's statement for a moment, then a smile crept across his face. "*Fluke*," he repeated, then began to laugh. "Ha. That's funny."

"What's funny?"

"Fluke?" Murray repeated.

"What about it?"

"*Fluke?* As in a whale's tail. We're gwonna cetch us a big fish, an' you said he's a *fluke* of nature. That's funny, James."

"Oh. Oh," James said, beginning to laugh at himself. "I get it now. No, I didn't mean anything by saying it that way. I don't really think about how big he might be, because we're just going by word of mouth from a bunch of assholes around town."

"Still funny though."

"I guess."

Murray and James fell into a more extended silence, enjoying the view of the lake spread out before them. Murray sniggered a couple of times at James's pun as it drifted back through his mind. James watched him surreptitiously as Murray glanced around a couple of times and admired his new outrigger unit.

"So, you don't think they's any other reasons why this fish got so big?" Murray asked.

"I don't know, Murray. There are no pictures to even prove he's for real. You know, sort of like the Loch Ness Monster."

"Oh, the Loch Ness Monster exists, James. I've seen pitchers of 'im in books before at the libree."

"What, those black-and-white grainy pictures that have been around ever since we were kiddie-boos?"

"Yeah."

"You ever think those pictures were artfully taken to raise somewhat of a mystery and imagination in people's minds as a way to drum up tourist business to the Loch Ness area?"

"Huh?"

"Murray, the Loch Ness Monster doesn't exist, alright?"

"Does *so*, motherfucker."

James cut his eyes over to Murray with a look that said *No, she doesn't, motherfucker,* and then backed it up by saying, "No, she doesn't, motherfucker." He gave an apologetic smile, as though sorry he had to break this bad news to him.

"Well, *you* can b'lieve what *you* like, *I* b'lieve he *does* exist." Murray drew the word 'does' out to really emphasize his conviction.

James laughed at his phrasing.

Murray asked, "What's so goddamn funny?"

"You called the Loch Ness Monster a '*he*.'"

"Yeah. So?"

"The Loch Ness Monster doesn't exist, but if *she* did, they consider *her* to be a *female*. That's why they call *her* Nessie." James laughed hard at Murray's blunder again.

"Whatever, dude. She, he, it—whatever *it* is exists, okay?"

"You believe it because you want monsters to exist in the world. That's your little kid's imagination working overtime, and that's fine. That's why you watch so many of those sci-fi monster and horror movies. You've been watching them since you were a kid."

"I have," Murray agreed. "And I would love to see our Loch Ness Monster here and maybe document this big fucker. I gots me a brand-new iPhone to do it with too." He patted the front right pocket of his jean shorts. "All these other fishermen have all their stories, but I'm gwonna get proof, same as you. And with my new phone, they won't be grainy or black-and-white like those pitchers in those books we looked at as kids. It will be in full color an' shit. Gwonna be awwwesome." He paused in his sermon as a new idea started to form in his head. "An' furthermore,"

Murray said, leaning into James to get his attention, "you say you don't b'lieve in monsters, yet you have this big fuckin' rig that you've made and attached to your boat. You've basically ruined the floorin' of it by boltin' it down to yer deckin'." He rapped his knuckles on the metal bar again. He looked up to the top of the metal pole; there was another metal attachment that anchored it to the roof of the boat. "For someone who don't b'lieve in monsters, especially in *Nessie*, you have really gone outta yer way with this contraption to hook the legend that lives in our lake."

James said, "Look, we both want this beast of a fish if it really exists. We just have our own ways of going about it. I make my own metal rod and reel, and you go and buy a new expensive rod and reel. These are just precautions we've both made in case there's a fish out there that's Loch-Ness-Monster big."

"You b'lieve what *you* want, and I'll b'lieve what *I* want. *I*, for one, for instance, b'lieve"—Murray looked around conspiratorially and over both shoulders before he continued—"that some company's dumpin' some type of toxic-waste shit in these waters."

"You do?" James asked, amused.

"Hell yeah, I do."

"Why you think that?"

Murray stood there, dumbfounded at his response. "Two reasons. One, 'cause Methuseler's so fuckin' big."

"In theory," James shot back. "Again, we're going by what people have said and have taken them and their stories at face value. But we have no proof whatsoever. Just big urban-legend tales about a legendary big fish."

"True. But *I* b'lieve their stories."

"Just like when we were teens and me, the Dewitt brothers and Sam Adkins took you snipe hunting, and left you off down there in the woods without a flashlight at two in the fucking morning." James started to belly laugh again at the joke his friends had played on Murray.

"Aw, shut up 'bout that. It ain't funny. Y'all keep bringin' that shit up to me. That wasn't a good night for me. I was sorta sick. I wasn't thinkin' straight. Fuck them guys." Murray lost his anger quickly as he ran out of steam. He laughed a little about some of the years of fun they'd had as boys. Then he got right back to what he'd been saying. "That's diff'rent. Snipeses ain't real. Nobody has pictures of them critters. But this damn fish is a diff'rent story."

"How so? I mean, no one has pictures of Methuselah."

Murray was pissed that James kept calling him out. "I don't know. He just is, dammit."

"What's the second reason? I'm curious."

"No, you're not. You're just pertendin', then you're gwonna make some more fun of me and prob'ly tell Sam and the Dewitts and everybody else down at the bar when I'm not there 'cause I promised Alice I wasn't gwonna go drink as much."

"No, c'mon, Murray. Tell me. I'm not gonna make fun of you. I'm always just having a little fun. It's nothing personal."

It took Murray some time to soften, but he finally gave in to James's coaxing. "Okay. Well, the second reason is that I have proof they're dumping shit into the lake."

"Bullhell."

"Swear to God Almighty on high."

Murray stood there, staring out at the water ahead of them, continuing to play with the fishing line. He wanted James to beg him a little more to tell him what he knew.

"Okay, Murray, I'll bite. What's this proof you have?" James asked, already writing this whole story off as a massive load of horse manure.

Murray turned back to James and struck an I'm-going-to-level-with-you pose. He held his hands up parallel to the deck of the ship, still holding his pole in one hand. It looked as though Murray was about to tell James he had just caught a fish that was as wide as he was—which wasn't that big, since Murray was so scrawny. "Okay, so ya know that German pharmaceutical company that was built in Breckenridge when we was teens?"

"Sure. Drexymeyer Industries. I haven't heard too much from them lately. Haven't really heard anything out of them since that facility went belly-up years ago."

"Exactly."

"What do you mean?"

Murray put on a little cocky air. "Why you think you ain't heard nothin' out of 'em?"

"Maybe because they keep a low profile about what they did inside those fences."

"*Do*," Murray emphasized as he leaned further into him.

"Do?" James asked. "I always thought they went out of business and shut that place down."

Murray leaned in again, his eyes dancing with conspiracy-theory knowledge. He looked James directly in the eyes and said, "So did everyone else in Breckenridge and other towns nearby. Doesn't mean they closed down, do it?"

"I don't know. You know something else we don't know about?"

"Oh, hell yeah. See, sometimes, when I leave Bowing's Landing, I don't go directly home. I just like to drive round at night to see what I can see."

"It's not good to drink and drive, Murray."

"I ain't drunk by that time, dammit. Just... still a little tipsy, is all. Buzzed some."

"Okay, okay, calm down."

"Well, sometimes, when I drive around, just for the fuck of it, I drive that back road on 441 that circles around to the back of Drexymeyer, and I spy on those fuckers out there."

"What did you see? Anything interesting?"

"No. Not the first three times I went. It was jus' dead as a tree that's been lighnin' struck. Just vacant lots and shit. Overgrown weeds and stuff."

"I know. They went out of business years after they built that place. What happened on the fourth trip?"

"The fourth time I went tooling by there." Murray paused for effect.

James's interest was piqued. "What did you see?"

Murray toyed with his fishing line again and turned to James. "I ain't told you this story? I thought I mentioned to you about this."

"No. You didn't. What the fuck happened?"

"Huh?" Murray said, pretending to check his memory. "Thought I did."

"Nope. Just get to the goddamn point."

Murray continued, "So, I come around that bend on 441, you know at the top of the hill there off to the left. You can see pretty much ever'thin' behind the fences from that angle. You know that section of road, or asphalt, they added there at the top of the hill?"

"Yeah, I know the place."

"Well, I pulled over there, kilt the engine, and got out. I sat on the hood of my truck and just, you know, smoked a li'l weed. Jus' surveyin' the Drexymeyer vacant lots from a bird's-eye view and lookin' out at the lights in the distance. The view's real pretty from up there at night, you know?"

"Yeah, I know. What happened?"

"Uh, I better not say. You're not gwonna b'lieve me anyway. You never do. You just think I'm makin' shit up all the time. Always callin' them conspiracy theories and shit like that."

"Murray, you're beginning to piss me off. If you don't tell me what the fuck happened, I'm going to set my fishing pole down and brain your ass in the face."

"Oh, shit, don't do that. I don't want that."

"Well, what happened?"

"Ground gave way."

"What?"

"Well, not so much as gave way as just lowered into the earth like at a forty-five, no, it was more like a thirty-degree sloped road that angled into the ground."

"Bull. Fucking. Shit. You're making this up."

"I'm tellin' ya, that's what I saw." Murray paused for a moment, then said, "Fine, if you don't b'lieve me and don't want to hear what happened, then you can just fish in silence. I'll go to the front of the boat. Nothin's bitin' on this side anyways. I might have better luck up here." He shuffle-stepped away from James as he mumbled under his breath, "Try and tell you God's honest truth about what went on three nights ago, and you think I'm makin' shit up."

"Three nights ago? This recently happened?"

"Yeah." Murray stayed silent, still facing away from James and waiting for James's cue to continue.

"You serious?" James asked. "Three nights ago?"

"If I'm lyin', I'm fuckin' dyin'. Swear to Almighty God on high. The ground gave way and tilted downward. You know, from my point of view up there, I could see into that hole at an angle. It was bright down in that openin', and there was stuff goin' on in there. Couldn't tell what it was because a big army transport came up that ramp and circled around to Drexymeyer's front entrance."

"What did you do?"

"What the hell do you think I did? I fuckin' got in my truck and followed their ass. Very discreetly, of course."

"Of course."

"Most of the time, I drove with my headlights off, you know, 'cause I could see their brake lights and shit. I didn't want them to know someone had seen what they was doin' or were gwonna do. They left Drexymeyer and continued on 441 down to 19 into Silver Ridge. They looped around on Lakeshore Drive to that big fuckin' mansion to the south side of this lake. You know which mansion house I'm talking about? We both eyeball it every time we go by there."

"I know it."

"Yeah, that one that seems so out of place on this lake. Big fuckin' monstrosity just sittin' out there for everyone to gawk at. Asshole. Some people are so show-offy with their money. Whoever lives there has some deep pockets with a whole lotta cash. And those deep pockets are doing a whole lot of testin' in underground laboratories that are right in front of the public eye. You know I'm right."

"Maybe. What the hell happened with the transport?"

"Oh, yeah, that. Well, I parked about a fourth of a mile from where they turned in on Lakeshore Drive, and I crept onto that mansion house property and down, well, I guess it was the west wall where nobody was. And I got 'tween the house and the bushes and crawled as close to the truck as I could. Four men was pullin' rusty fifty-five-gallon drums off that transport and loadin' them on the owner's boat. I heard one of the men tell another to get rid of all them barrels 'cause some audit thang the gov'ment was doin' was happenin' the next mornin'. He said they couldn't have anyone findin' those animal test subjects on the premises or the company would be ended for malpractice and inhuman testin' on animals. He said, if the gov'ment found out they've been fuckin' around with growth hormones testin' and shit like that, then Drexymeyer Industries would end a lot quicker than it'd gotten started. The other guy kept tellin' the one guy to calm down, that he would take care of all the ev'dence. I sat there frozen in fear, with my legs crampin' in the bushes. I watched a few guys leave on the boat, and about thirty minutes later, they come back, and it was empty."

"Really?"

"Swear to God. I'm tellin' ya, they dumped all those rusty barrels into Silver Ridge Lake."

"Why haven't you told me about this?"

Murray was too deep into the story to stop to discuss side questions. "And it's been leakin' out ever since. And that's prob'bly not the first time they've dumped shit in this lake. That's why there's all these reports about fish in this lake being so damn big."

"Why didn't you tell someone about this?"

"I couldn't, man."

"Why not?"

"I was goin' to, honest to God I was, but before I could crawl back down the side of the house and leave, I felt a piece of steel press against the base of my skull." Murray held two fingers and his thumb up like a pistol and placed the tip of his middle finger against the bottom right side of his head. "I swear to God, I almost shit my pants right then and there."

"What?" The story had all of a sudden taken a turn for the worse. James looked at Murray to see if he was pulling his leg or showed any tell-tale sign of bullshit.

Murray pressed on, his voice taking on a new edge of fear. He sped up his story. "I tensed up, thinkin' whoever had a gun to my head was gwonna pull that trigger at any moment."

"Jesus Christ."

"That's what I said. Then the guy whispered into my ear with a strange German accent, 'Goot morning, ahsshoole. I fink we have a peeping Tom on our hands.' I told him my name was Murray, not Tom. I know, ballsy of me, right? But I wanted him to know who I was."

"What did he say?"

"Again, in the German accent, he said, 'I don't give a fuck who you are, but you're goink to meet Mr. Vanarious.'" Murray's accent imitation, mixed with his redneck southern drawl, didn't come across very German, but it did nothing to kill the tension for James.

"Vanarious? Is that German?"

"I think so. They all had German accents. They would have to be, working for that company, right?"

"I guess."

Murray continued, "That guy brought me out of the bushes and made me get down on my knees while he called inside and reported what he'd found. About three minutes later, Mr. Vanarious came out of the back door to his mansion. He was wearin' a nice pair of dark blue pajamers an' a bathrobe. Real expensive-lookin'. He approached me weird too, you know, with his hands behind his back."

"Why the hell did he do that?"

"I don't know… I think he was deep in thought, tryin' to figure out what to do with me. When he stepped in front of me, I just lost it and started beggin' for my life. I told him that I hadn't seen anythin' and if I had seen somethin', I promised I wouldn't tell nobody. He said, and I will never forget these words, 'I know you won't say anything because you won't be able to.' I said, 'What the fuck you mean by that?' And he just simply rotated his arm around from behind his back and leveled the gun he was holdin' and placed it against my forehead and pulled the trigger."

James's head jerked to the side so quick it was as though he'd actually been shot in the head. He stared at Murray in dumb confusion.

Smiling broadly, Murray continued, "The bullet that was shot blew out the back of my skull—" but he couldn't finish the sentence and started laughing hysterically. Oh, it felt good to pull one over on James, who had in many ways over the years caused him to bear the brunt of so many jokes.

"Oh, you fucking son-of-a-bitch," James said.

Through his laughter, Murray managed to yell, "I story-sniped you, bitch!"

"You piece of shit asshole."

Murray continued laughing through James's tirade of obscenities.

"You lying whore." James was more pissed at himself for being led on this wild-goose chase than he was at Murray.

"You jus' got story-sniped. I own you. All those times you got me. I gotchu. I gotchu good. Wait till the Dewitts and Sam hear about this."

"Ha-ha. Very nicely done. That was a good one. You had me going. You should be a damn writer, the way you got me on that one."

The ruckus of Murray's joke and James's anger at being played finally died down. Eventually, they settled back into their quiet fishing modes again, although a snort of laughter escaped Murray's lips every now and again.

They caught a few, lost a few, kept a few, and threw some back. They talked of things going on in each other's lives, chatted about different football and baseball teams, and vented their frustrations with the players of each of those teams and their wins and losses.

When they had done all they could at Foster's Cove, they reeled in their lines. James geared the boat up and moved it to another part of the lake, where they did more of the same. Morning turned into noon and noon to mid-afternoon. They fished for a while in that spot, which brought some pretty big and exciting catches. Eventually, James moved the boat again. The waters here were darker, which meant they were deeper. It was calm and serene; a prime fishing spot for some major whoppers.

The shoreline in the vicinity was undeveloped, with no houses adorning it. There was just lush vegetation and tall trees peppered throughout.

James thought, *It's just a matter of time before new houses crop up all over that area. It would be a big moneymaker for some developers to buy up the land.*

The two men baited and cast their lines again. They fished for a while, and both had some minor nibbles at their bait.

Murray, thinking that his line had probably been in for too long and might need some new bait, reeled it in just to check. When it came out of the water, he saw his bait had been stolen. *Jesus Christ,* he thought. *How long has my line been down there without any bait on it? What a complete waste of time. Maybe it was nabbed durin' that last small tug. But that wasn't a very hard pull. Makes no damn sense.*

"Damn it! Buncha crooks," he muttered to himself. He reached into the cooler, pulled out the last dead fish, and attached it onto his hook. He rotated his pole behind him and made a half-assed cast. The fish dropped a few yards from the boat.

In less than a minute, his bait was snagged, and something ran with it. Murray reflexively jerked back hard on his pole. He felt the line grab and knew he'd hooked whatever had snagged his lure. But instead of being able to reel the line back in, it began to sing as it retreated away from him.

Startled, Murray began to furiously reel in his line, but this beast was pulling drag, and he was losing ground to it. It wasn't like any of the other large fish he'd caught in the past. Murray had the unsettling feeling that whatever he'd hooked was unusually large. He wasn't getting any traction with it, instead losing a great deal of line. He continued to fight with the fish, but was unable to reel him in. A few times, he almost lost his balance and was pulled forward out of the boat.

"Ain't gwonna get me like you did Old Bags, motherfucker," Murray said under his breath. "It jus' ain't gwonna happen."

At last—to Murray's astonishment—the fish turned back and headed straight for the boat. Reeling in the leviathan became easier, and Murray gave a thankful prayer for this strange turn of events. He wound the reel as fast and hard as could, but he saw the line getting closer to the hull, which unnerved him even more.

As the line drew near to the boat, the back of a monster fish crested out of the water. Murray and James didn't see its full head, but observed the oblong width and girth of the monstrosity; it told them instantly that Murray had bitten off more than he could chew.

Murray stared in wide-eyed wonder at its sheer size. It had to be Methuselah. He'd never seen a fish in these waters as big as the dark shape he'd just glimpsed. He gulped awkwardly, as though he were still eating his Chick-fil-A bagel sandwich.

James's eyes bulged in their sockets as this urban legend materialized right before him. He simultaneously disbelieved what he was seeing and couldn't discredit it. It was no trick of reflection in the water or anomaly playing tricks on his senses. This creature was big, huge, vast, and there was just enough time to grasp all of these facts before the enormous fish disappeared into the lake's depths with a vicious flick of its tail.

"He's goin' under the boat!" Murray exclaimed. He looked down over the side of the boat to follow his line.

"Unbelievable. I don't understand it. Fish always swim away from a boat, not toward it."

"Not this one. He's pretty pissed."

"Well, pull him out from under it and back to your side. You'll never get him if you don't."

"You think I don't know that? You saw how big he was. He was big as a car. He ain't doin' nothin' on account of me. I'm followin' his lead." Murray stepped to the back of the boat and pulled as hard as he could, trying to guide the fish back to the starboard side. The line was drawn as taut as it could go, and the pole bent in a severe 'U' shape.

"Well, if you don't get him back to this side you're going to lose your pole, or your line is going to—"

With a loud twang, the line snapped cleanly. Murray, who had been pulling hard, fell backward. His pole whipped in a fast arc and slapped hard against the port side of the boat's hull as he landed flat on his back. He released his pole, quickly rolled over, scrambled to the port side, and joined James, who was looking down into the water, waiting to see the fish from that side.

The boat rose a little way out of the water as the top of this fish's body scraped against the hull. James and Murray saw the dark grey shadow of something colossal right as it dove for deeper water. The scene was so ominous to both men that their hair stood on end.

"No fuckin' way," Murray said with awe in his voice.

"That was a big fucking fish."

"No shit. Did you see the size of the head on that thang? There's no way we're gwonna catch him with our poles."

As they searched the water, trying to see deep into the lake's gloom, James was secretly happy he'd added the downrigger to his boat. It was definitely the only chance they had at catching this leviathan.

They stood mesmerized, staring straight down at where the fish had disappeared, wondering if what they had seen was actually real or a figment of their imaginations. Before they realized it, that same shape was moving back up toward them. They only registered it just before the fish broke the surface of the water, a dark apparition that caused them to jerk upright and away in alarm.

As the fish's colossal head and open mouth surfaced, a significant release of air wafted over them. James and Murray grimaced at the stench and stepped away from the creature with caution, almost tripping over Murray's discarded rod and reel. They stood there in a reverent hush, disbelieving but mesmerized by what floated about six feet in front of them.

Methuselah's head floated like a swimmer treading water; he was working hard to keep it above water as he gazed fixedly at them. Methuselah seemed to be staring directly at Murray. But then, almost immediately, the fish turned slightly with a flick of his tail and fins and shifted his viewpoint to James. It looked as though Methuselah was as awestruck as they were.

"Why's he lookin' at us like that?" Murray whispered.

"I have no idea."

"I don't like the way he's starin' at us."

"Me either. Look at his fucking lips," James whispered back.

"Guess Maynard was right after all."

"Yeah."

Methuselah's fat lips did seem bloated with numerous hooks and a few random lures that had been snagged into him. There were even a few bobbers attached to lines coming out the sides of his mouth. Murray saw his own tackle, and the broken fishing line, had been added to the mix. The colors on most of the lures had faded, and many of the hooks had rusted over. And, as Maynard had stated and Murray had imagined, there was some sort of yellowish pus leaking from around the worst cases.

"Jesus Christ, he's ugly as shit," James whispered. "And that shit around his lips is really disgusting."

"Holy hell, why ain't I recordin' this?" Murray demanded as he reached for his phone a little too hastily. He pulled it from his front pocket and tapped the front screen to get to his camera.

By the time he got to the camera to film mode, Methuselah looked between the two men twice and then dove underwater again. To James, it almost looked like Methuselah was shaking his head against them catching any part of him on film. His dingy grey body rotated out of the water, and they got a better judgment of the beast's length and girth. Methuselah's mighty tail arched out of the water, and then with a powerful swish, he disappeared under the lake's surface again.

Murray had hit the record button, but only managed to film a grayish shape in dark water surrounded by splashes. It would be just like the people who had claimed to have caught footage or pictures of the famous Loch Ness Monster, only this time it would be in color.

"Fucking hell," he shouted when the fish was gone. He placed his phone on a small shelf behind the center console unit, then turned to grab his discarded rod. "What the hell do we do now?"

James was deep in thought, but said, "I don't know, but we're definitely gonna need some bigger bait."

"We ain't got no more. We used the last bit of it up on that last cast. Unless we use a couple of big fish we've caught as bait."

James wondered to himself, *Catch a big fish to catch an even bigger fish?* He began thinking of catfish and what kind of bait they were attracted to. Murray saw James's mind working overtime.

"What're you thinkin' about?"

"Nothing, just wondering how we can trick that big bastard."

Murray moved to the front of the boat, straining his eyes to see if he could catch any hint of the giant water-beast gliding underneath them. Meanwhile, as James searched for the answer, his eyes fell on the new fishing pole trawler contraption that he'd bolted to the deck.

Murray exclaimed, "Thar he is!" He was leaning over the bow, pointing into the water. "Jesus, that thing is ginormous. I don't know why more people haven't seen him. I mean, you can't miss that som'bitch."

James looked past his invention and refocused his eyes on Murray. A thought entered his mind. It was a hideous idea. Horrific. A terrible, evil idea that rooted him to the deck of the boat. He was afraid if he made any movement at all, his mind just might take him up on the suggested thought. Finally, he shook his head violently, and the idea went away— to a certain extent. It didn't completely leave; it still lurked there in the back of his mind, needling him. James hadn't even realized that as the grim thought was playing out, he had surveyed a full circle of the lake to see if anyone was in the vicinity.

"And now he's gone," Murray said. "He'll be back, hopefully. In the meantime, I'm going to step into the john and make a deposit into my account." Murray laughed at his shit joke as he disappeared below deck.

His cell phone began to vibrate. It was still sitting on the small platform behind the center console seat where he'd left it.

Forgetting that his iPhone was in his back pocket and thinking the vibrating phone was his own, James looked down and saw the name 'Virginia' on the screen. This wasn't alarming to him, and he leaned down and retrieved it. As he lifted the phone to his ear, he vaguely noticed that the picture of Virginia wasn't a photo of her he'd taken or even seen, for that matter. Still, this didn't register as alarming for the moment.

"Hey, babe, you've kinda caught me at a bad time. What's up?"

"Where are you?" Virginia said accusingly.

This attitude took James back a few steps. "What do you mean, *where am I?* I'm out here on Silver Ridge Lake fishing with Murray like I told you I was gonna be doing."

There was a moment of quiet. To James, it sort of felt like a guilty silence had set in on the other end. Then Virginia asked, "James? Is that you?"

"Uh, yeah, babe. It is me. That's who you dialed, isn't it? Who were you trying to get?"

There was another uncomfortable silence, but it wasn't as long as the original one. "Uh, nobody. I mean, sorry. I think I dialed the wrong number. I was trying to reach… Alice? Yes. Alice. Oh, I know what I did. I hit Murray's number instead. Their numbers are right next to each other on my phone. Same last name and all."

The picture finally registered in James's mind. *Must've been one Murray took with this phone when they were together*, James thought. Those last four words repeated again in James's mind, but at a louder volume. *When they were together.* He'd picked up Murray's phone, he realized.

Virginia continued, "Alice was going to come by here today while you two were out fishing, but she's not here yet. I was just trying to reach her to find out if she's alright."

"Okay," James said, thinking hard on this new development. Something didn't quite add up.

"Okay, *what*?"

"I don't know, babe. You tell me. You and Alice aren't really the best of friends. You hardly ever meet up or even talk to each other unless Murray and I are meeting, and you two just happen to be tagging along. Why the sudden change?"

Virginia's voice became defensive. "What's wrong with us getting together while you two are fishing?"

"Oh, nothing; I think it's great. I'm just shocked, that's all. I thought it would've been something you might've mentioned to me, is all."

"Honey, I don't tell you everything I do."

The statement hit James in an odd way. *Why would she say that to me?* He mulled her words over in his mind. *If you don't tell me everything you do,* he thought, *what are you doing that you're not telling me about?*

Virginia's voice came back on the line and brought James back to the present. "Sorry, James, my day is a little messed up because she hasn't shown up yet. I'm just frustrated with her."

She *hasn't shown up? Or Murray hasn't shown up yet?* He played it off for now.

"I do know what you mean. It's kind of like when Murray doesn't show up on the days we have plans because of his all-night drinking benders."

"Exactly." She hesitated, then tentatively asked, "Is Murray there?"

"Oh, yeah. He's here."

"Could I speak to him for a minute? I was just wondering if he knew what she was planning on doing today."

Something about the way she asked told him everything he needed to know.

"Um, well, he's kinda taking a shit in the bowels of the boat right now. Let me see if I can get him for you." When he lowered the phone from his ear, he glanced at it. He retrieved his own phone from its dwelling place and examined them both. They were both iPhone 10s. *That's weird*, he thought. *Identical phones.*

The door to the small bathroom opened again, and Murray climbed out. "Well, that one was quick. It jus' slid right out of my asshole, pretty as you please." He gave a sarcastic laugh at his own crudeness. "Almost didn't have to wipe my ass, it came out so perfectly. But I did, just as a precaution against an itchy butthole." He laughed even more as he lowered the galley roof. He turned and saw James staring down at something in each of his hands. Curiosity got the best of him; he stepped toward James and asked, "What'cha looking at? Something wrong?"

James turned to him as he slid his own iPhone 10 into the front pocket of his shorts. "Phone call for you," he said, then, "It's, uh, *my wife.*"

"Your wife?" Murray gave a little nervous chuckle. "What the hell does she want?"

"I don't know. I'm a little confused as to why she was calling *you* in the first place. You can let me know that when you're finished talking to her. Something about wanting to know where Alice is. Said they were going to meet today at some point while we were fishing? You know anything about that?"

Murray immediately started nodding and waved his arm as he reached out to take the phone from James. "Yeah, oh yeah, yeah, Alice mentioned somethin' to me about that when she dropped me off this mornin'. She not there yet?"

James said, "Apparently not, since my wife is calling *you* on your new cell phone."

Murray tried to grab the phone, but James's firm grip caused him to look up again. Their eyes met and held for a moment. Murray's were the ones that shifted away first. He added a little more tension and tentatively pulled the phone from James's tight grip. He put it to his ear, turned away from James, and stepped to the front of the boat again.

"Hey," Murray whispered.

"What the hell, Murray?"

"What?"

"You said you weren't going fishing today. You said you were coming by the house. Why didn't you let me know something?"

"I sent you a text message this mornin' tellin' you the plans for today were off and that I would explain everythin' later. You didn't get it?"

"No. I surely did *not* get your message. Why did you go fishing?"

"Alice and I got into a huge fight this mornin'. She was accusin' me of screwing around on her."

"Well, you are, Murray. With *me*. But *someone* didn't bother to tell me about this sudden change of plans. I've been waiting here all morning, thinking you were going to show up at any moment. Wasted the whole morning and part of the afternoon waiting on you. And then *I* call *you*, thinking you're nowhere near James, and he's the one who picks up your fucking phone! Why are you out there with him?"

"I had to go. It was the only excuse I could give Alice to get off the hook she had me wriggling on. She knew I wasn't goin' to be with anyone else, because she had to drive me here. She saw me get on the boat, and us leave the dock."

"But you didn't bother to tell me?"

"I'm telling you, I sent you a message. I don't know why it didn't go through. Could be the signal where we are is off, or somethin'."

"Whatever. It doesn't matter now. I see that fishing is a little more important to you than me."

"Don't do this. Don't be like this. My truck wouldn't start this mornin', so she had to drop me off at the pier. I barely got here in time before James left."

An exasperated breath. "You think James knows anything is going on between us?"

Murray looked around briefly and saw James messing with his new trawler. He turned back around to look out at the lake water.

"No, I don't think so; he's busy messing around with that dumbass outrigger he added to his boat. Thinks he's gwonna catch Methuseler with that damn thing."

"Well, I better go before he gets suspicious about why we're talking for so long."

"Sure. That makes sense. We'll get together soon." He raised his voice so James could hear him. "And when you hear from Alice, tell her to call me, okay?"

"I'll be sure to do that."

Murray hung up the phone, then immediately clicked on his text messages. The conversation between him and Virginia opened up again, and the text message he'd thought he had sent to Virginia sat waiting.

MS: Hey, girly. Can't meet today. I had to go fishing with James as originally planned. Not really my choice. I'll explain it all later when I see you. You go do something fun since I can't be there with you today. Sorry. I'll see you soon.

He remembered back to when James had asked him to untie the ropes from the dock. In his haste to untie them, he'd punched send but probably hadn't made complete contact with the icon or hadn't applied enough pressure, and the message had never been sent. Murray cursed himself for being so stupid and in such a hurry. In disgust, he deleted the unsent message and shoved his phone into his front pocket again.

"You get everything worked out with Virginia?" James asked. There was no suspicion in his voice—just a natural conversational tone.

"Huh?" Murray said, turning to James. "Oh, yeah. I's just tellin' Virginia that Alice went to see her momma over at Breckenridge today instead. She'd told me this mornin' on the way to the marina that she was plannin' on goin'. Guess she just forgot to tell Virginia. Alice probably just forgot to call her. She prob'ly has her phone turned off is the reason Virginia couldn't get a holt of her."

"Oh, really?"

"Yeah, why?"

"Did Alice follow any army transport on her way to Breckenridge?"

"What?" Murray said, not following.

"Did Alice stop to watch someone drop some rusty fifty-five-gallon drums of growth hormone animal test subjects into the Silver Ridge

Lake? Because what it sounds like is that you're just giving me another horse-shit story like you did earlier today."

"Naw, man. What are you talkin' 'bout? That was jus' a joke story."

"Is it, Murray? It's just a snipe joke story?"

"Yeah, man. Honest to God. I was just foolin' with ya."

"Just seems weird to *me*... that our wives don't really associate with each other unless they have to, and I just now find out today that they had plans to *hang out* with each other after my wife calls you on your cell phone. A cell phone that is exactly the same as mine."

"What's so weird about that?" Murray asked. "I think it's good they're gettin' together. That's good, ain't it? You have to start somewheres, right?"

"Oh, yeah. You have to start *somewhere*."

Murray stepped to the part of the boat that was the furthest away from James, who watched him go. *He's avoiding the situation.* If anything screamed guilt, that was it. His eyes narrowed as he thought about what had come to light, then he said, "Hey, Murray. I'm going to ask you one question, and I want the truth, no matter how hard it may be to tell me. Okay?"

Murray knew what was coming, but he played dumb. "Sure. Okay."

"Are you and Virginia fucking around with each other behind my back?"

Murray immediately started laughing at the accusation. "See, I knew you were gwonna ask that. I knew you were gwonna be suspicious of that. Hell no, man. I wouldn't do that to you!"

"Then why is she calling you?"

"She wanted to know where Alice is. Honest. They was gettin' together today for some goddamn reason or another. I didn't ask her why, though it would be interesting to know."

"Alice and Virginia getting together? That doesn't seem odd to you?"

"Yeah, a little, maybe, but I don't see what's so wrong with it."

"Nothing wrong with it. It just seems odd she was calling you about Alice."

"Well, she is my wife. I guess she thought I might know where Alice was."

James switched gears on him. "When did you get your phone?"

"My what?"

"Don't play dumb. You heard me. Your *phone*. Your new iPhone 10. When did you get it?"

"I don't know. A few days ago. Alice got it for me. Said she thought it might help me think to call her more often when I'm out."

"A few days ago, huh?" James began to think. *If Murray's lying to me… Virginia actually gave* him *the phone. Virginia gave him his before she even gave me mine.* His anger was building up inside, but he was careful to not let it show outwardly. "So," he said, pulling his phone from his pocket and holding it up. "If I call Alice right now and ask her if she gave you a new cell phone, she would confirm it?"

There was a long, pregnant pause, then an audible gulp from Murray. And there it was: the famous cough before the lie.

Murray was tense and noticeably nervous, but then he straightened. He placed his hands on his hips and looked James in the eye. He nodded.

"Sure. Yeah. Go ahead and call her if you like. I'll wait. But my question is, why do you need Alice's number in your phone? Are you fucking my wife behind my back?"

"Maybe so, Murray. Maybe I am." They locked eyes with each other, then James said firmly, "The reason I have your wife's number on my phone is to keep tabs on *you,* since you're always late whenever we make plans to do anything. I always call her to find out if you're going to be a no-show or not. She calls me when she's worried about you, after you've been out drinking at all hours of the night. It's only because of you, Murray. Only because of you."

Murray called his bluff. "Oh, really, James? Is it really all because of me?"

James ignored him and countered. "Just so you know, I don't think *Alice* gave you your phone. I think *Virginia* gave it to you, because *my wife* gave me one of my own." James angled his phone for Murray to see it better.

"Oh. Oh, shit."

"What do you mean by 'oh, oh shit'? Did Virginia forget to mention to you that she got me one of my own?"

"Yeah—I mean—fuck."

James smiled grimly. "That's the key word and action in this conversation, isn't it? Whether or not you're fucking my wife. And these things," he said, wagging his phone by his face again, "are her way of keeping tabs on us, I guess. What are we going to do about this situation, huh?"

"Look, James, before you do anything crazy, just let me explain."

"Who said anything about me doing anything crazy? We're just talking here. I just wanted to know if it was true."

"Well, Virginia and I, we was—"

James released a huge breath of air, as though he'd been holding it for a while. To Murray, it seemed to contain a lot of relief. James cut him off before he could get too far into his explanation.

"I don't want to hear it, Murray. I don't need the play-by-play of what you and my wife do when you two are together. I just wanted a yes or no answer, and I just got my answer."

"So that's it?"

"Yeah, that's it," James said evenly, and turned away. "I'll deal with all of this in my own way."

Just like I have, Murray thought as he stared at James. *I should confront him about what I know to be goin' on between him and Alice, but I've never been able to bring it up.*

Instead, he asked, "Are you mad at me?"

James was looking out over the boat's motors and taking in the surrounding lake vista. When he heard Murray's dumbass question, a seething breath of air escaped his clenched teeth. He took a moment to compose himself, then turned to look back at Murray. A slight smile crept onto his lips.

"No, Murray, I'm not mad at you," James lied. "If I wanted anyone fucking my wife, I would want it to be my best friend, right?"

"Yeah, I guess. Me too," Murray said with a knowing smile.

Murray's phrasing struck James in an odd way, and he couldn't hide his immediate thought process. It came out on his face before he could mask it. *Does he know about Alice and me? Surely not. Fuck, this is such a weird conversation.*

Murray turned away and stepped toward the back of the boat.

As James watched him go, he thought about Virginia, the woman he loved… to a certain extent. If he really searched his heart, he knew he wasn't happy; neither of them were. He and Virginia were more or less just roommates now. They used to be crazy in love, he knew that, but somewhere over the years, they had slowly drifted apart. It had started with an argument where both parties felt they were in the right, and neither one of them had ever offered an apology. More arguments over stupid subjects had caused them to drift even farther apart until they both realized they were more distant than they could have imagined.

They both knew it would be too much work to even try to get back to what they had once had. James would never have admitted it, but he felt a secret, bitter hatred towards Virginia sometimes. His marriage was a failure, and this relationship was doomed; more to the point, he knew it was already over. That inward bitterness had festered deep inside him, and now it was permeating his whole body.

James wondered whether Murray was trying to see Methuselah, if by a slim chance he had come back around to the back to the stern. Maybe a little distance was what they needed; they needed a lot more than this boat could give them, but they were stuck here until the fishing trip was over. Maybe they should call it a day.

The evil plan that had occurred to him earlier clicked inside his head as the boiling rage bubbled to the surface.

Moving about without any real conscious decision or effort, James felt himself turn to the downrigger. As if in a dream, he saw himself bend to pick up the hook, which was lying at the base of the metal pole he'd anchored to the deck. Without any hesitation, he grabbed the handle that was tied to the rope line and snatched it up, then turned back to Murray. James raised the hook high as he cleared the distance between them and slapped it down on Murray's left shoulder.

At first, Murray didn't know what had hit him; it startled him but didn't completely alarm him. He glanced to his left and saw the metal hook—the sleekness of the hardened steel, the sharpness of the point— and his heart sank, his body instantly engulfed in fear.

"What the—"

But James had already placed his left hand on Murray's back. With a mighty yank of his right hand, he jerked the hook back toward himself. The hook was sharp, and easily stabbed through the top of Murray's pectoral muscle.

Murray let out an unearthly yell of agony as he dropped to the deck of the ship and squirmed around as if in an epileptic fit. "Oh Jesus, James! NO!" he yelled. He was writhing as though a faith healer had just hit him with the Holy Ghost's healing power. "What the fuck are you doin'?"

"I told you I would deal with all this in my own way. Well, this is me dealing with it."

"Jesus. God, no. Please," Murray begged.

The hook had not yet come through Murray's back as expected, and James realized that it had stopped when it had hit Murray's shoulder blade.

James was having a hard time controlling his bait. Murray was flapping around worse than a fish an angler was trying to get off a hook. James leaned over and punched him in the face. This seemed to daze Murray a bit. Since James was standing above him, he simply jerked up on the hook to maintain his balance. The hook point turned upward as it scraped along the inside of Murray's shoulder blade and finally punched through and out the top of his shoulder muscle.

Murray continued to wriggle and flop around on the deck of the ship, but James kept pulling up on the hook, not allowing him to escape.

James was mentally assessing the situation as he held Murray down. He looked to the back of the ship, wondering how far away the fish had gone. *Is Methuselah still around? Is there still time? Did I just fuck my life up doing this to Murray? Shit, this is the lowest thing I've ever done. Fuck it! Too late now.*

"Oh, Jesus Christ, James, what the fuck are you doin'?" Murray bellowed.

"I'm goin' fishing. Remember when I said we needed bigger bait?" James didn't give Murray time to answer. "Well, guess what? You're the fucking bait." He jerked Murray up by the hook with one hand and grabbed his shirt with the other.

Murray, desperate to get loose, punched, slapped and kicked at

James, but James had too much control over his body, holding him in submission by the handle of the hook.

James awkwardly shuffle-stepped to the controls with his unruly burden and turned on the ignition switch. He pushed the throttle forward. The engines turned on and kicked into a slightly higher gear as the propellers began to spin. The boat started to move away from the spot where they were currently floating.

"What the fuck are you doin' this?" Murray yelled as he struggled against James, who was pulling him to the back of the boat. "This really has nothin' to do with fishin', does it? This is all about Virginia, isn't it?"

James said, "Sort of. You've heard the saying 'kill two birds with one stone.' Well, I'm dealing with two problems with one piece of bait." Not wanting to discuss the subject any longer, he shoved Murray again to the stern.

"We ain't ready to cetch a fish this size, James," Murray said in a defeated voice. "No one in this marina is ready to take on that beast."

James jerked him up and closer to his face. "You're gonna get out there, and he's gonna come for you. You're going to hook him, and I'm gonna reel him in, then I'm going to celebrate."

"Wadder yer mean, celebrate?" Murray said as he reached up and feebly tried to unhook himself from the contraption that James had skewered him with.

James grabbed his hand and flung it away from the hook. "C'mon now, don't do that."

"I don't wanna celebrate with you, you asshole," Murray blubbered. "I'm gwonna take this hook and—" he reached for it again, but his hand fell. "And... and I'm gwonna shove it up your ass, you fucker."

"No, you're not. You're going to do nothing of the sort. You're gonna get out there and hook me that fucking fish."

James made a movement to shove Murray overboard. Murray winced in agony, yelled out, and crouched as low as he could to stop the action. James countered again instantly, grabbed hold of his shirt with one hand and his arm with his other, took a half-turn, and flung Murray out of the boat.

"And don't come back until you do!" he yelled.

He stepped to the contraption and flipped the lock mechanism switch on it. As the boat moved away, James unreeled more rope as it pulled Murray along. There wasn't a lot of slack because of Murray's body weight and the tension James was keeping on the line. There was also enough pulling pressure to keep Murray from being able to unhook himself. He was flailing around in the water, barely being dragged along.

"C'mon, you big fucker," James said, surveying the waters. "Where are you? I have a big morsel for you to take in." He pulled the gear up to neutral, and the boat stopped but continued to idle. Feeling like there was enough slack in the line, he put the lock mechanism back into place.

When the boat stopped, the pain pulling on Murray's shoulder eased slightly, and he was left floating on the water.

"Help!" Murray yelled as he feebly splashed around with one arm. He couldn't raise the other above his head. He continued to shout non-sensical pleas for anyone to come to his aid.

Nothing was happening on the surface; everything was still except for Murray's splashing around.

James said, "Good. That's good, Murray! Splash all you want! Get that dumb bastard's attention!" He moved the throttle up into the half-way point again. The boat picked up speed, and the hook in Murray's shoulder jerked against his clavicle.

The pain levels in Murray's body went into overdrive, and he yelled out loud and long. To alleviate the agony as much as he could, he grabbed on to the hook for dear life and pulled back on it to quell the extreme discomfort in his shoulder.

James dragged Murray the length of a football field to get a consistent drag and tease with his bait, then he pulled the throttle back to neutral again. The boat rode the swell of water that caught up with them, then settled back on the lake's surface.

James hoped that the combination of Murray's thrashing and his dragging Murray across the water would be enough to attract Methuselah's attention, but he was really beginning to doubt the choices he'd made. *Would a fish that big really eat a man whole? It's not the usual way to get them to bite. Methuselah looks more like a catfish, and most catfish trawl the bottom of the lakes for the dead bait that's just sitting down there. Jesus, am I going about this all wrong? What the fuck was I thinking? How is this downrigger I've invented going to actually hook him? Most of the hook is in Murray—definitely not enough to get Methuselah. That will all have to be Murray's doing, if he's smart enough.*

Murray's mind, on the other hand, was going ballistic. *What did I do to deserve this? I know I've had some moments with Virginia, but it's not worth killin' me over, is it? Is a fuckin' fish worth breakin' up our friendship over? I swear to God if I ever get out of this alive, I'm gwonna fuckin' kill him ba—*

Murray felt something clamp down on his ankle and give it a hard jerk.

"What the fuck?" he yelled, then thought, *Jesus, that's tight.* He spun around in the direction he had been pulled and instinctively kicked out with his other foot. He made contact with something fleshy, and it was a pretty big object from what he could tell. His leg and foot being under-water didn't allow for any real force, but whatever he had kicked had let go of his ankle.

Something grabbed hold of his other foot and jerked back even harder. Murray was pulled beneath the surface of the water. He barely had time to catch a new breath of air. He turned his head in the direction he'd been pulled.

Methuselah was right there in front of him in all his glory, a vast, ugly monstrosity not entirely concealed by the lake water. There was just enough of his bulkiness revealed by the mid-afternoon sun for Murray to witness him.

Murray screamed in fear, and at the sheer size and grandeur of the fish, expelling the last bit of air from his lungs. He kicked out again, and Methuselah let go of him, angled his big body away, and disappeared into the deeper darkness of the lake waters.

Murray desperately needed air. He frantically scrambled for the sur-face, but hadn't realized he'd been jerked so far under. He opened his mouth as he broke through the water's surface and breathed in deeply. He got a half-breath of air and an equal half-mouthful of disgusting lake water. He spluttered against the muddy taste—like stale rain infused with mold—as the eerie intuition that he just might drown out here began to set in.

Drowned first, then eaten, he thought with a hopeless dread.

Something struck him in the center of his back. Again, he spun in the direction of what had hit him. All he saw was the big dark grey body of the giant creature circle away from him with a hard swish of his tail. Water slapped him in the face as the fish retreated.

He's toyin' with me, Murray thought. *Like those type fish do with bait. Jesus Christ, he's gwonna toy with me until he drowns me.* A thought hit him square in his head. *Is this what my life turned out to be? Is this all I amounted to? Just a meal for some big ol' dumb fish. Fuck that. I'm not dyin' out here toda—*

Another hard hit to his back. It pushed him about five feet across the surface before the creature turned and angled away again.

I hafta get away from this thang, Murray thought. He had a bright idea.

"James! Punch it!" he yelled, giving James the best 'go forward' motion that he could deliver. The thing was nibbling at his ankle again. Then, all of a sudden, its mouth was all the way up to the middle of his thigh.

"FUCK!" Murray yelled as he kicked out with his other leg. He barely had enough room to maneuver as he placed his foot on the fish's bottom lip and stomped down as hard as he could. Panic consumed him, and tears of fear poured from his eyes. Desperation gripped him as tightly as Methuselah as he yelled out again. "James! For the love of God! Floor it!" He gave him the frantic 'go forward' motion again.

James was looking back, and had seen a blur of black crest out of the water. Even from this distance, it startled and also scared him a little for Murray's sake. He saw Murray's frantic arm motion and wondered, *Does he want me to go forward? Is that what he's tellin' me? Okay, hang on to your ass.*

The thought came to James that Murray didn't have much choice in the matter.

He pushed the lever out of neutral and slowly up to half speed. The boat began to move away, which pulled the slack out of the rope.

Murray breathed an inward sign of relief. *Thank God, James got my messa—*

The vice grip of pain tightened in Murray's shoulder as he was dragged along, face-down in the water. He kicked his body over so he could at least breathe while he tried to unhook himself before Methuselah came back around and took him all the way in. Murray moved his arms up and grabbed the hook as best he could, holding on as the pain ratcheted up. His shoulder was going to be fucked up for the rest for his life, thanks to James. It was a wonder his collarbone hadn't been broken with the crazy amount of force that had been put on it. *I'm still going to kill James for doing this,* Murray promised himself.

After James had traveled about the length of two football fields, he dropped it back down to neutral again. *Let's see what that gets us. C'mon, Murray, don't let me down.*

As soon as the force pulling Murray stopped, he swiftly gave the hook a tough, clean pull downward in a counter-clockwise motion that brought the hook completely out. And, oh, Jesus, did it hurt. Hell was definitely a place, and that place was in the center of his shoulder. The trauma nearly caused him to pass out as he fought against the agony. His life depended on him staying awake. Murray was overwhelmingly glad that this hook didn't have a barb on the opposite side like most fish-hooks.

He continued to grasp the hook and rope for dear life. If he let go now, he would never get back to the boat. This was the only lifeline he had.

Come at me one more time, you ugly piecea shit, Murray thought. *I'm gwonna hook you, and I'm gwonna hook you hard. And then I'm gwonna kill James. And then I'm gwonna go home and make love to two ladies.*

There was a splash behind Murray, and he turned. Methuselah was right there, cresting halfway out of the water and coming down on Murray with the front half of his body. The ugly open mouth was working up and down as though Methuselah hadn't eaten in months, and Murray was the only meal in sight. The weight dropping on him wasn't something he'd expected, and he almost passed out again from the combination of fear and shock. Once underwater, the fish readjusted and came at Murray again. And Murray, putting his plan in action, allowed himself to be eaten.

The fish snatched at him three times; first, when its mouth closed down around his calves, then again when it took him in up to his thighs, and a final time when it moved up and clamped down around his waist.

Methuselah didn't seem to have any teeth, as is the case with catfish, but the inside rim of his mouth was as coarse as Brillo pads. Gigantic as he was, the texture felt like a cheese grater scraping across Murray's skin. Every time Methuselah closed his mouth, it was like the extremely powerful and tight hugs he remembered receiving from his grandmother as a child. Boa-constrictor tight, crushing, and almost suffocating.

Jesus, I'm glad I ain't battlin' no goddamn shark. I would've already been done for. But this fucker is gwonna realize he's bitten off more than he can chew.

Murray frantically looked around and searched the fish's mouth for the best place to drive the hook home, but it was incredibly dark down here. He knew he had to hurry. One more jerk forward, and he would literally be fish food. He'd been a fisherman for most of his adult life, though, and his knowledge of fish anatomy kicked in. *There it is,* he thought. To him, everything appeared black and white like those Loch Ness Monster pictures from yesteryear. He rotated his body as best he could to the left side of the fish's mouth.

The fish took another gulp, and Murray was up to his chest.

Fuck! he thought. *I have to hook this som'bitch in some way.*

The fish was diving deep now. If he didn't get this hook in immediately, it would be ripped from his hands, and that would be all she wrote.

Placing the hook in what he thought was the best spot, Murray pushed hard with the palm of his left hand as he push-pulled with his right. His shoulder screamed in agony as he drove it home. *I hope you choke on this, you bastard.*

Methuselah lurched hard and angled upward.

Murray fought against the fish's quick movements, but couldn't manage to hold on to the hook. Methuselah's movement was hard and fast, and as he swam upward, Murray slid backward and down the short sliding board of the fish's gullet into his stomach. This was the one part Murray hadn't foreseen. An overwhelming sense of hopelessness overtook him as Methuselah thrashed out of Silver Ridge Lake and slapped his jaws shut.

James turned just in time to see Methuselah leap completely out of the water. He rose a good five to six feet above the lake's surface before he splashed back down.

"Mother of God!" James said aloud and in awe-struck wonder. "I got him!" He cheered as loudly and excitedly as he had ever done in his life. "I fucking got him! Murray came through for me. Holy fucking shit, we got you, you dumb bastard!" Peals of laughter erupted from him as James danced around the cabin of the boat for a second or two. Then he became serious again. *Hooked him, but not totally caught him.*

James wheeled to the controls and threw the lever from neutral into some sort of forward motion. He didn't realize just how far he'd thrown the throttle because he was already turning back to the reel he'd invented, starting to try and reel Methuselah to him in some way. The motors revved hard. Because of Methuselah's weight, when the propellers hit that abrupt high gear, the boat's back end was forced straight down into the water. They weren't gaining enough forward motion.

James noticed the lowering stern was dangerously close to dropping below the waterline. He frantically moved to the controls and pulled the throttle back to neutral. The boat slowed and returned to its original position. Trying again, he moved the throttle forward but at a much lower register. It was easier going at a slower pace, but there was a bigger chance of the creature shaking himself off the hook. The boat pulled ahead at a sluggish pace, dragging a thrashing Methuselah behind it. James continued to reel his prey in as best he could, but the fish's weight made it tough, and Methuselah was fighting hard to get loose. James continued to ramp up the speed, and eventually, he was towing and reeling in his gigantic catch.

∽

Utter darkness surrounded Murray when he splashed down into a slimy, slightly rubbery cocoon. Murray wasn't disoriented; he knew he was in Methuselah's stomach.

The stench that hit his nostrils upon arrival was more than Murray could take. Two whiffs of this disgusting filth hole were some of the most ungodly odors he'd ever smelled. Such combinations as busted-open coffins mixed with construction-worker porta-potties or mass graves unearthed in a landfill coupled with manure and compost didn't do this hell justice. It smelled of death, and his stomach turned over and threatened to release what was inside. He clenched his teeth and choked back the vomit.

There was barely any room to move. As he turned over, his shoulder scraped against the greasy, cushiony roof of this prison. Something sharp ripped his soaked shirt and sliced his skin. He winced at the pain as he focused on composing himself.

The thrashing of this monstrosity was doing a number on his stomach. He'd been a fisherman most of his life and had been out on many boats—even deep-sea fishing charters—and he'd never had any experience with being seasick, but his stomach was rolling hard now. Murray finally lost control, and everything within him spewed out into Methuselah's belly. He retched again, and the last of the chicken, egg, and cheese bagel and Coke from Chick-fil-A came up and out. It didn't taste as good the second time around; he grimaced and spat his mouth as clean as he could.

There didn't seem to be much air down here, and he took deep breaths through his mouth to pull more into his lungs. This brought more of the putrid stench and hot fumes of whatever made up the contents of Methuselah's belly. Murray continued to dry heave, and he hoped and prayed that this big motherfucker would do the same for him.

Murray's hands kept feeling a strange texture, like multiple strands of cotton thread across each other. His body involuntarily shuddered against the feeling, but his mind couldn't latch on to what the strands actually were.

He turned completely over and tried to kneel, but there was no room. The roof pressed hard into his shoulders and along with it, sharp spikes pressed against his back. He gritted his teeth against the needle pricks and tried to crawl back up Methuselah's slimy esophagus. Before he could, Methuselah lurched hard, and Murray was pitched against one of the walls of this creature's belly. Something slashed his arm. Actually, two somethings.

"Ow, shit! God damn it. Fuck! What are those things?"

Something splashed in the muck around his thighs; make that a few things. He couldn't see anything in here, it was so dark.

Was that a snake or another fish? What the—

The splashing came again, and something rubbed against his arm. It was scaly and slimy. Murray yelled out in alarm and punched near where the thing had tried to grab him. This action gained him more thin lacerations on his arm, and he pulled back against the stings.

Methuselah jerked again, and Murray was tumbling around as though he were in an automobile rolling ass-over-tea-kettle down a mountainside.

As Murray tumbled, something started biting him again. Little sharp slashes kept nipping at him, and it fucking hurt. Whatever was biting him, its small barbs kept digging in, pricking his skin, then pulling free as he was thrown in another direction. He knew he was bleeding in numerous places, especially around his shoulders and back, where James's hay-baling hook had punched through. He just wanted to be out of the fucking fish's body, and he begged God to make this creature sick enough to throw him up.

Finally, the thrashing and sharp movements were all Murray could take. He was slammed this way and that, nauseatingly dizzy, and he fell into an even deeper darkness as he submitted to unconsciousness.

James was on the deck of *The Big One*, observing the big one he had barely managed to pull aboard. He was leaning over with his hands on his knees, heaving ragged breaths of air. This battle with Methuselah had been the biggest and toughest he'd ever had with a single fish. His arms and shoulders were on fire, as though he'd done a thousand curls and shoulder presses with dumbbells that were slightly more than he could handle.

Winning this war had come down to two things. One was just

exhaustion and who would give up first. James had had a small advantage in that he had a lock mechanism on the spool piece, so he wasn't going to lose any line during the battle. He could take small breaks, but he'd had to watch Methuselah because that fish wasn't as dumb as James had initially thought. Methuselah kept trying to swim under the boat. The first and second time Methuselah tried that action, it had almost capsized *The Big One*. James had barely had time to run the ship out ahead of him to kill that severe angle of force Methuselah was trying to make. With each consecutive dive, James had gunned the boat again to counter Methuselah's move. This had angered Methuselah, who had thrashed harder.

The second reason for this win was being able to pull Methuselah aboard his boat. It had to be done, because Methuselah was going to keep fighting. That was inevitable. There was just no way James could get Methuselah close enough to the boat to do so, and Methuselah wouldn't keep still enough for him to try. It came down to a solid metal bar that James kept on the boat for self-defense. He'd never had to use it in a fight until now, and he never would've thought he would have to use it to catch Methuselah, but it was the only way to get him aboard. Using the bar as a lever to turn the spool piece, he had used his body weight to push down and pull up. Sometimes he placed the bar in the middle of the spool and cranked it like a tire iron, as though he were taking lug nuts off his truck.

Even then, he'd barely been able to raise Methuselah up high enough to pull him up out of the lake and onto the boat. But with one final, agonizing, full-body crank, the spool piece had turned just enough to where the bloated body of Methuselah moved high enough to swing free of the bow and drop to the back deck of the boat.

No one is going to believe this. But they'll have to, because I have living proof right here. I have to get him back and string him up on the pier scales and see how much this mother weighs.

Methuselah's head was closest to the main controls. His huge mouth was gaping open, working eagerly. His top fin was near the port side, lying upon the gunwale, and his belly was closest, nearly touching the starboard side. His tail was lying across the transom and up over the motor housings, hanging off the stern.

Unthinking, James leaned in close and stared deep into Methuselah's saucer-sized eyeball. "I got you. I got you, you ugly son-of-a-bitch."

Methuselah's huge eye rotated toward James and held his gaze for a moment; then the fish lurched on the boat, swung his monster head up toward James and snapped at him.

James jerked his head back just as the big fish's mouth snapped shut. The new and rusty fish-hooks from unlucky fishermen rattled faintly, like ghost chains in the attic of a haunted house.

"Oooohhh-who-who-whooooo boy!" James said, drawing out a surprised, relieved laugh. "That was close. You almost got me there, you fat fucker!" He let out a Ric Flair 'woo' yell and crouched in a low stance as he held out his arms before him, shooting the creature double middle-finger birds. "Fuck you, you piece-of-shit fish. I. Got. You. And I'm taking your ugly ass home."

James turned around and looked at the open water for any sign of Murray. Seeing only calm waters now, he felt a pang of guilt. Murray had probably drowned out there somewhere. He shook his head, turned, and carefully stepped to the controls.

He was about to crank the engines again and point *The Big One* back to port, but all of a sudden he felt extremely exhausted. He realized his heart was hammering against the inside of his chest as though he'd just drunk a gallon of espresso. He didn't feel as though he could make the trek back to the marina yet. He had to lie down, or he was simply going to collapse or have a heart attack.

Just a little nap will do me wonders, he thought.

He wondered about Methuselah and whether he would flap himself free while he went below for a snooze. The fish still had the hook embedded deep in its mouth, and James had the rope it was attached to reeled all the way in and locked. This bad boy wasn't going anywhere, even if he flapped around a little bit. James had been impressed that Murray had found a place to drive that hook home.

Confident that Methuselah would still be there after his power nap, James stepped below deck to the small bed in the bottom of the ship and immediately drifted off to sleep.

୶

Some time later, a nightmare dissipated from James's mind as he ripped himself awake. His best friend's name tore out of him in a scream as he sat up in the little bed below deck. His heart was beating arrhythmically, but that was nothing compared to the way it had been before this nap. This pounding only had to do with the terror of the dream. But the nightmare faded just as quickly as he awoke. There were no fragmented images to grasp on to—not that he really wanted to. Instead, he just clutched at his chest in desperation, scared of the unknown.

He pushed himself to the edge of the bed and placed his elbows on his knees. A pang of guilt unlike anything he'd ever felt seized his body. Whatever had happened between him and Murray could've been worked out, even if it broke up their friendship.

Murray didn't deserve what I did to him. Not by a long shot. But I can't go back and undo what I've done, even though now I wish I could.

James shook his head and forced Murray to another part of his mind. He sat up straighter. His whole body ached, as though he'd worked out too long and too hard. His arms hurt the worst, but parts of his legs, back, and shoulders were locked up as well. He slowly stretched them out to get the circulation moving within them better. He arched his back, and his vertebrae popped. It felt good—damn good.

He glanced at his watch and noticed it was close to 4:30am. He blinked in confusion.

"What the fuck?" he exclaimed. "Impossible." *When I stepped down here, the sun was just beginning to set. Did I sleep the entire night?*

He opened the cabin door and moved up a couple of steps to the main deck, only to be confronted by Methuselah's glassy-eyed, blank stare.

"Oh, Jesus Christ," James said as he stumble-stepped backward, almost tripping back into the bedroom area. "You scared me." *That was spooky.* He tentatively moved back up the stairs.

A stench James could've done without smelling met him on the top deck. It wafted from the great fish's lolling, open mouth.

"Oh, God. I think I'm going to be sick. That's really rank. I've got to get home and figure out what I'm going to do with this beast. Let's go, Methuselah. Let's go get famous."

James stepped to the controls as best he could, since Methuselah's massive body was blocking the way. He cranked the twin engines and slowly pushed the throttle into a higher gear. He made sure to give the boat a slow ramp-up because he didn't want to burn the engines out, hitting them with the heavy weight that was now sitting on his boat. He didn't want to have to wait on anyone to find him; they would have to tow his ass back to the marina if he screwed up his motors. This was a delicate situation on all accounts.

Finally, when the engines were moving them at a fairly decent clip, he turned the controls toward the marina and home.

Murray woke out of darkness into the darkness of his confined space. His body was bunched up tight in the fetal position, and he was drenched from head to toe in a slimy, rank-smelling muck. The sensation that had awakened him seemed to be small bugs swarming all over his body, and every single one of those creatures was biting and devouring him. He was tingling in many places, but that sensation was barely noticeable because the rest of his body was simply on fire. He reached over and scratched his arm to alleviate the harsh burning underneath his skin. He felt nothing but slickness as he did so. The scratching did nothing to soothe the burning; if anything, it just made it worse. A dread deeper than what was already possessing him washed over his body as something seemed to give way on his forearm.

He was extremely cramped. The space he was in was so constricting, it felt as though he was in an amniotic sack. He tried to roll over, and as he did, his arm slid over something slick above him. A different type of pain seared his arm in a few places. It was that cutting sensation again. Anytime he moved, something bit or nipped at him. He flinched back the other way. Everywhere he touched seemed to sting him in return. The feeling of claustrophobia was fully engaged. He began to panic. Tears were already free-falling down his face. He had to get out of here, but he was completely disoriented and didn't know which way was an escape.

An idea hit him. He maneuvered his hand to his pocket and carefully slid it in, managing to grab his cell phone. He had no idea if it would work with all the water he'd been submerged in. He carefully pulled it out of his muck-filled pocket and moved his hands up near his chest. He gently examined the phone with his fingers, but his sense of touch didn't seem to be working right. At times he wondered if he was even holding anything at all. At other times—in different areas of his hands— everything felt normal. Hoping his intuitions were correct, he pressed a button, and the main screen came on and immediately blinded him. He quickly closed his eyes again to adjust to the bright light. A bight rect- angle was all he saw behind his eyelids. He swung his phone away from his face and blinked. Bringing the phone back to his face, he carefully slid his finger weakly over the main screen to unlock it. He clicked the flashlight icon, and it flared on.

What Murray saw in the light of his iPhone flashlight scared the absolute hell out of him. He simultaneously pissed and shat himself. Lying in this chamber of horrors inside this legendary beast of a fish, Murray saw hundreds upon hundreds of lures of all shapes and sizes.

Murray thought back to when he and James had witnessed this levi- athan break the surface of the water for a few seconds to stare at them. They'd got a good look at him and the numerous lures that were hooked into Methuselah's fat lips.

But here, not an inch above his face and all throughout the fish's stomach lining, were multitudes of rusty and gleaming hooks. Years upon years of tug-of-war had been played out with fishermen's lines, and Methuselah had won on every occasion. Some lures were haphazardly hanging down, and others had worked themselves into and fastened firmly over time to the stomach tissue. The lures were of all shapes and sizes and a tapestry of color. Many of them still had some sort of rotted bait hanging loosely from them; others had fresher meat from the things this monster had eaten. Murray finally saw and realized that the spi- der-web strands were the filigreed fishing line that was still attached to many of the lures. As the ingested food had sloshed around, the hooks had grabbed hold and ripped at the food, and who knew, maybe even helped in this beast's digestion process.

Then Murray's eyes fell on his hand, and his heart sank lower in his body. He slowly swung the flashlight to his hand and arm as he realized what the full-body burning sensation really was.

Digestion!

The word screamed out in Murray's mind. That single word—just a common, everyday word—in these circumstances scared him to death.

The pain was not bugs or parasites biting him, but Methuselah's stomach acids breaking down every fiber of his being from outside in. He knew now that the feeling of giving way on his forearm when he'd scratched it to relieve the itchy and burning sensation had been his weakened skin peeling away. With this realization, he rotated the flashlight over toward his right arm and looked. Stark, raw and ravaged red muscle stared back at him.

His body seemed to light up in new agony, and Murray Stockton let out the loudest wail he'd ever voiced in his thirty-five years on this earth.

⌘

James turned at the sound of something behind him. He didn't know what it was, but it was very faint and distant. He was moving at a decent and steady clip now, far from the place Murray had gone under and disappeared. Methuselah was still on the stern of his boat—thank God—and he was still unmoving. The sound that had caught his attention didn't sound like a big-ass fish trying to shake himself hard enough to get back into the water—he knew exactly what that sounded like.

James listened again, his ears pricking to grasp the faintest sound. He listened to the engines churning hard, but nothing seemed wrong with the way they were working. He had worked on his boat the day before this trip, so everything was in order with their hydraulics. He looked up and saw birds calling out above him. They were keeping pace with the boat, hoping that a piece of food would be thrown their way. Maybe they even wanted a piece of Methuselah. Other birds were in the far distance, calling back. He looked behind him and out at the flat plane of lake water, thinking he'd heard Murray screaming for him to come back and get him. Then he scoffed at the idea. It had been hours since the incident; Murray couldn't tread water for that long. He'd probably drowned from the blood loss and trauma of being thrown around the lake like a rag doll by an angry fish.

A stab of guilt struck him, and he genuinely felt sorry for the guy. *Poor Murray. I hated to do it, but it's for the best. And it all worked out to my advantage. I have no idea what I'm going to say to Alice about him. She knew we went out together. I have no idea how long she watched, but if she thought Murray was cheating on her, she probably stood there at her car until we were way out into the lake. She wanted to make sure he was definitely gone. I could say we came back at lunch for whatever reason, and I dropped him off then went back out in the lake on my own. Play it off like I have no idea where he went. Maybe to get a few beers. That could work. I'll go with that if I can't think of anything better.*

Finally, hearing no other curious sounds, James shrugged his shoulders and turned back, facing the blowing wind as he continued back to the marina. As he moved across the lake toward home, he continued putting his story together of the disappearance of Murray Stockton.

James sat on a bench that was built into the main pier, breathing heavily. He'd just had another battle hoisting Methuselah on the scale, which maxed out at one ton. James was seated near the big fish, which hung upside down by his massive tail from the most heavy-duty piece of rope James could find. It hadn't been as bad as catching him, but it had been a struggle. He had managed eventually; the two-ton metal come-along cable pulley system with two hooks had done most of the work.

James was studying his cell phone screen, trying to figure out how to bring up the video to capture his prize catch, when a couple of half-digested fish slid out of Methuselah's open mouth. They landed on the pier, flopping and flapping weakly a few times, then fell still.

"Awww shit, that's gross," James said.

A work boot came out next and dropped near the dead fish.

James stopped, frozen stiff, as he stared closer at the boot. It looked waterlogged and was covered in slime, so the yellowish hue of the Caterpillar name brand had been discolored. That other thing he noticed was that the laces were untied and very loose, the way Murray always wore his boots.

That was Murray's. No doubt about it. Methuselah must've toyed with him a good bit before Murray got off the hook and drowned. Damn, that really sucks, Murray. Sorry, man.

James pocketed his phone as he stepped over to the monstrosity. When he got closer, he glanced around to make sure no one was watching this early in the morning and simply kicked the boot over the pier into the water. He did the same for the couple of fish that lay there, unmoving, in all the half-digested watery goo that was still oozing from Methuselah's mouth.

He glanced at the knife he'd used to cut the rope, which he'd stabbed into the railing during his frantic attempt to hoist Methuselah up. He thought about retrieving it and putting it back into his pocket before he started his poses with his catch, but his eyes drifted back to the fish, and he forgot about it. He turned from Methuselah and pulled out his phone again as he walked to the far side of the pier. He wanted to prop his phone up on the pier and record a video so he could prove that he'd actually caught this big bitch of a fish.

Behind James, a bloody, wrinkled foot slowly slid down and out of the fish's mouth. The foot was connected to an extremely wilted and raw-muscled leg, which continued to slide free. Another foot, still wearing a work boot matching the one James had just kicked off the pier, followed closely behind.

James pulled up his camera app and touched the screen to change to video mode.

With a long, slow suction sound like that of a barnyard boot stepping through thick muck, the remaining, ravaged upper torso of Murray Stockton birthed itself from Methuselah's mouth. He landed hard on the dock with a grunt of agony.

James heard the thump of something heavy dropping on the wood planking behind him.

"Jaaaaaaaames," a voice called out in a long, mournful dirge that seemed to drift on the early morning breeze. The voice was guttural, from another world, and sounded strangely demonic.

James sucked in a mouthful of air and whirled around. His heart began pumping in double time, and his body broke out in an instant icy sweat. He was intently focused on the creature that was slowly unrolling itself from the cloudy goo and the hundreds of individual threads of fishing line that slowly dripped and slid from its body.

Body? James thought. There was almost nothing left of this body. Murray Stockton looked like a nightmarish marionette that had been clever enough to snip the hundreds of clear strands that operated every one of his muscle movements. As the half-digested apocalyptic zombie staggered forward, the fishing lines slid away from his body, and the extremely loose sections of skin that were barely hanging on peeled away with them.

James didn't even register it when his phone slipped from his hands and landed on the deck.

Murray's guttural and broken smoker's voice whispered again, on an unhinged jaw that didn't quite work right, "Jaaaames… whyyy did ya… dooooo… thiiis… to meeee?"

"Murray?" James croaked.

Murray grinned as though to answer his question, but to James, it came off more as a leer. The anger on Murray's face was etched with unfathomable hate. A lot of the flesh around his mouth had been eaten away by the fish's stomach acids, and many of Murray's teeth could be seen above and below his wilted lips. The zombie's face looked as though something had sucked it off, chewed it up, then spat it back onto his head and worked it around into some half-assed semblance of a face. The figure's head bobbled up and down spastically, as though he sat on the dashboard of a car traveling extremely unstable ground.

James couldn't believe Murray was asking him this question. He must know why. "Why'd I do it?" he echoed, incredulity painting his voice. "'Cause you were fuckin' my wife, you asshole!"

The Murray creature crept closer on hindered muscle control. It locked eyes with James as it did so. "Iiii ooonlyyy diiid thaat… beeee-cauuuse yoou… fuucked miiine firssst."

The slurred words were like a gut-punch to James's kidneys, and he inhaled in shock. *That's why he was with Virginia? He knew? Why didn't he ever say anything to me about it?*

The nightmare denizen's teeth chattered together like a wind-up toy, and James was left wondering if Murray was laughing at him. All of a sudden, Murray lunged at James. James wasn't expecting the figure's quick movement; he had just enough time to swing his arms up and over his head and skirt around Murray like an experienced matador.

"Jesus Christ," he shouted in alarm. "Get the fuck away from me!"

The lurching figure lost his balance and crumpled to the ground, crashing into some crates and fish-netting decorations. Murray rotated as he flung the containers away from him as best he could with almost useless arms. Pieces of his skin clung to some of the netting and peeled away as he moved to get up. Murray still felt as though someone had lit him on fire; a firestorm of agony was consuming him. He forced that burning sensation as far into the back recesses of his mind as possible. His only focus and determination now was to get James in some way.

No one does this… to me… and gets away… with it, he thought in ragged, disconnected pieces.

He managed to stand, turning to James again and starting after him in a shaky, undead shuffle. The connective tissue that was continuing to be eaten away underneath other sections of skin slid from his body and clumped in a trail as he made his way down the pier. His open wounds leaked and splattered blood in crazy, zig-zagged patterns, leaving something like a Jackson Pollack canvas in his wake.

"Jesus Christ, what happened to you?" James exclaimed.

As he retreated from this nightmare creature, something caught the heel of his boat shoe—maybe a raised nail, or a warped board from the constant barrage of the rain and heat. James threw his arms back to brace his fall, but he landed hard on his butt. As he scrambled to get up, he heard several quick shuffle-steps along with some heavy grunts and labored breathing.

When James looked up, Murray was there, leaning down, hovering over him. Blood leaked from his open wounds as more chunks of flesh shook free and slopped onto James's bare legs, shorts, and the pier around them. Murray's jaws snapped shut, and his teeth clapped together as he leaned in close enough to kiss James.

James cried out in alarm. He slid away on his butt, then crab-walked backward across the pier in a flurry of arms and legs. "Get the fuck away from me!" he shouted.

Murray fought to regain his balance in a malfunctioning-robot fashion. He carefully and very deliberately readjusted as he rose on broken-hinged joints, then began his lurching walk again.

"Noooooo," he said in his battery-acid-choked voice. "Gwonnnaaa giiitt chooooo."

Two quick shuffle-steps, then one long slide with a drag of his barely useable foot.

James screamed again, "I said, get the fuck away from me, Murray!"

"Giiitt chooooo... goooood."

With a bobble-head jitter, Murray looked over to where the great fish had been hoisted. He saw a knife standing straight up out of the pier railing, where he assumed James had stabbed it some time earlier that morning. James had either forgotten or wasn't paying attention to what was directly behind him and hanging above him.

He's gwonna wish... he had it now... just like I wisht... I had one... when I was... inside Methu—

Hanging dormant near the crouching figure, long, clear strands of oily saliva continued to drip out of Methuselah's mouth in steady streams as he watched a new meal crawl toward him. The fish's eyes seemed to bulge in their sockets with expectation.

Hangin'... above... James... Murray thought, with backfiring brain synapses. He took a few quick and eager sliding steps toward the banister railing, but lost his balance. The railing caught him across the sternum like a punch to his chest. This took some of the air from his almost unusable lungs, and he breathed in deep, hoarse, ragged breaths. He feebly pushed himself back to his feet.

James Lory had never seen anything so bizarre and horrifying in his life. He knew no one would ever believe this story, and he wished to God he'd been able to set his phone up to capture the whole thing on video. He couldn't take his eyes off this new, dissolving Murray.

The knife James had stabbed into the railing was within Murray's reach. He feebly reached out and grasped it. The lack of sensation in his fingers and palms was even worse—almost non-existent—than it had been when he'd woken in the belly of Methuselah. He reverently handled the knife, as though it was a gift from God. He knew this was his last and only chance at revenge. If he dropped this knife, there would never be another chance at payback; he had to make this moment count. He focused as much as was left of his mind on the knife and the conscious effort to carefully pry it out of the railing.

Hoping against all hope that he was going to crush the hell out of James with Methuselah's body, Murray swung the knife with as much strength as he could manage.

There was an audible twang as the knife nicked the rope strands. They snapped under the strain of Methuselah's weight, and he dropped straight down onto James's frozen body.

As Methuselah fell, his mouth gaped wide, as if to welcome this new, huge bite of food. The fish only remained in the headstand for a second or two, and then crashed down on his side. The pier shook from the weight. As the monster fell sideways, he upended himself to get more of James's struggling body into his mouth.

Murray's eyes went wide with shock at the movement. This was even better than he could have wished. Just to hear the panicked screams from James and to see his legs kicking wildly put a wicked smile on Murray's disintegrating face.

Still feeling the rope around his tail, Methuselah flapped ceaselessly as he took more and more of James into his mouth. The rope finally unraveled, but didn't slide completely off, whipping around as Methuselah continued to flop around the decking. The fish aimed his body toward the closest section of the pier, where he could make it back into the water.

With one last tremendous and final flap, Methuselah flipped up, head-first, as he took the last of James's body into his mouth. His jaws slapped shut as he landed on the handrail of the deck. The handrail was unable to support the fish's weight, and it, as well as part of the decking under it, disintegrated and gave away completely. The great fish—along with James Lory—toppled over the railing and disappeared into Silver Ridge Lake with a humongous splash.

Murray stared in wide-eyed fascination, transfixed. Even through all the agony, he managed a burning grin.

Nothing remained of the great fish now; he had already swum back out into deeper water. The only evidence of his presence was the oily goo on the decking, and the bits and pieces of Murray's own flesh.

Murray looked down at the knife in his hand. Needing it no longer, he held it over the railing and let it slide from his desensitized fingers.

He stood for a long while, just staring down at the agitated waves that lapped at the pier below. When the rockiness of the bay calmed to a flat, even plane, Murray finally turned away from the water. Giving the missing section of the pier a wide berth, he moved toward the end of the dock in a low, painful crouch and humpbacked stride. He walked the rest of the way down the pier, using the handrail with both hands for support.

At the end of the pier, he stood for another long moment as he breathed in the fresh lake breeze that blew in from the south. After smelling the bowels of Methuselah for as long as he had, this breeze was incredibly refreshing. Tears of relief began to flow from his sagging eyes. Then, as his mind and body continued to shut the rest of the way down to death, he moved to sit. The movement was awkward, excruciating, and he took his time about it.

When he had finally settled his body into as comfortable a position as he could, Murray looked out at the lake again. He had just enough brainpower to realize that what he was looking at was a beautiful vista. He saw the birds flying—mostly hovering, their wings spread out—not too far from where he sat. He was mesmerized, like a little kid seeing something new and interesting for the first time. Those birds were just floating on the wind with not a care in the world. They called out to him. He thought they were telling him to come fly with them. He wished he could go back in time and know the little bit of what he knew now. He knew he would definitely make some different life choices. He knew he would've steered clear from ever becoming friends with James Lory. His life would've had a happier ending, or at least he thought it would have. His thoughts turned to Alice, whom he loved, and to James's wife, Virginia, to whom he'd made love for the simple reason that James had cheated with Alice first.

Should've... jus' confronted... him 'bout that, Murray thought. *He might not have... called me on... what I did. Doesn't matter... now. What's done is... done and can't... be undone. All that is... left for... me is to... just di—*

Murray's mind and body simultaneously shut down, and he went dark. As his body relaxed, his arms slid forward. The weight of his head and shoulder folded him forward at the waist. Top-heavy, he rolled forward and fell from the pier. For a brief time, as the birds had requested of him, he was flying with them. Murray joined James and Methuselah's world with a mediocre splash.

The few birds that were hovering near him seemed to cry out in alarm at his falling headlong into the water. Voicing their opinion on the matter, they tilted their wings, caught an updraft and circled away for an early-morning breakfast somewhere else across the bay.

OFF THE BEATEN PATH - THE ENDING

RACHEL KIRKLAND WAS in the forest again, standing smack-dab in the middle of the trail. She had sworn to heaven, hell and herself that she would never again walk its path, yet here she was.

This could be a huge mistake on my part, Rachel thought, second-guessing herself for the hundredth time. *But we made the choice to come back here. It has to be done this way.*

The forest surrounding the trail was as amazingly beautiful as it had been when she'd traveled it that nightmare day eight years ago. It was summer now, and the forest was bathed in high afternoon sunlight that filtered through the trees. All around her was a myriad of different shades of green, not the tapestry of fall colors it had been the first time she had been down this path.

As she stood on the trail, her fingers looped around the straps of her backpack, she felt that the woods were denser now. Maybe it was because it had been fall back then and some of the trees had already lost a few leaves.

The events that had transpired eight years ago were beginning to emerge from way back in her mind where she had pushed them in an effort to forget. She shook her head and forced them back again, refusing to relive those moments.

I can't dwell on the past. Now is not the best time to dig up dead memories, she thought. *But no matter how hard I try, I just can't completely forget what happened back then.*

"What's the matter?" a voice asked.

"Hmm?" Rachel asked, turning to see Gregory Dumont stepping over to her. He was smiling that gorgeous smile that used to thrill her and always made her heart jump a little. Recently, however, it had been failing to excite her.

The devil's smile, she thought.

He stared at her intently for a few seconds. "I said, 'What's that matter?' You seemed so deep in thought. You look worried, babe." He leaned into her and whispered in a hushed, conspiratorial tone, "What's your big secret?"

Rachel was still thinking of her memory from eight years ago and said a little too harshly, "I don't have a secret."

Surprised, Gregory took two small steps away from her. "Oh, hey, wait. I was just kidding, Rachel." He laughed a little.

Rachel gave him a fake laugh that sounded real enough and quickly said, "Ha-ha, very funny. No, seriously, it's nothing. Sorry."

He tutted a few times. "Touchy, touchy," he said, then smiled.

Wanting to smooth over the misunderstanding, Rachel said, "I'm sorry. I was just looking at the foliage. This trail is just so beautiful. It's been so long since I've seen it."

Gregory's voice rose a little too eagerly. "Oh, you've hiked this trail before?"

Fuck, she thought. *I shouldn't have said that.*

Finding her voice quickly, she stuttered but managed to say, "Ah, no. No, not at all. A, uh, a friend of mine has been here. I saw some of her pictures of this park on Facebook a while back. I've always wanted to come out here and see it for myself. And, well, you know, here we are." She threw out her hand as though the forest had just happened to materialize around them.

"Oh, well, good. You scared me there for a second," Gregory said.

"What do you mean?"

"You know I always like doing things together with you that we both haven't done. I would've been a little disappointed if you'd experienced this trail and its awesomeness already…" Gregory let the statement hang out there on the warm summer air, then added, "Or with someone else."

That was a fucking odd statement, Rachel thought. She said, "What's that supposed to mean?"

"Oh, nothing. Nothing. I just like doing things together with you, that's all."

"Well, what if I had hiked this trail with some other guy?" She tilted her head and raised her eyebrow. "What then?"

He leaned forward and replied in the same playful tone. "Have you?"

"No," she said evenly, right on the heels of his question.

"Then it's not a problem."

Rachel cut the playful banter. "But if I had?"

"Then it would totally be okay, as I know that is or was in your past. I would just hate that we couldn't have this experience together. That's all."

"Well, what happened in the past is my past. That's not as important as what's happening right now, in the present, right?" She hated herself for saying that, knowing it indicated to Gregory that there was a hint of a future between them. And that was so far from the truth.

"Fair enough," he said, and stepped into her. "You're right. Nothing is as important as this moment. The present." He wrapped his arms around her, leaned in, and kissed her deeply.

Rachel forced herself to kiss him back with as much passion as her body could work up, inwardly cringing.

If he sticks his tongue into his mouth, she thought, *I'm going to be sick.* She knew she had to keep pretending. She had to keep acting just a little longer. She couldn't reveal her true intentions, at least not right now. *Remember, you're not doing this for yourself. You're doing it for—*

"Oooh, gross," a little voice said to their left.

Gregory and Rachel guiltily jerked their lips apart.

Oh, Jesus Christ, thank you, Rachel prayed. *Thank you, God, for small favors.*

They looked down at the little girl standing near them. Her arms were folded across her small chest and an exaggerated frown was set upon her face.

"Quit doing kissy-face with my mommy," she said. "It's *extremely* gross."

Gregory leaned down into the little girl's face and said, "If I stop doing kissy-face with your mommy, I'll have to do kissy-face with you." He did a little jump and spread his legs wide, then raised his arms out, curling his fingers into exaggerated claws.

Startled by the threat of being kissed and the 'monster' he'd become, the little girl squealed, turned from him, and ran down the path.

"Evelyn!" Rachel said, calling after her daughter. "He's not going to kiss you." She stopped in her tracks and thought about what her other daughter, Lynette, had told her last week. Then she thought about how weird Gregory's statement to Evelyn had sounded.

Wait, where is Lynette?

A meat-cleaver of panic chopped into her brain as she spun in a three-hundred-sixty-degree view of the forest. Lynette was nowhere in sight.

"Lynette!" Rachel called out. She spun in the opposite direction and looked around again. *"Lynette!"*

A little way down the trail, Gregory had just scooped Evelyn up in his 'claws'. He lifted her high above his head in victory, then pulled her down onto his face. Her shirt had pulled up in the lift and he put his mouth to her tummy. His growls were replaced by a loud fart noise as he pressed his mouth firmly to her belly and blew air against it as hard as he could. Evelyn's screams were replaced with fits of laughter.

Rachel didn't like the way it looked. She didn't like that he was taking these liberties with her daughters.

Daughter, she corrected herself. *From what Lynette said. God help me if I'm wrong and Lynette made the story up for some reason. No! I don't believe she would do that. She was telling me the truth.*

"Gregory! Evelyn! Stop it!"

As soon as she yelled at them, she knew it was too harsh. She inwardly scolded herself. *You have to keep pretending for just a little while longer. You can do this. Don't ruin it.*

Gregory pulled his face away from Evelyn's stomach and set her down as he turned to Rachel.

"What the hell is that all about? We're just playing here. You don't have to get so pissed at us."

"Yeah, Mom. He was just zerberting me," Evelyn said. "That tickled."

Gregory leaned down and asked, "Did you like the zerbert monster?"

Evelyn did a little excited jump back, then immediately leaned forward. "Yeah. He was really scary."

Rachel smiled at her adorable mannerisms.

"Well, I'll just have to make sure he comes zerberting on you some more."

Gregory's statement drained the smile from Rachel's face. *Not if I can fucking help it.* "Gregory, could you stop playing for just a minute and help me find Lynette? I haven't seen her for the last ten minutes."

"I'm sure she's around here somewhere," Gregory said, mimicking Rachel's turn and looking all around. "She probably just ran down the trail a little ways ahead of us." He jogged a little further himself, calling out to her, "Lynette!"

"Oh yeah? How do you know that?"

Gregory turned and jogged backward. "I don't know. I'm just using a little deductive reasoning. Our girls have been in front of us for most of the hike. I'm just assuming she hasn't looped around and backtracked on us while we were talking, so she has to be up this way."

My girls, Rachel thought. *They're not your girls. They never will be your girls.*

While one part of her mind panicked about Lynette's disappearance, the rest was still thinking about Gregory.

Gregory Dumont, a man who had been nothing short of perfect since they had started seeing each other. Gregory, who had been so loving to her twins. Any single mom would be envious to land such a great daddy figure for her kids...

"Rachel?" Gregory called.

"Yeah," Rachel replied, pulled from her thoughts. She gave a little disoriented shake of her head, then focused on him again.

"You okay?" he asked.

"Yeah. No, I'm fine," she said.

"You don't look fine. You look as though you're a million miles away. You feeling okay?"

"Of course. Just worried about Lynette."

"We'll find her."

Evelyn's sweet voice called out, "I found her!"

Gregory flourished his hands, as though he was the magician that had just conjured Lynette out of nowhere. "See," he said. "I told you we would."

Evelyn was standing at a high point on the trail, pointing somewhere below—an area Rachel couldn't see from her current vantage point.

"She's down there at the water's edge," Evelyn explained, and began running in the direction she'd pointed.

Water's edge? Rachel thought.

She broke into a fast run. She passed Gregory—who was watching her with intense curiosity—and reached the spot where Evelyn had been standing. Now Rachel could see both girls. Evelyn was running up behind Lynette, who was already crouched at the lake's edge. They both peered down at their reflection in the water.

"Lynette!" Rachel called. "Get away from the water!" She knew she was panicking, but she couldn't stop herself, and she ran after Evelyn.

When she reached them she heard giggling, mostly from Evelyn. She grabbed Lynette and turned her round. She was about to gently but firmly tear into her about running away like she'd done and tell her never to do that shit again, but then she saw tears running down Lynette's face.

"Oh, baby, what's wrong?" Rachel begged.

Lynette shrugged, then said, "I don't know."

"You're crying."

"Yeah, because—" Lynette began, but then stopped as she glanced over to see Gregory standing at the top of the trail. She diverted her eyes away from him.

"She okay?" Gregory called.

Rachel glanced at him as he stood there, looking down at them. She shifted her body, using it to shield Lynette from him while she composed herself.

Not wanting to draw attention to Lynette's tears, she gave a simple wave and said, "Yep. She's good."

"Tell him I was just looking at the little fish," Lynette prompted. There was utter fear in her voice as she turned away from him. Rachel glanced back into the water and saw little minnows darting back and forth. She also saw Lynette's reflection and that she was quickly wiping away the tears.

Rachel called back over to Gregory, "She was just looking at the little fish swimming here at the edge of the water."

Gregory was slowly making his way over to them. Rachel turned quickly to Lynette and gently turned her back into her. "Dry your eyes, little one. I know why you're crying. I told you we would get him back, didn't I?"

"Yes, ma'am."

"And I always keep my promises. That's why we're here. It won't be much longer, and then he'll never be able to hurt you ever again."

Lynette gave a tentative smile. "You promise?"

"With all my heart, I promise. No one, and I mean no one, hurts my babies and gets away with it."

Lynette looked down at her hands and said, "Thank you, Mommy. I love you."

"I love you too, baby."

They heard the crunch of brittle sticks behind them, then Gregory said, "What are you three talking about?"

Lynette glanced his way again and Rachel saw her smile fade, replaced with dread and sadness. She turned and looked out at the lake again—not down at the fish, but somewhere off to the distant shoreline.

Evelyn jumped in and said, "They're telling secrets to each other."

"Oh, really?" Gregory asked.

"Yep, I overheard what they said. But since it's their secret, and mine too, I guess, I can't say. It wouldn't be right."

"Oh," Gregory said, obviously not expecting this. "Well, then. I feel ganged up on." He leaned down to Evelyn. "Just so you know… I have a secret too."

"Really?" Evelyn said. "What's your secret?"

Gregory smiled. "Are you going to tell me yours?"

Evelyn looked to her mother to see if it was okay. Rachel was staring back at her, but gave her no prompts. Evelyn looked back at Gregory and shook her head emphatically.

"It wouldn't be right to tell."

Gregory knelt to Evelyn's level. "That's okay. We both can have our secrets." He put a finger to her small chest and tapped it gently, driving his point home. "There is nothing wrong with that. But I have a very sneaky suspicion that I will be telling my secret to you gals a little later today." On the word 'today' he tapped her nose, making her scrunch it up.

"When?" Evelyn asked.

"When the time is right," he said, then smiled again. He turned to Rachel and winked.

She tried to smile back, but there was no honesty behind it, and she hoped Gregory couldn't tell.

Gregory moved to Lynette and said, "Hey, sweetheart. You've been quiet for most of the trip. You feeling okay?" He rubbed the back of her head with his fingers, then dropped them lower and stroked her back. Lynette turned away from his touch.

"Oh, she's fine," Rachel said, scooping Lynette up and heading back to the trail. As she went, she said, "Come on, you guys. Let's go. We can talk on the trail. We have lots to see yet."

Evelyn skipped after her mother, leaving Gregory at the water's edge, staring back at them with a mix of bewilderment, uneasiness, and confusion.

When he caught up with them, they were all holding hands, Rachel in between her two girls. Gregory stepped between Rachel and Evelyn's hands, broke them apart, and took each of theirs in his.

"Mind if I join in on all this fun?"

Rachel turned to him. "No. Not at all."

"Good. I was feeling a little left out—you three women walking hand in hand. I didn't feel like a part of this family."

"You're not," Evelyn said, evenly and without reservation.

"Oh, wow," Gregory said.

Rachel jumped in as he spoke. "Evelyn. That was rude. You apologize to Gregory."

"Oh, it's okay, Rachel. She can say that. She can say whatever she wants or feels. I know I'm the odd man out with you beautiful ladies and probably always will be. She didn't hurt my feelings. But I'm curious… why did you say that?"

"Just because," Evelyn said innocently as she skipped beside him. Her head was lightly flopping from side to side to the beat of each skip. They all waited for her to continue.

"Because why, Evelyn?" Gregory asked eventually.

"Because Mommy, Lynette, and me have been together for as long as I can remember. We've never met our daddy. He left us a long time ago. Mommy doesn't see a lot of men. Well, she doesn't really see anybody. Except you."

"I guess that makes me a lucky guy."

"Why?" Evelyn asked.

"Yeah. Why, Gregory?" Rachel asked, her interest piqued.

Gregory looked over to Rachel and said, "Because you're such a beautiful woman. I guess I just feel lucky that you want to be here with me and not any other guy. I mean, you could have any man you want—"

Rachel didn't cut him off, but exhaled loudly as she rolled her eyes and shook her head in disgust.

"Don't do that," Gregory commanded gently. "You always do that. Please don't shake off my compliments. You may not see yourself in that way or feel that way, but I do."

Gritting her teeth, Rachel nodded and mumbled, "Sorry."

Gregory continued, "I'm serious. You could have any man you want, but you've consented to be here with me, and have allowed me to be with you and your girls. That is, unless you're seeing some other guy I don't know about behind my back."

Rachel shook her head emphatically. It was the only honest answer she had given him recently.

"Good," he said, nodding. "That's—that's good to hear." Gregory looked back over to Evelyn. "Your daddy, whoever he was, was very stupid to leave you three. If I ever got a chance to be your daddy, I would never leave you. I would be the best daddy you could ever wish for."

Evelyn grew excited. "Yeah, that's what I meant earlier! You would have to ask Mommy to marry you. You would have to get her a ring. That's the way it works. That's when you can be part of the family. When both of you get married."

On edge, Rachel broke in, "Oh, well, I don't think either one of us is ready for that." Something Gregory had said had struck a nerve within her. It was only a small thing, but she couldn't stop thinking about it.

Gregory just said, 'Your daddy, whoever he was, was very stupid to leave you three.' Why did he say 'was', not 'is'? Does Gregory know Stuart is dead? Did Gregory know him? I told everyone that Stuart just upped and left me. Left them.

A loud, cat-like cry reverberated from out of the tree line off to their right, the sound bringing Rachel immediately from her thoughts. The pitch dropped to a long, guttural, purr-growl that caused all of them to freeze in their tracks.

Gregory whispered, "Is that a fucking mountain lion?"

"That's what I was thinking," Rachel whispered back.

"Where the fuck is it?"

The sound had definitely come from in front of them. They searched the woods ahead for the animal that had made it.

"Right there," Rachel whispered, seeing the underbrush shake slightly.

The mountain lion slunk from out the dense scrub about thirty yards in front of them. As soon as it stepped out, it became extremely wary of them. It crouched tensely at the edge of the trail by a big boulder whose tip was jutting out of the ground, eyeing them cautiously as it continued growling its guttural purr.

"Mommy?" Lynette said, starting to whine.

"Quiet!" Rachel whispered harshly, and squeezed her hand. Very calmly and slowly, she put her hands on the shoulder straps of her backpack and began to slide them from her shoulders. "Girls," she whispered, "get behind me. Do it slowly. Remember your ears."

Gregory looked at her, confused. The big cat kept up that deep, guttural purring.

Both girls did as their mother ordered. They crept cautiously behind her, huddling at the back of Rachel's legs, and plugged their ears with their fingers. Though their movements were minimal, the mountain lion cried out again and took two warning steps closer to them.

Rachel stared directly into the mountain lion's eyes. It was growling, crouching ready to spring. Rachel pulled her backpack in front of her until she held it over her chest. She continued to maintain eye contact with the creature as she slid her hand inside.

The mountain lion sprang, launching itself at them. Gregory turned and ran as fast as he could in the opposite direction, leaving Rachel and the girls behind to fend for themselves.

Rachel pulled her 9mm Luger smoothly from her backpack and leveled it on the charging cat, letting the bag drop between her legs. She brought her left hand up, bracing her shooting hand; she knew she had to steady the jumpy recoil it usually gave her.

She fired four times, and each shot found its mark: first in the side of the neck, then in the lower jaw. At that point, the fight was mostly taken out of the big cat and he began to slow. The last two she fired were clean head-shots: one above its right eye and the other into the bridge of its nose.

Rachel's mind was instantly thrown back in time to something Stuart had said to her eight years ago about the gun he'd been carrying. *Please don't be mad if I want to protect you from anything out here that could possibly harm you… and eventually our little one.*

Huh, she thought. *Guess even though he was an asshole and a psychotic murderer, he was right about this.* She was glad she'd lost her fear of guns since then, though her heart was filled with deep remorse that she'd had to put the big cat down. Why couldn't it have just slunk off across the path, back into the woods, and left them alone?

It was either him or us, she thought. She would've done something different if she'd had the chance, but the speed of the mountain lion hadn't given her any time to pop off a warning shot. Rachel didn't even know if a cat that size would have been scared off by a gunshot. Still, she wished she hadn't had to kill it.

But nothing is going to come between my girls and me. I would give my life for these two miracles.

"Mommy?" Lynette asked, pulling her pink earplugs from her ears. "Are we okay?"

Evelyn mimicked her sister, pulling out a pair of purple earplugs. They both stuck their ear protection into their respective pockets and looked over at the fallen animal.

Rachel was still in her shooter's stance, her gun still aimed at the unmoving lion. At the sound of Lynette's voice, she relaxed and dropped her arms to her sides, though she kept an eye on the big cat as she knelt and hugged her girls tightly.

"Yes, kiddo. We're okay now. You're safe."

"You have a gun?" Gregory called from behind them. It sounded more like an accusation.

Rachel turned. He was about forty yards down the trail—forty yards away from the danger she and the girls had just been in. He was heading back to them, which meant he had run further down the trail before he'd stopped.

Rachel turned and faced him. "You ran?" she shot back at him. "You just left us here and ran?"

"Babe, I thought you and the girls were right behind me."

"Oh, bullshit! You did not. You fucking left us. There is no way these girls could run faster than you. You didn't even try to protect them. You were just protecting yourself, you son-of-a-bitch."

"You have a gun," Gregory pointed out.

"You didn't know that, you coward."

"C'mon, now; that fucking mountain lion scared the shit out of me."

"Watch your mouth in front of my girls."

"Sorry," he said to Rachel. "Sorry, girls." Then he was right back on the subject of guns. "What is that? A Sig Sauer? Glock?"

"It's a fucking Luger, you asshole. What difference does it make what I'm carrying?"

"You have a license for that thing?"

"What the fuck? Yes, I have a goddamn license to conceal and carry, but who gives a fuck if I have one or not? You the fucking cops? You gonna turn me in if I don't have the correct paperwork?"

"No, baby, calm down. I just… I'm shocked, that's all. I didn't know you were into guns, that's all. You saved my life. Our lives."

She looked at Gregory directly. "Well, just know that I only had my girls in mind when I shot that cat." She looked over at the mountain lion to make sure it was still down for the count, then back to Gregory. "Evelyn and Lynette were the only thing on my mind—not you."

"Can I see it?" he asked. He held out his hand as he approached.

"What, my gun?"

"Yeah."

"No," Rachel said simply. She stooped and picked up her backpack, shoving her Luger back inside. "Nobody touches my gun except me. I have the permit for it, so I should be the only one who handles it."

"That's a wise choice," Gregory said. "Smart." He couldn't meet her eyes. "So, I guess we should head back to the car," he added. "Call it a day."

"Why?"

"I just thought your heart wasn't in it, after…"

"No. We're going to finish this hike. This"—she pointed to the big cat—"was just a little hiccup in today's plans. What shall we do with it?"

Gregory stared at her blankly, seeming to go into a trance.

"Gregory?"

"Huh?"

"Are you listening to me? I fucking hate it when you drift off like that. You didn't hear anything I said."

"I heard you. I just zoned out there for a second."

"Then what did I say?"

"I'm sorry. I don't know. I meant, I heard you, but I didn't comprehend it because I was reliving that scary moment again."

"Don't fucking do that again. Pay attention to me when I'm talking to you. It's fucking rude."

"Sure. Yeah. No problem. I can do better. Could you please repeat what you said?" There was a good deal of sass in his voice. Gregory never liked being lectured. "Honestly, Rachel, I'm just a little shaken up from the attack, but I'm listening now."

Rachel looked at him suspiciously. *Let it go,* she told herself. *This isn't the fight you're trying to win.*

She held out a hand toward the dead animal. "I just asked you about the mountain lion."

"What about it?"

"We can't just leave it here on the trail, Gregory."

"Why not? Animals die all the time."

"It was shot. It didn't just die. What if someone else comes along and finds it?"

"What if they do?"

"I shot it in self-defense, but I don't have a hunting license to kill one. I would just feel better if you moved it into the woods where it can't be seen."

"Cover up your crime, huh?" he said, giving her a smile she didn't like.

"I just don't want to alarm any other hikers that might be out today, that's all."

"You want me to do your dirty work?"

"I just saved your ass. I think it's the least you could do."

"Oh, Jesus Christ. Fine, I'll take care of it."

Gregory went to the big cat. He grasped the scruff of the cat's neck with one hand, and with the other a handful of skin near its tail. He jerked it up as though he were doing a deadlift and began to drag it away from the trail. It was almost too heavy for him. When he was a little way from them, he did a half-turn as though throwing a bale of hay onto a tractor and flung the mountain lion away into some thick brush.

Rachel didn't like the way Gregory manhandled the big cat; there was no honor or respect for the creature. It was as though he didn't give two shits about the animal. Sure, she was grateful that he had agreed to move it, but his attitude was unpleasant. It was just one more sign amongst many that she didn't want to waste any more time with this man.

She slung her backpack over her shoulders and set the straps straight as Gregory returned to her and the twins, swiping at his hands to dislodge the cat hairs that clung to them. They all walked in silence for a while, deep in their own thoughts.

A mournful wail echoed through the forest.

Gregory, Rachel and the girls slowed their stride until they stopped and slowly looked around. They couldn't figure out where the cry was coming from.

"What the hell is that?" Gregory asked.

"Not sure, but it sounds like an animal."

"It sounds awful," Lynette muttered toward the ground.

Evelyn said, "Mommy, is that animal hurt?"

"I think so," Rachel said, patting Evelyn's head and stroking her little ponytail.

"Sounds like it's coming from this way," Gregory said, leaving the main path and pushing himself around a grouping of slender trees that grew in a cluster.

Rachel looked further down the trail and saw the blue strand she'd tied around the tree yesterday when she'd been up here. It was the one she'd marked as the turning point to get to the Sanctuary.

Fuck, she thought. *What now? At least Gregory's still heading in roughly the right direction. Looks like he's cutting across the woods. Hopefully, he'll intersect that smaller path I made.*

She didn't like it, but she followed Gregory anyway. "C'mon, girls. Let's see if we can find that hurt animal. Stay close to me at all times, okay?" They carefully moved off the beaten path and around the trees Gregory had just passed.

The agonized cry from the wounded animal drifted through the woods again. Both the twins covered their ears so they wouldn't have to listen to the mournful lament as they walked.

Lynette pleaded, "Make it stop, Mommy. Please, make it stop."

"We will, honey," Rachel said over her shoulder. "We will. We just have to find where it's coming from."

"You promise?"

"Yes. I promise."

They moved as fast as they could through the trees, underbrush, and briars.

Gregory finally stepped out of the thick woods onto the small rabbit trail that Rachel had been hoping he would find. The long, low, guttural bleat rolled out across the forest valley again. It was louder now, and sounded like it was full of sorrow and woe.

"This way," Gregory said, and shot off in an urgent run. Rachel and the girls had to really move to keep up with him.

From the moment Rachel had heard the animal's cry, a sickening mixture of dread and guilt had flooded her body. She'd instinctively known it was coming from the Sanctuary. Though she didn't know what animal was making the sound, she had a horrible feeling she knew what had happened to it.

Gregory stepped from the thick tree line into a small, circular patch of thigh-high grass and bushes: a little field out here in the middle of nowhere. Rachel and the girls quickly followed.

Rachel remembered the first time she'd pushed through this line of trees, and how even and neat everything had been. Now these trees had been subjected to eight years of weather, wind and the wilds of nature. Some of the pine trees were still standing strong and tall, but many had fallen or been uprooted and turned to rot. There was none of the seclusion that had been here the first time. The huge oak tree still stood sentinel to the left, growing out of the sea of waving grass and brush.

The mournful cry was louder now that the woods weren't suppressing the sound, and it seemed to be coming from the far side of this small patch of land. An even smaller trodden path of folded grass cut through the center of this field. Gregory moved onto it to find out what was making the sound.

Rachel stooped quickly and took turns looking at both girls directly. She pulled their hands away from their ears so they could hear her clearly. "I want you two to stay here while Gregory and I find out what's making that noise. It may not be safe, and I don't want you to see whatever is making the sound. Do you understand?"

"Okay. We'll stay here," Lynette said, and stuck her fingers back into her ears.

Evelyn just nodded and did the same.

"Good. We'll be right back."

Rachel stood and caught up with Gregory as he neared the other side of the field.

Close to the huge tree was a smaller area of grass that had been trampled flat and partially cleared. There was also an open rectangular hole that cut straight down into the earth. Curving around the back and side of the hole was a huge half-moon mound of dirt.

"Is that a fucking grave?" Gregory demanded. He looked over at Rachel, who was staring at the grave in mock surprise.

"Don't look at me," she said defiantly. "I have no idea."

He seemed unconvinced, but apparently decided to let it go. "Well, that's definitely something you don't see every day," he muttered.

The inhuman, pain-filled cry wailed from the hole.

Gregory and Rachel crept closer. They saw movement, and Rachel's heart sank with dread. She'd been afraid this was what she was going to find.

They saw the antlers first. The horns moved back and forth on a weary head. Then they saw the head pull back and up, and a loud bray cut loose from the buck's mouth. He cut his cry short when he saw the two human faces peer over the lip of the opening above him. The pitiful, pain-filled eyes widened expectantly with a possible hope of help.

Gregory and Rachel looked down on the pathetic animal, not knowing what to do. Impatient at their odd stillness, the buck brayed again, loud and long.

"Make it stop, Mommy," Evelyn said. "He's in pain. Make it stop."

"Evelyn!" Rachel yelled in alarm when she turned and saw her daughter behind her, staring down into the grave. She and Gregory had been so focused on what they were seeing that they hadn't heard Evelyn sneaking up behind them to investigate the matter for herself.

Rachel rushed to her daughter, covered her eyes, and whisked her away to the far edge of the high grass, where Lynette was still standing with her fingers in her ears. She set Evelyn down and stooped to her level. "What did I tell you? You weren't supposed to see that."

Evelyn bowed her head. "I just wanted to help. Can he get out? Is he hurt? He sounds hurt. Are you going to help him?"

"I'm going to talk to Gregory. We're going to figure out the best thing to do for the animal. Stay here with Lynette, and do not come over here until I say it's okay. Now, do I make myself completely clear?"

The girls were quiet.

"Okay?" she insisted.

"Okay, Mommy. We'll stay here," Evelyn said. Lynette just nodded.

"Alright, then. I'll be right back."

Rachel walked back to Gregory, who was standing near the hole with his hands on his hips. He threw a hand up as she approached and gestured toward the animal.

"He's really badly off. His back leg is broken clean in two. He can't make the jump out of that fucking hole without the use of both his back legs."

"Anything we can do to help him?"

"If I had some rope, maybe." He looked up at the big limbs of the oak tree above him. "If it were long enough, I could throw it around that limb up there, then drop a slipknot around one of his horns—if he would stay still long enough. But then again, we—"

"Don't have any rope," Rachel said.

"Yeah. I'm not going to risk toppling in onto his horns by trying to pull him out. That son-of-a-bitch would be heavy for me. And he wouldn't know I was trying to help him. He would fight me."

"So we only have one option," Rachel said.

"Yeah."

"Put him out of his misery."

"Yeah, because even if he got out, without his back leg being set and healing properly, it's just a matter of time before he's dinner for another animal—or just dies because he can't function properly with a fucked-up back leg."

The animal bleated again. It wasn't as loud, but they could hear the plea in his voice. The buck shook his antlers at them in agitation, adding to the already numerous grooves in the grave walls. Clumps of dirt sifted down onto his body. It was a pitiful sight.

Gregory exclaimed, "Who the fuck digs a hole out here in the middle of nowhere? It was stupid to just leave it uncovered like this."

Rachel didn't answer, but part of her felt that his comment was directed at her. She just stared down at the exhausted deer. Her heart went out to the poor animal. *It's all my fault you're down there. I'm the one to blame, and I'm so sorry,* she thought, hoping somehow the deer would telepathically hear her apology.

"Rachel? Did you hear me?"

Rachel turned to see Gregory staring at her. "Uh, what?"

"Apparently, I'm not the only one who zones out during a conversation. You do it too. So quit giving me shit about it." He didn't give her a chance to disagree. "I said, do *you* want *me* to put the animal out of its misery, or would you like to do the honors?"

"There's no honor in this."

"I don't mind doing it for you if you want me to." He held out his hand, palm up. "You just need to let me borrow your gun."

Rachel stared at his open hand, feeling as if the devil was asking her to give him her soul.

"No," she said quickly. "It's my gun. I can do it. I'll take care of it."

Gregory stuck his hands out in surrender and gave a slight bow as he backed away from the grave. "Suit yourself," he said. "I'll leave you to it, then. I'll be right over here if you need me."

Rachel watched him walk away with furrowed eyebrows. She slid her backpack from her shoulders and placed it on the ground between her legs, found the handle of her Luger, pulled it from its holster, then stood again.

"I'm sorry I did this to you," she whispered softly, just loudly enough for the buck to hear her. "I'm sorry for the pain I caused you, but this was all for somebody else. I'm sorry I have to do this to you now. Please forgive me."

The deer was looking up at her with a strained tilt of his head. She aimed down into the hole to a point right underneath the deer's eye and pulled the trigger. The deer gave a startled jump as the bullet hit; that was all it took. It fell over backward, dead. Its head caught the grave wall at a weird angle; one antler drilled into the earth, leaving the other to stick out into the grave.

Rachel fired another bullet into his heart for good measure. She didn't think she could deal with this creature coming to again and starting its loud braying of pain.

She stood there a few moments longer, half expecting the big deer to move. When it didn't, she ejected the clip from the gun, leaned down to retrieve another clip from the side pocket of her backpack, and jammed it home as she stood again. She always liked to have a full clip in her gun, just in case.

"So," Gregory said. "This is the place where you buried Stuart Monroe's body."

The statement made the bottom drop out from Rachel's world. She had barely thought of Stuart since the fight for her life eight years ago. After the police interviews and interrogations, she'd only spoken his name a few times to her daughters to tell them as little about their dad as she could. Now his name had been spoken by someone who wouldn't even have known Stuart. That was, unless that someone had been lying to her... She wheeled around to face him.

"Slowly, Rachel," he said calmly. "And make no movement with that gun in your hand. I swear to God I will not hesitate to shoot if I feel you are a threat to me."

Rachel stared down the barrel of the gun Gregory was aiming at her.

"There she is," he said. "Why don't you go ahead and chuck that gun over here in my direction? Don't want you to get any crazy O.K. Corral gunslinging ideas like you did with that fucking mountain lion earlier. You can imagine it was a major shock to my system when I heard that boom. Why the fuck do you have a gun, Rachel?"

"For exactly that reason. Protection from anything that might be out here that could possibly harm my girls and me." She was echoing Stuart's words from eight years ago. He'd been lying then, but as it turned out, he'd been right. She was glad now that she had gotten over her fear of firearms and spent so long practicing at the gun range. "What, did my gun scare you?"

"I'll be honest, it did make my butt pucker a little bit. But I'm not giving this situation any chance of becoming a showdown. Just go ahead and throw your gun over here to me."

Rachel was about to toss the gun close to Gregory's feet when she caught a hint of pink and a brief flash of purple move in the tall grass behind him. It was one of her girls. They hadn't listened to her again; one or both had already crept back through the tall grass to be nosey about this situation. Rachel made a split-second decision. She pitched the gun in an underhanded toss, but flipped it a little harder and higher than necessary. It sailed over Gregory's head and slightly too far to his right for him to catch it. It landed behind him.

Gregory didn't move to retrieve it. He gave her a pissy look. "Seriously? You bitch. You did that on purpose."

Rachel spoke urgently and in a flustered tone to keep his attention on her. "I'm—I'm sorry. I'm just a little worked up from the mountain lion encounter earlier." She turned and gestured toward the grave. "And having to kill that buck, and now you, whoever you are—I mean, my God, I have no idea who you are. Pulling a gun on me. Where the fuck did *you* get a gun?"

"We're even now," he said, grinning. "Ankle holster. It's police issue. I never go anywhere without my Walther PPS. It's gotten me out of a number of sticky situations. But when I started dating you, I had to go without it a few more times than I wanted just so you wouldn't get suspicious about me. Talk about feeling naked. I was feeling really lost without this baby."

"You had a fucking gun when that mountain lion attacked us, and you chose to run rather than take it down?"

"Hey, let me just be upfront and clear the fucking air about everything. I don't give a fuck about you or your little bitch twins." He exhaled sharply, as though cleansing himself of that confession. "God damn, that felt really good to say. I've wanted to say that for a long time now."

Rachel stood there, furious and shocked in equal measure.

Gregory continued, "I would've used it if that big fucking pussycat had gotten through you three bitches. But if there was any chance you had survived, I still had some questions for you about Stuart Monroe, and I was going to ask them. And you're going to answer them."

"You're a cop, aren't you?" Rachel asked in a defeated tone.

Gregory smiled cockily. He took a few confident steps toward Rachel, nodded, and said, "Detective, actually."

"Detective?" Working the word around in her mind and saying it aloud didn't help her believe this.

"Detective Conklin, to be exact. Michael Conklin. I do a lot of undercover work. Sorry, I don't have my credentials with me to prove it. Guess you'll just have to take my word for it."

Rachel couldn't believe she'd been played again by another guy. Her anger was making her tense. She told herself to loosen up, or this wasn't going to play out well.

You're getting too hot-headed. Downplay it. She gave a little laugh, and it felt good. *Put it right back in his fucking face,* she thought. *Make him second-guess himself.*

She laughed at him again, a little harder this time. "You mean to tell me that you faked who you are to get close to me to find out where I hid my ex-boyfriend's body?" She laughed again, even louder. "You think *I* had something to do with Stuart Monroe's disappearance?"

"I know you did. It's one of those gut feelings cops get. I have it. I've always had it. Ever since the cold case file dropped onto my desk about a year ago."

"Cold case file? They never found him? I thought they might have located him way out in some obscure place, living a non-existent life. Thought that case was closed years ago."

"Non-existent? Somewhere like here," Gregory—Michael—said, pointing to the ground with his free hand. "But not living."

Rachel mentally cursed herself for choosing that. She continued calmly. "I hate to be the bearer of bad news, *Michael,* but you've wasted a little over two months of both of our lives. So stupid. Stuart just up and left me high and dry after I told him I was pregnant. That's what I told the other detectives eight years ago. And that's what I'm telling you."

"Because that's the story you worked up back then. So convenient, isn't it?"

Rachel ignored his comment. She looked down at her hands with sadness. "I've always wished Stuart could've known how great our girls turned out."

Unfortunately, Michael wasn't buying it. "Oh, wow, Rachel. You're good. You've had a lot of practice. Do you sit in front of the mirror and practice these phrases and that poker face? That's brilliant acting, but do me a favor: cut the bullshit and tell me where Stuart is. I know he's around here somewhere."

"Well, if you know I'm so *guilty* of this crime you're accusing me of, why don't you just get your crime scene investigators out here and dig this fucking place up?"

"Oh, you can bet your sweet ass on it. That's the first thing we'll do just as soon as you're in custody." He leaned down and pulled his pant leg up high enough to remove a pair of handcuffs that were holstered there. He stood again with the cuffs and waved them around. "We're going to canvass this whole goddamn area." He tossed the handcuffs over to her; they landed at her feet with a clink. "Go ahead, babe. Do me a favor and put those silver bracelets on."

Rachel picked up the cuffs and rolled them around on her index finger. She looked back up to him. "How about *you* do *me* a favor, Michael, and, um..." She turned slightly toward the grave and chucked the handcuffs over her shoulder. "Go fuck yourself."

The handcuffs dropped into the grave with a slight rattle and a barely audible thunk as they landed on the carcass of the buck.

"Oh-ho-ho, you fucking bitch," Michael said. He rubbed his head in frustration with the upper receiver of the gun then dropped it to his side. He took another step toward Rachel.

"And when your people come out here and find nothing, and *then* I tell them you sexually molested my daughter—which I *do* have proof of..." She reached around, pulling her cell phone from her back pocket and waggling it toward him. "On here is Lynette's recorded testimony about the incident. Who do you think will be arrested then, huh?"

To her shock, a broad grin broke out on his face. "So I was right."

"What are you talking about?"

He shook his head in disbelief, but his smile remained. "It took me doing something that horrific to your daughter for you to bring me up here to get rid of my body. The place where I hoped you buried Stuart. I fucking knew you would do that. Believe me when I say this, but I really hated to do that to Lynette. She's a sweet kid and all, but that's not really me."

So there it is. There's his confession. He's admitting to what Lynette told me he did to her.

Rachel felt her body go rigid. It was all she could do not to charge

Gregory, or Michael, or whoever the fuck he was, and claw his eyes out. She would sink her fingernails into his neck and rip his throat out. She would push her fingers so far back into his eye-sockets that she'd feel grey matter. She would take him apart piece by slow, painful piece. But Rachel knew that if she charged him, Michael would take her down before she could get to him, just as she had with the mountain lion. Her fists were clenched at her sides, and she spoke through clenched teeth.

"You... sexually molested... my daughter... to get a reaction out of me... for me to bring you up here... where you think I buried my ex-boyfriend?"

"Yes, I did. And apparently, it worked." He paused to let that truth sink in for her. "You know, molesting your daughter was a decision I battled with for a few weeks. That was such a hard decision. Not that it didn't feel good, mind you. But—" He gave an exaggerated full-body shudder, stuck his tongue out and made a gagging sound. "It's not my style. I don't see how child molesters do that shit all the time. It's pretty sick."

Rachel whispered, "How do you live with yourself?"

"Just one day at a time. You wouldn't believe some of the things I've had to do in the past to capture a suspect I believe is guilty. I've pretended to be someone else, planted evidence—you name it, I've done it. Doing Lynette may have been one of the worst things I've ever done, but you can always bet on me that I'll get my man... or in your case, *woman*. These are the sins I have to live with."

"And that sin against Lynette will be the death of you," Rachel promised him.

"Did you just threaten a police officer? I believe you did. We're going to have to add that to the rap sheet I've already started for you."

Rachel felt like she was going to be sick. This was all too much. The first time she'd been here, she'd discovered the man she'd thought she loved was a serial killer. She'd had to fight for her life—and her babies' lives—against him. It had completely turned her world upside down when Lynette had broken down and told her about Gregory's despicable actions. The man she'd trusted and fallen for, who had always been such a perfect gentleman to her girls, had betrayed her—and them—in the worst way possible. Now there were *more* lies? This wasn't worse than what he'd done to Lynette, but she couldn't believe she'd missed the signs again.

"Oh, you fucking son-of-a-bitch," she gasped. "Next chance I get… I am going to fucking kill you. How's that for fucking threatening you?"

"Kill me? Like you did Stuart?" Michael said, pointing to the space directly behind her. "Is that what that goddamn hole is for? You dug one for me because I diddled your daughter?"

She wanted to scream. *You're goddamn right I dug it for you. And I dug it extra deep, too, to make sure you're closer to hell, since that's where you're going when I end you, you sick fuck. I'm going to make damn sure you never come back the way that asshole Stuart did. When you die, you die for good! I'm going to erase your shitty existence from the world! And I might just shit on your grave before I leave this cursed place for the last goddamn time!*

But she didn't tell him any of that. All she was able to say through ragged breaths as she straightened again was, "I have… no idea what you're… talking about. I didn't kill… and bury my ex-boyfriend… out here in the fucking… woods. You've got your facts… all mixed up."

At that moment, Lynette and Evelyn stepped out of the high grass behind Michael. Rachel froze at the movement, but she didn't move her eyes or turn her head in that direction. She didn't want to give them away.

Michael scoffed at her comment and looked off to his left, contemplating his next words. Rachel thought, *Am I making him second-guess his intuition? Does he actually think his research is all wrong?*

She gambled a swift glance over Michael's right shoulder. Lynette was looking directly at her and smiling, for some reason. The little girl pressed an index finger to her pursed lips to tell Rachel to be quiet. Then Lynette looked intently at the ground.

What the hell is she doing? Rachel thought.

Lynette took a careful and quiet step into the trampled grass. Then she took another. Evelyn followed her like it was a game.

Oh, if you're doing what I think you are doing, you are such a smart little girl.

Rachel looked back at Michael and shifted her stance to focus his attention on her. He eyed her suspiciously. A chickadee called from somewhere off to their right; another small animal scampered in the brush behind Rachel. Everything else was deathly quiet.

"No. I don't believe you," Michael said. He jabbed his gun forward to emphasize his words. "My facts are right in line with everything that happened before. You want to know why?"

She had to keep him talking. "I would love to hear your theory," she said.

Michael continued almost before she had finished speaking. "Here's where you fucked up in the grand scheme of things and in your cover-up of Stuart."

"Please, enlighten me."

"You named your twins after the two girlfriends who disappeared that Stuart dated before you." He flipped out his left thumb and said, "Lynette." Then he flipped out his index finger and said, "And Evelyn."

Lynette and Evelyn stopped behind him, as if Gregory had turned and was talking to them directly.

Rachel set her poker face. She shrugged her shoulder and raised her eyebrows as if to say, 'Yeah, and?' Deep inside, she cringed. *Oh, fuck. I never thought about it like that. I just wanted those two lost ladies to live on in some way, since their lives were cut short so soon. No other names sounded as perfect. But it's true. I have to hand it to him. That is a good gut instinct.*

"God. Damn. So implacable," Michael said with amazement in his voice. "Unwavering. Such a great actress. You should be in the movies."

Rachel noticed that Lynette and Evelyn were creeping closer to Michael. If she didn't do something drastic, he was going to see them out of the corner of his eye. If that happened, he'd turn and hold the gun on them, then he would corral them over to her so he could keep track of them.

Would he shoot three times? One bullet in the heart for each of us? Or would he make them headshots? Or would he shoot six times and give us head and center shots, just to be an evil bastard? How will today end? Will we end up here with the other Evelyn and Lynette, and with Stuart and the deer? Will the satisfaction of just knowing the whole story of where Stuart and his exes are buried be enough for Michael? Does he have to get the credit of solving this cold case to better himself with all his law enforcement buddies?

Would he make one of the girls go to him and force a confession out of me while he holds his gun to her head?

Rachel didn't like the frantic thoughts. She tried to block them out. She made a decision, praying it was going to work on Michael and his ego.

She took a few steps to her right and said, "Okay, Michael, I'll level with you. Let's talk this out once and for all." She looked back and saw he'd turned his head toward her and away from the girls. He was ultra-wary of her.

"What's the catch here?" he asked cautiously.

"There's no catch. I'm just tired of keeping these secrets."

Lynette and Evelyn had stopped in mid-stride, obviously wondering what their mother was doing. Seeing her move further away from them and then noticing Gregory following her movement, they understood. They took another tentative step toward where their mom had thrown her gun.

Rachel continued, raising her voice a little to cover up any sounds her girls might make. "You are extremely wrong about one part of this reconstructed crime scene you obviously pride yourself on figuring out."

Still unsure, Michael raised his gun again and aimed it at Rachel. "Well, why don't you just spill your guts about the matter and explain my mistake to me."

"You see the area I'm standing on right now?"

"What of it?"

"About four, maybe five feet down is where I buried Stuart Monroe eight years ago."

"I fucking knew it." He scoffed. "Tell me I'm wrong again."

"You *are* wrong, Michael; you're dead wrong, because the grave that was dug eight years ago was open for *me*."

"What?"

"Yeah. Stuart was a serial killer who loved beautiful women and being in relationships with them, but he couldn't handle the reality of being a real family man. When we hiked up here, it was a few days after I told him I was pregnant. Of course, at that time I didn't know I was going to be blessed with twins, but Stuart didn't like the fact that I was going to have even one child. So he thought he was going to put me in a fucking hole."

"Right there?" Michael asked, with a nod of his head toward where Rachel was now standing.

"Yeah, as best I can tell after eight years have gone by. I mean, this place looked so much better than it does now. I swear he had it groomed to perfection. He was really fucked up in the head."

As Rachel droned on, saying anything that came to her mind, she risked another glance and saw that Lynette and Evelyn were almost where her gun had landed. She needed to pull his attention a little further left.

"What did you mean earlier when you said Stuart was a serial killer?"

"Oh, you didn't figure that out, *Michael?* You smart detective, you. You didn't put two and two together and realize that Lynette and Evelyn were pregnant before they disappeared? That was the reason Stuart got rid of them. It's just like you accusing me of making Stuart disappear. Why? I don't know. You didn't think that maybe he made the girlfriends of just a few months disappear? I would think that would be a basic first deduction. I thought family or romantic interests would be the ones the police always look at first. That's why I was questioned so thoroughly after Stuart disappeared. That's Basic Detective 101. That information had to be in each of their missing person files. And you call yourself a detective!"

Lynette took one last step, then stooped and picked up Rachel's gun. She didn't examine it or roll it over in her hands; she simply let it hang at her side. Then she took a few careful side steps to move further in behind Gregory.

Rachel took a few more steps to her right and stopped when she was standing—to her best guess, with all the high grass—between where Evelyn and Lynette's bodies lay.

"Right here and right there is where Lynette and Evelyn are buried." She pointed straight down, then back over to where Stuart's grave was and said, "That's where he wanted me. Right in line with his other two victims. All of us right in a neat little row, where he could come visit us and chat us up when things in life got to be too difficult for him."

"That's pretty sick," Michael said.

"It's no worse than what you did to my daughter. And some might say that was far worse. You think there's *ever* a time that it's okay to do what you did to Lynette?! To do that to *any* child, for that matter?"

"Oh, get over it, Rachel. I didn't do that much to her. Just enough to get her to tattle-tale on me to get you to bring me out here to Stuart's burial site. I didn't mean any hurt to Lynette."

"You raped my little girl, you fucking son-of-a-bitch!"

"She never said no, so technically, I didn't."

Rachel's fury consumed her. It was all she could do to stand there. Michael was too far gone to reason with. He had somehow justified his horrific actions in the name of solving the case.

"I knew if I could get you pissed off enough at me that you would do it, and I see you're really fucking livid," he went on. "And here we are." He gestured at the Sanctuary.

Rachel added, right on the heels of his statement, "And I made damn sure that if we did come here, no matter what, we were going to be leaving here without you."

"What the fuck you talking about?" Michael asked. Rachel's confident, angry words sort of scared him. All of a sudden, he began to think that maybe he hadn't thought everything through. He realized that it was amazingly quiet out here in this little field, and they were all a long way from home. Michael didn't like the smirk Rachel was giving him beneath all of her anger, either. It was like she knew something he didn't.

Then it came to him.

"Wait, where are the girls?"

Before Michael could turn, a soft, timid voice spoke up from behind him. "Drop your gun, mister."

Michael stared at Rachel, who simply raised her eyebrow and gave a slight shrug of her shoulders as if to say, *You're fucked.*

He glanced over his shoulder and saw the twins behind him. He felt a dread deep in his loins as well as a chill that hit him in two waves, one for each of the girls standing there.

He registered Lynette first, and the look on her face did not match the voice in which she had just spoken to him. An intense anger had creased her baby features. One eye was closed, and the other was open and looking across the gunsight that was aimed at the center of his chest. He immediately knew it was Rachel's gun. The thing he hadn't expected was the way Lynette was standing. She was in a perfect shooter's stance. One foot slightly forward, the other one back just a skoosh to help brace herself against the recoil.

The next sight made his blood stop in his veins. It was Evelyn. She was standing innocently behind and a little to the left of her sister. Evelyn's mouth and eyes were scrunched up, and her fingers were already in her ears, as though expecting a report at any moment from the gun her sister was holding.

Michael's voice went up an octave when he saw them. "Hey, girls. What are you doing?"

Lynette took a small step forward and regained her shooter's stance. "Playing Good Girls, Bad Guys. I said, drop your gun."

Evelyn dropped her hands away from her head long enough to say, "We're the good girls. You're the bad guy." She stuck her tongue out at Gregory, then jammed her fingers in her ears again.

Rachel said, "I think you better do what she says. She has an amazing aim for a kid her size."

Michael glanced over his shoulder at Rachel and gave her a scoff. He turned back to Lynette and said, "Wow. You got Mommy's gun, don't'cha?"

"Yes. And I know how to use it. Mommy taught me. Drop yours."

"Mommy… taught you… to shoot a Luger?"

"Yes."

Evelyn unplugged her ears and joined in on the conversation again. "She taught me to shoot too." She returned her fingers to her ears.

Gregory suddenly remembered something he'd noticed during the mountain lion attack: seeing the girls pull their hands down from their ears and put their hands in their pockets. They'd been pocketing their earplugs.

Rachel brought Lynette up here with her gun to let Lynette take some pop shots at me for what I did to her. And they brought earplugs.

He gave a quick, embarrassed chuckle. "Well, it looks like I've been misinformed." He glanced back at Rachel again, then back to the girls and said, "Can you imagine what the guys at the office would say if they saw me now in this situation?"

"I don't care," Lynette said evenly.

The comment pissed Michael off. He took a tentative step toward Lynette and held out his hand. "Why don't you just give me that kidney-buster before you hurt yourself and your little sister there."

Without hesitation, Lynette dropped her aim from the center of his chest to his right thigh and squeezed the trigger. The gun bucked in Lynette's little hands, and her arms moved high with the recoil. Her arms went with it, controlled it, then leveled the gun back down on Michael, but this time she stopped her aim on the center of his face.

Evelyn took her fingers from her ears and cheered loudly as she jumped into the air. "You got him!" As soon as she landed, she fell silent and stuck her fingers back into her ears, as though she knew more gunshots were going to follow.

Michael, still in shock that the gun had gone off at all, was bemused by Evelyn and her strange reaction. He held up his hands. "Okay, now… hold on a second," he began, but stopped when he realized something was off with his body. He looked down at his thigh. Blood trickled down the front of his leg.

She did indeed get me, Michael thought.

And with that realization came the ungodly pain of the gunshot. As he stared at his bullet wound, he began to yell. His scream crescendoed as the pain swelled. Michael took a stumbling step back and fell on his ass in the trampled grassy area closer to the open grave.

He could only ask stupidly, "Why… why… why did you shoot me?"

Lynette told him in a monotone voice. "Because you hurt me. You hurt me bad. Mommy asked me what I wanted to do about it, and I said I wanted to hurt you back. Mommy told me the story about my daddy and what he tried to do to her. Then she told me what she did to him. We talked about it, and we decided to do the same to you. That's why we're up here."

"This is bullshit," he said. He pushed himself off the ground and hopped backward on his good leg to put a little distance between him and the girl who still had Rachel's gun trained on him. He stopped and tested how much weight he could put on the injured leg. It was a fair amount, but he still kept it guarded.

Lynette asked, "Are you going to drop the gun, or do you want another bullet hole in you?"

Michael didn't want to relinquish his gun, but she had the drop on him. Maybe he could make a gamble and talk them down.

"Alright, alright," he said, surrendering and dropping the gun at his feet. "You got me. You win. The good girls win. Game over."

As soon as his gun hit the ground, Evelyn ran to retrieve his weapon. Rachel saw the eagerness and yelled, "Evelyn! Don't!" but it was too late.

Michael had already dropped to the ground and grabbed his gun with the same hand before Evelyn could reach it. He grabbed and spun Evelyn back toward Lynette with the other hand, looping his arm around Evelyn's middle and leveling the gun to the side of her head. He pushed through the pain in his right leg as he forced himself to his knees. The whole movement was nothing short of sloppy, but that was the way it was done in the field. You had to get down and dirty sometimes just to survive.

"Oh, you fucking bitches! You're all fucked in the head," he snapped. "Especially you." He jerked his gun at Lynette, then pointed it at Evelyn's temple again. "This whole goddamn story of Stuart and you"—he glanced over at Rachel—"teaching your girls to kill. Fuck you, Rachel. And you, you little cunt, why don't *you* fucking drop the gun?"

Lynette remained focused, keeping her aim on him. Michael shifted his weight to his bad leg long enough to throw the knee of his good leg out in front of him, and her gun moved up with him as he got to his feet.

"I said, drop the fucking gun, or I'm going to show you the inside of your sister's head. You want to see her brains, you little bitch? Drop. The. Gun!"

Michael had Evelyn wrapped up tight and pulled high on his chest now. He was peeking out from behind her neck and shoulder, and his gun was pressed tight against her temple.

He saw Lynette's eyes shift. Then he saw her hands guide the gun lower, leveling it directly on the center of his crotch.

He immediately realized his mistake. By pulling Evelyn so high to cover his chest and head, there was nothing protecting him below.

Lynette squeezed the trigger. The gun boomed and bucked up again in the little girl's hands. The bullet went between Evelyn's dangling feet, entered Michael's lower abdomen, and exited the backside of his ass. He felt something splinter within his pelvis and thought that maybe the bullet had shattered bone. The shot and his scream echoed across the forest valley together.

Michael's body went limp with the shock of being shot in the dick. He simultaneously dropped Evelyn—who landed on her feet—and fell to his knees again. Dropping his gun, he brought both hands into the center of his crotch. Blood began to soak his pants, making it look like he had just pissed himself, then seeped between his fingers. He doubled over in the dirt in anguish, his forehead pressed into the earth as he sobbed uncontrollably.

Evelyn snatched up Michael's gun, dashed away from him, and took her place at Lynette's side. Just like her sister, Evelyn took up a perfect shooter's stance, with her right leg back, her left leg forward, and her gun aimed down on Michael, rolling around in the dirt.

The girls waited.

Rachel waited.

A bird flew across the sky above them, crying out.

Finally, Michael sat up.

"Aww, shit," he said, and sucked in a mouthful of air. "You got me." He chuckled and winced through the pain. "You got me right in my fun zone. Awww, damn, your mom was right. You are a crack shot. Shot me right in my cock. God! Damn! That fucking hurt!"

He glanced over at Rachel, who looked on with her arms folded across her chest, a proud momma smile on her face.

Not a worry on her face, he thought. *That right there is fucking creepy as shit. If she were standing anywhere else, like at a playground, that look would be one of a proud mother watching her babies having some innocent fun on the swings or the monkey bars.*

Michael half-heartedly wagged a finger at Rachel and then at the girls. He began to laugh again. "I believe you ladies have me at a slight disadvantage." He continued to laugh, finding that sentence hilarious.

He'd heard the line of dialogue in a movie or two somewhere along the way; he just couldn't figure out which one.

I've been in crazy situations before, but there is no getting out of this one.

If these were going to be his last words—and he doubted these bitches were ever going to tell anyone what he said—then why not? He laughed some more, though the movement of his body irritated the injuries in his leg and crotch.

He looked back at Rachel. "I think this is one cold case I should've never warmed up."

"You would've probably had a much longer life if you hadn't," Rachel agreed.

Michael pushed himself up onto his knees again. It took a lot of doing, with a hole in his leg and his lower abdomen bullet-shredded. He continued on, forcing himself into a standing position. He looked to the sky and took the deepest breath of his life. He wasn't going to die on his knees, groveling in front of those two little shit-sluts.

I'm going to die like a real man, he thought. *On my feet with my head in the forest air.* He breathed in deeply again.

"Oh, God, that smells good," he said. "The clean, fresh smell of the green forest surrounding us." He looked down at the two girls and asked, "So… what now?"

Evelyn said, "You die for what you did to my sister."

"Oh yeah?" he said, leaning down slightly to Evelyn with a sarcastic waggle of his head. "Well, you're all g-going to hell for this," he stammered through the pain.

"You first," Lynette said.

Michael whipped round to her. He threw his bloody left hand up in front of himself and yelled, "Wait!"

But it was too late. Lynette had squeezed the trigger.

The bullet ripped through Michael's hand between his thumb and index finger. His head snapped back as the bullet entered his face right below his left eye. It scrambled the contents of his brain and exited the back of his head, ripping away the back part of his skull and the whipped contents within.

Michael's body jumped and shuddered as he stumbled back—arms and legs pinwheeling—into the grave. He disappeared from the girls' view, but Rachel saw that he didn't land all the way at the bottom of the hole.

She was confused at first and stepped forward, then immediately understood.

The deer.

Michael had fallen onto the antler that was sticking up in the center of the pit. It had punctured his back, slid deep into his body, and exited the front of his chest as just a little blood-covered period.

Her daughters joined her at the edge of the grave.

Michael's face was blank; he wasn't even staring up at them. The way he had fallen into the hole had rotated his torso over and slumped it against the wall of the grave. His eyes looked diagonally across to the far corner of the rectangular hole he was in. To Rachel, it looked like the most uncomfortable position to die possible, and that made her very happy.

Lynette didn't say anything, but simply raised her gun with both hands and fired into the grave again. The bullet hit Michael in the chest. She fired again, this time into Michael's crotch for the second time. She took turns shooting Michael in the chest, the head, and the crotch until her gun was empty. Even then, she continued to pull the trigger.

Evelyn joined in with her sister's fun, firing into the hole with Michael's gun, but she stopped when her gun was empty.

Rachel went to Lynette, grabbed her hands, and gently pulled the gun from her grasp. Even with the gun out of her hand, Lynette's small trigger finger continued to twitch. Rachel pulled her into a tight embrace.

"Oh, baby, it's okay. You're safe now. We got the bad guy. He can never hurt you again."

A soft moan from Lynette, then, "You promise?"

Rachel stroked her long hair as she rocked her gently. "I promise, baby. It's over now. You're safe. No one will ever hurt you like that ever again."

"Good," Lynette whispered, and mewled into Rachel's ear again.

Rachel closed her eyes for a long moment and held her heartbroken daughter in an all-encompassing hug. When she finally opened her eyes again, she saw Evelyn still staring down into the grave. Rachel blinked a few times to make sure she wasn't imagining what she was witnessing.

Evelyn was focused on Michael's bullet-riddled body with a broad smile upon her face. It was a look of elation, wonder, and excitement.

Rachel, unnerved, watched her for a few moments, waiting for her to get her fill, but she just continued to stare. And smile. Finally, Rachel couldn't take it anymore.

"Evelyn," she called gently.

Evelyn lost the smile and looked over at Rachel for a second. "Huh?"

Rachel didn't exactly know what to say, and couldn't keep Evelyn distracted long enough; her daughter looked down into the grave again.

Rachel tried again. "What are you doing?"

"Looking at Gregory."

"Well… stop that. Come over here with Lynette and me. Give us a big hug."

"Okay."

Evelyn moved to her mom, but her gaze lingered on Michael as she did so. Finally, she turned, set the gun down on the ground, and joined Lynette in their mother's arms.

"Yeah, quit looking into the grave. You don't need to do that anymore."

Evelyn asked, "Why?"

Rachel didn't really know how to explain, but opted for, "Because it's over. It's all over now."

"Really?"

"Yes. It's over for good."

Rachel hugged her twins tightly and silently thanked God for her two little angels.

After a while, she slowly pulled away from them. They felt her movement, released their mother, and stepped back in unison. She smiled at them, and they smiled back in their individual, adorable ways.

"Mommy?" Evelyn said.

"Yes, sweetie," Rachel said, turning to look into Evelyn's angelic face.

"This was fun. Can we do it again sometime?"

"Uh, what?"

"I was just wondering who we're going to bring up here next time!"

Rachel's heart plummeted into the pit of her stomach. A pang of grief hurt her heart. "Oh, no, sweetie. This was just a one-time thing. We did what we came here to do because Gregory was a bad man that needed to be stopped from hurting your sister, um, you, and other little girls out there. We won't be doing this again. Do you understand?"

Evelyn was frowning in confusion. "But what if you meet another man who isn't nice to us? Would we come back up here then and do it again?"

"No, baby. No."

"Why not?"

"Well, let's just say your mother is a terrible judge of character, especially when it comes to men. I just don't know how to pick the right man for me... or for us. I won't be going out with any more men for a very long time. Maybe not until you two are out of college. Maybe never again."

"That's a long time," Lynette said. "Won't you be lonely?"

"No. Not at all. Not if I have you two by my side. We don't need a man in our lives, because we can take care of ourselves. I will be the luckiest woman in the world if you two stand by me."

"We'll always be here for you, Mommy," Lynette said.

"Yeah. Always," Evelyn added.

Rachel smiled with pride. "Good. Then we'll be the best family ever." She glanced over to the open grave again. She still had the arduous task of burying that molesting asshole for good.

Better to do it now and get it over with. Alright, up and at 'em, girl.

Rachel looked directly at each of the girls. She wanted them to know she meant business. "Now, why don't you two go down that little path we came up? Just go that way a little way, and sit on the trail and wait for me while I tidy up around here."

"You're going to bury him, aren't you?" Lynette asked.

Rachel released a deep, frustrated sigh. She'd known there were conversations she'd have to have with her daughters one day—discussions about growing into womanhood, monthly cycles, the difference between male and female bodies, the whole talk about sex and where babies come from. She'd never thought the first life lesson she would chat with them about would be about covering your tracks by burying a child molester in a pre-dug grave way out in the middle of nowhere.

"Yes, I am going to bury Gregory, because that's what you do to dead people."

"And animals," Evelyn added. "You know, the deer."

Lynette chimed in, "And the mountain lion. Don't forget about the mountain lion."

Fuck, Rachel thought. *I did forget about it.* She nodded and agreed, "And animals."

"I'm tired," Lynette said with a weary sigh. "I wanna go home."

"That's okay. You don't have to do anything but rest now. We're going home soon. Go with your sister like I said and wait for me to join you. Do not wander off. Do you understand?"

"Yes, ma'am."

"I want to help you," Evelyn said eagerly.

"No, baby. This is something I have to do. I need you to sit with your sister and comfort her. You've both been through a lot today."

"But I'm not tired!"

"I know, but Lynette needs you right now. She needs you much more than I need help with Michael."

"Michael?" Evelyn asked quickly. "His name is Gregory, Mommy."

"Yes, Gregory," she said, correcting herself. "Now go. Sit with your sister."

"Okay," Evelyn said reluctantly. She grabbed Lynette's hand. They moved toward the thin trail leading through the high grass that came up to their waists.

"Comfort your sister. I won't be long, and then we can go and forget about this place forever."

"Okay, Mommy. We will."

"Don't go far."

"Okay. We'll be right over here playing."

"Thank you. I'll be there as soon as I can wrap things up here."

As soon as the girls moved away into the tall grass, Rachel went to a grassy area behind the large oak tree. She unwrapped a spade, rake, shovel, and hoe that she'd covered over with branches that had fallen during past storms. She carried the tools back to the open grave and threw them down, picked the shovel back up, and immediately began to shovel the mound of dirt back into the hole.

She worked feverishly, throwing shovelful after shovelful into the grave. She made sure to pack and fill the dirt in, around, and underneath the deer and Michael's body. She didn't want any pockets of weak earth to cave in under somebody or some animal who might walk over this grave after they were gone.

After the girls and I leave here today, we will never return here under any circumstances. I mean it this time.

Her muscles began to ache and burn, but she let her anger propel her. She worked up a sweat that drenched her armpits, her chest, and brow. Her hair became matted, sticking to her face as she worked.

As she buried Michael, images from eight years ago played out in vivid clarity as if they had only happened a few moments ago. She stopped suddenly as a blanket of fear wrapped her body up in a sudden panic, remembering how she'd buried Stuart with his keys.

She came back to the present and felt around in her jeans pockets, but found no keys. That blanket of panic wrapped itself around her a little bit tighter. She looked over to her backpack, then it came to her; she had stuck them down into one of its side pockets for safekeeping. She went to her backpack, unzipped the pocket, and looked just to make sure they were there, safe and sound where she had stashed them.

She took another mental note of anything she might be forgetting.

Michael's billfold?

She didn't know if he had one in his back pocket—or anything in his pockets, for that matter—but it really didn't matter; once he was buried, he would be gone for good. The woods would grow back up out of this grave and around this area, and this shithead would be forgotten in the same way Stuart had been forgotten by the few friends he'd had.

Michael's keys?

If they were in his pocket down there in the grave, it was of no concern to her. Rachel had made sure that it was her car they'd driven into the mountains. She hadn't wanted to have to get rid of another automobile piece by piece as she had done with Stuart's years ago.

Michael's handcuffs? In the grave, buried with him. Best place for them, I guess.

"His credentials?" she said aloud, remembering what he'd said. "They're probably at his house. On his nightstand or bureau. And that is okay if they're there."

As she continued to shovel, Rachel worked out the story of what she and the girls would say to the authorities when they did start asking questions about Michael Conklin, but then other questions began to nag at her.

Was this a sole undercover mission for Michael? If it was and he knew I might try to kill him for molesting Lynette, did he tell anyone else about his plans in case he went missing? Or was he such a confident detective that he wanted to work this case on his own? If others in the department were involved in this case, would he even chance them knowing that he'd committed his first offense as a child molester? Was this his first offense? Surely no one in his department would allow him to do that just so he could trick me into bringing him up here? That is unless Michael had a partner who's just as amoral as he was...

She knew the future would answer these questions in its own time. She and the girls would just have to wait and see what unfolded for them. But they would be ready; they would come up with a solid story by which all three of them would abide.

When Rachel had leveled out all the excess dirt that wouldn't fit in the grave because of Michael's and the buck's bodies, she took leaves, sticks and some of the long grass blades that had been broken and trampled and spread them all around until this whole area was lightly covered. Anyone passing through here might think something had happened, but she doubted that anyone would guess four bodies lay beneath the soil.

Rachel stepped away from her handiwork and came to the conclusion that she could do no more. Mother Nature herself would have to help her out and camouflage the rest.

As she hooked her arms into her backpack and turned to pick up her tools, she heard Evelyn's voice. "Mommy?"

"Yes, baby. I'm coming."

Evelyn stepped out of the high grass into the smaller clearing and asked, "What's taking so long?"

"I just finished up, baby. You and Lynette ready?"

"We've been ready." Evelyn saw the ground beyond her mother and ran forward to observe the leveled landscape. "Wow! You did all that?"

"Yeah... It took me a little longer than I was expecting. I had to make sure no one would suspect anything, you know?"

"You did good, Mommy. It looks real neat."

"Well, thank you, baby. I'm just trying to protect us."

"I know."

"Where's Lynette?"

"She's through there a little ways," Evelyn said, giving a noncommittal point behind her. "She's sitting on a tree stump thingy waiting on us."

"Then let's go get her. Let's get out of here and get home."

"Can I help you carry something?"

"Uh, sure. How about this rake... and, um, this hoe?" Rachel held them out.

"Okay," Evelyn said. She took one in each hand, then skipped back into the high grass. Rachel followed, carrying the spade and shovel in each of her hands. As she moved away, she peered back over her shoulder to view this area for one last and final time.

There was a sadness about this little sanctuary—as Stuart had liked to call it. Maybe it was because only Rachel knew the history of this evil place, and the pain it had caused the original Lynette and Evelyn and their unborn and unnamed babies.

And then there's all the pain it's caused me, Rachel thought as she looked over the terrain. *The physical pain of the fight when I struggled with Stuart for my life. The mental drain when I realized I had murdered someone; in self-defense, of course, but murder nonetheless. And let's not forget about the emotional distress of burying him. I harbored all that anguish inside me as I carried my girls during my pregnancy.*

The image of Evelyn smiling as she looked down into Michael's grave came back to Rachel's mind again.

Did what I did here years ago have adverse consequences for my girls? Did getting punched in the stomach by Stuart cause some kind of mental condition? Did one or both of my girls inherit Stuart's serial killer gene? Is that even hereditary?

She remembered Evelyn cheering as Michael was shot for the first time.

Is Evelyn going to grow up and be a female version of Stuart? Good Lord, I hope not. What happened here today is heavy for any mind to comprehend, let alone a young, impressionable, seven-year-old. She shook her head at her thoughts, then continued to look out over the overgrown graveyard. A pang of guilt stabbed into her. *In hindsight, now that it's all over... I shouldn't have even involved my girls with any of this shit. I should've handled it all myself, then they wouldn't have even been exposed to—*

"Mommy?" Evelyn said again as her tiny hand slipped around Rachel's dirt-encrusted wrist. Rachel realized she had stopped as she became lost in her thoughts. She turned from the Sanctuary and looked back down into Evelyn's sweet, innocent-looking face. "You coming?"

"Of course, baby. I'm right behind you."

"Well, come on," Evelyn said, tugging lightly on her mother's hand. "We have lots to talk about."

"What do you mean?"

"Uh, duh, Mommy. People will ask questions about Gregory. What are we going to tell them?"

Rachel's heart filled with dread, and her eyes began to tear up. She turned away from Evelyn and looked back at the sanctuary again, blinking the tears away.

It could just be an innocent deduction from a smart little mind. Please, God, let it be that, she prayed. *She's just thinking ahead, as I've been doing. Even though what we did was bad, it was right.*

She wasn't totally convinced. Deep down, she had a sneaky suspicion that Evelyn had enjoyed this excursion a little too much and wanted to continue doing so. Rachel knew that in the coming days her work would be cut out for her. She would have to keep her eyes on both of the girls, but especially Evelyn, to see if they started doing anything that remotely resembled past serial killers' patterns of behavior.

"You're right. We have a lot to talk about," she agreed. "We all have to get the story straight in our minds if we want to remain together." She quickly wiped away her tears with a dirty hand and composed herself as best she could. Turning away from the overgrown area, she let Evelyn lead her from the evil place that was way off the beaten path.

They found Lynette sitting erect on a small stump, her back straight and her hands neatly folded on her lap. She was staring out into the woods, but she wasn't focused on any particular thing. Rachel knew she was reliving what had just transpired. It had been that way for her too all those years ago. It had played out regularly in her mind for weeks before the horror had started to fade and the normality of life had allowed her to relax.

"Hey, sweetie. You doing alright?"

Lynette turned to her mother. "I'm fine," she said with an exhausted smile.

Rachel smiled in return. "There's that smile I've been missing."

"I finally found it again," Lynette said. "You helped me find it. I think today was really good for me."

Rachel didn't really know what to say to that. "Uh, well, ah, that's good, honey. That's really great to hear."

"I'm ready to go home now," Lynette announced. "Can we? I don't like this place much anymore."

"Of course we can."

Lynette stood, robot-like, and in a slight daze, began to lead them back to Rachel's car.

As they went, Rachel removed the blue strands she had tied to the trees yesterday when she'd hiked back up here to find the Sanctuary and dig Gregory's—Michael's—grave. With the blue ropes gone, she felt more at ease that even the smallest signs they had ever been here were disappearing.

As much to herself as to her daughters, Rachel said, "Things will get better for us, I promise you that. After that day here with your dad, things for me got a million times better."

"Really?" Evelyn asked.

"How?" Lynette asked.

Rachel smiled and said, "Because I gave birth to you two girls."

Broad grins replaced the girls' confusion. "If I didn't have you two little angels in my life, life itself wouldn't be worth living."

"I love you, Mommy," Lynette said, grabbing Rachel's wrist.

"I love you, too, Lynette. And you too, Evelyn," Rachel replied, wishing she could squeeze their hands tight.

"I love you too."

"There's nothing in this world I wouldn't do for you girls."

"And there is nothing we wouldn't do for you either, Mommy," Evelyn said, smiling. "Just like we did today." She held out her hand again and she and Rachel linked index fingers as best they could, since they were each currently carrying a rake and a shovel.

Free of Michael, Michael's gun, and the trail of blue markers, Rachel walked wrist-in-hand with Lynette and fingers linked with Evelyn as they made their way back down the path. She let her daughters lead her into whatever new life awaited them once they left these woods—forever.

ACKNOWLEDGEMENTS

I have to thank everyone who was a major supporter of my first novel, *Soul Dreams*. I am deeply indebted and humbled to everyone who has purchased, read, and left a review on social media for my first novel. Also, a special thanks to those individuals who have recommended it or bought extra copies to give to their friends and family members as a gift. I appreciate all of you for your love, encouragement, and support. It means the absolute world to me.

I must thank Joe's Place Bookstore and everyone who worked there. I say worked, as it is sadly now closed. Thank you for allowing me to shelve a few copies of *Soul Dreams* for the public to purchase. Also, a huge thank you for all the vanilla lattes and pimento cheese bagels you made for me while I worked on this novella collection in the big room upstairs. Here's to (lifting my coffee cup): Alix, Anne, Becky, Elissa, Emily, Kat, Logan, Mary, Patty, Sarah, and Nola. You guys are so awesome. Cheers!

I am so thankful to have been able to work with Damonza.com again and have them help me design my book cover and bookmark for this project; they also helped with the formatting for *Off the Beaten Path*. The first time I worked with this company was when I published *Soul Dreams*. They were so accommodating with all the nit-picky details that I wanted to have incorporated in the cover; they always came through for me and gave me exactly what I wanted. Such a great company to work with. If you are looking for a great cover for your project, check them out at www.damonza.com.

Double high-fives to Jason Underwood for beta-reading *Off the Beaten Path – The Beginning* years ago when I was first working on it. Some of his suggestions are intertwined within that first story, so thank you for all your feedback and suggestions. This is your story too, brother.

A big thank you to Chris Cashon for answering a few questions that arose during the writing of *Dead Bait*. Chris is a long-time friend and an amazing actor. He also knows his IT and computer material better than anyone else I know, and always comes through with helping me with Photoshop needs. He was gracious enough to design the 4x6 thank-you note/social media reminder card insert in this book. (You probably have the insert if you received a copy from me).

Huge high-five to Max Dodson for his help in *Dead Bait* and *Frostbite*. Max is a colleague I worked with for years at Fluor Corporation, Jacobs Engineering Group, and O'Neal Engineering, as well as a friend who knows everything about fishing and boating. He also plays a mean guitar and is in a band called Throwing Bones, so look them up and check them out if you are ever in Greenville, South Carolina. They are usually playing in bars or clubs downtown.

Special thanks to Landon Hyder for helping out with some of my questions during the writing of *Rage*. The answers you gave and the added pictures of your BMW helped to write that story. Landon is a long-time friend from all the way back in our high school days at Bob Jones Academy. He plays a mean game of golf as well.

Special thanks to Bill Kennedy for answering questions that came up about police procedures in *Rage* and in both *Off the Beaten Path* stories. Bill is a former police officer with the Mauldin Police Department in South Carolina. He is now a real-estate agent with Keller Williams Realty in Greenville, South Carolina. Contact him if you need to buy a house in the Upstate of South Carolina (or anywhere for that matter). He can help you find your dream home.

A huge kick-ass thanks to Silas James Rowland for helping with a few questions that came up during the writing of *Dead Bait*. I also wanted to thank Silas for helping me out with the most recent photo-shoot he did for me at Joe's Place Bookstore to promote this book. Thank you for making me look my best. Silas is an amazing screenwriter, actor, director, producer, and filmmaker in Greenville, South Carolina. This guy is blowing up. He's gonna be huge. Check him and his work out at www.greenglasscapture.com.

Deepest thanks to Shane Willimon for his donations to help get this collection edited and published. Thank you for your continued encouragement and your belief in me as a writer as I navigate this publishing world with my works.

Special thank you to Instagram friend and fellow author Evan Bond, who passed on some of his sage advice about marketing. I appreciate you sharing with me some of your secrets. Your help and suggestions have been beneficial, so deep gratitude to you on that front. Evan specializes in thriller/suspense novels with such titles as *Echoes of the Past*, *Death Can Wait* and *Getaway*, and his on-going Ethan McCormick series: *To the Wolves* and *Sins of the Mother*. You can find out all the details about Evan and his works at www.evanbondauthor.com.

Much gratitude goes out to Emma O'Connell of www.emmasedit.com. It is a hard thing for a writer to let go of their work and simply trust someone with the story or stories they have worked so tirelessly on, but I trusted Emma, and my stories are so much better because of it. Emma was such a joy to work with. She tells you what works and what doesn't. It's that plain and simple. Not only that, but she gives you the reasoning behind all her suggestions. Her edits are seamless and took my stories to a whole new level. She works hard not to change your story, but to enhance it. There is a certain flow that seems to entwine her suggestions to make my stories read smoother; that was the first thing I noticed when reading my stories after her first edits were made to them. She actually made my writing better (and I have no problem saying that). She is a master editor and I count myself lucky to have found her. Emma made me look like a seasoned professional. I would be honored to work with her again. If you are looking for an editor, look no further because Emma O'Connell is who you should go with. Drop her a line at emma@emmasedit.com. Tell her I sent you her way.

Special thank-you shout-out to Ellie Owen. Ellie is what I consider to be Emma O'Connell's 'fresh-eyes' grammar and punctuation sidekick. She was called in for a second look at grammar and punctuation on these stories. I learned so much from the edits she brought to the table; edits that I will continue to use for years to come. I appreciate everything that Ellie suggested story-wise and all the remaining grammatical errors she found and corrected. So, working with Emma, you get to work with Ellie as well. That's a bonus.

A colossal thank you and the highest of fives goes to my good friend, Lee Bagwell, for helping me out with the writing of *Dead Bait*. I also wanted to thank Lee for being a sounding board to just let me talk out the storylines of most, if not all, of these novellas. Lee was such an immense help in just letting me ramble freely and allow myself to come to the story's conclusion. Thank you for the times you have given me input on some of the stories. All your suggestions or hinted directions led me to reach specific story points or outlined moments during my writing process. Lee's intuition about story is second to none.

And last, but definitely not least by a long shot, a huge thank you to my wife, Laurie Jones, for being the very first reader of all these tales and discussing them with me at length. It's always such an enjoyable time conversing with you about these stories over a hot cup of coffee. Your attention to story detail is very much appreciated. You, just like Lee, were very influential in helping these stories remain real. Thank you for being honest with me in telling me what you felt worked and what didn't, and for proofing some of the stories for grammar and punctuation in the beginning stages of final edits. You are, without a doubt, the best ever. I love you.

Wofford Lee Jones
Joe's Place Bookstore
Friday, October 4, 2019

Photo Credit: Silas James Rowland of Green Glass Capture
Photo Location: Joe's Place Bookstore

ABOUT THE AUTHOR

Wofford Lee Jones is the author of the supernatural thriller *Soul Dreams* and this collection of horror stories *Off the Beaten Path*. He is currently at work on his third book, a Halloween based horror novella, *Hell Night in Hopewell*. He works at Yates Construction as a designer by day; by night and on the weekends, he writes every chance he gets. He enjoys photography, watching theatre and movies, traveling, reading (especially supporting his indie author friends out there), drinking coffee, and unnerving his readers with his dark, delicious, and disturbing stories. He lives in Greenville, South Carolina, with his wife Laurie and their four-legged son, Baxter.

For more information about
Wofford Lee Jones and his writing,
please go to his website:
www.woffordleejones.com

If you enjoyed *Off the Beaten Path*, or my previous novel, *Soul Dreams,* please go to any social media you use and help me promote my books. Self-published (or indie) authors have the full weight of marketing and promoting their projects on their shoulders, but we can't reach everyone ourselves. Please take a photo of this book and post it on the social media avenues you frequent. Please leave a short review on such spaces as Amazon, Instagram, Facebook, Goodreads, Twitter, etc. (but, please, don't give away any spoilers). If you know of people who read books in this genre, consider buying them a copy as a gift for their birthday, Christmas, or some other holiday. Please help me and other indie authors promote our works. I would be indebted to you for your help.

Thank you so much for your help in advance.
I appreciate you.

Until next time,

Wofford Lee Jones